DATE		
JUL 2 4 2006	APR 2 2 2008	
SEP 1 0 2006	AUG 0 1 2008	
OCT 0 4 2006		
DEC 0 4 2006		
MAR 1 5 2007		
MAY 0 9 2007		
JUN 0 2 2007		

MAGDALENE

ANGELA HUNT

TYNDALE HOUSE PUBLISHERS, INC., CAROL STREAM, ILLINOIS

Visit Tyndale's exciting Web site at www.tyndale.com

TYNDALE is a registered trademark of Tyndale House Publishers, Inc.

Tyndale's quill logo is a registered trademark of Tyndale House Publishers, Inc.

Magdalene

Cover Art; private colletion/Agnew's, London/Bridgeman Library.

Designed by Jessie McGrath

Scripture quotations are taken from the *Holy Bible,* New Living Translation, copyright © 1996, 2004. Used by permission of Tyndale House Publishers, Inc., Carol Stream, Illinois 60188. All rights reserved.

Scripture quotations are taken from the *Holy Bible,* New International Version®. NIV®. Copyright 1973, 1978, 1984 by International Bible Society. Used by permission of Zondervan. All rights reserved.

This novel is a work of fiction. Names, characters, places, and incidents are either the product of the author's imagination or are used fictitiously. Any resemblance to actual events, locales, organizations, or persons, living or dead, is entirely coincidental and beyond the intent of either the author or publisher.

Library of Congress Cataloging-in-Publication Data
Hunt, Angela Elwell, date.
    Magdalene / Angela Hunt.
      p. cm.
    ISBN-13: 978-1-4143-1028-2 (sc)
    ISBN-10: 1-4143-1028-5 (sc)
    1. Mary Magdalene, Saint—Fiction. 2. Bible. N.T.—History of Biblical events—Fiction
3. Christian women saints—Fiction. 4. Palestine—Fiction. I. Title.
    PS3558.U46747M34 2006
813'.54—dc22   2005035154

Printed in the United States of America

11   10   09   08   07   06
 7   6   5   4   3   2   1

God of forgiveness,
do not forgive those murderers of Jewish children here.
—Elie Wiesel at Auschwitz, January 1995

Wilt thou forgive that sin where I begun,
Which is my sin, though it were done before?
Wilt thou forgive those sins, through which I run
And do them still: though still I do deplore?
When thou hast done, thou hast not done,
For, I have more.
—John Donne, "A Hymn to God the Father"

CHAPTER ONE

SILENCE, AS HEAVY AS DOOM, wraps itself around me as two guards lead me into the lower-level judgment hall. When I fold my hands, the chink of my chains disturbs the quiet.

My judge, Flavius Gemellus, senior centurion of the *Cohors Secunda Italica Civum Romanorum*, looks up from the rolls of parchment on his desk, his eyes narrow. I don't blame him for being annoyed. I am not a Roman citizen, so I have no right to a trial. Besides, I have already confessed and am ready to die.

My appearance in this dimly lit stone chamber is a formality, an exercise in Roman diligence before the application of Roman justice.

The centurion's eyes flick automatically over my form, register my sober tunic and veil, then return to an unfurled parchment in his hand. "State your name for the record."

"Mary," I say, using the Greek form for the scribe's benefit. "But my people call me Miryam. Miryam of Magdala."

My judge looks up again, his eyes raking my face. "You are . . . Syrian?"

"I am a daughter of Isra'el. From a territory called *Galil*, or Galilee."

He nods. "Galilee is part of the Syrian province. So detail your crime."

"You want me to begin at the beginning?"

The surly centurion is apparently in no mood for small talk. "If I had my way, you would already be in the arena. But since the emperor insists that we record the history of every condemned prisoner, give us your story."

I lower my gaze to collect my thoughts. The flagstone in this dank chamber is wet and streaked with mud; a rat scuttles into the shadows beneath the scribe's table. Roman citizens undoubtedly stand trial in better surroundings, but I have no complaints. I am here of my own volition . . . and I'm ready to meet my Lord.

At the thought of entering eternity, a weary smile crosses my face.

"You have nothing to smile about." The guard at my right brandishes a flail in my direction, but I doubt he'll use it. I am an old woman, worn to a nub by my wearisome journey to Rome.

"I am called many things," I say, deliberately letting my mind run backward, "but because Miryam is such a common name, most people call me the Magdalene. I grew up on the shores of Lake Kinnereth, which you know as the Sea of Galilee, where my father arranged my marriage to Yaakov, a fine man. HaShem, the Holy One, favored us with two fine sons—"

The centurion lifts his hand to catch the scribe's attention. "Wait—I've never heard of this God. Who is HaShem?"

I lower my gaze in respect, but not for the Roman. "The God of Isra'el, whose name is too holy to pronounce. *HaShem* means 'the name.'"

"Fine. But we don't need your life history. Speak of your crime, woman. That's all we need to record."

I hold his gaze without flinching. "But you cannot understand my crime unless you understand my history."

The scribe lowers his stylus and frowns at me from beneath a fringe of graying hair. Clearly he'd rather send me to the lions than transcribe my story, but I have an important tale to tell. The apostles have been sharing their stories for years; this is *my* chance to bear witness to all that transpired in Eretz-Yisrael when Pilate governed Judea.

I return my attention to the centurion at the desk. His distinctive helmet sits on the edge of the table, its red-plumed crest before me like an open eye. The officer's dark gaze studies me from shadowy circles beneath brown hair generously flecked with gray. Though I have not even begun to explain my presence in this horrid place, he glares at me like an avenging angel.

I wonder at the source of his anger—does he hate me or my people?

The barrel-chested guard moves toward me. "She's stalling. She's afraid of what waits for her in the arena."

"I'm not afraid of anything out there." Again, an unbidden smile tugs at my lips. "I'm afraid for you. All of you."

The centurion snorts with the half-strangled mirth of a man who rarely laughs. "Why would you say that? We've broken no law."

"Rome—and Romans—have broken the laws of the one true God, the maker of heaven and earth. But you are not alone. I have broken them, too."

The guard opens his mouth to protest again, but my interrogator silences him with a look. The centurion glances toward the door behind me, then crosses his arms and leans back in his chair. "Take your stations by the door; we will let her talk. She might prove interesting."

Grateful for this small miracle, I close my eyes. "My story begins in Magdala, a city by the sea. . . ."

CHAPTER TWO

I SHOULD HAVE KNOWN better than to journey to the market in the heat of the day. When the sun climbed directly overhead, anyone with the sense of a goat took cover beneath a shady tree or ducked indoors. But that morning Binyamin had almost crawled into the fire pit beneath my dye pots so, after scolding him and wiping ashes from his drool-covered fingers, I delayed my departure for the market to thank the Holy One, blessed be he, that I'd turned in time to stop my younger son from burning himself.

With Binyamin tucked in a sling, I blinked in the sting of a hot wind and wound through the mostly deserted aisles of the market-place. After passing the stalls of ironworkers, woodcutters, and bread bakers, I found Rachel, my pregnant daughter-in-law, leaning against a stack of folded fabrics.

Because ours was the only stall covered with a thatched roof, three other women had taken advantage of my absence to crowd into the rectangle of shade. I recognized them as I approached: the tall one sold figs; the old one, oil; and the lame one, wine. The lame woman, Devorah, once sold me a bottle of bitter wine. I hadn't ventured near her booth since.

"*Shalom aleikhem*, Miryam," the tall woman called as she struggled to rise. "And peace be with your daughter-in-law for taking pity on us who were about to melt."

"Peace be with you." I gave them a tight smile and patted the sling in which young Binyamin rested. Hospitality required that I invite them to stay, but I had no time for idle talk. I needed to speak to Rachel, and the spot of shade was not big enough for all of us.

"Good trading to you." I bowed as each woman reluctantly vacated our booth. "May the Holy One of Isra'el, blessed be he, make you prosperous."

When the last interloper had moved away, I knelt on the woven mat and untied the sling knotted at my shoulder. "Has the Roman woman come?"

Rachel's dark eyes danced. "Not yet, but she sent a servant to tell me she would arrive at midday. She probably wants to avoid the crowds."

"Ah."

I didn't know much about Romans in those days, but everyone in our village knew that the women who traveled with Roman soldiers weren't—how shall I say this?—proper *wives*. The legionnaires of Rome, my Yaakov once told me, weren't allowed to marry lest they be distracted from their duty to the army. Of course, that didn't stop the centurions from keeping their mistresses nearby. Bands of harlots frequently followed companies on patrol, so even the lowliest Roman soldier could indulge his desires . . . though not with any sort of woman I'd welcome into my home.

I didn't care what the soldiers did when they weren't terrorizing our people. Romans were *goyim,* or Gentiles, and Gentiles were heathens; everyone knew that.

I placed my younger son on the mat and looked around the quiet square. The women in the next booth had covered their baskets of salted fish; the woolworkers had settled linen sheets over their stacks of wool. They would return when the sun slipped toward the west; then goods and money would again be exchanged in the Magdala marketplace.

"Miryam." Rachel nudged me and held out her arms for the baby. "Behind you—the Roman woman."

I turned my back to the approaching litter for a last-minute check of my bright blue tunic. Fortunately, Binyamin had not spilled anything on me. I ran my fingers along the edge of the veil covering my head, tucked a few straggling hairs out of sight, then turned to greet my visitor.

The pretty lady who traveled in the company of a Roman centurion had been in Magdala only a few days. Apparently she had spotted my exceptional wares through the curtains of her litter as she traversed the marketplace; in that hour she had finally come to buy.

The litter bearers halted and a white linen curtain lifted. A dainty face, framed by a riot of black curls, smiled out at me. "You are the dyer of wool and silk?"

The woman spoke perfect Greek, so I answered in the same tongue. "I am. And you are?"

"The lady Carina." She swung her feet out of the conveyance and stood, her red sandals a stark contrast to the beige dust of our market square.

My eyes lifted to drink in the details of her costume. All sorts of foreigners came through Magdala, but rarely had I seen a woman as beautifully dressed. My prospective customer wore a tunic of a splendid yellow silk bordered with golden fringe. She had chosen to cover this with a blue *palla*, folded lengthwise and fastened at each shoulder with a golden clasp. To protect her pale skin from the hot sun, she also wore a short cape over her upper arms.

I was studying my visitor's apparel so intently that I missed her next comment, but another nudge from Rachel broke my concentration. "I'm sorry; what did you say?"

The young lady smiled, so perhaps she was accustomed to being openly admired. "I asked if I might know your name."

"I am Miryam." I imitated her smile, wanting desperately to appear as competent as whatever dyer had provided her current garments. "Wife of Yaakov, mother of Avram and Binyamin, mother-in-law to Rachel—if you should ever need to ask for me."

The woman's pale hand drifted toward a covered stack. "May I?"

"Certainly."

I whisked the protective linen away, exposing several lengths of wool and silk. The silk came to us from elsewhere for dyeing, but workers in Magdala spun and wove the fine wool. Our town was known for two things—no, three: salted fish, expertly dyed fabrics, and corruption. I'd heard it whispered that the religious authorities in Jerusalem thought Magdala's virtue had been spoiled by too much trafficking with Gentiles, but no city in Judea opened her gates to more foreigners than Jerusalem.

The lady knelt. Her hand caressed the wool, then fingered the silk. "I wonder . . ."

"Yes?"

"The other day I glimpsed a lovely scarlet fabric here. I glanced away, but when I looked again, the material had changed to a deep purple. Did I see two different kinds of cloth?"

My heart sang with delight. "You saw a fabric so unique it can only be purchased in this booth. Not long ago I discovered that by combining a red dye with blue I could create a silk that shimmers scarlet in one light and purple in another. The secret process is long and involves several dyes, but I'm sure you'll agree the effect is worth the effort."

A knowing smile dimpled her cheek. "I do agree. A miracle, surely, that a cloth can vary in color."

"Miracles are of the Holy One, blessed be he," I corrected her. "The cloth is merely the product of a highly skilled dyer."

"A dyer who must command a very high price."

"A woman with such an eye for color demands a high price indeed. So high that common people cannot afford such cloth. I have been saving that fabric for a customer with discernment, an exalted station, and the beauty to complement it."

"I'm sure you have." Her gaze trailed lightly over a stack of blue and green silk, but I could tell she wasn't interested in those colors. Her mind had filled with purple and scarlet. She lifted her gaze. "Would you mind if I examined it?"

"Of course not. I have it safely put away, to protect it from dust."

I stepped over Binyamin, who played silently, and reached into the calfskin bag hanging at the back of our booth. I pulled out a generous length of the shimmering silk and nearly tripped over Binyamin as I moved forward to spread the fabric over our other goods.

The Roman lady caressed the silk and brushed it against her cheek, then smiled as she pulled it into the sun. Draping the material between her fingers, she shifted the folds and laughed as the crimson deepened to a purple as intense as any cloth that ever graced a caesar.

"The fabric—" I knelt and pulled a lower edge into the shade— "begins crimson; do you see? But the heat of the sun brings out the purple hues."

She clutched the cloth to her chest and closed her eyes. "I must have it. How much?"

In truth, I had not set a price, knowing that few people in Magdala could afford such luxury. But this was a Roman centurion's woman, so perhaps I should set my hopes high. . . .

"Ten denarii," I told her.

Her eyes flew open. "Silver?"

I laughed. "Gold. Ten gold denarii."

She drew in a quick breath. I expected her to counter with an offer of one or two denarii, which I, after pretending to be insulted, would answer with a price of six. If all went well, I might sell the remarkable fabric for five denarii, half the price of a small house in our town.

But the lady surprised me. "You will come to the inn and pick up your money," she said, gathering the fabric into her arms. "Tonight."

I shook my head. I knew she wouldn't understand, for Romans go where they will and think nothing of it, but no respectable daughter of Avraham would enter a Gentile home, even a temporary abode. And Yaakov would bar the opening of our courtyard before he'd let this woman into our house. I caught a silken edge and held it tight. "You will send a servant to my house with the money. When your servant comes, my husband will give him the silk."

She pressed her painted lips together, then nodded. "It shall be as you say." She let the fabric fall; I reeled it in and thrust it into Rachel's arms for proper folding.

We stood, each of us satisfied with our half of the bargain. The Roman lady climbed back into her litter and murmured a command to her slaves, but not before casting one last longing look at the crimson-and-purple bundle in Rachel's embrace.

Chapter Three

ATTICUS AURELIUS, THE CENTURION commanding the second century of the Cohors Secunda Italica Civum Romanorum, pauses to catch his breath outside the doorway to the judgment hall. The woman standing before Flavius speaks Greek with the broad accent of a Galilean, an inflection he never expected to hear in Rome.

He had intended to arrive before the proceeding began, but his tardiness might work to his benefit. From this rear vantage point he can study the woman and listen without being observed.

He peers through the arched opening and examines the prisoner. Her clothing disguises any distinguishing characteristics, but the crackle in her voice suggests she is older. Her tunic and head covering, a square of fabric no devout Jewish woman would appear in public without, are plain and unadorned. Nothing in her voice or form kindles a memory. Why has she confessed to such a heinous crime?

He moves into the hall, hoping to slip in unnoticed, but Flavius lifts a finger and nods in silent greeting. The woman hesitates, then glances over her shoulder and catches Atticus's eye. Her expression changes as something tightens the corner of her mouth, and for some reason her gaze sends a flush of heat to his face. He looks away, then sinks onto a bench and studies his hands as if he has no interest in the proceeding.

Yet he is vitally interested. This woman is an enemy of Rome; she is *his* enemy. But most of the people he met in the region of Galilee scarcely ventured beyond the walls of their villages. The rugged fishermen braved the unpredictable waters of their inland sea with admirable courage, but the women tended to keep to themselves.

The woman turns back to Flavius, but a tremor now fills her voice. Atticus squints at the back of her head, trying to place her face and features. In younger days, she would have been striking, even beautiful. Did he know her in Galilee? in Caesarea? Perhaps he met her in Jerusalem.

Or . . . perhaps she is insane and he never met her at all.

He considers her crime and is again perplexed. Insanity would explain the charge against her, but her calm voice is both powerful and gentle. Her language is precise and rational, and she speaks Greek with apparent ease, emphasizing a word now and then with a restrained gesture.

Nothing about her suggests madness or wide-eyed fanaticism.

Atticus transfers his gaze to the scribe, who listens with a bored expression, his stylus moving over the papyrus in short, quick strokes. Flavius sits in the seat of judgment, his arms folded, his legs extended and crossed.

Atticus leans forward, hoping for another look at the woman's face. As if she senses his presence, she turns slightly and meets his eye, but this time she doesn't falter and her resolute gaze lacks even a trace of panic or fear. She wouldn't be here unless she deserved death, but why would she confess to a capital crime?

Chapter Four

As a breeze swept away the heat of midday and the other merchants reappeared, I made Rachel lie down in the shade of the stall. "Get some rest," I told her, realizing that I would be holding my first grandchild within a month. "It should be quiet this afternoon, but if Rekhav tries to buy anything, you must refuse her. She has not paid what she owes us from the last time she visited."

When Rachel gratefully sank to the mat, I wrapped Binyamin in my arms and walked toward the lake. The smell of water and the tang of fresh fish reached me before I could even see the silver waves of Galilee.

Fishermen crowded the shore, unloading their catches, as salters filled their baskets with the palm-sized fish that abounded in those waters. I averted my eyes from the sight of so many bare-chested men and walked directly to the place where my Yaakov stored his boat.

As always, my heart leapt at the sight of my dear husband. His skin shone like oiled olive wood as he stood at the bow and tugged on his nets. He called something to Avram, our firstborn, and smiled when he saw me.

"You have brought Binyamin," he said, holding out his arms.

Glad to be rid of the weight on my breast, I leaned across the shallows and handed our sleepy son to his father. Yaakov held the boy above his head and called to him, but though Binyamin smiled, he did not greet his father like other babies his age.

As always, a shadow of concern filled Yaakov's eyes as he returned our son to my arms.

"There now, Binyamin." His eyes crinkled at the corners when he caught my gaze. "Go with your mama while I clean the boat."

So . . . once again, we were going to avoid talking about Binyamin's refusal to babble. Yaakov kept telling me not to worry, all would be well, but my husband was always looking for miracles.

In all my forty years, I had never seen one.

Avram splashed into the water and called a greeting before hauling a basket of fish from the stern to the shore. He would take the day's catch to the salter, then join Rachel at the market stall.

I settled beneath a shade tree and bounced the baby on my knees. "You did well today."

"We did." Yaakov paused, his hands on his hips, as if trying to remember what he'd been about to do before I appeared. "A nice haul. But one of the nets ripped; it must have caught on something under the boat."

I looked at the sky, where the sun had retreated behind a cloud bank. "It's a good day for mending."

Yaakov grunted a reply and gathered a net into his arms, then leapt out of the boat and splashed toward me. After settling in the shade, he spread the net on his lap and showed me the broken strings.

I clucked in sympathy. "It'll mend."

"I think so."

While he pulled out his twine and tools, I told him of the Lady Carina and her fascination with the purple cloth. I did not tell him she had asked me to meet her at the inn.

"Ten gold denarii?" His dark eyes glittered above his beard. "It's too much."

"She agreed to pay. What can I do if she refuses to bargain?"

"You tell her you've had a change of heart; then you lower the price."

"Why should I deprive her of wearing the most expensive tunic in Galil? A thing is worth whatever the buyer is willing to pay for it."

"A thing is worth a fair price, no more. When her servant comes tonight, you will tell him the price is five gold denarii. And the lady will *still* be wearing the most expensive tunic in Isra'el."

I rolled my eyes and pretended to pout, but I actually felt grateful for my husband's intervention. Despite her ignorance, I had liked the lady Carina and had no wish to cheat her.

When Binyamin made a fist and rubbed at his eye, I dropped my hand onto Yaakov's sun-warmed back. "I should go home. The baby wants a nap."

"Go then." My husband's eyes went soft with affection. "I'll be along later."

"I'll have your dinner ready."

Reluctantly, I left the thick shade and stepped into the bright sun. I noticed that I had the road to myself—not a Roman chariot in sight. As a thin ribbon of sweat wandered down my back, I felt myself longing for the comforting atmosphere of our house. My business kept me busy in the marketplace three days a week, but I always loved coming home.

I hadn't traveled more than forty paces when I spotted Avram standing on the edge of the road with a group of men. Like him, several wore sleeveless tunics over their bare chests, the uniform of fishermen. Two others wore the broad *tzitziyot* and *tefillin*—fringes and phylacteries—of Pharisees. Those two would not be happy to see me, a woman, walking alone in the sight of so many men.

I lowered my head in a modest posture and quickened my pace, but an overheard comment from my son halted me in midstep.

"I will obey all six hundred thirteen commandments in the Torah—" Avram's voice rolled with the thunder of an offended rabbi—"when the people of Isra'el join me in honoring the creator of those commandments. We will not have the Holy One, blessed be he, as our king until we throw off the Roman oppressors."

What was he *thinking?* I turned toward the men and closed my eyes, momentarily wishing that Avram had been born as compliant as Binyamin. Such talk would get him into trouble with the rabbi *and* the Romans. A good thing none of the legionnaires had been around to hear him.

Despite the heat, my forearms pebbled with gooseflesh when I heard the distinct crunch of hobnails on pavement. Shifting slightly, I glanced up the road . . . and saw bare legs, thickly strapped sandals, the tip of a sheathed sword.

A soldier was coming toward us.

I stepped off the pavement, but I could not let the Roman pass while Avram spouted belligerencies only a few feet away. Desperate to protect my firstborn, I lifted my head and boldly stared at the interloper. The plumed half-circle crest on his helmet told me he was a centurion; the hard lines of his face assured me he would resent my son's aggressive talk.

The Roman officer walked with his left hand on the hilt of his sword; the other hand swung free at his side. Beneath his helmet, his face looked like a stretch of sunbaked desert trenched by deep ravines.

The man ignored my defiant eyes and continued his advance. He probably wanted to buy fish; soldiers often snacked on the dried sardines sold at the water's edge. Perhaps he hadn't heard Avram's rash comment.

I stood at the side of the road and pretended to examine Binyamin, who drowsed against my breast. I clenched my jaw, *willing* Avram and his companions to be silent as the empty air between us vibrated and the silence filled with dread.

My elder son and his companions parted when they saw the Roman. They stepped off the pavement, but they did not retreat. They stood at the edge of the road, their faces signaling silent contempt for the oncoming centurion.

The heathen did not slow, but turned his head to regard the men with an unnerving and implacable expression. Deliberately meeting their eyes, he seemed to hold their scorn in his grip while his mouth took on an unpleasant twist. After a long moment, he lifted his chin and looked away.

I exhaled a pent-up breath, then winced as a soft, wet sound reached my ear.

No. Not that.

I peered at Avram, whose lips were still curled as the back of his hand rose to wipe his chin.

I looked at the centurion and saw a shining circle of spittle on the Roman's sandal.

Binyamin began to whimper as my hand rose to my mouth. *HaShem, Holy One, please, not Avram, not now, not here—*

The Roman turned. I saw the slight squint of his eye, the sideward movement of his jaw, the throbbing pulse in his neck.

But he did not move toward my foolish son. He scowled at the group, his brows knitting together. Then he pressed his lips into a flat line and continued toward the lake.

As one, Avram and the others watched the Roman until he disappeared among the trees; then Avram howled in laughter.

If he'd been ten years younger, I'd have dragged him home by the ear.

As it was, all I could do was hold my younger son close and hurry toward the safe shelter of my home.

I was still trembling with impotent rage when I heard Hadassah's lilting voice.

"Miryam? Can I help with dinner?"

I straightened and looked into the courtyard. My neighbor's fifteen-year-old daughter stood at the gate, her eyes alight with expectation.

I couldn't stop a smile. "Come in, dear one."

She whirled into the room with the energy of youth, then paused to peer into Binyamin's basket. "Oh, Miryam, he looks like a sleeping angel. He grows sweeter every day."

"I would have to agree."

"Do you think I'll ever have a baby?"

I lifted a brow. "Don't you think that's a question for your mother?"

Hadassah shrugged. "Mother wants me to get married; she's eager for grandchildren. But Father insists he's not ready to let me go."

I returned my attention to the mess of vegetables I was cleaning for the stewpot. "Surely your father knows what's best."

"I don't want to get married now." Hadassah sank to the rug, propping her chin on her elbow. "I haven't wanted to get married since . . . well, you know. It's hard to find anyone who measures up to him."

I pulled a handful of lentils from my bowl and paused before dropping them into the pot. "You have to think of someone besides Avram. He's married to Rachel and he's happy. Besides, he's too old for you."

"Avraham wasn't too old for Sarah. And Yitzhak was *years* older than Rivkah!"

I smiled as she continued to name examples of aged patriarchs and their younger wives. In truth, the girl's prattle lightened my spirit. Seeing my headstrong firstborn through her adoring eyes helped me forget how furious I was with him.

"And my father is *twenty* years older than my mother—"

I held up a hand to interrupt her. "Will you pour some water into the pot, please?"

She sprang up and grabbed the pitcher, then tipped it into the pot. Something in the gesture reminded me of myself in younger days.

"You know," I said, smiling at a memory, "I was once quite taken with a man . . . who wasn't Yaakov."

The dark lashes that shadowed her cheeks flew up. "You *were?*"

"Yes. I was betrothed to a young man from another village. Hoshea was handsome and kind, and our fathers arranged everything. But before he came to take me to his father's house—" I shot a glance at Hadassah, who stood frozen in a paralysis of astonishment—"I heard he had walked alone with another girl from my village. I promptly begged my father to break our arrangement, of course."

Hadassah lowered the pitcher to the floor. "What—what happened next?"

"Hoshea came to my house and begged my father's forgiveness. He said he'd made a mistake, but he hadn't soiled the other girl's honor or hurt my good name. But if I couldn't trust him in simple things, how could I trust him in more important matters? So my father ended the betrothal, and soon afterward Yaakov's father spoke to my father. And now all is as it should be. Yaakov was meant to be my husband."

Hadassah gaped at me, her luminous eyes wide with wonder. "And what happened to Hoshea?"

I shrugged. "I suppose he married a girl from his village—probably someone who doesn't know the first thing about dyeing fabrics. So you see, Hadassah, the Holy One knows what he is doing."

"Yaakov is a blessed man to have married a merchant, a dyer, and a good wife." She checked the water level in the pot, then tipped the pitcher again. "I know you're the best mother in the entire world. You raised *such* a fine son."

"If the Holy One, blessed be he, wills it, I will raise *two* fine sons," I said. "Now, that's enough water and enough foolishness. Your father is a wise man and he will arrange a good marriage for you. And when you are betrothed, you will come to see your father's choice as everything you need in a husband—"

"Not unless he's as handsome as Avram and as practical as you." Hadassah stood and returned the pitcher to its place, then bent to kiss my cheek. "I'd better help Mother; she'll be looking for me. And she wants you to taste her fig bread. She's trying something new."

"I'll see her tomorrow." I waved the high-spirited girl out the door, then sat in a room that suddenly seemed far too silent.

Like my youngest child.

Chapter Five

By the glow of lamplight I set the stewpot on a chunk of wood in the center of our rug. I had already nursed Binyamin, who played quietly by his father as Yaakov and Avram sank to their usual spots across from each other.

Rachel offered bread to Yaakov, who took it and recited the blessing: *"Baruch Atah* Adonai *Elohenu Melech Ha'olam, hamotzi Lechem Min Ha'aretz."* Blessed are you, Lord our God, King of the universe, who brings forth bread from the earth.

Having given thanks, Yaakov tore the flat loaf, gave half to Avram, and dipped his half in the pot.

As a woman, I should have waited, but as a mother I had to speak my mind. "Your son—" I bent to catch Yaakov's eye—"nearly brought the wrath of the Romans down on us today. I was so terrified my heart nearly stopped."

Yaakov blinked. "Binyamin?"

"Not Binyamin. This one!" I pointed at Avram, who flinched

beneath my trembling finger. "This long-eared, big-mouthed fool who cares more about hearing himself boast than preserving his family!"

"Mother!" Avram twisted his face into a look of aggrieved dismay. "You misunderstand me. I am only zealous for the Holy One, blessed be he, who will free Isra'el when we are brave enough to stand up to our oppressors."

"Did that Roman in the road oppress you? The man wanted fish; he came alone to the lake. He was minding his own business, as peaceful as a new morning, and you spat on him!"

Yaakov blinked again. "You did *what?*"

"I demonstrated my disdain for him and his obnoxious fellows," Avram said, his voice hard and flat. "He came into our territory alone and unafraid. You should have seen the look on his face! His bearing alone was an affront to all who call themselves sons of Avraham, Yitzhak, and Yaakov. His presence was an insult to Isra'el, so I let him know that while our people might be under Rome's bondage, we are not broken."

Yaakov stared at our son, his hand hovering over the pot of lentils. "You must be wise, Avram," he said finally, dipping his bread into the pot. "You must choose your battles with care. I do not think you were meant to strike at Rome today."

"How will we know when it is time to strike?" Avram persisted, his eyes blazing. "The Holy One, blessed be he, will equip us when we muster the courage, but how are we to rouse the people when men like you refuse to—"

"Avram!" Though he was a grown man, I could not bear to see my son insult his father. Yaakov was no coward—after all, he had been married to me for nearly twenty-five years, and I am not known for soft words. "You must not speak to your father in that tone."

"I meant no disrespect." Avram's eyes flashed from me to his father. "But I will continue to do all I can to rouse Isra'el to action. Only when we have mustered the will to strike against the Romans will the Holy One, blessed be he, free us from the domination of these caesars."

Frustrated by my son's dangerous ideas, I lifted my dye-stained hands to a heaven that had grown stony with silence. "You think HaShem is watching us now? You think he cares? Not now, he doesn't. He has left us, Avram; he has left us to find our own way. How long have the prophets been silent? How long has it been since we were promised a deliverer? Generations, my son. HaShem is no longer with us."

"Miryam—" Yaakov's voice cracked with weariness—"you do not know what you are saying. Sit down."

"I cannot sit." Still trembling with the terror of the afternoon, I crossed my arms and glared at my family. Poor Binyamin, thankfully, could not understand these things, but Rachel should have talked sense into her husband months ago. Yaakov, light of my life, was too gentle to restrain our firstborn, so the job of hobbling that stubborn mule had fallen to me.

"Do not leave this house tomorrow—" I glared at Avram—"if you are going to persist in this foolish behavior. HaShem is not working to save Isra'el, not now."

A flush raced across my son's face like a fever. "Were the prophets wrong, then? Is there no hope for us? no Messiah coming?"

"If he does come, he's certainly not coming to Magdala." I pulled my veil from its hook and flung it over my head. "One thing I know for certain: it is better to do one's work and not make trouble than to persist in foolish dreams."

When no one responded, I folded my arms and stepped out into the blessed coolness of the courtyard.

I loved my family, but on some days I longed for the freedom to run away.

⋄⟶═◉═⟶⋄

I was pacing in the courtyard, my jaw tight, when I heard a rap at the gate. I pushed past the milking goat and my dye pots and peered over the stone wall. A beardless man in a short white tunic stood there. A Roman.

"My lady wishes to conclude her business with you," the man said, peering at me from beneath a sweaty clump of thinning brown hair.

In the anxiety of the afternoon, I had nearly forgotten about my arrangement with Lady Carina.

I glanced toward the house. I ought to call Yaakov to conclude this transaction, but I was still irritated with him for trying to dismiss my concerns about Avram. I turned back to the slave. "Did you bring the payment?"

Uncertainty crept into his expression. "My lady wants you to come with me. You will bring the package; she will pay you on delivery."

I bristled. Had that woman forgotten our agreement, or had she deliberately decided to ignore my wishes? I ought to send this servant away and go back inside, but how could I walk away from so much money?

I bade the servant wait, then crossed to the wooden trunks where we stored our fabrics. I knew I shouldn't go out alone, especially after dark, but the men were still eating—I could hear their baritone voices and Rachel's soft murmur through the window.

Yaakov might not even realize I'd gone out if I returned quickly. And I'd be in the company of this servant. . . .

I fumbled through stacks of woolens and linens and pulled out the variable crimson silk. After smoothing my tunic, I tucked the bundle under my arm and slipped out of the gate.

The servant moved through the streets at a brisk pace, granting no consideration for my shorter steps. A full moon lit our way, shining on the homes of my neighbors—buildings of dressed stone and brick, some palatial and embellished by rows of pillars, others small and plain. Like ghostly presences, cloud shadows crawled across the street and slid up the walls, shading the rooftops where many of Magdala's citizens had retreated to enjoy the cool of the night.

My gaze drifted up a stone staircase when I recognized the familiar voice of my closest neighbor. "Yes, she makes a lovely yellow," Yudit was telling someone on the rooftop to my right. "But her prices are high; don't you think?"

I lifted my chin. Yudit had to be talking about me. For some time I had suspected that she coveted my business—or at least my customers. I would have been happy to demonstrate my dyeing techniques to her or Hadassah, but Yudit had always been too proud to ask.

She would squirm with envy when she heard what I'd received for the silk.

After we passed the well at the town center, the servant knocked at the inn's courtyard gate. My excitement swelled into alarm when I heard the sound of masculine voices from behind the wall—several Gentiles, speaking Greek. If they'd been Israelites, they'd have been speaking Hebrew or Aramaic.

When a serving girl opened the gate, I stepped into the courtyard and spied a knot of soldiers gathered around a fig tree. Some of the tension slipped out of my shoulders when I realized that they seemed at ease. More importantly, the centurion I'd seen on the road was not among them.

I drew a deep breath as we moved into the main hall. The servant ushered me into an opulent room with tile floors, sumptuous wall hangings, and a brightly tiled table. I waited in an incense-scented silence until the Roman lady breezed in from an adjoining chamber.

"Miryam," she said, extending her hand as she glided toward a delicately carved chair. "How good of you to come. Will you have a seat?"

A plain stool stood across from the ornate seat the lady had chosen. I followed my hostess's example and sat, positioning my package on my lap. I folded my arms and tried to behave as if I visited wealthy Roman customers every night.

"Would you care for something to drink?" The words had scarcely left Lady Carina's lips when a servant brought in a tray with two bronze goblets. Not wanting to insult my customer, I accepted a cup and waited until she drank before sipping the liquid.

She'd given me a cup of Judean wine, yet not even that sweet nectar could counteract the tension still tightening my nerves. I lowered the goblet to the tiled floor and straightened my posture. "I would like to conclude our transaction. I have a family waiting at home."

Inexplicably, my hostess's gaze darted toward the doorway through which she'd come. She gave me an indulgent smile, like a woman amused by the antics of a simpleminded slave. "I like you, Miryam. When I met you this afternoon, I thought you an extraordinary creature. You're nothing like the other Jewish women I've seen. They're so silent when I'm around."

I forced a smile. "You must not have visited the well early in the morning. You would not think our women silent if you had."

She leaned to the right, resting both arms on a curved armrest.

"You are more like the women of Rome. We are strong, taught to model ourselves after the goddesses who reside in our temples."

Her mention of goddesses caught me by surprise. I had heard that the Romans employed all sorts of perverse graven images in their rituals and superstitions, but I had never heard talk of goddesses. Still, very little surprised me about heathens.

I tilted my head and tried to formulate a reply that would fall between offensive disinterest and overt fawning. "These goddesses—" I chose my words carefully—"do they help you run a household?"

She tipped her head back and laughed. "Help? By all the gods, no! They are too envious, revengeful, and demanding. Yet my favorite is Viriplaca, the goddess of domestic life."

"If she does not help you . . . then why do you worship her?"

The lady's smile flattened. "She appeases the man of the house and turns his angry mood to gentleness. For even Viriplaca must submit to the head of the home." She lifted her goblet and smiled at me, her bright eyes twinkling over the rim. "Drink, Miryam. Business need not be dull."

Relaxed by the wine and intrigued by the lovely surroundings and a taste of forbidden knowledge, I lifted my goblet and drank. When I lowered the empty cup, the room had gone softer, the light fainter, and my blood had warmed in my veins.

She nodded at the bundle in my arms. "Did you bring the fabric?"

I unwrapped the linen covering enough to expose a flash of silk. In the coolness of this chamber, the fabric glowed like the deep scarlet of an overripe grape.

"May I see it?"

I gave her the bundle. Purring like a kitten, she stood and shook out the folds, then brought one gathered corner to her shoulder so the remaining length draped over her slender form.

"It's wonderful." Her voice descended to a low and breathy note. "This will make a robe fit for an empress."

"And an emperor." I pointed toward the excess length splashed over the tiles. "You could also have a tunic made for—well, the head of your household. Or anyone."

"Ah." She lifted a brow as if to acknowledge my tact. "Excellent. Thank you, Miryam, for delivering this."

Her servant reappeared and stood at my right as if ready to escort me out. I hesitated, uncertain how to proceed. Had Lady Carina forgotten the other half of our transaction?

I fixed her in my gaze. "I do not believe we have concluded our exchange."

"Will the color change in lamplight, do you think?"

"But we are not done—the agreed-upon price was ten gold denarii."

When a sly smile curved her cheek, I knew Yaakov was right— I should lower the price. I took a deep breath and began again. "For you, Lady Carina, I have decided to be generous. This exquisite fabric will be yours and yours alone for five gold denarii."

Again she smiled but made no move to fetch her purse or ask her servant for assistance. Instead, her plump mouth curled as if on the edge of laughter. "Do you value your life, Miryam?"

Stunned by the question, I couldn't answer.

"If one were to assign a value to your life, would it equal five denarii? ten? perhaps even twenty?"

The truth hit me: *She's not going to pay a single quadrans. And I can do nothing about it.*

Still, I pressed for justice. "I know we are different sorts of women, but I have established a good reputation in Magdala. My fabrics are of excellent quality; the colors are pure and worth every coin—"

She cut me off with an abrupt nod. "I could have had one of the legionnaires fetch the silk from your house, but I like you, Miryam. So I have paid for it with your life."

I stared at her through a blank moment in which my head swarmed with words. Then the truth struck with the force of a blow.

She belonged to a Roman soldier. A centurion . . . whose men had been gathering in the courtyard.

Not waiting for an escort, I whirled and grabbed up my tunic for the run home.

⋄⟩═◉═⟨⋄

I heard the bedlam well before I reached our house. Screams and shouts filled the night that had been quiet only a few moments before; smoke and heat rolled through air that had been cooled by an evening breeze. When I turned the corner and scrambled toward our house, I saw the shadowed forms of my neighbors before the mud-dabbed wall of our courtyard. Beyond the wall, a wind-tattered fire sawed about in the darkness.

My trunks, my fabrics, my dyes. The Romans were burning everything.

A scream clawed in my throat. I raced forward, but had barely penetrated the crowd when muscular arms caught and held me.

"Miryam." Yudit's broken voice rasped in my ear. "Miryam, you are too late. They are gone."

I turned to see my neighbor, her eyes wide and wet. Hadassah stood behind her, pale and shivering.

A sudden darkness bloomed behind my eyes. "What do you mean? Where did they go?"

"Come see."

When the pressure on my arms eased, I realized that Uriah,

Yudit's husband, had been holding me. With Yudit's arm about my waist, I tottered forward and saw four soot-streaked men emerging from our courtyard. They laid the bloody body of my husband next to the lifeless form of my firstborn. Rachel lay next to her husband. All three had been killed by a bloody slice across the throat . . . and some beast had also slashed Rachel's expanded belly.

Her womb yawned like a gaping mouth.

Black emptiness rushed up at me like the bottom of a well. Strong hands snatched at my arms, but I fell anyway, landing on my hands and knees in the dust.

This could not be happening. I lifted my eyes and beheld fire shadows dancing on the faces of my loved ones. Beyond their lifeless bodies, flames spun in the wind with whoofs and puffs and streams of sparks that whirled off into terrible darkness—

"Binyamin!" I struggled to my feet and lurched toward the burning house. "My baby!"

"No, Miryam!" Uriah caught my arms in a viselike grip. "The fire is too hot."

"But Binyamin! He's still inside!"

Uriah shook his head. "We came as soon as we heard Rachel's screams. They killed everyone before they started the fire."

"They?" My gaze moved into his. "Romans?"

Concern flitted along with confusion in his eyes as he dipped his head in a reluctant nod.

My mind spun with bewilderment, until the events of the day fitted together like broken pieces of pottery.

Avram had instigated this. His moment of temper had goaded the prowling lion, and the lion had come back to devour us. Though Avram's sin was great, greater was the sin of Lady Carina, who had condemned me to outlive my children.

Yet greatest of all was the sin of the men who had wielded their swords in my home. They had murdered my husband, my son, my daughter-in-law, my grandchild, and my precious Binyamin.

I tore at my hair, ripped my tunic, and fell to the earth, helpless and weeping as sparks rose from my home to dance hot and red among the stars.

Chapter Six

Atticus locks an arm on his crossed leg as the woman's words wash through him, tightening his muscles like the grip of a nightmare.

He will never forget that night. He does not remember seeing this woman, but he remembers the fishermen . . . and the pregnant girl. . . .

Under their centurion's order, his eight-man contubernium left the camp and reported to the inn where Gaius was staying with his mistress. Gaius led them to a house in Magdala, then stood outside the courtyard and ordered the insolent young fisherman to surrender.

But the young man didn't appear. Another Jew came into the courtyard, an older man with a graying beard, forelocks, and one of those Jewish shawls around his neck. For an instant, Atticus was certain the fellow would offer an apology, but the man had the temerity to ask what crime his son had committed.

Obviously, the older man had no experience with Roman discipline. Never one to tolerate anything less than instant obedience, Gaius signaled Atticus, who, as *tesserarius*, directed the group to follow him into the house. With his sword drawn, Atticus strode into the courtyard and pushed the man aside. One of his comrades took hold of the older man while Atticus led the others of his contubernium inside the building.

He wasn't sure what Gaius had expected to find—armed rebels, perhaps?—but Atticus saw a family gathered around the remains of their supper. The young man leapt to his feet and stepped in front of a screaming pregnant woman. The Jew picked up a rusted iron sword and tried to strike, but Atticus parried the blow with ease, clearing a path for two of his comrades. They laughed as they caught the woman and dragged her out to the courtyard.

The younger man, so defiant a moment before, raced after her and broke when he saw a Roman dagger at his wife's throat. He lowered his sword and wept. Two other soldiers forced him to his knees.

Alone inside the small house, Atticus searched to be sure no one remained. The home seemed prosperous; colorful garments filled the trunks and the scent of meat rose from the supper kettle. Hard to believe that these people could be serious enemies of Rome. Aside from the single sword, Atticus found no weapons.

He was about to leave when a large basket against the wall gave a slight shiver. He caught his breath and tightened his grip on his blade. A small man could fit in such a basket. He could be waiting to spring and attack the moment a soldier turned his back. . . .

Atticus steadied his weapon and moved forward with purposeful intent. After reaching the wall, he nudged the basket with the flat of his blade, then flipped the lid with an upward stroke. The straw cover flew off, and in the dim lamplight he saw that the basket *had* been used as a hiding place . . . and the sight of the person inside sapped the killing strength of his arm.

The basket had concealed a wide-eyed, nearly bald baby.

Atticus glanced toward the doorway, through which he could hear the laughter of his comrades and the agonized cries of the Jews. If he carried this baby into the courtyard, Gaius would kill it in front of the young woman, for the child had to be hers.

He stared in fascination as the child blinked at him, its wide forehead knitting in what looked like bewilderment. Then the baby began to cry, a wail that sent a pang of nostalgia shuddering through Atticus's frame.

Quintus. The name leapt unbidden into his thoughts, binding him to this child as if Quintus and this baby were one and the same.

"Shh." Atticus sheathed his sword and lifted the baby from the basket. The light wool blanket fell away, revealing the child's gender, and Atticus took the sight as confirmation. A boy, like Quinn.

But unlike Quinn, this child would have a chance.

When Atticus had taken the *sacramentum*, the vow of a Roman soldier, he had sworn to kill anything—be it animal, barbarian, or Roman—when commanded to do so. But he'd never thought he'd be ordered to kill an innocent babe.

He lowered the child back into the basket and pulled a cloak from one of the trunks. Knotting the soft wool at his shoulder, he created a sling like the ones he'd seen on the local women. Then he set the baby in the sling and adjusted his cloak so its folds covered the odd lump under his arm.

Confusion reigned outside. In a moment men would fire the house. Pandemonium would infect the neighborhood as shocked onlookers hurried to protect their homes from the flames.

Under the cover of darkness, Atticus would slip out and return to their camp outside the city gates. A group of harlots had been following them since Tyre. Perhaps one of them would see to the child until he could find the boy a proper home.

If the gods were merciful, this innocent one would be spared Quinn's sad fate.

Chapter Seven

WHAT DO YOU MEAN, that story has nothing to do with why I'm standing in this judgment hall? That story has *everything* to do with why I am here. What you call my *crime* has its roots in that night.

I'm not sure what I did while my house burned—my memory of the rest of that night is spotty. I do remember sitting in my neighbor's house the next morning as Yudit and several other women washed the bodies of my loved ones. I wanted to help, but every time I stood to reach for a basin, my knees went soft and my vision clouded.

Sweet Hadassah hovered near like a shadow, her eyes red-rimmed with weeping. Occasionally she would kneel on the mat where Avram lay and fresh tears would sparkle in her long lashes.

Because the Law forbids us to eat meat or drink wine, to put on the phylacteries or engage in study as long as a corpse remains in the house, Uriah and the men waited outside, leaving the dead in our charge. Several neighborhood women prepared food in the courtyard, and occasionally those who were tending my dead family stepped out to eat.

I could not even think about food. Something in me was amazed to discover I could still breathe.

My people have a tradition—so they will not be tormented by painful talk, mourners are greeted with silence until they instigate a conversation. So none of the other women spoke to me, though they often peered at me from the edges of their veils.

Respecting my grief, Yudit oversaw the ritual cleansing for Yaakov, Avram, and Rachel. To another neighbor she pointed out a small linen bag and remarked that it contained ashes and a jumble of small bones, all Uriah could find of Binyamin and the body of Rachel's infant. Though she meant to be helpful, her words pierced my heart like a dagger. Cremation has never been practiced among my people; only heathens burn their beloved ones.

The women sang low songs of mourning as they scrubbed dried blood from Yaakov's throat. I tried to sing with them, but my throat tightened whenever I drew a deep breath. My fingers twitched as Yudit lowered lovely Rachel's eyelids and applied the chin band to keep her mouth closed. My heart broke when Hadassah dropped the square linen napkin over Avram's strong features.

My family, formed over seasons of joy and struggle, had been destroyed in moments by foreign conquerors. I turned my face to the wall lest my neighbors see the storm of hate raging behind my eyes.

The rabbi entered, bringing with him a basket of aloe and myrrh. This he gave to Yudit, who would slip handfuls of the fragrant herbs into the linen wrappings over my loved ones, not to slow the body's return to dust but to counter the vile smell of death.

With stiff dignity, the rabbi walked toward me. I lifted my gaze to meet his. "Rabbi."

He folded his hands. "A sad day, Miryam. But the Holy One, blessed be he, is a just judge."

How many times had I heard him murmur that phrase to a grieving wife? "An unjust day," I countered, hearing an unexpected note of iron in my voice. "Where is the justice of HaShem in this?"

The women's songs ceased as waves of silence spread from those nearest me to the crowd in the courtyard.

The rabbi parted his hands, his dark eyes peering out from deep sockets like caves of bone. "Where was the Almighty when Job faced total destruction? Where was he when the Babylonians burned our Temple? Where was he when our fathers cried out in Egyptian bondage? He was there, Miryam. He was waiting."

"For what?" A thread of hysteria lined my voice, but I couldn't hold my tongue. "I don't care about Job and our fathers and our Temple; I need to know why HaShem didn't save Yaakov and Avram and Rachel and Binyamin and the baby."

"We cannot understand HaShem. He is not a man, that he should behave like one."

"Then how am I supposed to understand anything? I need to know *why*, Rabbi. I need a reason for this. Where is the Holy One when we need him? What's the use in following a God who's so far above us we can't even speak his name?"

The old rabbi's face closed, as if guarding a secret. Again, he folded his hands. "His ways are high above our ways, his thoughts high above our thoughts."

Heaven help me, I wanted to strike the man. My fists clenched, but I managed to close my eyes and look away. Let them all think I was too grief stricken to speak further. Let them imagine that I accepted the rabbi's wisdom.

In truth, I accepted nothing.

❖❖

"Yitgadal ve-Yitkadash Shmei Rabbah . . ."

"Magnified and sanctified be his great name throughout the world which he has created according to His will."

When the rabbi and ten men had finished saying the Kaddish, the prayer for the dead, I walked out of Uriah's house with only my rage and grief for support. The hired mourners and musicians stopped their wailing and flute playing as I passed, erect and dry-eyed, but they began their ministrations with renewed vigor when the weeping women followed me. Behind the women, several leaders of Magdala carried biers supporting the bodies of Yaakov, Avram, and Rachel. A smaller bier held the pitiful bag of ashes and bones.

I walked with my head high, sustained not by hope of the resurrection but by a burgeoning hope of justice. Surely Roman soldiers couldn't come into a town and annihilate a family without cause! While Avram *had* provoked a centurion earlier in the day, his rash action should not have resulted in execution.

Because death had entered the world through a woman, with a stately step I led the ever-growing parade of mourners down the street, through the city gates, and over the dusty road that led to Magdala's burial site. No goats grazed on that land, no children played on those sloping hills. I couldn't even recall ever seeing a bird roosting in that desolate area.

I walked past the small columns used to mark the graves of poorer people, then paused before the family crypt sheltering the bones of Yaakov's parents and grandparents. In that cave, hewn out of hillside rock, my husband and I had laid two baby girls who had died before living a full year. One of them would have been Hadassah's age if—

Too many *ifs.* If Avram hadn't been so foolish; if Yaakov hadn't been so mild. If the men had lingered on the sea yesterday, if the

Romans had never come to our land, if the Holy One of Isra'el would fulfill his overdue promises . . . life would be better.

I had to trade all my *ifs* for one hard fact: by sunset, everyone I loved would sleep within that stone chamber.

I stepped aside as the bier carriers approached. Several men moved forward with sharp staves to roll the stone away from the entrance. Silence fell over the crowd as they levered the huge rock onto its side, opening the passage that led into the tomb.

I bent and glanced inside. Three niches had been cut in the wall to my left, three to my right, and three opposite the entrance. Six of these held adult bodies; the remaining spaces would be filled today.

The pitiful little bag would rest with my baby girls on a slab in the center of the chamber.

I straightened, then moved toward my family members. The carriers lowered the first bier, allowing me to trail my fingertips over the linen covering my beloved husband's face. Through the linen, I glimpsed the dark circle of the birthmark near his brow. How many times had I kissed that spot because my heart had been too full for words? How could I begin a new day without tugging his beard to wake him? How could I go to the lake without expecting to find Yaakov waiting at the shore?

A flash of loneliness stabbed at me, but I closed my eyes to the pain and moved to the next bier. Avram, my son. So much like Yaakov, too much like me. If only the fire of my stubborn independence had blazed less brightly in him!

A new anguish seared my heart when I pressed my fingertips to the linen over Rachel's lovely face. She had left her people in Bethsaida to make a home with us, and I had grown truly fond of my gentle daughter-in-law. I had surrendered Avram to a woman who brought him joy, and I had yearned to hold her babe in my arms.

How could HaShem let the Romans rip that hope from me?

I closed my eyes and stepped back to allow the bier carriers to enter the tomb. Behind my closed eyelids I felt the threat of tears. My head had swollen with them; the inside of my nose tasted like the sea each time I drew a breath.

Inside the tomb, the bier carriers arranged the bodies with care; Uriah wanted to be sure that Rachel rested in the niche above Avram.

Behind me, the professional mourners beat their chests and wailed while the flautists blew their melancholy tunes. Beside me, I felt the pressure of a hand. I opened my eyes and saw Hadassah, who slipped beneath my arm, then reached up and stroked my cheek with her fingertips.

Like blood out of a wound, a keening wail rose from the bottom of my heart and ripped through the graveyard. I lowered my face to Hadassah's slender shoulder and went quietly and thoroughly to pieces.

CHAPTER EIGHT

"SOMETHING'S WRONG, I tell you. Look at him."

Atticus stared at the Syrian girl who'd been in the band of women following their century ever since Tyre. Because she seemed a pleasant sort, he'd placed the baby in her keeping while they marched, but in that hour every trace of good humor and patience had vanished from the curve of her mouth and the depths of her eyes.

He glanced at the baby, who sat on a blanket at her feet. The little one kept rubbing his eyes as if he was tired, but nothing else seemed amiss. "What do you mean?"

The girl screamed. The shrill sound made Atticus flinch and startled two soldiers at the supply wagon, but the little boy didn't even blink.

The girl sank to the blanket, then pulled a pouch of salted fish from a fabric bag. "This child is deaf."

"How can you be sure? Maybe he has a placid nature."

"No one is this calm, Atticus—not even you." The girl broke off a piece of fish, then tucked her hair behind her ear and smiled. "I don't know why you became a soldier. You're not like these other men."

Atticus ignored the personal observation and lowered himself to the blanket. "Is there some medicine I can give him? Could our physician help?"

She lifted a bare shoulder in a shrug. "You'd be taking a big risk, wouldn't you? What would they do if they knew you had a baby?"

"I don't have a baby."

"Then what do you call this person on the blanket? He's not tall enough to be a centurion."

Atticus gave her a black look. "I meant to say he's not *my* baby."

"Then whose is he? He has to belong to somebody."

Atticus breathed hard and tried not to look at the girl as she chewed a piece of fish. Her thick dark hair hung in graceful curves over her shoulders, and her sleeveless tunic exposed her slender arms. He had hoped she'd form an attachment to the child and drift toward one of the cities they passed through, but here she was, unhappy with her new responsibility and as persistent as an itch.

"Doesn't matter where I found him. No one's looking for him and he's not hurting anything. He's quiet."

She spat the fish into her hand, plucked out a bone, and offered the chewed meat to the mostly toothless child. "He's *too* quiet— that's what I'm trying to tell you. This baby is not right. If you were hoping to use him as a servant one day, maybe you'd be better off getting rid of him."

Atticus clenched his jaw as a spasm of disgust rose from his core. "If you don't want to help me, I'll find someone who will. Surely one of those other harlots you travel with—"

She lifted her hand, exposing nail-bitten fingertips. "I didn't say I didn't like the baby; I was only thinking of you. If this child will get you in trouble, perhaps you could leave him in a field—"

Atticus caught and gripped her arm. In a fury, he lowered his head and stared into her brown eyes. "I will not abandon this boy."

She trembled in his grip, but she did not avert her gaze. "Then you take care of him. Here." She smacked the remaining fish against his knee. "Feed him yourself."

He released her. "I will. Consider yourself relieved of this obligation."

He thought she would leave—he almost *hoped* she would leave, but after a moment the storm clouds left her face.

"Come now, Atticus, be serious." Her smile shimmered like sunbeams on the surface of the River Tiber. "You can't take care of a baby and be in Caesar's army. You are not a free man."

He lifted a brow. "And *you* are free to do as you choose?"

She reached into her bag again and pulled out a loaf, then pinched a piece of soft bread from the crusty shell. "You didn't leave a bruise on my arm, did you? A big oaf like you could hurt me without even knowing it."

"I didn't hurt you. I didn't want to hurt you."

She chewed a piece of bread, then offered it to the hungry boy. "I'll help you with the baby, Atticus; don't worry. I like him."

Atticus broke off a piece of fish and offered it to the child, who took it into his mouth and screwed up his face in displeasure.

The young woman laughed as she crooked her finger inside the baby's mouth. "You have to chew it first, at least until he gets a few more teeth. Chew it and be sure to spit out the bones—he might choke on them. And give him goat's milk, unless you can find a nursing mother who'll help you out."

Atticus nodded.

"Now——how long are we going to be in Caesarea?"

Atticus pulled the baby's fist from his mouth and gave the child a bit of bread crust to chew on. "Since Caesarea is our home base, we'll remain there as long as it suits the governor."

"Can I come see you?"

He snorted. "The fortress is not as relaxed as this camp."

"But surely a man like you can find a way to see his woman."

He stiffened, unnerved by the sudden shift in her perceptions. Since when had she become *his* woman?

She must have intuited his thoughts. "If I'm going to help you take care of this child," she said, arching her brows into triangles, "then you're going to help take care of me."

Atticus drew a deep breath. A soldier had little time for anything but marching, training, and following orders. Though he'd concentrated on serving the Imperial Roman Army for the last five years, he wouldn't be free to think about a wife and family for at least twenty years more.

When he didn't answer, she dropped her hand to the top of the baby's round head. "I'll go with you to Caesarea and we'll look out for each other. Agreed?"

"Listen, girl——"

"Cyrilla." She leaned toward him, her gaze as soft as a caress. "My name is Cyrilla."

"I am a soldier, a common legionnaire. I can't afford a mistress."

"You are a gentle man and you like babies. Don't you like women?"

He looked away and swallowed hard, feeling his cheeks blaze as though they'd been seared by a torch. Out of all the women who followed their camp, what had possessed him to approach *this* outspoken wench? "I like women. But I need to remain . . . unattached."

"Really." The girl pursed her lips in a thoughtful expression, then smiled as two of Atticus's tentmates approached.

"We're lonely." Flavius tossed the girl a smile. "Would you give a dusty soldier a kiss for keeping you safe on this long march?"

While the girl rose to collect a quadrans for her affections, Atticus stretched out on one elbow and considered the baby.

Could he trust the girl with this child? Cyrilla was a mess, altogether too blunt and thoroughly impractical. But she knew babies and she was traveling with a half dozen other women. Surely they'd make sure she took proper care of this little orphan.

The boy looked at him, blinked, and brought the drool-softened crust to his mouth.

With his arms locked around the girl's waist, Flavius released a heavy sigh. "'Tis a sad sight," he said, pitching his voice to reach Atticus's ear, "when the biggest, broadest soldier in the Cohors Secunda Italica Civum Romanorum cares more for a tiny sack of skin than he does for a lovely lady."

Atticus ignored the jibe. Flavius wouldn't understand.

Chapter Nine

Our law sets limits for grieving: we are allowed three days for weeping, seven for lamenting, thirty for abstaining from laundered garments and from cutting the hair. Whoever does not mourn as the Law prescribes is considered callous.

After the burial of my family, I set about the business of mourning. For seven days I did not wash, anoint myself, put on shoes, or engage in my trade. The first three days I tried to weep, but though my soul roiled with grief, I could not cry.

I sat dry-eyed in the blackened doorway of my house and received condolences from the leading citizens of Magdala. Some of my neighbors praised my husband, son, and daughter-in-law; others cursed the Romans. Some wondered aloud what I had done for HaShem to punish me so severely.

Hadassah sat with me, breathing in the acrid scent of ashes and not speaking. Sometimes she would weep and sprinkle dust over her veil; at other times she shook her head at the blackened remains of what had been a flowering vine in my courtyard. But if anger stirred her soul, she gave no sign of it.

The townspeople tried to help me salvage bits and pieces of my life. Uriah discovered Yaakov's staff in a corner of the courtyard; it had miraculously escaped the flames. One woman brought a tortoiseshell comb Rachel had lent her; she wept as she laid it at my feet. Another woman brought a square of vermillion silk she had taken from our stall and not yet paid for. I stared at the silk in surprise, unable to believe I had forgotten about a debt owed.

Our worldly goods should have gone to Avram; on that day they belonged to me. As my husband's only heir, I owned the ruined shell of a house, several stained dye pots, a boat and its nets, an empty stall at the marketplace, a purse of coins (unearthed from its hiding place under a piece of pavement), a gnarled staff, a comb, and the clothes on my back.

When the seven days of deep mourning had passed, I walked out of my courtyard and asked Uriah to discover anything he could about the Roman centurion who'd stayed at the inn. He returned to my house an hour later and said that the Romans had moved on after the fire—presumably to Caesarea or perhaps to Jerusalem. In any case, the centurion was Gaius Cabilenus; his mistress was Lady Carina.

I knew the lady.

"What of the other one?" Hadassah interrupted. "I saw them, Father, and one man was bigger than the rest. He went into the house first; he led the way for the others."

I lifted a brow. "Who was that?"

Uriah's face bore an inward look of deep abstraction. Whatever he'd seen that night, he was seeing it again. "There was a big man," he admitted, his voice sounding as if it came from far away. "A regular Sha'ul, he stood a head taller than the others. The one called Gaius gave the orders, but the giant went forth to meet your husband, he of blessed memory."

"The giant's name." A hair of irritation lined my voice. "Do you know his name?"

Uriah looked at Hadassah, then nodded. "I heard the others praising him. They called him Atticus."

I closed my eyes and quietly committed both names to memory. Gaius Cabilenus, the centurion with a spoiled mistress and a merciless pride. And Atticus, the giant who had invaded my home and inspired his comrades to murder my family.

Hadassah waited for her father to leave; then her brow wrinkled. "What are you going to do?"

I gave the girl a wan smile. "I will . . . rebuild, I suppose."

"That's not what I meant." She placed her hand over mine. "I know you and I recognize the look in your eye. You have a plan . . . and I hope it is not dangerous."

I hesitated, wavering between the sin of deception and the sin of unwomanly behavior. My desire for justice tipped the scales. "I have been wronged, Hadassah." I lowered my voice. "There will be no justice for me in Magdala."

She patted my hand. "I know you are sad, but you should talk to the rabbi. He will remind you that the Law says we are not to take vengeance or bear a grudge. He will help you accept—"

"The Law says we are not to bear a grudge against any of *our* people, and the Romans are not our people. No, the rabbi holds no answers for me, and I cannot accept what has happened. So there is only one place I can go."

I did not expect her to answer. I never dreamed a girl of her youth would guess my intention, but Hadassah knew me better than I had guessed. "You would go . . . to Tiberias?"

I blinked at her, then felt the corner of my mouth twist. "Why not? It is not a long journey."

"But that city is—" she shivered—"unclean."

I blew out a breath. "Do you think I care about clean and unclean at a time like this? So Herod built his city on a graveyard . . . I have just placed my entire *family* in a tomb and buried my heart with them. Let me be unclean; I don't care!"

Hadassah glanced over her shoulder, doubtless wishing her father would return to talk me out of this notion, but he had left the courtyard.

With no one to call on for help, she squared her slender shoulders and licked her dry lips. "Herod is a dog, an Edomite. If Father were here, he would tell you that no daughter of Isra'el should waste her time with him. Yaakov of blessed memory would rend his clothes if he knew you were thinking of going to see this vile king."

"If Yaakov had rent his clothes over Avram's foolishness, my family might be alive today." Though I knew the words must have stung her young heart, I closed my eyes and lifted my face to the blazing sun. "My family cries out to me. I am the next-of-kin avenger, so the Law compels me to avenge their murders."

"Would you keep a law that commands you to kill *Romans?*" Hadassah's eyes went wide. "The Law says you must put a murderer to death when you meet him, but if HaShem is merciful, you will never meet those Romans again. Take your case to the rabbi and see if he doesn't agree."

"The rabbi is helpless; the leaders of this town are powerless against the Romans. Herod is the authority in Galil, so to Herod I must go."

Hadassah shook her head. "Don't go, Miryam. You can remain here; my family will help you rebuild your house. My father will speak for you. We will be your family, and in time your grief will pass."

Only the habit of womanly silence kept me from laughing in my young friend's face. Did she think her father could command me? Within an hour of bringing me into his home, my dear Yaakov had realized that I would not be commanded. Yet we lived in love for twenty-five years.

Hadassah's heart would recover quickly from loss; the love she had borne my Avram went no deeper than infatuation. Yet I had known and loved my family members completely, and I could not mourn them until I achieved justice for them.

I would walk away from Uriah's authority, but not yet, for I did not wish to seem ungrateful for his help. My neighbors had been good to me. They had taken me in when I had nowhere to go; they had held me upright when my limbs were paralyzed with shock and grief.

So I bowed my head and pressed my palm to the trampled earth that had once been a flowering courtyard. A shard of pottery jutted between my splayed fingers—a broken dye pot, the perfect symbol of my shattered dreams.

Since my family could not be restored, I would have justice.

Chapter Ten

Atticus had felt a cloud of fatigue lift when Caesarea, proud capital of the territory of Judea, finally came into view. Built by Herod the Great in honor of Caesar, the city rose from the Mediterranean shore like a jewel in a glittering setting.

The guards at the city gate snapped to attention when the century's trumpet blared. An answering horn shrilled from the watchtower, followed by a welcoming shout. The signifier, the officer who carried the century's standard, a thunderbolt, quickened his pace and separated from the main columns to march directly behind the centurion's mount.

Atticus straightened his spine as they proceeded into the city. Though they had been on a routine patrol, probably prompted by nothing more than Pilate's wish to intimidate the unruly populace, dozens of Caesarean citizens poured from their homes to cheer the century's arrival. Women waved from marble balconies; men lifted their arms in salute.

Atticus breathed deeply of the air, grateful to be back in a place that even *smelled* like Rome. The delicious scents of pork and lamb wafted from braziers as slaves prepared the evening meal. A sewer system kept the streets clean, and servants kept the dust at bay with buckets of sparkling cold water brought via aqueduct from Mount Carmel, seven miles away.

Gleaming palaces rose from neat streets, and beyond the hippodrome he could see the artificial harbor that provided a port for the growing shipping industry. Women in spotless white tunics smiled at him from beneath mountains of curls, unlike the modest Jewish women, who had peered at him from beneath veils designed to conceal every wisp of hair.

Because Caesarea would always remind him of Rome, it would always feel like home.

Following Gaius, Atticus and his comrades marched into the garrison, then stood at attention. At the sound of their centurion's curt dismissal, the men let out a shout and scattered over the training ground, most of them hastening to the barracks.

Atticus wandered toward the gate and peered through an opening in the stone wall. They'd left the Syrian women near a grove when they broke camp this morning. Would they reach the city before nightfall? Would Cyrilla be able to find food for the baby?

He worried about her. The girl was entirely too unpredictable, but none of the other women had evidenced any interest in surrogate motherhood. He couldn't really blame them. How could they care for a baby when they struggled to feed themselves?

But Cyrilla had been willing . . . and able. She looked too young to have borne a child herself, so at some point in her life she must have cared for younger siblings.

Atticus had considered the baby's situation throughout most of the long march back to Caesarea. He couldn't keep a child in the barracks, so he'd have to find a reputable nurse. Which meant he'd have to pay a woman to care for the baby; which meant that most of his three hundred thirty denarii a year would go to care for the boy.

His situation could have been worse. A common legionnaire received only two hundred twenty-five denarii a year, but Atticus had received pay and a half since being promoted to tesserarius.

Raising a child would be difficult but not impossible. Given Flavius's garrulous tongue, it *had* been impossible to keep news of the child from the others of his eight-man contubernium. But his closest comrades had enveloped him in a kindly conspiracy, so Atticus's secret did not reach Gaius or anyone from the other nine contubernia of their century on the trek through Judea.

Only once had Atticus feared that his small stowaway would be discovered. Pleading for a stretch of uninterrupted sleep, Cyrilla had crept in and out of Atticus's tent, leaving the child with him for the night. Though the little boy did not babble like a normal toddler, he cried when he was frightened or uncomfortable, and the sight of so many strange men set the boy to wailing. When the guards came around to investigate, Atticus tucked the baby behind him while he and Flavius burst into song, lifting the praises of Romulus and Remus, the famous twins reared by a she-wolf.

"Remember Romulus," Atticus sang, leering drunkenly at one of the guards, "for without him there would be no Rome to rule the nations, impose the law of peace, or tame the proud in war."

The guards had laughed and moved away, but the next morning Atticus heard one of them remark that his singing would be more likely to insult Romulus than to praise him.

If any of his comrades had disapproved of their unexpected mascot, Atticus doubted they would have dared voice an opinion. The gods had gifted him with a gentle nature, but few men glimpsed it behind his impressive frame.

Though no man had ever been able to wrestle him to the ground, Atticus wondered if a child might prove to be his undoing in the barracks. Four hundred eighty men, all members of the Cohors Secunda Italica Civum Romanorum, lived and worked in the garrison at Caesarea. Surely one small child could be hidden among so many until he could find a woman to care for the boy.

If only the girl would bring the baby soon.

* ══◈══ *

They had enjoyed less than an hour of rest when a message came from Gaius—the century was to stand for inspection immediately. The procurator of Judea wished to examine the century that had just returned from Tyre.

Atticus glanced uneasily around the large barracks, where men lay sprawled over their straw-filled mattresses. A few minutes before the messenger arrived, Flavius had murmured something about a visitor and disappeared. He'd be in for a beating if he didn't return in time for the inspection.

Atticus stood and pulled on the dusty armor he'd recently unbuckled. "Anyone seen Flavius?"

His friend's own voice replied: "Ho, Atticus! Look!" Flavius barreled around a corner, pushing a small wheeled wagon, the sort of cart vendors used to sell goods on the street.

Atticus regarded his best friend with barely disguised irritation. "You're late. Gaius wants us on the field for an inspection."

"I'm not late. And I haven't removed my armor, so I'm more prepared than you."

Atticus sighed and picked up his sword belt. He had neither the energy nor the desire to debate the matter, and he was worried about the girl and the baby. Where *were* they? He had assumed the girl would have sense enough to come to the fortress, but who could tell what sort of scattered thoughts ran through her head.

Flavius leaned one arm on the covered cart and grinned like a well-fed fox. "Well?"

"What?"

"Aren't you curious?"

Atticus frowned. "We don't have time for games. If you were as clever as you think you are, you'd be cleaning the dust off your shield."

"You're no fun, Atticus. No fun at all." Flavius lifted his voice and glanced around the room. "Would anyone like to see the souvenir I've brought from Tyre?"

Several of the men stopped polishing their armor long enough to look up. Satisfied that he had an audience, Flavius whipped the linen covering away.

Despite his irritation, Atticus glanced inside—and saw Cyrilla crouching in the cart with the baby on her lap. Atticus looked up, not knowing whether to thank his friend or curse him. "Are you crazy?"

Flavius answered with an impenitent grin. "I found her outside the gate. She wanted to come in, so—" he extended his hand—"here she is, with your boy."

Scowling, Atticus extended his hands and took the baby, then helped Cyrilla out of the cart. The men of his contubernium laughed and moved away; others of his century clapped and whistled.

"Leave it to Atticus to bring a woman into the barracks!"

"Atticus! I didn't know you had a son!"

"Fast worker, that one. He'll be a centurion in no time."

Atticus ignored their comments and set the baby on his straw-filled mattress.

Flavius crossed his arms. "Are you planning to leave him there?" Atticus bit his lip as he fastened the belt beneath his banded armor. "He'll be fine."

"He's fine *now*. What are you going to do when he squalls?"

"He won't squall."

"How do you know? He'll cry, and this time I won't be able to sing a hymn to Romulus."

"Then what would you have me do?"

When Flavius flinched before the anger in his eyes, Atticus immediately regretted his outburst. He did not often lose his temper.

"He will be quiet." Atticus smiled at the boy and laid him flat on his stomach, then knelt and rested his hand in the small of the boy's back. "He'll sleep during the inspection. When it's over, we'll come back and get him something to eat. Tomorrow I'll look about and find a nurse in the—"

"Have you forgotten about me?"

He glanced at the girl, whose color was higher than the temperature of the room warranted. She stood with her hands on her hips, expecting an answer . . . to what question? Atticus tilted a brow at Flavius. "You brought her in. What happens next?"

Flavius sank to his own mattress. "She'll wait with the baby, I suppose; then I'll sneak her out. Don't worry about it."

Atticus shook his head. A toddling baby might make a little noise and soil a bit of straw, but a woman could get them into all kinds of trouble. A soldier's life centered on discipline, and while women might be enjoyed anywhere a soldier found them, they weren't supposed to be found in the barracks. He pointed at the girl. "She can't stay."

"Why not?"

"She's a woman."

Flavius nodded. "So? That's a baby."

"He's a boy. In a few years, with some training, he could be useful to us."

"The woman could be useful to us now."

"Stop talking about me as if I have no ears!" Cyrilla swallowed hard, lifted her chin, and boldly met Atticus's gaze. "Did you think I promised to care for this child for only a few days? We made a deal, you and I. We promised to look after each other."

Atticus shook his head. "I told you I was a soldier. I have sworn fealty to Rome alone."

"Yet you would swear to take care of this baby! You made a promise, Atticus. You gave me your word!"

Atticus would have argued further, but a trumpet blast from the training ground ended the debate. Exhaling between his teeth, he strapped on his sandals, hoping the baby would fall asleep and the wanton girl would vanish in the next few minutes.

But the brown-eyed urchin wanted nothing to do with sleep. The toddler pushed himself into a sitting position and watched Atticus fasten his sandals. Then he gave the girl who knelt beside him a wet, toothless smile.

And Atticus saw that he had been defeated.

Gaius Cabilenus, who had served Rome's army for more than twenty years, marched before his century, hands behind his back, his eyes sharp and accusing. Beside him walked Pontius Pilate, procurator of Judea, and his lovely wife, Lady Claudia Procula.

As a tesserarius, Atticus stood in the front row and tried to calm his racing heart while he stared straight ahead and focused on empty air.

Pilate had questions, which he asked in a calm voice all the more intimidating for its control. How had the centurion found things in the region of Galilee? Had the Jews settled down from their recent uprising over the matter of Caesar's standards? Had the men observed any signs of activity among the *sicarii*?

"The so-called dagger men," Gaius answered, "describe themselves as zealous for their God, but their efforts are not organized. They still exist, however, particularly in Galilee. The people of that region are stiff-necked and strong. They would rather die for honor than work for favor."

Pilate chuckled. "I think everyone in Judea fits that description."

He paused, smiling at his own joke, and Atticus urged himself to be patient. In a moment Gaius would release them and he could get back to the barracks—

"There was one bit of trouble," the centurion said, a frown settling over his features. "We handled it swiftly."

Pilate showed his teeth in an expression that was not a smile. "Go on."

"It happened in Magdala. One man openly insulted Rome and her leaders, but we took action to ensure that he will never do so again."

Pilate regarded Gaius with a perplexed expression, as if a question had entered his mind without the courage to ask it. Finally the procurator nodded. "Good. I want no more trouble during my tenure."

The governor cast another long look over the eighty assembled men. In a silence resulting from the holding of breath, Atticus watched the procurator as he turned, smiled at his wife, and opened his mouth to speak.

In that instant, however, an unexpected wail echoed from the garrison.

Pilate's eyes darted toward Gaius. "Centurion! Does one of your servants have a *child* in the barracks?"

Gaius's features hardened. "Not to my knowledge, sir."

"Find the source of that noise."

Gaius dispatched two men from the back row. Atticus closed his eyes, already feeling the blows of the centurion's staff on his back. He would be punished for this, beaten until it hurt to draw breath.

He lifted one eye in a squint. Pilate's face had darkened like thunderclouds, but the Lady Procula was searching the garrison doorway with keen interest. Cyrilla had proven herself resourceful, so perhaps she would find a hiding place. . . .

A moment later the men returned with the Syrian girl secured between them. The baby rode on her hip, his long tunic wet with tears and drool.

Atticus stifled a groan.

Gaius thrust his hands behind his back and glared at the girl. "Whose are you?"

She lifted her chin—and though he wanted to crawl under a rock, something in Atticus had to admire her audacity.

"I am a free woman," she said. "I'm called Cyrilla."

"Who brought you to the barracks?"

She rolled her eyes in an expression that might have been charming in another time and place. "I brought myself."

Atticus exhaled softly. Beside him, Flavius was sweating like old cheese.

"That baby."

Every man in the formation strained to hear Lady Procula's soft voice.

"Tell me, girl—how old is your little one?"

For the first time, uncertainty entered the young woman's face. "About . . . a year?"

"I see. And who might the father be?"

"The baby is . . . his."

Without looking, Atticus knew she had pointed to him.

"Tesserarius!"

Atticus stepped forward, snapped to attention, and met his centurion's gaze. Gaius's features had twisted into an expression of exceptional malignity. "Sir!"

"Is this your child?"

Atticus blurted out the only available answer: "Apparently it is."

Gaius's eyes appeared to be in danger of dropping out of his face. "What do you mean?"

The procurator's wife spared Atticus from answering when she stepped between Gaius's hot gaze and Atticus's confusion. Lady Procula gave Atticus a smile, then stretched out her bare arm and touched her husband's shoulder. "I think," she said, displaying remarkable courage, "that this soldier has spent considerable time with this young woman, and due to the will of the gods, they now have a baby. Would my assumption be correct, legionnaire?"

Atticus reluctantly shifted his attention to the lady's oval face. He felt like a trespasser, allowing his eyes to behold loveliness belonging to another man, but her face shone with kindness and he stood in sore need of compassion.

Though the picture she had painted was neither entirely accurate nor entirely a lie, it was . . . useful. If Gaius guessed that the child had come from the house in Magdala, the baby was as good as dead. If anyone realized the boy was deaf—well, no one wanted to invest in a child who would never be of any use.

He dipped his chin in an abrupt nod. "My lady, you are wise."

She gave him a sly half smile, then turned to her husband. "Please, my lord," she said, her voice low and intense, "they are common people and do not know any better. No harm has been done, and surely we can find some useful service for the girl? Let her be my handmaid and she can care for her child. The soldier is still a soldier; you have lost nothing."

Pilate's stony face softened at his wife's entreaty. "I suppose we can always use another servant." He lifted his wife's hand and squeezed it. "Take the woman and child with you, my dear, and do with them as you will."

Cyrilla's brow wrinkled. "But—"

"Go!" Atticus hissed under his breath. "Be grateful for mercy and be off!"

As the governor's wife glided toward the piazza, Cyrilla shifted the baby on her hip and hurried toward the white marble balustrade.

With a mixture of relief and longing, Atticus watched them depart. He'd escaped a beating—for the moment—but now he felt responsible for the baby *and* the girl.

"See?" Flavius muttered under his breath. "I told you not to worry."

Atticus wanted to smack him.

Chapter Eleven

After a full month of mourning, I slipped away from Uriah's house under the soft cover of dawn. I carried nothing but a leather scrip and Yaakov's staff. I lingered in the shadows by the city gates until they opened, and then I set out on the paved road that paralleled the curving shore of the sea and led to Tiberias.

After the arrival of our conquerors, miles of paved paths had begun to penetrate Judea. Though I disliked the Romans, even I had to admit that travel had become safer with this pagan improvement. Where roads led into major cities, heathen engineers provided raised walkways for pedestrians. Drainage tunnels kept the layered pavement dry and smooth. Mile markers informed a traveler of his location. Yaakov told me that a man could purchase maps of all these roads in the shops of Rome, but I had never seen such a thing in the region of Galilee.

Most people marveled at the highways, but my elder son had resented anything created to aid our conquerors. Though we walked on the roads, if we spied a Roman chariot or a contingent of soldiers in the distance, we had to leave the pavement and stumble through overgrown grass until the roadway cleared.

I saw no Romans the morning I set out for Tiberias, so I walked with a quick and light step. I had heard many things about the city, most of them negative. Herod Antipas had built himself a wonder, the men of Magdala said, ostensibly to honor the emperor, but actually to honor himself. Antipas had cleared a burial ground near the shore, he had renamed our beloved Sea of Galilee after Tiberias, and he had enticed residents to his city with offers of free land, free housing, and freedom from taxation. No self-respecting child of Avraham would live on an unclean burial ground, but through bribery and force Herod had managed to build a citizenry for Tiberias.

I pushed all thoughts of his impure city from my mind and clung to the hope that Antipas still wanted to be respected by his people, most of whom were people of Isra'el. If so, he would hear my plea and take action on my behalf.

I walked with brisk steps, not stopping to greet any of the early rising fishermen or merchants headed to the wharves along the shore. No proper woman traveled alone, so I was relieved to spot a party of men, women, and children on the road ahead. I quickened my step until I reached the women; then I asked if I could join them for the day's journey.

The oldest woman in the group took in my appearance with one swift glance. After wishing me *shalom aleikhem*, she said, "Do we know you? Are you from Capernaum?"

"Magdala," I answered, firmly holding her gaze to show I had nothing to hide. "I am Miryam, wife of Yaakov, but my husband has been killed and I must seek recourse from the king."

The old woman's brows lifted, but she didn't object to my company. The others offered me polite smiles, then resumed talking among themselves. They seemed to intuit that I wanted company, not conversation.

Heat covered the road like a blanket. To the east, the dazzling sun reflected off the lake, forcing us to squint every time we lifted our gazes from the pavement. The men at the head of our group talked and laughed with loud voices, gesturing frequently in the direction of Jerusalem. I don't think any of them were even aware of my presence.

We walked all morning, stopping at midday to rest in the shade of a grove. While the men watered the pack animals, we women drank from the sea and splashed our faces. I nibbled at the bread I'd packed in my scrip and wiped my neck with a damp cloth. One of the women started toward me as if she wanted to make conversation, but I rebuffed her with a frown.

Soon after returning to our journey, I sensed a commotion among the men, and within moments I understood why. A tax collector stood in the road, watching our approach with calculating eyes. After he counted our number, the sun-lined grooves beside his mouth deepened into a lazy, smug smile.

I could almost taste the tension in the air as each of us walked by the complacent publican and paid the toll tax. I had never had to pay it myself—Yaakov had always handled these things when we went up to Jerusalem—but I knew only part of this payment would find its way into Roman coffers. Tax collectors asked for whatever amount they chose, and anyone who did not submit ran the risk of persecution.

As the towers of Herod's gleaming city came into view, the leaders of our party turned toward an unpaved path that led west. They would not enter the king's unclean monstrosity but would skirt it and look for a sheltered place to camp for the night.

The old woman sought me out. "Are you sure you must leave us?" she asked, her eyes searching my face.

"Yes. But thank you for your concern."

Her smile was more like a wrinkle with brown teeth in it. "Then may the Holy One of our fathers, blessed be he, guide and direct you and keep you from all dangers on your way, bring blessing to the work of your hands, and return you home in peace."

I bowed my head and realized I was crying only when I tasted the salt of tears on my lips. I stood in the road with dust swirling around my ankles until the group had moved on.

CHAPTER TWELVE

WHEN THE GROUP FROM Capernaum had gone, I blinked tears from my eyes and considered the city that lay only a short distance away. Intersected by two formidable watchtowers, the stone wall encircling Herod's infamous settlement loomed above me. Embroidered flags fluttered from the towers, ensigns that bore images of the reeds growing at the water's edge. Because the sun had not yet set, the city gates stood open, the wooden doors pushed flat against the towers, their iron hinges gleaming like dull silver in the fading light. A passage between the towers led into the heart of the city, but armed guards in yellow tunics and mailed armor blocked my way.

How I wished I could disguise myself as one of the sparrows flitting in and out of the gate without attracting attention!

I must admit, the sight of Herod's guards unnerved me far more than the hawkeyed sentries who watched over the entrance of a typical Israelite city. At least these were not Romans. From their features, they appeared to be Idumean, descended from the same Edomite tribe as Herod and his kin.

A ray of hope sprouted through my despair—perhaps the guards and merchants gathered at this gate wouldn't care that I had arrived without husband, father, or brother as an escort.

I turned as if looking for someone on the road behind me, then stepped beneath a shade tree to study the situation. Outside the gate, several men stood around wagons and two-wheeled carriages for hire. A pair of horses stamped the earth as a team of oxen chewed hay and blankly regarded the horizon. A publican lounged on a rock, ready to tax anyone who wanted to pass through the gate, and a pair of guards stood at the entrance, swords dangling from their belts and daggers sheathed on their forearms.

I took a deep breath, gathered my slippery courage, and stepped forward. An earthen mound outlined a drainage ditch that curved toward the city wall while a cloud of flies buzzed around a dead dog that lay half in the water. If Herod cared so much for his beautiful Tiberias, why didn't he have someone remove this spectacle of death from his front gate?

As I lifted my veil to shield my nostrils from the stench, I felt the sharp eyes of the guards probing me. Doubtless they would think it strange that a Hebrew woman would approach the gates alone. Would they turn me away?

I could almost feel intrusive questions rising off the heathen strangers. If stopped, I could tell them the truth about why I'd come, but they might not believe me. I could say my husband waited within the walls, but if I told one lie, I'd have to buttress it with another.

At thirty paces from the gate, a guard strode out to meet me. "Halt!" he commanded in Greek. "Who are you?"

I lifted wide eyes and pretended confusion.

"Where is your man, woman?" He jabbed his index finger at me and raised his voice as if I were hard of hearing. "What business brings you here?"

I glanced past him to the passage that would lead me to Herod. I could see a busy road at the end of the stone tunnel, but at least twenty long steps lay between me and the safety of that street. I didn't think I could bolt and run without being caught.

A lifetime of training in modesty fell away as I lifted my gaze and directly addressed the guard. "My name is Miryam of Magdala."

"I asked your business, not your name."

"I have come to seek an audience with my king."

The corner of the guard's mouth lifted in a smirk. "A woman alone?"

"Please. I have a petition to set before Herod."

I held my breath as he stepped back, his gaze raking over my form. I thought I caught a glimmer of kindness in his eye, but before he could speak, another guard called from a group of men squatting on the ground: "Send that one away! Tiberias has more than enough of her kind!"

My cheeks burned as though they'd been seared by a candle flame. Mortified by the man's comment and his assumption, I turned and walked away as swiftly as my tired legs could carry me, then darted into a grove. This sheltering place might have to serve as my abode for the night.

I crouched on the ground and nibbled at my thumbnail. I'd come so far; how could HaShem allow me to be turned away when I was so close to reaching my goal?

The sun was teetering on the rim of the western horizon when the creak and rumble of wooden wheels interrupted my thoughts. A man and his wagon approached, pulled by a team of oxen. From the length of his beard and the tzitziyot on the edges of his robe, I knew he was a child of Avraham.

I ran toward his wagon like a rabbit seeking a burrow. "Please, friend, let me hide among your wares. I have to enter the city."

The startled man's hand automatically went to his belt, where he'd probably hidden a dagger among the folds of his tunic. Like the guard at the gate, he glanced around for the husband I'd lost, but this fellow, at least, did not question my virtue.

He called a low command to the oxen, which chuffed and grumbled to a stop. "Hurry." Without once looking at my face, the man glanced toward the horizon. "They will close the gates in a moment."

Thanking him with a nod, I ran to the back of the wagon and climbed in, then sat with my knees pressed close to my chest, insinuating myself into the space between two rows of baskets. The familiar scent of salted fish brought a wry smile—this man had probably come from Magdala.

As the wheels creaked and rumbled, I held my breath and prayed that HaShem would close the guards' eyes. The prayer held no power, though, no conviction. HaShem had failed to protect my family last month, so why should he act on my behalf now?

With each turn of the wheels, I saw the guard's taut face on the backs of my eyelids. What would he do if he found me? Would he strike me down as carelessly as Roman soldiers had struck my family?

When the odor of dead dog invaded the scent of salted fish, I bit down on my curled index finger and tried to stifle a shiver. The wagon slowed and stopped. I heard the low rumble of men's voices, then the sound of hobnails scraping against pavement. The guard was walking to the back of the wagon.

HaShem, King of the universe, blind his eyes . . .

"Wait a minute."

Gooseflesh formed on my arms as I recognized the guard's rasping voice. I closed my eyes at the sound of a creaking basket and a sudden rush of fresh air.

"Do you always make your wife ride in the back?"

I looked out to see the guard convulsed in raucous laughter. He must have glimpsed my form behind the baskets, but apparently he didn't think it unusual for a woman to be tossed into a wagon like so many other marketplace goods.

My newfound friend didn't answer, but with a swish of his flail, the oxen strained against their harness and we rumbled through the stone passageway.

I leaned against the baskets and breathed in the odor of fish while fresh perspiration chilled my skin. But I had reached Tiberias.

I owed my success, at least in part, to ignorance: to the Idumean guards at the gate, one Hebrew woman looked much like any other.

✦══◉══✦

After thanking my rescuer, I slipped out of the wagon and found myself in a city even bigger than Magdala. The tower entrance opened to a large public square, where several streets converged in a busy hub.

Despite its many reported sins, Tiberias appeared to gleam with prosperity. I walked past dozens of sellers who were putting away the produce of their fields, orchards, and dairies. Across the road, foreign merchants secured their exotic wares. One woman called to me, suggesting that I exchange my plain tunic for a silken gown and a Roman palla—as if I would ever wear *anything* Roman dogs had produced. I averted my gaze and walked faster, turning into another alley, this one occupied by goldsmiths, metalworkers, and sculptors, each calling persuasive promises to those who would linger to buy in the remaining moments of daylight.

The sky, streaked by this time with orange and gold and red, seemed to be descending over the city like the lid of a brightly lined jewel box. I bit my lip as I considered the horizon. I needed a place to spend the night, and I had no idea how to find accommodation in a heathen settlement. In a Hebrew village, a visiting stranger could go to the well and wait for an invitation to lodge with a family—our rabbis say that whenever a stranger stands at our door, the Holy One, blessed be he, stands at our right hand.

I wasn't sure I could count on any kind of hospitality in Herod's heathen city.

I passed an inn—a tall building with a large courtyard for animals—and lingered at the gate, wondering if I dared enter. I was about to inquire about a night's lodging, but the sight of a painted woman with free-flowing hair stopped me cold. I'd rather sleep under the stars than in a place where evil flourished so openly.

I turned another corner, then blinked at the sight of a building that had to be Herod's palace. The structure's opulence had not been exaggerated—white-marble pillars separated the building from the street while gleaming tiles paved the walkway. The palace's decadence had not been exaggerated, either—the builders had carved animal figures into the stone walls, directly violating our laws against graven images.

Yaakov would have fainted dead away at the sight, as would half the men in Magdala. How could Herod claim to represent our people when he blatantly ignored our laws and convictions? Bad enough that I'd seen statues in the merchant stalls, but to have images carved into a *building* . . .

I slowed my step as I approached the well. What was I doing in this place? I had come to Tiberias to seek justice for my murdered family, but could justice exist in a pagan place like this?

I listened to the sounds around me with rising dismay. Somewhere in the distance, a baby cried; not far away, a woman sobbed. The scents of incense rose from pagan altars and mingled with the aroma of roasting lamb and the odor of bleating goats. Tiberias offered something for everyone, apparently. Would it offer anything for me?

Night lights had begun to glow in windows along the city streets by the time I sat and smoothed my veil, hoping to present an image of respectable virtue. Dust covered my tunic and my feet were gray with grime, but again I felt a flicker of hope.

Without help from anyone in Magdala, I'd entered Herod's city. All that remained was to gain an audience with the king, present my case, and rest in the conviction that Antipas would seek out and punish the Romans who had destroyed my family.

To my left, the sky blazed crimson and gold. I crossed my legs and pasted a placid, harmless expression on my face even though the story of the men who visited Lot in Sodom reminded me that evil roamed in darkness, especially in pagan cities.

Dread strummed a shiver from my soul. Far down the street, a pair of men approached. One man kept his eyes lowered as he walked, but the other man stared at me, his eyes bold and possessive. I stood and faced the well; I pulled up the rope and drew out the bucket, pretending to be engaged in my task. I must not let them know I was unprotected. . . .

I flinched when a hand gripped my wrist.

"Do you need a place to stay?"

A woman stood to my left—a young woman with dark eyes and urgency in her voice.

I nodded.

"Will you pay for a night's lodging?"

I blinked. The woman appeared to be Hebrew—she wore a modest tunic and a veil covered her hair. I'd never heard of Israelites charging for their hospitality, but perhaps things were different in this city. "I'll pay."

"Come. Quickly." She tugged on my sleeve, urging me away.

She led me to a small door in a long row of attached buildings of various sizes and shapes. Diamonds of light marked the lattice at the window, and a wooden door hung at an angle on leather hinges. Before opening the door, she paused and held out her hand. For an instant I stared at her palm like a simpleton; then I pulled my purse from my belt and gave her a quadrans—a coin which, I noticed, had been ornamented with Herod's Galilean reeds.

"My name is Dodi," she said, her fingers closing around the money. "My husband and I run an inn—for Israelites." She opened the door and led me into a wide room, dimly lit but scattered with clean-smelling straw. A young family—husband, wife, and two small children—had taken refuge in one corner. A donkey stood in the opposite corner, idly munching a mouthful of oats.

I thanked my hostess and smiled at the young mother.

"Are you alone?" the innkeeper asked, looking out the door.

I moved to an empty spot in the straw and tugged my veil from my head. "I am."

"But your husband—"

"Is dead. I have come here to ask Herod to punish those responsible for murdering my family."

Dodi snapped her mouth shut, then bolted the door. The young husband watched me with wary eyes.

My hostess came closer, the hem of her tunic swishing over the floor. "Would you like water? a basin to wash your hands and feet?"

"Please."

"Are you hungry?" The woman tilted her face toward the light, and for the first time I saw a shade of concern in her eyes.

The tension in my shoulders began to fade. "I've had nothing to eat since noon."

"I have a stew. Sit and rest; I'll bring what you need."

Without further urging, I knelt, heaped an armful of straw into a bundle and placed the bundle between my back and the wall. It felt good to stretch my legs, and after a few minutes of allowing my muscles to relax, I leaned forward to unlace my sandals.

Across the room, the young husband cleared his throat. "Do you really think he will see you?"

I looked up, surprised he would speak to a woman—and a stranger. "Who?"

"Herod. What makes you think he will see you?"

I tugged off my right shoe. "I am one of his subjects, and I have a complaint about an injustice. Why wouldn't he see me?"

The man's expression shifted into a smirk. "Surely you don't believe Herod cares a whit for us. Did you look at this city? The people speak Greek, the guards are Edomite, and did you see the amphitheater at the Eastern Gate? Herod stages spectacles there. Heathen entertainments."

I pulled off my left shoe and let it fall. "I saw no amphitheater, and I hear Greek spoken in my own city. And Herod *is* our king."

"Bah." The young man spat out his disagreement, then lowered his voice. "He is an imbecile and a profligate. You will be lucky if his steward even notices you."

"Then I will wait outside his gate until I am as gray as his pagan statues." I lifted my chin and smiled as Dodi brought me a basin of water and a towel. "Perhaps you know a way to gain an audience with the king?"

"Why would you think such a thing?"

I shrugged. "You run an inn. People must come here to seek an audience with Herod. Surely you know how such a thing can be arranged."

Dodi set the basin on the floor. She stepped back, hands on hips, and watched as I washed my hands, then lowered a dusty foot into the cool water. As I closed my eyes, relaxing in the refreshing sensation of liquid on my skin, I heard her sigh.

"I know nothing of such things, but my husband might. He's at the palace now."

My eyes flew open. "He works for Herod?"

"For several years Tirza has tended the king's horses. I could ask him to put in a word for you with the steward. Other than that, there's nothing I can offer."

I nodded my thanks, then lowered my other foot into the small basin and splashed water over my ankle. My sandals had worn painful blisters on the heels of both feet, but each mile had brought me closer to my goal.

This pain would be a small price to pay for justice.

CHAPTER THIRTEEN

MY HOST, A ROUGH-BEARDED, brawny man known as Tirza, scowled when his wife told him why I'd come to Tiberias. "She wants to see Herod?" he asked, his brows shooting up to his hairline. "She thinks she can walk right in and talk to a king?"

Dodi held up a soothing hand. "She has come all the way from Magdala. She is a widow and she seeks justice. Surely you can do this one thing to help her."

Without warning, the man's gaze shifted and locked on me, focusing with bold intensity. "You have truly come alone?"

I spread my arms. "Do you see an assassin hiding under my cloak?"

"I wouldn't be so bold in the king's presence." The corner of his mouth quirked. "I'll see what I can do. You'll have to wait at the gate until the king receives petitioners in his judgment hall. You may have to wait many days."

I nodded in gratitude as his wife handed me a blanket. "I am facing a lifetime without my family. I can wait a few days."

I slept like a dead woman that night, waking only when one of the young couple's children tapped my shoulder. When I woke at the touch of those stubby fingers, I breathed in the scent of little boy and looked into wide eyes that looked like Binyamin's. For an instant my bitter reality vanished; then memory surged and I cried out, startling the child into running back to his mother.

I sat up and struggled to swallow the sob that rose in my throat. Lest I alarm the others, I turned, allowing the curtain of my hair to hide the tears that trickled over my cheeks in an overflow of feeling.

"He was worried about you," the young mother called, settling the toddler on her lap. "You have been sleeping a long time."

"I was tired." Despite my resolve, my voice wavered. I wiped the wetness from my face and looked toward the latticed window. Indirect sunlight brightened the space while street sounds poured through the opening. Already I could hear the babble of voices and the bleating of goats. "I . . . am not used to sleeping so long." I stood, brushed straw from my tunic, then turned to see if I could help my hostess.

Dodi knelt on a woven rug, where several small loaves of bread waited in a bowl. She caught my gaze and smiled. "You should eat." She pointed toward the food. "My husband has remembered your request. He said you should go to Herod's courtyard and remain there until the steward summons you."

I thanked her, accepted a loaf from her bowl, and gratefully took a bite. The sight of food had awakened my appetite, and I felt ravenous. Dodi was a good cook, and the fruit-filled bread was as good as anything I'd ever eaten in Magdala.

When I had finished eating, I pulled my veil from the straw and shook it out, then smiled at the young mother and her children. "Will you travel today?"

She nodded, but her lips flattened to a thin line, as if she dreaded the prospect. "We are traveling to Jerusalem. My husband's father was at the Temple when he fell ill. He needs us to bring him back to Bethsaida."

"You are a long way from home."

"Yes." She pinched a bit of bread from a loaf, chewed it, then transferred it to her little boy's gaping mouth. "I have seen so much of the land . . . too much, really."

I smiled. "Before this, I had only journeyed from Magdala to Jerusalem and back. Though I had heard stories of Tiberias, I had no idea the city was really—" *This bad*, I wanted to say. Instead I shrugged. "—so interesting."

After finishing my breakfast and washing my face, I thanked my hostess and stepped out onto the street.

"Watch out!"

I whirled in time to see a runaway donkey trotting toward me. I flattened myself against the side of the house as the beast and his frustrated owner passed. Drawing a deep breath, I checked to be sure my veil still covered my hair and tried to arrange my face in pleasing lines.

Before Herod, I would have to appear as a rational and aggrieved woman. He would have to understand that I was no beggar, no slave, no uncivilized farmer's wife. I was Miryam of Magdala, seller of fine fabrics and widow of Yaakov the fisherman. With my husband and son, I had held a place of honor among my countrymen until a company of rogue soldiers took everything from me.

I might not be Roman, but I knew injustice when I saw it. And I had been most grievously wronged.

⋅→⟨══◎══⟩←⋅

After an hour of standing, I shifted on my feet and crossed my arms. A crowd had gathered around Herod's gates since the early morning, yet none of the guards had moved from their positions. No one had opened Herod's door either, which meant the king was either busy with other things or determined to ignore his waiting subjects.

Out of a dozen people standing at the entrance to Herod's court-yard, I was one of only two women. The other woman was young and also alone. At one point I moved toward her and touched her arm, intending to make conversation, but her eyes flew up at me like a pair of blackbirds scared out of safe hiding.

I backed away, seeing that I had alarmed her. "Excuse me."

She lowered her gaze, hanging her head so the edge of her veil obscured her features. Yet she hadn't been quick enough to prevent me from seeing the ugly bruise marring her eye and cheek.

Without being told, I knew what had brought her to Herod's door. This poor child had a cruel husband or father and apparently felt she had no recourse but an appeal to the king.

I clicked my tongue against my teeth. Why was no one defending this child? Where was the girl's mother?

That question brought visions of *my* children rippling in its wake: Avram and Rachel and my precious Binyamin. They slept in their tomb, awaiting justice. I was their only advocate, and I could not fail them.

The wound of their loss, still so fresh, opened like a painful scab, and I closed my eyes lest I sob before a dozen strangers. I had left my home and friends to come to this place; I had ignored almost every standard of virtuous conduct. Must I also expose my tattered heart to heathens?

The sun had climbed high in the sky before Herod's tall doors opened. The crowd around me surged forward, propelled by the heat and whatever had compelled them to seek an audience with the king, but the two stern guards did not grant us passage.

Instead, an olive-skinned face appeared in the opening between the double doors. "Your king is busy." The messenger squinted, peering at us as if he were gauging our propensity for violence. "Herod bids you all go home and come again tomorrow."

"Tomorrow will be too late!" the man next to me cried. "The merchant who cheated me will be too far away from the city."

The messenger stepped back into the cool shade of the hall while his jeweled hand flapped us away. "Go home, all of you."

Unwilling to believe I had heard the man correctly, I threaded my way through the crowd. Hadn't Tirza told the steward about me? I had come such a long way and braved so many trials—

"Wait. Wait!" As the door was closing, I thrust my foot into the opening.

A guard gripped my arm, but the messenger held up a hand, his nostrils flaring as he looked down the length of his nose at me. "Remove your foot, woman."

"Wait, please. Tirza knows me. I am Miryam from Magdala and I must speak to the king."

His look of disapproval deepened. "I told you to go home."

"I have no home—not anymore."

"Remove your foot or I'll ask one of the guards to chop it off."

I slid my sandal out of the way. When the door closed with a final thump, the closest guard's eyes blazed down into mine. "You heard the steward," he said, his voice gruff. "You should go."

"But I've received no answer."

"Come again tomorrow, then."

I shook my head and wearily stepped aside. I had a choice— return home or remain in Tiberias until I could present my case. I missed Magdala and hated Herod's city, but for the sake of my loved ones I could not leave.

I trudged over the flagstone street and knocked again on Tirza's door. Dodi opened it and did not seem surprised to see me.

I sank to a section of clean-swept floor. Without speaking, the innkeeper's wife swept up the remaining soiled straw from the previous night. The scent of goat hung heavily in the air.

"The children have gone," Dodi finally said, her gaze roving over the area the young family had occupied. "I will miss them."

I lowered my head into my hands and wept.

⋄⟩══◈══⟨⋄

Except for the Shabbat, which I quietly observed with Tirza and Dodi, for the next several days I presented myself at Herod's gate and waited among the heathens until late afternoon. The coins in my purse dwindled; the faces outside Herod's palace became far too familiar. Many of those who sought an audience with the king gave up and went on their way, but I would not be swayed from my quest.

So I waited.

Each night, Tirza provided another excuse for his inability to act on my behalf—either Herod had not gone to the stables that day, or Tirza had not been called into the palace. Or Herod *had* gone to the stables but had been too busy to listen to his groom, or the king had walked by the stables but had been too angry to speak to anyone.

Every night I gritted my teeth, thanked Tirza for remembering my cause, and promised to wait another day.

I also learned to invest my time more wisely. When I realized that Herod did not rise until long after sunrise, I wandered the boulevards of Tiberias before joining the crowd at the palace gates. I examined the goods of cloth makers and visited the booths of other weavers and dyers. I smiled in quiet pleasure when I realized that though the leading dyer of Tiberias had managed to produce a deep and lovely purple, his silk would not project a crimson hue no matter how carefully one shaded it from the sun.

So many times I would see something and find myself thinking, *I must remember to tell Yaakov about this.* On those occasions, sorrow fell on me like a weight, encumbering my limbs and curbing my enthusiasm for everything but justice.

One morning, when the heaviness in my chest felt like a millstone, I paused at a booth where a young woman with dark skin stood beside a skeletal tree dripping with amulets.

"My lady," she said, bowing as I struggled to restrain a sudden rush of tears, "have you been visited by grief and sadness? Perhaps your heart is filled with despair. My amulets, blessed by the gods, can drive such awful feelings into the abyss."

I waved my hands and backed away, repelled as much by her words as by the sight of so many graven images swinging in the breeze. But as the days passed and the girl's invitation became familiar, I lingered in the music of the tinkling amulets.

On my eleventh day in Tiberias, the girl met my gaze and smiled. "I am Marisa," she told me, tossing a clicking mass of beaded hair over her shoulder. "Formerly a slave, now a free woman."

I'd never met a freed slave. Few Hebrews in Magdala kept slaves, and none were as exotic looking as this girl.

She must have seen the question in my eyes. "My master bought me in Egypt and brought me here. I thought I would die of loneliness in this place, so I prayed to Isis for wisdom." She reached out and cupped an elaborately carved amulet. "One night my master lay down near the fire. I had fallen asleep, but the stench of burning hair woke me. I sat up, saw my master's hair afire, and beat out the flames with my hands. My master was so grateful he granted my freedom."

She looked at me with an odd mingling of wariness and amusement. "Have you been praying for something?"

I hesitated, then nodded.

Marisa gave me a bright-eyed glance, full of shrewdness. "Perhaps you have been praying to the wrong god."

I took a half step back and forced a laugh. She was a persuasive saleswoman, but I did not need an amulet. No daughter of Avraham should even look upon a graven image. I lifted a brow. "If you were so lonely, why didn't you go back to Egypt when you were granted your freedom?"

She spread her hands. "How was I supposed to get back to the land of my birth? I remained here because Isis told me she would take care of me no matter where I lived. As long as I have Isis and a place to sleep, I am home."

I glanced up the street and felt my pulse quicken. The gate leading to Herod's courtyard had opened.

"I have to go." Hope and anticipation brightened my voice as I called my farewell. "A prosperous day to you, Marisa."

———◇———

Herod's bejeweled steward was scanning the crowd when I arrived, breathless and flushed. My heart did a double beat when I saw Tirza standing behind him in the open doorway. The keeper of the king's stable bent to whisper in the steward's ear; then the haughty man pointed to me. "You, woman—come forward. And you, the merchant from Jerusalem. All the rest of you must go home; the king will see no one else today."

Taking a deep, unsteady breath, I stepped forward as the grumbling crowd dissipated. The merchant from Jerusalem, a tall man in a richly embroidered robe, shifted a polished wooden box from one arm to the other, then charged toward the steward without even glancing at me.

I followed without a word. As a woman, I was accustomed to being invisible.

The steward, who introduced himself as Chuza, led us through a grand hall of polished stone and white marble. I found myself drifting closer to Tirza, the only familiar face in sight. But like an animal that senses danger, he slipped though another door and disappeared, leaving me alone.

The steward barked out a warning when my footsteps faltered: "Do not linger! Do not look around! Follow me without delay!"

Not wanting to be scolded again, I lowered my gaze and tucked my hands into my sleeves.

Finally we halted before a pair of double doors gleaming with pounded brass. More animal figures—dogs and bears and lions— had been etched into the metal, while the center of each door featured a commanding figure with a bow and spear. I didn't have to be told I was looking at a graven representation of Herod himself.

"Wait here," Chuza hissed. He opened the doors slightly, releasing a stream of music into the hall, then disappeared, only to reappear a moment later.

He spoke first to the merchant. "Drop your gift at Herod's feet, then step back and bow. Do not speak unless spoken to. Answer any question in as few words as possible. And do not approach the king under any circumstances."

The merchant blew out his cheeks. "But how will I know if he wishes to obtain more of my goods?"

"He'll tell you. As for you, woman—" Chuza turned to me—"do not speak unless Herod notices you. Do not lift your eyes when talking to the king. Do not look upon his face. State your case and wait for the king's answer. Do you understand?"

Not certain what to do with my eyes, I met the steward's gaze and immediately looked down. "I understand."

"All right, then." The little man turned and pulled the doors wide. The merchant lifted his chin and strode into a room filled with the rhythmic pounding of drums. Following like his shadow, I padded after him.

I nearly ran into the merchant when he stopped to lay his gift at Herod's feet. Realizing I had followed too closely, I retreated and stood in silence, chin down, eyes scrolling upward, ears tuned to catch the slightest whisper.

I had never beheld anything like the scene that met my eyes.

At first I thought I had stepped outdoors. Vivid paintings of a grassy wilderness adorned the walls behind several couches, where two men and a woman reclined around a small table. Clouds drifted through a blue sky painted on the ceiling over my head, and the soft breath of fans made me feel as though I had been ushered into the cool shade of a meadow by the lake.

Behind the young girls who stirred the air with their fans, a trio of slaves beat a series of graduated drums while a flautist piped a slithering melody. Near them, to my right, a lithe woman with pale skin moved her bare arms and legs and hips in time to the rhythm, bracelets jangling as she narrowed her eyes and grimaced at the men on the couches.

Those men had eyes for no one else. I did not think they even noticed our arrival.

I felt a blush burn my cheek. Because my business frequently brought me into contact with heathen foreigners, I had always considered myself sophisticated, but I had never seen anything like this lewd display of flesh and form. Even the prostitutes who occasionally tarried around Magdala's city gates would never advertise their bodies as this young woman did.

The merchant from Jerusalem lost all custody of his eyes. For a long moment he stared at the writhing girl. Then he snapped to his senses and remembered the steward's instructions. He bowed before the king, pointedly lingering beside the wooden coffer on the floor.

Movement from the heaviest man on the couches caught my attention. He wore a tunic of white silk and a cloak of deep purple, while a circlet of golden leaves crowned his brow. Every finger gleamed with gold; even his toes shone in the glow of lamplight. His hair had been oiled and set into tiny curls above a wide forehead and a soft, round chin.

He was a rounder, softer version of the warrior depicted on the brass doors: Herod Antipas.

Amid the thump of drums and the jangle of bracelets, my heart began to pound in my chest. Had I committed a foolish act by coming to this pagan palace? My murdered family cried out for vengeance, but why couldn't HaShem lead me to someone more virtuous than Antipas?

My heart sank with swift disappointment. I had heard stories about this king, but I didn't want to believe them. Stories can be exaggerated and rumors can be false, but one look at the Idumean king convinced me that I'd been sheltered from the full and terrible truth.

Rumor held that Antipas was as vicious as his father, and no one had forgotten the elder Herod's murder of his favorite wife, Mariamne; her two sons, Alexander and Aristobulus; and, only five days before his death, his oldest son, Antipater. On his deathbed, the elder Herod had ordered the nobles assembled around him in his last moments to be executed, so his death might be attended by universal mourning.

Some said he had once ordered the massacre of every baby boy in a small village called *Beit Lechem*, or Bethlehem. I would have thought such an act too barbarous for a descendant of Avraham, but the Herods were Edomites, and violence flowed through the blood of Esau's offspring.

That thought brought another in its shadow, with a chill that struck deep in the pit of my stomach. If Herod the Great had killed scores of Hebrew babies without a second thought, could I expect his son to value the life of *my* baby boy?

I peered around the edge of my veil as the king leaned toward the merchant's box, curiosity evident in his fleshy face. On the couch across from him, the heavily painted lady lifted her arm, touched her hennaed hands to her lips, and dramatically stifled a yawn. "Herod," she said, her voice a purr in the room, "must we put up with these common folk while Salome is dancing?"

The king ignored her and gestured to the merchant. "Who are you and what have you brought me?"

"Long life and peace to you, my king." The merchant lifted his head from the floor. "I have traveled many days to bring you this token of my esteem." With great care he raised the lid of the wooden box, exposing a golden crown. With one hand he lifted it from its silken bed and presented it to Herod.

The king tossed a gloating look at the woman, then removed the gold circlet he wore. The new crown was a cunning design; the goldsmith had skillfully hammered his material to resemble the reeds Herod had chosen to represent his magnificent city. From where I stood the narrow stalks looked almost lifelike.

Herod positioned the crown on his head, then shifted it so the thickest section of golden reeds rested squarely above his brows. "Herodias?" He grinned. "What do you think?"

The woman couldn't have looked more bored. "Why do you want to wear a crown of weeds?"

The brightness that had lit Herod's face dissipated. Pouting like a spoiled child, the king lifted the crown and unceremoniously tossed it back in the box.

"Does the gift not please you?" The worried merchant pressed his hands together. "If not, we could make something else, a representation more fitting to your august position. I could take this back to Jerusalem and have it reshaped into something more to your taste—"

Thought worked in Herod's eyes as his squint tightened. "Few men bring gifts without also bringing a request," he said, one fat hand falling to his dimpled knee. "What is your request?"

The merchant bowed his head again. "We would ask . . . that is, we would like to ask—"

"Do not exhaust my patience."

"When you come to Jerusalem, will you wear the crown we have made? We would be honored to be known as Herod's goldsmith; we would be respected if all Jerusalem recognized the jeweler who had fashioned the crown that graces your head."

Herod sat up, swung his legs to the floor, and rested both hands on his knees. He regarded the merchant with eyes from which a film of boredom had been peeled away.

"I will wear your crown," he finally said, a smile tugging at the corners of his mouth, "but I will keep this one to amuse my dear wife. By the time I leave for the festivals of the high holy days in Jerusalem, you will furnish me with two additional crowns—one for me and one for Herodias. They will not be simple gold, but gold studded with rubies and other precious stones. They must be the most elegant crowns Eretz-Yisrael has ever seen."

The merchant's hands began to tremble. "Oh—oh yes, of course. But *two* crowns with precious stones—the cost will be high!"

"Not as high as the honor I am bestowing on you." The king's dark eyes flicked toward Herodias, before returning to the merchant. "You may go."

The merchant bowed his way out of the room, nearly running into me in the process. For a moment I was tempted to scurry away in his shadow, but memories of Yaakov, Avram, and Binyamin compelled me to stay.

Herod reclined again on his couch and reached for a plate laden with pastry and fruit. Herodias, however, had seen me—one woman will always see another.

"Herod." She caught his gaze, then tilted her head toward me. "Another waits for you."

The king popped a pastry onto his tongue, dusted his hands, and turned to me, his cheeks distended. He measured me with a cool, appraising look, then mumbled around the delicacies in his mouth, "What do you want, woman?"

I fell to my knees in the heat of his pitiless gaze. "Merciful king, my soul is greatly troubled. I have come from Magdala with a request."

I could not lift my head, but in the play of shadows on the floor I saw Herod turn to his wife. "Has there been trouble in Magdala?"

"Ask *her*," Herodias answered.

"Look at me, woman."

I trembled, but did as he commanded.

"What is this trouble?"

I tried to summon the words, but they clotted in my throat. I had come so far, waited so long, and carried such a heavy burden. This odious toad could avenge the deaths of my family, so why wouldn't my tongue cooperate with my will?

Because terror had seized me. The Romans who attacked my family had been cruel, but Herod had been so cruel for so long that he wouldn't hesitate to order *my* death if I insulted him. He had probably killed others for less.

I gulped back my fear. "If it please the king—"

"It would please the king if you would get on with it."

Herodias giggled.

I drew a long, quivering breath, mastering the panic that shook me. "If it please the king, I come to you as a woman who has been most unjustly injured. Murder, oh king, has been committed in your territory. My husband, my two sons, and my daughter-in-law were most foully killed only a month ago."

"Murder?" Herod put on the look of a man who has just been knocked over by a charging goat. "In my territory?"

Scarcely daring to breathe, I nodded.

"Was this murder provoked in any way?"

The question stole my breath. *Provoked?* "I'm not sure what you mean," I confessed, "but neither my husband nor my sons did anything to injure the men who treated them so abominably."

"Then you shall have the justice you seek." Herod leaned forward, his weight on one elbow. "But first I must know—what sort of Jews kill an entire family without help? Have you a pair of Samsons living up there in Magdala?"

Herodias laughed aloud, and at the sound of her mirth my fear shifted to irritation.

"The murderers are not Samsons, oh king, and neither are they children of Avraham. They are Roman soldiers; one is a centurion and the other is one of his officers."

Herod's heavy jaw fell open before he recovered from his surprise. "You're sure about this?"

"Yes, my king. The Romans were passing through the area and camped outside our city. My neighbors investigated the matter on my behalf. Others were involved, of course, but those two were the leaders."

Herod squeezed his eyes so tight his entire face seemed about to collapse on itself. "Roman centurions do not go around the country-side murdering Judean citizens. Rome wants to govern a peaceful people, and murder is not peaceful."

The tide had turned—a moment ago I'd had Herod's promise to help, but the edge in his voice suggested he was about to change his mind. I would have to regain his cooperation quickly.

"Perhaps, sir, the centurion thought he had cause to act, though I'm sure you'll agree his motivation was baseless and his reaction exaggerated beyond the bounds of reason. My son is—was—quick-tempered. Though he said nothing against this Roman, I witnessed something between them earlier that day."

Herod opened one eye in a cautious slit. "Go on."

"It was nothing important, my king."

"Nothing is nothing, and yet you saw something. So speak, woman."

"I saw my son Avram . . . spit at the centurion's sandal."

"He *spat* at him?" Tremors of mirth fractured Herodias's voice.

Desperate to have Herod understand, I unleashed the torrent of words bubbling in my throat: "Avram spat at the man's sandal—*on* his sandal. But the centurion, this Gaius, did not protest. Instead he came back under cover of darkness and struck an innocent family at supper! With his men, with this giant, Atticus, he slaughtered my loved ones and burned my home! He took everything I had, every-one I cared about."

When Herod lifted his hand, the drums and dancing ceased. I heard only my pulse battering my ears; then the king signaled the guards by the door and pointed to me. For a wild and hopeful instant I thought his gesture meant those men would be dispatched to take up my cause. The guards strode forward and stood at my right and left hand.

The king leaned back and reached for another pastry. "Take her away."

Courage returned as my heart pumped indignation and outrage through my veins. "My king!" I screamed the words, for what did I have to lose? "They killed my daughter-in-law; they ripped the baby from her womb, dashed its brains against a doorpost, and fed its body to the flames! They behaved like animals in one of your peaceful cities, and you will do nothing to intercede for me?"

Slowly, Herod chewed, his eyes narrowing with fury. Hope flared again; then I realized his anger burned toward me, not the Romans, and in a moment I would insult him beyond his capacity for mercy.

I yielded to the sobs that clogged my throat and collapsed as the guards dragged me from Herod's hall. When we passed the bronze doors at the courtyard, Tirza stepped forward and squeezed my arm so tightly I whimpered in pain.

"Do you value *your* life, woman?" he snarled in my ear. "If I'd known who you came to accuse, I would never have acted on your behalf."

"This is not justice." I wiped my cheeks with the back of my hand as the guards left me in Tirza's custody and slammed the doors. "If Herod does nothing, justice does not exist in Judea."

"Who said it did?" Tirza's voice remained low and controlled. "Herod rules at Rome's pleasure; don't you understand? He would no sooner act against a Roman centurion than he would walk through the streets naked. You have committed a great folly, woman, and I am sorry to have spoken for you."

"But I had hoped—"

"Hope is for children and fools. Now get safely away before Herod remembers your insults and seeks you out."

Still holding my arm, Tirza marched me through the courtyard and thrust me into the street. I found myself standing in the hot sun with an empty scrip around my shoulder.

My horrible losses, combined with the heaviness of defeat, left me with an inexpressible feeling of hopelessness. I trudged from Herod's palace and wandered through the streets until I found a trough for animals. I sank to the mud at its edge and splashed water on my tear-streaked face, then sat motionless as a man tied his donkey to a nearby post and walked away without speaking.

The animal drank deeply, ignoring me. A horsefly buzzed around the beast's ears, then settled on my damp hand.

I stared at the vile fly and considered the raw sores of my aching heart. Where could I go from here? Magdala held nothing for me but memories and charred ruins. I felt nothing for Tiberias and I had no connections with any other place or people in Eretz-Yisrael.

In only one month, everything I had been—wife, mother, merchant—had been destroyed. Nothing remained but skin, bones, and bitterness.

I had lost myself.

Not wanting to see Tirza or Dodi again, I slid backward until my spine rested against a wall, then hugged my knees to my chest. With nowhere else to go, I would sit and wait for sunset. Perhaps, if I was lucky, one of the heathens would attempt to rob me and, finding nothing valuable in my purse, would take my life instead.

Chapter Fourteen

The invitation had startled Atticus. In honor of his wife's birthday, Pontius Pilate, procurator of Judea, wished to invite all officers under his command—centurions and all *principales*, including those with the rank of signifier, optio, or tesserarius—to a banquet at the palace.

He and Flavius retreated immediately to the baths, where they scraped off the day's grime before dressing in clean tunics and polished armor.

"Do you think they'll have meat?" Atticus asked, thinking of the plate of unground corn, or *frumentum,* that awaited the soldiers at the barracks.

"Who cares?" Flavius waggled his brows. "I want to know if they'll have dancing girls."

With light hearts they climbed the steps to the palace, left their helmets in the care of a slave, and entered the grand banquet hall. The governor's steward had outdone himself. Lamps gleamed from niches in the wall and freestanding pillars, brightening the room nearly as well as the sun itself. White linen cushions covered every reclining couch, and several tables groaned beneath platters of every imaginable delicacy—including, Atticus noticed—beef and chicken and fish. *Meat.*

Atticus washed his hands in a laver of rose petal–scented water, then accepted a linen hand towel from a servant. A group of harpists stood behind fan-bearing servants, filling the air with a warm, continuous ripple like flowing water. The men stood, hungry and waiting, until the guest of honor appeared on her husband's arm. Smiling at the assembled soldiers, the Lady Procula followed her husband to a raised dais; then she reclined on her couch.

Atticus looked at Flavius, who nodded in Gaius's direction. Their centurion was more accustomed to patrician living than they, so they sat when he sat; they ate when he lifted his first bite off a tray.

As the group relaxed, Atticus lifted his goblet and realized that all six centurions and eighteen principales of their cohort had accepted the governor's invitation. Who wouldn't? Not often were they treated to pastries, meat, and music in a single night.

After dinner, a trio of dancing girls entertained the men, much to Flavius's delight. After the dancing, when Pilate should have dismissed his guests, Gaius Cabilenus stood and moved to the center of the room, awaiting the governor's attention.

Atticus watched his centurion with a mixture of pride and anxiety. What was Gaius doing? The other centurions had toasted Lady Procula's health and praised her beauty, but none of them had risked this sort of attention.

Pilate leaned forward, the fold of his toga looped over one arm. "What say you, Gaius?"

"If it please the governor and my lady Procula—" Gaius bowed low—"may I present the Lady Carina? She has a gift for our governor's wife."

Pilate nodded, granting permission, and a pair of doors opened at the back of the room. A lovely woman entered, an exotic beauty whose dark hair spilled from a knot at the top of her head and splashed on her bare shoulders.

Flavius nudged Atticus with his elbow. Most of the men in their century had met the lady Carina and none of them liked her. The woman whined constantly when she traveled with the army, yet she refused to remain behind.

Tonight, however, Gaius's mistress radiated gracious elegance. She came into the hall and sank to one knee at Gaius's side, then pulled a mass of cloth from a white bag at her side.

"In honor of my lady's birthday," she said, her mouth twisting in something not quite a smile, "may I present a most remarkable and unique fabric?"

Flavius nudged Atticus again. "I heard about this," he said, concealing his mouth behind his upraised goblet. "She didn't want to give that silk away, but Gaius commanded her. He said it wasn't fitting that she should wear more purple than the governor's wife."

Atticus lifted a brow. "That fabric is red."

Flavius raised a brow, then barked a laugh. "Maybe the vixen pulled a switch."

Gaius took the folded material from his mistress's hands and presented it to Lady Procula. "To honor you, my lady. This extraordinary fabric changes from crimson to the deepest purple you can imagine."

Procula smiled at her husband, then accepted Gaius's gift. She ran her hand over the cloth and tugged on a corner, spilling its length onto the floor. "It is lovely, centurion. But how does it change?"

"Light, my lady. It changes when exposed to the light."

Still smiling, Procula held the fabric aloft, angling it toward the nearest lamp, but the fabric remained crimson.

Atticus glanced at Flavius, who shrugged and took another sip of wine.

Gaius tried to smile, but the corners of his mouth only wobbled precariously. "Perhaps you have to wear it. Perhaps it takes time."

Though a frown settled over Pilate's face, the Lady Procula inclined her head in what looked like sincere gratitude. "Thank you, Gaius and Carina, for thinking of me. This is a lovely silk. I may use some of it to make a cloak for Pilate." She kissed her husband's scowling cheek, then dismissed Gaius and his mistress with a wave of her hand. "Everyone, please, eat your fill before departing. Thank you so much for sharing this evening."

Atticus turned back to the table to see what remained of their feast. He was reaching for the last bite of candied apple when he caught Flavius's eye.

"And that," his friend said, keeping his voice low, "is why it doesn't pay to keep a woman or give fancy gifts to your betters. A gift horse is likely to turn and kick you in the rear."

Atticus popped the apple into his mouth. "I'm not likely to be giving anyone a horse and I don't have a woman."

"Oh yes you do."

"Cyrilla's not my woman; she's Quinn's nurse."

"She'll be your woman soon enough," Flavius answered, grinning. "And mark my words, women are where trouble always begins."

CHAPTER FIFTEEN

I DON'T KNOW HOW long I sat there, but at some point before daybreak I dozed off amid the bleating of livestock.

A gentle touch woke me. I looked up, expecting to see Dodi or another Hebrew woman, but Marisa, the Egyptian ex-slave, knelt by my side. "You are lost," she said. "Come with me."

I might have refused, but stern looks from a pair of herders convinced me they weren't happy I had crowded their goats at the trough. So I rose and followed the Egyptian girl, wandering through the streets and alleys until we reached her stall in the marketplace. She pulled aside a woven grass mat, then bade me enter her small space. She pointed to an empty spot on a carpet. "Sit."

Too depleted to argue, I obeyed and sank to the ground behind the dead tree that held the young woman's wares. Marisa's stall was clean and well swept, and there I could breathe deeply without inhaling the scents of animals.

She poured a cup of cool water from a stone jug, then broke off a handful of bread and handed both bread and cup to me.

Though my stomach growled, I shook my head. "I can't take your food."

"Isis has provided. So take, eat, and restore your strength."

I hesitated only a moment before obeying. The water tasted like fine wine; the bread had a delicious crust and a soft interior. "This—" I pointed to the bread—"is wonderful."

She laughed. "Now I *know* you were hungry."

Marisa squatted across from me and nibbled on a bit of crust, then stood to help a bareheaded woman who stopped to inquire about her amulets. After the customer had purchased three—one for herself and one for each of her daughters—Marisa returned. "Are you feeling better?"

"Yes. Thank you." I looked at her through gritty eyes that felt as though they'd shed every tear and all feeling. "I should be going."

"You will wait here. There's no need to return to that horrid man at the inn."

I gaped at her. "How did you know where I—?"

"Isis told me. She tells me all kinds of things."

I blinked while Marisa stood to help another customer. Isis was a foreign god, a man-made bit of stone or wood and an anathema to any Israelite . . . or so I'd been taught.

I had grown up in a village where from age six boys were schooled in the Tanach, our Scriptures, and taught to respect the one invisible God above all created things. Though women were forbidden to learn Torah, my father recognized that HaShem had blessed me with a curious and quick mind. Perhaps he'd realized that one day I would need to know the Law in order to teach my own sons, so he never forbade me from listening as he instructed my brothers.

With them, I memorized passages of Scripture, but they studied the words of the prophets at my father's knee while I learned Torah as I swept the floor around them.

After age six, my brothers studied with our rabbi at the synagogue. Because I never went to school, I didn't learn as much as my brothers, but I knew the stories of the prophets. I knew how our forefathers had fallen into idol worship and heathen practices. HaShem had burned with anger toward us, and we had been exiled from our Promised Land for seventy years.

Was HaShem *still* angry with us? For though we lived in the land promised to Avraham, Yitzhak, and Yaakov, we worked and worshiped under the ruthless hand of a foreign emperor. We remained at the mercies of his spineless vassals who did nothing to avenge our wrongs or punish those who struck us without just cause.

I lifted my eyes to Marisa's dead tree and its fingerlike branches. The unblinking eyes of stone faces stared down at me, each of them promising—what? What could these stone idols grant that the God of our fathers could not?

Justice.

Revenge.

Satisfaction.

The voices brushed by me with the gentleness of a whisper, but the effect was as great as if they'd shouted in my ear. For no reason I could name, those three words raised the hairs at the back of my neck.

Marisa finished with her customer, slipped coins into her purse, then knelt by my side. I gave her a brief, distracted glance and tried to smile. "Did you hear them?"

She tilted her head. "Who?"

"Never mind."

She studied me, then took my hand with a smile far more warming than the rising sun. "What," she whispered, "do you want most in the world?"

Speaking in the low voice reserved for secret things, I told her. She smiled.

And a lifetime of service to the God of Avraham, Yitzhak, and Yaakov fell away as I leaned forward to listen.

CHAPTER SIXTEEN

THE STONE AMULET WAS A SMALL THING, no bigger than my thumbnail. It dangled from a thin leather strip and tucked between my breasts. My secret. My hope.

My Yaakov, he of blessed memory, would be furious to know I had put on an amulet. But my husband could no longer forbid me anything. The man who had failed to teach his son how to hold his tongue had been gathered to his fathers, a group of devout Hebrews who had gone to their graves awaiting deliverance from on high.

After accepting the amulet from Marisa, I tried to explain my previous reticence. "I was raised as a daughter of Avraham," I told her. "I obeyed my father, listened to my mother, observed the Shabbat and the law of Moses. But I never understood why women were not allowed to learn like men. I once heard the rabbi tell my brothers that it would be better for the words of the Law to be burned than be delivered to a woman."

Marisa said nothing, but from the look in her eye I knew she understood. We had much in common, this ex-slave and I. We had both been born female; we had both come to maturity in a type of bondage, though mine had been a gentler servitude. Now Marisa had shown me a path to freedom.

The hopelessness I'd felt after my audience with Herod evolved into renewed determination. My desire for justice had not dimmed, and since neither my king nor my prayers to my father's God had had any effect, I felt no guilt in seeking another source of help. So I slipped an amulet around my neck, and each morning I followed Marisa's example and spilled grain onto the small stone altar outside her stall.

For several days I remained in Tiberias, working in Marisa's booth and listening to her tales of the spirit world. In many ways I felt like a child again, but this time I was free to learn at my instructor's knee. The gods were just like people, Marisa said; they suffered from jealousies and rivalries and anger. If we pleased them, they might be persuaded to help us; if we angered them, they would work mischief in our lives. Though we could not see their faces, they were always near. Sometimes, if we focused and listened carefully, we could hear them speak.

One night, as the stars hid their faces behind a dark cloud, I lay in Marisa's stall and again promised an entire pantheon of deities that I would give anything, *be* anything, if they would help me avenge my family's murders.

A muffled cry cut into my thoughts. I rose on one elbow and checked Marisa, who often cried out in her sleep, but she remained still, long strands of her beaded hair draped over her dreaming face.

Again, a noise—an unmistakable bleat of pain and terror followed by a rumbling growl. I sat upright and peered over the edge of the grass mat that separated us from the road and saw nothing alarming. Night lights burned in the houses across the way; a lone watchman paced at the end of the street. I was about to lie back down when I heard the familiar sound of hobnails grinding against pavement.

A Roman soldier in a red tunic stepped out from the alley and looked toward the roving night watchman. His sharp and surly profile, outlined against the shadows, gave him the appearance of a bird of prey. He placed his hands on his hips, glanced left and right, then strode down the street with the unconscious arrogance of a conquering warrior.

That's when I knew what he'd done.

With my heart in my throat, I slipped beneath the mat and crept toward the alley. Somewhere a family was missing a daughter; one day a husband would refuse his promised bride. Because unless I was mistaken, that Roman pig had found an unescorted girl on the street and dragged her to this place.

I peered into the shadows. "Hello?"

No answer.

"I won't hurt you. I am Miryam, and I can help."

I leaned forward, straining to see through the darkness; then I heard a mewling wail.

I stepped into utter blackness and swung my arms wide until my feet encountered something. I knelt and opened my arms to the injured innocent I sought.

"Dear one." I smoothed her hair from her wet face; the brute had torn her veil away. "Come, let me help you."

She shuddered in my embrace. She would not speak or cling to me, so I supported her as best I could and pulled her into the light.

Marisa had awakened by the time I reached the booth. Without a word she reached out to the girl within my arms, then bade her lie down.

While Marisa murmured incantations and tended to the girl's pain, I stared down the empty street and felt a cold knot form in my stomach. The girl at my feet was no young woman—she was yet a child, probably only eleven or twelve years old. Her clothing told me she was Hebrew; her bruised face told me she'd suffered violence as well as humiliation.

Marisa caught my eye, not daring to speak what we both knew: the life this girl had dreamed of would never come to pass.

Silence loomed between us like a heavy mist; then I turned and strode out of the stall. My fear had vanished, replaced by a glorious rage. What did I care if I met a Roman soldier in the street? Let one of the vile dogs assault me, and I would die cursing him.

I strode toward the city gates, determined to be done with this wretched place. Hatred—and a desire for justice—boiled in my soul. When I reached the barrier of the tall wooden doors, I lifted my fist and begged any god that would answer to take my hate and use it to avenge my family. I screamed at the sky, tore at my tunic, allowed my anger and hatred to pour out in a flood of vituperation.

The tower guards called out warnings, but I ignored them. I might have cursed Herod and the Romans until the guards arrested me, but an unexpected gust of wind whirled around my feet and sent an anticipatory shiver rippling through my limbs. The wind ruffled the hem of my tunic and moved upward, caressing my knees, my hips, my shoulders. I opened my mouth and breathed it in, inhaling a scent like the freshness of a spring morning. And in that instant, I felt satisfied. Empowered. Filled with hope.

I had not won my battle, but I no longer felt alone. Enchanted and elated, I walked back to the marketplace and stopped in front of Marisa's amulet-laden tree.

I was standing there, lost in a pleasant daze, when I heard a woman's laughter. I turned, expecting to see Marisa and the girl, but they were neither in the street nor in the booth. I stood alone, accompanied only by my determination and the flickering watch lights from a half-dozen houses.

As light and lovely as rainwater, the sound rippled again in my ears, before warming my shoulders and tingling the length of my arms. Laughter floated up from *my* throat, warm and rich, yet I had not consciously produced the sound. I was not drunk. I felt a long way from any kind of humor, yet something . . . or someone . . . laughed within me.

A sense of unease crept into my consciousness like a plume of smoke. My heart nearly stopped when I heard a voice: *Poor woman, do you want your family avenged? Call on me and I will help you.*

I stumbled backward, astonished by the whisper echoing in my head. I could see no one in the street shadows, not even a night watchman. The voice did not belong to Marisa or one of the other merchants; it seemed to come from *inside* my head. . . .

Hot as it was, I felt as though a trickle of mountain water had slid down my spine. I gathered my tattered courage and whispered into the shadows, "Who are you?"

Again, laughter spilled in my head, accompanied this time by a musical female voice: *I am Natar, friend of Isis, a friend to you. Do you truly want justice for your family?*

Though my heart raged like a wild thing trapped in a cage, I nodded. "I do."

Then I will help you.

I had heard promises of help before; I would not be easily won. I jerked my chin at my unseen ally. "Prove it."

In the rising wind, the voice commanded, *Go to Tirza's inn.*

I made my way along the silent street and halted when one of the night watchmen appeared in the moonlight. He stopped, observing me, and spoke in a low voice so as not to wake those who slept just beyond the open windows. "What are you doing here, woman?"

I pointed up the road. "I'm on my way to Tirza's house."

The watchman stepped closer and held his lamp aloft. I squinted under his scrutiny, half afraid he would look through my eyes and see Natar, but he appeared satisfied and lowered his lamp. "Be off with you. But do not wander the streets after dark in Herod's city."

I bowed, then walked to the innkeeper's dwelling. I hesitated at the threshold, listening for some last-minute instruction from the voice that had sent me, yet I heard nothing but the wind.

I rapped on the door. Sounds of movement came from the latticed window. Dodi peered at me through a crack in the doorway. Her eyes widened when she recognized me. "Miryam?"

"May I come in?"

She opened the door wider. "Do you need a place to sleep?"

I shook my head. "In truth, I'm not sure why I've come."

I looked around the dimly lit surroundings. Two men slept near the windows, their shoulders covered with woolen blankets. A rough grumble seeped from beneath the curtain separating the front room from the cooking area.

Dodi's brow wrinkled as she regarded me. "Are you a healer?"

"Is someone sick?"

"Tirza. He came home yesterday with pain in his chest. I've dosed him with herbs and covered him with blankets, but still he moans and mumbles and struggles for breath."

I closed my eyes and listened. Had Natar sent me to help the man who had practically tossed me into the street?

"May I see him?"

Dodi led me to the back of the house, where Tirza lay under a blanket on a mound of straw. Perspiration dotted his forehead and upper lip; his eyes were closed against the lamplight shining from a niche in the wall. He opened his eyes, but gave no sign that he recognized me or his wife.

Not knowing what else to do, I knelt by the big man's side. Natar remained silent within me, so I whispered, "I came. Now what do I do?"

The voice did not answer, and I could feel the pressure of Dodi's eyes on me. If I kept talking to myself she would think I had gone mad.

I lifted my head and caught her eye. "Do not be frightened. I think . . . I think I have been visited by one of the gods. She sent me to you, so I'm hoping she'll tell me what to do."

Dodi's face drew into a pale knot of apprehension. With one hand at her throat, she stepped back and squatted behind her cook pot.

I closed my eyes and begged Natar for direction. "I came. I obeyed. Now you must tell me what to do."

An icy quiver ascended to the back of my neck when the voice answered: *Will you obey?*

"Of course, I'm here."

No matter what happens?

"No matter what."

Show him your hand.

My hand? What good would that do? I lifted my arm before Tirza's closed eyes; nothing happened. In order to keep from appearing foolish before Dodi, I teased a strand of hair from Tirza's fevered brow, then dipped a cloth in water and wiped his face. At my touch he lifted his lids, recognition flickering in his eyes.

Show him your hand!

Why? I glanced at my hands; they appeared ordinary and unremarkable.

"Tirza, are you better?" I reached for the water jug, thinking I would give the man a drink, but before I could ask Dodi for a cup, unseen fingers closed around my throat. I tried to speak and couldn't; I tried to draw breath and could not.

You must learn to obey! Show him your hand!

In desperation I thrust out my hand and watched my tingling palm fill with a bloodred image of the angular face on my amulet.

Poor Tirza! As the pressure on my neck eased, the sick man's eyes bulged and his skin flushed. I clenched my palm and tucked my bloody hand behind my back, but after a horrible interval of choking and gurgling, Tirza's head lolled away from me, his eyes as blank as windows.

Dodi stumbled to us and found her husband dead. The hostess who had always treated me with respect stared in disbelief for a long moment, then turned on me. "You killed him." She glared at me with burning, reproachful eyes. "You came here to destroy Tirza, not to heal him."

"No, I—"

"You were angry because Herod wouldn't listen. So you came here to punish my husband."

I tried to protest, but the woman wouldn't listen, so I ran outside and stood quivering in the street as Dodi's keening wails shattered the night silence.

I trembled in every limb. What if Dodi accused me before Herod? She could say I killed her husband with sorcery—and in that moment, I wondered if I had. If the people of Tiberias had suddenly surged out of their houses to stone me, I would not have protested.

I smothered a sob and fled.

Chapter Seventeen

After completing a twenty-mile march in five hours, Atticus led a company of auxiliary recruits back to the training square and ordered them to stand in formation. When they had stopped shuffling, he strolled in front of them, nodding when he saw a particularly alert face.

"And so your life as a soldier begins," he said, locking his hands behind his back as he eyed the Samaritan trainees. "Nothing is more important to the Roman army than soldiers who can march. An army split by stragglers is always in danger from the enemy. When you are accustomed to this pace, carrying your full load, we will increase our speed and cover a distance of twenty-four miles in this same period."

None of the men protested, but he saw more than one pair of shoulders droop. They were tired, but they'd grow strong in time.

"All right," he said, confident of a good start. "You are dismissed."

The men answered with a salute and a rousing shout, then broke formation and ambled toward the barracks.

Atticus smiled as Flavius approached, a broad grin on his face. "How goes the training?"

"About as I expected."

"They look a little thin to me. I'm surprised they can march at all."

"Don't underestimate them. These men are accustomed to the heat and the desert. What they find strange is organization."

Flavius rubbed a hand across his face as he watched the last of the stragglers disappear into the barracks. "I know you have a soft spot for the locals, but I'd feel better if we were training Romans to march beside us. You can't trust these people."

Atticus was about to remark that the army had to recruit locals in order to fill its garrisons, but Flavius interrupted, jerking his head to draw Atticus away from a group of soldiers coming from the governor's house.

When they had walked far enough that they couldn't be overheard, Flavius folded his hands into his armpits, then lifted a brow. "Has Gaius spoken to you?"

Atticus flinched. "Have I done something wrong?"

"No, no." He bit his lip. "I can't say more."

"Flavius, you can't drop a question like that and not expect me to—"

"Hush, he comes now. You've heard nothing from me."

Bewildered, Atticus turned to see the centurion striding across the square, his sandals kicking up dust as he approached.

"Atticus Aurelius." The centurion nodded in greeting. "I've been watching you."

Atticus snapped to attention. "Sir, have I done something to displease you?"

"Quite the contrary, I think you are an exemplary soldier. You have handled the duties of tesserarius very well."

"Thank you, sir."

The centurion answered with an impersonal nod, then tipped his face toward the sun. "Am I correct in assuming you would like to progress further in leadership? Perhaps even to the centurionate?"

Atticus resisted the urge to look at Flavius. "Yes, sir. I have given my life to Rome; I will serve as long as the empire needs me."

"Excellent. Then at sunset the two of you must meet me at the garrison gate. Tell no one where you are going. And do not be late."

The centurion walked away, leaving Atticus speechless. Flavius gripped his arm. "It's happening. I think we've been selected for initiation."

Atticus smiled, but something cold slid down his back, leaving a faint feeling of unease along his spine. The army of Rome demanded everything from its men—their minds, their bodies, even their souls. Every soldier worshiped Jupiter, Juno, and Minerva, the gods of the established state religions. But whispers of another cult, a secret society who worshiped Mithras, occasionally floated through the barracks.

Rumor held that only those who had joined the Mithras cult could be promoted to the centurionate . . . and only those who passed a merciless initiation rite could join the cult.

Atticus wanted to rise through the ranks . . . but what price would his ambition demand?

⊸⊱══◉══⊰⊶

Crouching behind a hedge in Pilate's garden, Atticus watched the Syrian girl comfort the weeping baby and felt a pang of some indefinable emotion. What was it about women that gave them the advantage in nurturing? He lacked breasts that could feed a child, but so did Cyrilla; the girl had been forced to rely on a goat for milk. His lap wasn't as soft as a woman's, but he did have a strong pair of shoulders, capable hands, and legs that could march a full day without wearying. He had a reasonably quick mind, nimble fingers, and ears to hear when a baby cried.

So why did the boy settle so easily into the girl's arms and wail so miserably in his?

"You can come out, Atticus," Cyrilla called, not looking up.

He stiffened, momentarily abashed, then released the hedge and rose to his full height. "How did you know I was there?"

A smile curved her lips as she watched him approach. "When a cloud passes before the sun, I feel the shade. When you enter the garden, I feel the earth rumble." She laughed softly. "You walk this way almost every afternoon. And since my lady rests at this hour, I thought it would be a nice time for us to have a private word with you—when you can get away, that is."

Atticus sat next to her on the bench and looked at the child in her arms. The boy had put on weight in the last few weeks.

"He looks good," Atticus said, hoping she'd take his comment as a compliment.

Cyrilla smiled, then ran a hand over the hair she had pulled into a knot at the nape of her neck. "By the way, soldier, this child needs a name."

Atticus frowned. "Well . . . what do you call him?"

She lifted one shoulder in a shrug. "I call him *sweetness*, but that's not a proper name. The right of naming belongs to you. I've been waiting to ask you about it."

Atticus stared at a green hedge. She'd waited for him? Something in him warmed to hear it; something else in him worried. A soldier could not form attachments.

He turned. "Do you like the name Quintus?"

She tilted her head. "That's a Roman name."

"So? I'm a Roman soldier."

"Atticus . . ." A flash of humor crossed her face. "The boy is Hebrew. I saw that the first time I held him."

Atticus swallowed the lump that had risen in his throat and crossed his arms. Foolish of him, really, to think no one would notice. The Jews' bizarre rite of circumcision had marked the boy forever. He imagined the boy as a young man at the baths, fending off intrusive questions or fearing to lower his towel. . . .

"Quintus," Cyrilla said, apparently harboring no troublesome thoughts about future humiliations. "Quintus it shall be. And I will keep your secret, Atticus. As far as I'm concerned, this boy is your son."

He studied the young woman next to him. Cyrilla's countenance seemed to have improved remarkably since the last time he saw her. Her cheeks were fuller and rounded, though her wide brown eyes still seemed to occupy most of the available space.

"*Auuuuuuuu.*" The baby interrupted with a long, drawn-out sound, then looked at Atticus and flashed a wet smile.

"New teeth?" Atticus gingerly touched the boy's lower lip. "*Two* new teeth?"

Cyrilla bounced the newly named boy on her knee. "Quintus will be grown before you know it."

-◊-══◉══-◊-

Atticus had just finished telling Flavius how much the boy had grown when Gaius stepped from a pool of shadow and intercepted them at the gate. "Legionnaires," the centurion asked, all traces of friendliness absent from his eyes, "do you wish to advance in the service of Rome? Do you wish to join a brotherhood where rank and mutual obligation are not based on social codes but on the secret bonds of a closed circle?"

Atticus wanted to look at his friend, but instinct told him any sign of hesitation would not be well received. "I do," he answered, relieved to hear Flavius reply in the same way.

"Are you," Gaius continued, a muscle clenching along his jaw, "willing to undergo the seven trials that lead to the sacrament of joining? Do you swear upon your life to keep these rites secret?"

Again, Atticus and Flavius answered in the affirmative.

"Then do not speak, but follow me."

Atticus fell into step behind the centurion, and only when they had gone ten paces did he dare glance at his companion. Flavius grinned, but a tide of anxiety surged behind his eyes, and Atticus was sure Flavius could see the same dark currents behind his.

They walked over two miles, then turned into a gated garden. After leading them around a fountain and past several formal hedges, Gaius led them down a stone stairway that ended at a rough-hewn door. The centurion knocked and murmured something; a moment later, the door opened.

Atticus drank in the sights without speaking. From hearing rumors in the barracks he knew they had entered a mithraeum, an underground temple dedicated to Mithras and built to resemble a cave.

When they reached another door, Gaius turned. "Do you swear upon pain of death never to reveal what you see here? Do you swear never to divulge the names of the brothers gathered in this inner chamber?"

Atticus and Flavius swore an oath.

For the first time, the flicker of a smile crossed the centurion's face. "Then enter. And prepare to test your strength in honor of Mithras."

Atticus had to duck in order to enter the underground chamber. The rectangular room was not large, but its builders had done an artful job with the vaulted ceiling. An aisle ran lengthwise down the center of the temple, with stone benches on either side. Soldiers filled the benches, each man wearing his uniform and a mask. Atticus couldn't have identified them if he'd wanted to, though several wore the distinctive helmets of centurions.

A man wearing a bull mask stood at the front of the room. "The initiates will come forward."

Together, Atticus and Flavius approached what appeared to be a stone altar.

"Mithras," the priest continued, "god born of a rock and destined to secure the salvation of the world, bids you follow him. As the god Apollo, through the agency of a raven, bid Mithras to slay the bull from the region of the moon, I bid you slay your enemies and rejoice with your blood brothers. Everyone you see here has endured the trials of fire, water, hunger, cold, flagellation, bloodletting, and branding. If you are willing to endure these tests and accept our sacrament, kneel before me. If you are not willing, turn now and go, knowing that if you ever speak of this you will most certainly forfeit your life."

Atticus felt a bead of perspiration trace a cold path from his armpit to his rib, but he did not turn, nor did he look at Flavius. He had given his life to Rome and in exchange had been granted a place of security . . . and monotony. If he were to advance past endless days of peacetime drilling, marching, and training, he would have to endure this initiation. He had been born a Roman citizen, so the army offered him more advantages than it offered the uncivilized auxiliaries who filled the barracks at Caesarea, but without an edge he could never compete with the patrician sons of senators for leadership positions.

Mithras offered what he sought.

He bent his knees and knelt on the cool stone, then lifted his gaze and met the eyes of the man who stared out from behind the bull mask. "I am willing."

Beside him, Flavius echoed the same words.

The priest's eyes narrowed. "Prepare yourself. Mithras holds the power of the unconquered and unconquerable sun, so as you prove yourself deserving of him, you will prove yourself worthy to symbolize the courage, success, and confidence of your brother soldiers. We will demand your self-control, virtue, loyalty, and blood. These tests will determine whether you are able to give what we require."

The priest extended his hand toward another masked soldier, who pointed to a dark tunnel. Atticus glanced at Flavius and saw the lump in his friend's throat bob once as he swallowed.

With his nerves at full stretch, Atticus rose and walked into the tunnel.

Chapter Eighteen

Sticky wetness covered my hands, stained my cloak, and dotted my veil. Pools of crimson liquid had coagulated on the rocky hill and seeped into the hem of my tunic. I looked around, but I could see no sign of the animal that had been slaughtered here.

I hesitated, blinking with bafflement. Was this Yom Kippur, the day when the priest entered the Holy of Holies to offer the blood of a sacrificed bull as the *kapparah*, or atonement, for our sins? I had no idea how many days had passed since Tirza's death, but I had sinned—I knew it. I had erred in going to Herod, in wearing the amulet, in turning my back on the Holy One of Isra'el, blessed be he.

But how could I return to the truth? How could I rid myself of the evil that had infected my heart, mind, and body?

The gods I'd called upon would not release me, and they delighted in blood. Their voices buzzed in my brain; they rejoiced at signs of carnage. They swirled around me like wasps, tickling my ears and settling on my shoulders. Like a dog that chases its tail, I swatted at them and ended up slapping myself.

Their jubilation turned to jeers. Many of them had come to live in my head; they kept me company through days and nights. Though I never saw them, they spoke in loud rants and soft purrs, masculine growls and womanly whispers. Occasionally they called each other by name—Ba-ath, Qin-ah, Avah, Az-aph, Katakritos, Ge-ah—but one voice overruled them all: Natar.

She is ours. We have a home!

The voices surrounded me, mingling in amiable insult and agreement.

She obeyed; she opened the door.

She toyed with the dead man; he sealed the bargain.

Her heart brims with anger and hate!

She loves us! She needs us!

She is me; I am she.

She is lost to the one whose name must not be spoken. She is us; we have won!

Frantic with frustration, I smacked my ears, ground my knuckles into my cheeks, and pressed my thumbs into my eye sockets in an attempt to pop the voices out of my head. I yanked at my hair, hoping I could pull the intruders out by the fistful, but despite my pain and blood and blindness, they remained, a whirling cacophony of feverish celebration.

"Leave me alone! Go away!"

I opened my blurry eyes and saw Marisa staring at me, her face deadly pale except for two desert roses, one growing in each cheek. She squatted on the other side of the booth, her hands pressed to the carpet as if she might spring up at any instant.

I exhaled a trembling breath. I'd been dreaming. The craggy hill, the blood, the pain—nothing but a dream.

But I lifted my right hand and found it smeared with blood and tangled hanks of hair. I touched my left hand to my scalp and winced when my fingertips encountered raw flesh.

I gaped at Marisa, whose expression mirrored my bewilderment. "Can you help me?"

She flung up both hands and turned away. "Go!" she cried, hiding her face as if the mere sight of my distress could spread contagion. "Get away!"

"But—"

"You are a curse! Leave me!"

I rose to my hands and knees in silence. The voices began to babble again. I covered my ears and rocked back on my heels as they taunted and tortured, but Marisa's scream overpowered them all: "Go away or I shall call for Herod's guards!"

Somehow I staggered to my feet. The sun had barely begun to brighten the sky, so perhaps I could flee the city before Marisa sounded a warning. I could understand why Dodi might think me guilty of murder, but how could Marisa think me dangerous? She had introduced me to the voices.

The Egyptian? She is nothing, a pawn.

Why should we trouble ourselves over her? She has always belonged to us, but you, daughter of Avraham, are our crown jewel!

"Go away go away go away go away!" I pressed my hands over my ears and staggered down the street, understanding only one thing: I had to leave Tiberias. The city had become an anathema to me.

I hesitated outside a baker's booth as the voices raged. Somehow I managed to take a deep breath and focus on escape. "If you want to survive, you must be silent." I spoke aloud for the sheer pleasure of hearing my voice in a pitch more vital than the others'. "If you draw attention to us as we pass through the gate, the guards might take us before Herod."

I closed my eyes, steeling myself to my task, and by some miracle the voices faded. I blew out a breath, relieved by the rare and concentrated silence. My thoughts settled into a single rhythm; my breathing returned to a normal pattern.

So. The gods *could* cooperate with mortals.

I wrapped my veil around my wounded head and made my way to the well in the center of town. I would wash my hands and face, then slip into the stream of morning travelers leaving the city. Tiberias had given me nothing, so I might as well return to Magdala, where I owned property and might yet have a few friends.

After reaching the well, I pulled on the rope and brought up the bucket, then plunged my bloodstained hands into the cleansing water.

Chapter Nineteen

Because nothing but fiery light licked at the bare stone walls, Atticus had no idea how long he and Flavius remained in the temple chamber. Certainly days passed—perhaps a week or more.

He only knew that if given the opportunity to suffer for Mithras again, he would walk out of the temple and never look back.

Seven trials, the priest had said: fire, water, hunger, cold, flagellation, bloodletting, branding. Endured one at a time, a man might be able to bear each ordeal without complaint, but when endured in combination, any man would vent his agony.

After entering the smaller chamber, he and Flavius had been instructed to remove their armor and their tunics. Exposed to the elements and away from the warming sun, they began to feel the sting of cold from their first hour in the initiation room. Hunger reared its head soon after their arrival, for no one offered either of them food or drink. Instead they were chained to the wall and left with only each other for company.

For a while Atticus and Flavius talked to keep up their spirits, but as the hours wore on Atticus couldn't help but wonder if the initiation was some kind of joke. Had Gaius heard that Atticus had taken a baby from the condemned Jews' house? Was this an elaborate form of punishment? The centurion was the sort who would bear an insult quietly and strike when his opponent least expected it. He was also the sort who would think nothing of destroying an enemy and anyone close to him.

Flavius fell silent, then began to snore. Atticus yanked on his chains and strained to see his friend, unable to believe Flavius could fall asleep in an upright position. *His* nerves had stretched too tightly to allow any kind of rest; his thoughts had gone cold and sharp, focused like the point of an awl.

When Pilate had found Cyrilla and the baby, Gaius must have doubted the picture the governor's wife presented. He must have sent spies through the ranks, and one of them might have talked to a man from Atticus's contubernium. Maybe they'd gone out drinking one night, and Atticus's comrade had loosened his tongue after too much ale and let it slip that the baby was Jewish and from Magdala, and Gaius had put the pieces of the puzzle together.

Atticus's thoughts returned to the afternoon and his meeting with Cyrilla and Quintus in the palace garden. They had both seemed happy, so no one had stepped forward to threaten them . . . yet. But perhaps Gaius was at the palace now, informing the procurator that the young child under his wife's supervision was a despised Jew and the handmaid a harlot. Pilate would be so furious he might have them both killed or sold into slavery. . . .

These jagged and painful thoughts kept Atticus company until Flavius snorted and roused himself.

Atticus lifted his head from the stone wall. "Don't go to sleep again."

"What? I've been awake."

"No, you've been snoring. I need to talk to you about something important."

"Not the best time, Atticus."

"I'm serious. I've been thinking. What if this is Gaius's way of punishing us?"

Flavius grinned, but Atticus thought he saw a faint flicker of unease in the depths of his eyes. "What are you talking about?"

"I think Gaius found out about the baby. I think he's going to kill us. I'm sorry you got involved—" He clamped his mouth shut when the swollen wooden door scraped against the floor and two soldiers entered, each wearing an animal mask. One of them carried a *flagellum*, a leather whip whose thongs had been weighted with bits of bone and lead.

The taller man tapped the whip against his palm while the other stepped up to release Atticus from his chains. Behind the mask, Atticus saw a grim smile in the man's eyes.

From his spot on the wall, Flavius's grin wavered. "You're not really going to use that on us, are you? We're Roman citizens."

"You're Roman soldiers," came the gruff response. "You'll bear what you must in order to be accepted by Mithras. If you want to avoid pain, speak now. If you want out at any time during the trial, all you have to do is say so."

Surely that was a jest. For this was punishment, the discipline Gaius had ordained for Atticus first, then for Flavius.

Unless . . . maybe Gaius *didn't* know about the baby. Maybe the centurion had only intuited that something was amiss among his men, and this torture was an attempt to get Atticus or Flavius to confess how they'd been breaking rules ever since Magdala.

Atticus pressed his lips together and tried not to think about the whip as the shorter man secured him between two pillars. He'd suffered dozens of blows from Gaius's staff during training, and narrow scars from errant swords laced his arms. But he'd never felt the sting and rip of a flagellum. The lead ball would leave bruises; the sharp bits of bone would tear his flesh.

He stood as tense and quivering as a just-fired bowstring, but his voice was calm when he asked, "How many blows?"

"Seven."

Seven . . . unless he broke and confessed his crime. If he broke, though, he'd certainly doom Cyrilla and Quintus.

He turned and looked at the man with the flail. "Whenever you're ready, then."

CHAPTER TWENTY

BY THE TIME THE SUN had risen halfway over the Sea of Galilee, I had joined a group of travelers en route to Gennesaret. Their journey would take them through Magdala, so I walked behind them, avoiding conversation as much as possible.

One of the older women, however, seemed determined to keep me company. I caught her peeking at me as she walked beside the road, and finally she lingered until I reached her side. Then she matched my stride and clucked in sympathy. "My dear, does he hit you often?"

The question startled me. "What?"

"Your husband. Who else would strike you?"

I blinked at her. "My husband is dead."

The woman's forehead knit in puzzlement. "Then who——?"

I waved her away, warding off further attempts at conversation. "I am fine. And I want to be alone."

Because I knew she would feel it her duty to persist, I left the group and walked toward the lakeshore. When I reached the reeds, I stood with my back to the travelers until the dust of their passage stretched far down the road.

Only then did I kneel to stare into a puddle on the sand. I hadn't been able to imagine what the woman saw in my face, but in the reflection of still water I beheld bruises—deep purple splotches under my eyes, by my temples, and at the base of my ears— the results of my battering myself as I tried to silence the tumult in my head.

I sank to the wet sand and let my hand fall into the water. Why was I bothering with this journey? I had no family to care for, no business to oversee. My king, the authority who should have come to my aid, had refused to help me. The voices who'd promised miracles had betrayed me, driving me from the small shelter I had found . . . and the woman who'd shown me a bit of kindness.

I lifted my face to the breeze and listened to a plane tree rattle its leaves. Why not walk into the sea and lose myself beneath the waves? Why not follow Yaakov, Avram, Rachel, and my beloved Binyamin into the valley of death?

I rose on shaky knees and considered the blue-green waters of Galilee. In the distance, two fishing boats were rowing their way toward the markets that lined the northern shores. The wind had picked up, whipping the waters and painting whitecaps on the waves. Sudden storms frequently assailed this sea; boats often swamped in minutes.

I'd find it hard to swim in choppy water, if by some chance I changed my mind. The heaving sea would drag me down; the rising wind would push me away from shore. And though some in Magdala might hear of a middle-aged woman's drowning and speculate, they would never know for certain what I'd done.

She's looking at the water! Do you think she wants to die?

Stop her!

Yes! Don't let her die! Where would we go?

Stop, woman! You can't do this to us!

Come now, Miryam, you aren't that brave!

Run away from the water! Come back to us!

An eel of fear wriggled in my gut, but I ignored it and took another step toward oblivion. Should I remove my sandals? A foolish question, perhaps, but a practical one.

Forget about your shoes. Back away!

You idiot! You bring a curse upon yourself!

You are not brave enough for this! You are a fool!

Vulture! Sorceress!

I smiled. As a little girl I had run barefoot over these sands and splashed with abandon in these waters, but since reaching maturity I had not dipped a toe into the sea.

I would keep my sandals on, and my cloak, and my veil. The more items I wore, the heavier I would be. I would sink as soon as my strength gave out, and I would pass from this life as unremarkably as the hundreds of small fish Yaakov used to harvest from these waters every day.

I parted the reeds and waded through the greenish brown scum that coated the surface at the shore. I took another step . . . and another. The voices in my head howled in protest, but I clapped my hands over my ears and grimaced in my determination to ignore them.

Moving steadily forward, I stared at the sun-spangled sea and tried to listen for the familiar shush of waves brushing the shore. Invisible hands twisted my stomach and pounded my heart, but I persisted, striding through every twinge and pain.

Soon my agony would be over. Soon I would join my family in

Sh'ol, where together we would await the Day of Judgment. If my sins then kept me from my family, at least I had put an end to my pain.

The wind blew harder, flattening my garments against me. The swells of the sea looked like rolling hills. Out on the lake, fishing boats labored over the peaks of the waves as men struggled to haul in their nets before the unexpected storm capsized the ship.

I pressed on, shivering as the water laid a cold hand against the womb that had carried my children. The water rose, its touch increasingly intimate, caressing my waist, my chest. I could scarcely focus, for inside my head the voices of foreign gods shrieked and caterwauled and hissed more violently than ever.

I lowered my arms, content to know nothing could stop me. I trailed my hands over the surface, creating little waves that rippled at my wrists, and noticed how the water shimmered with crimson streaks from a slanting sun. The incoming waves slapped at me, but I welcomed them.

I had been born at the edge of this sea. . . . It seemed fitting that I die in its depths.

I tipped my head back to navigate a path between the swells and felt the sand beneath my feet give way. As the water closed over my face, my head, my first instinct—reinforced by the screaming entities in my head—was to fight to the surface, but with a supreme effort I straightened my arms and released the air in my chest. Silvery bubbles rose from my pursed lips and the taste of water filled my nose. I lifted my face toward the silvery surface and saw the world I had known slide away.

The voices cursed me in languages I'd never heard, but they could do nothing to stop me. I crossed my arms over my chest and lowered my gaze to the murky bottom.

I believe I even smiled.

CHAPTER TWENTY-ONE

ATTICUS STIFFENS AS THE WOMAN drifts into a heavy silence. He stands and walks toward her, then stops at her side. "You didn't die."

The woman smiles, impressed, perhaps, with his grasp of the obvious. "No. But . . . I wonder if you could spare a cup of water? I am not accustomed to talking so long."

He gestures for the guard at the door. "Water for the prisoner. Be quick with it."

He sinks to the bench at the woman's side and studies her face. For one who has suffered so much, her face is barely lined, her hairline only touched with gray. He notices again the shape and color of her eyes. She looks like any other older Jewish woman from Galilee, but there is something about her . . .

He clears his throat. "You were well treated on your journey to Rome?"

One corner of her mouth twists. "For a prisoner, yes."

Atticus glances at the scribe. "You are recording all of her story? The emperor will want a complete history."

The scribe flushes and points to a scrawled page. "A most protracted story. I have yet to hear the details of her crime."

The woman's gaze, as unfathomable as the ocean depths, rests on Atticus as she responds. "I'm not finished."

The room swells with silence as Atticus brings his hand to his jaw and tries to make sense of the woman's tale. Broken pieces from a distant past are fitting together, but still he cannot see the entire picture.

He sits without speaking until the guard brings a metal cup and hands it to Atticus. He rises and offers it to the woman, who swallows greedily, perhaps realizing it may be the last cup she will be offered in this life.

From the desk, Flavius clears his throat. "Perhaps, centurion, you would like to interrogate this prisoner? I will relinquish my place if you say the word—"

"No, Flavius, please continue. I'd rather listen to her testimony."

Atticus returns to his bench and sits in full view of the prisoner. No point in hiding behind her now. He wants to watch as she tells her story; he wants an explanation for her presence in this place of judgment.

When the woman hands the cup back to the guard, Flavius urges her to continue. "You tried to commit suicide."

"I did. In foolish ignorance I thought an *end* to life was an *answer* to life. Later I discovered the flaw in my reasoning . . . but not before I had other occasions to long for death."

After glancing uneasily in Atticus's direction, Flavius pinches the bridge of his nose and closes his eyes. "Continue, then. And, scribe, take it all down."

The woman draws a deep breath and continues.

Chapter Twenty-two

I awoke in the bow of a fishing boat.

Due to the rising wind and the howling in my head, I had failed to notice a pair of fishermen in a small boat to the south. My first recollection of them is among a score of memories I'd rather not revisit . . . but to fully appreciate the silver threads in a fabric, you must weave in dark threads as well.

The men had left me in the boat and gone ashore, perhaps thinking me dead. I sat up, bracing myself against the hull, and tried to visualize where I had come ashore. I guessed I was still south of Magdala, near the fish markets.

I spied one of the men just past the reeds; he was singing as he fastened the lids on baskets borne by his donkey. The second man stepped out from behind a tree, exchanged a word with his partner, and led the donkey away.

I ducked back inside the boat and grimaced. The voices remained with me; I could hear their gloating laughter and quiet murmurs. Somehow, they had won.

I lay quite still, struggling to listen over the slap of the waves against the vessel and the insistent noises in my skull. When the sound of the fisherman's singing faded, I lifted my gaze and peeked at the shore.

Unfortunately, the fisherman hadn't gone—he'd only stopped singing to tie on his sandals. His eyes widened when he saw me; then he tightened the knot in his shoe and hurried toward the boat.

I turned away in a panic. How would I explain what I'd done? Virtuous women did not wander about the countryside alone, and they certainly didn't try to drown themselves in the sea.

For practical reasons, I very much wanted to be regarded as a virtuous woman.

"You're awake, then." The fisherman's voice echoed with wonder. "By heaven's throne, we'd given you up for dead."

I drew a deep breath and sat up, then winced as Natar hissed in my ear. I smacked the meaty part of my palm to the side of my head in an effort to stop the vibrations.

"Are you all right? Come out of there and let me have a look at you."

With my limbs weak and trembling, I could not move. The fisherman's broad fist gripped my arm; his other hand tugged at my belt and hauled me out of the boat.

When he released me on shore, I tried to stand, but my legs felt as weak as a newborn lamb's. I crumpled to the earth, and at the touch of solid ground my voices erupted in such gleeful gibbering that I cringed and thrust both hands against my ears.

The man spoke, but I couldn't hear a word over the racket in my skull. I squinted at him, trying to read his lips, but I couldn't tell if he spoke Greek or Aramaic. I finally turned toward the muddy grass, cushioning my elbows in the soft soil as I sought the comfort of warm earth. There I was, a lone woman, confused, disheveled, and defenseless. . . .

When he touched me, I thought immediately of that poor girl in Tiberias. She had been more vulnerable than I; she would be far more damaged. I was already a shattered vessel, a home fit only for unpleasant pagan gods.

The fisherman thought I was one of those women who lingers by busy roads and makes her living in the most primitive way imaginable. And so he smiled and his hand went to my neck. My voices trilled at his touch. Several of them shrieked my dead husband's name, and for an instant I thought I had found my way to death's shore and that Yaakov, he of blessed memory, was waiting for me. . . .

But the moment the stranger's mouth touched my skin, I knew the shore was not Sh'ol, nor was that stranger my husband. I drifted into a dark place as my ears filled with the taunting hoots of the invaders who had bedeviled my soul.

Chapter Twenty-three

Fire, water, hunger, cold, flagellation, bloodletting. Branding of the shoulder with the images of a dog, a snake, and a scorpion. Atticus endured them all in the dark initiation chamber, where time stopped and the outside world ceased to exist. At times pain rose slowly inside him like a wave, cresting, sending streamers of anguish in every direction; at other times agony crackled over his back like heat lightning.

During the water test, in which his tormentors held his head under water far longer than he would have imagined possible, he couldn't find enough air to push out the scream clawing in his throat. During the trial by fire, in which the torturers held torches to the soles of his feet, he screamed until he thought he would wake Julius Caesar.

But through it all, he did not betray Quintus, nor did he ask for mercy.

After being branded, when Atticus had wearied of breathing the odors of blood, sweat, and seared skin, the swollen door opened again. Four masked soldiers entered; two of them carried new togas and armor.

Atticus closed his eyes, relieved at this tangible sign of the real world's return.

Along with their armor and tunics, he and Flavius were given raven masks to indicate their rank. "But before you put them on," the priest said, his now-familiar voice scraping across Atticus's frayed nerves, "there is one more rite of initiation." Again, the eyes behind the mask smiled. "Follow me."

Atticus avoided looking at Flavius as they stepped out of the chamber and walked back to the central temple. As before, masked soldiers in full uniform filled the benches, and for a moment Atticus wondered if they had moved since that first night.

"Our Mithras," the priest intoned, "was commanded by Apollo to slay the bull that represented the fullness of life. In the *taurobolium*, you must slay the bull and be immersed in its blood in order to partake of its life-giving properties and join us in fellowship. Will you do this?"

Atticus lifted his gaze. Behind the priest, a deep bowl had been cut into the earth; above the bowl, someone had erected a slatted wooden bridge. A bull had been led onto the bridge and tethered between two posts. The bull blew gustily, then lowered its great head to bellow in displeasure.

Flavius did not hesitate. "I will slay the bull."

Atticus nodded. "I will, too."

"Then take up your swords and strike in the name of Mithras!"

Atticus glanced to the right, where two swords waited on a stone altar. He reached for the first and waited for Flavius to take the second; then they stepped down the curving slope of the bowl and looked up through the wooden slats.

The bull tossed his head and bounced in agitation. Atticus nodded at Flavius; then they thrust their swords through the slats and pulled, piercing and slitting the bull's exposed belly. Above the bull's death roar Atticus heard his own triumphant shout.

Blood and entrails showered down upon them in a crimson spatter. Atticus looked at his friend, chagrined and a little amazed that deprivation and trials could ignite a bloodthirsty fire in his veins, but Flavius's eyes were aflame with exultation. Atticus felt the same, though he took less joy in the ritualistic slaughter than in the simple fact that the trials had been tests, not a sinister plan to break his spirit and force him to betray the people he'd promised to protect.

Together they knelt, tipped their heads back, and opened their mouths to drink the baptism of blood. At the altar, the priest recited a prayer to Mithras, then pronounced that Atticus Aurelius and Flavius Gemellus had passed their trials and experienced the taurobolium. As a result, they were now *renatus in aeternum*, reborn for all eternity.

CHAPTER TWENTY-FOUR

EVENING SHADOWS HAD STRETCHED across the ground by the time I reached the fishing stalls outside Magdala. I trudged past overturned boats and empty booths and dragged my feet over paths I had crossed a thousand times with Avram and Yaakov and Rachel. When I reached the city gates, I leaned my bruised cheek against them, not at all surprised to discover I'd been locked out.

Too late to call for the watchman. Magdala was not Tiberias; we did not keep a man in the watchtower all night. Whichever husband had drawn tower duty had already gone home to his wife, his children, and a good night's rest.

No choice but to sleep under the stars . . . if I could find a place to lay my head.

I turned and wearily considered the landscape. A half-moon the color of bleached bone hung in the eastern sky, but the shadows under the plane trees were cold and blue. I shivered. The moon cast strange shadows across the sands, and in the shifting shapes I could see the unspeakable things mentioned by the voices in my head. As invisible creatures prowled through the darkness and murmured under the voice of the wind, my heart trembled like an animal in a cage of ribs.

I gulped back a sob and ran for the security of the gated graveyard. There, at least, I would rest with my beloved Yaakov, Avram, Rachel, and Binyamin. And if in the morning the women of Magdala found me dead among the tombs, they would wonder how I'd come to be there, but they would not mourn my loss.

They would only remind each other that a woman is nothing without her family.

CHAPTER TWENTY-FIVE

FAMILY. THE WORD SNAPS ATTICUS back to a time when he had been training a group of recruits outside the barracks when a slave approached and asked for a private word. After Atticus dismissed his recruits, the slave informed him that Lady Procula wished to see him at once.

He would have rushed directly into the governor's hall, but the slave suggested that he clean up before going to the house. Atticus obeyed the suggestion, but barely—he splashed water on his damp hair, dried his face on his tunic, and pulled his cloak over his sweaty shoulders before striding toward the palace.

The servant ushered him into a cool room where tall doorways allowed a breeze to enter. Low couches encircled a short-legged table bearing a pitcher, several cups, and a plate of fruit.

Atticus thrust his hands behind his back and resisted the urge to pace. He could think of no reason for Pilate's wife to summon any of the legionnaires who guarded her home, so this must have something to do with the child.

Had the boy fallen ill? The thought struck like a rock dropped into a pool, sending ripples of anxiety in every direction.

A door opened and in walked Pilate's wife, a vision in gold and silk. Cyrilla, with the baby on her hip, followed in Procula's shimmering wake. The baby, thank the gods, looked healthy and whole.

Quintus regarded Atticus with wide eyes, then broke into a smile. Atticus had to force himself not to rush forward and scoop the toddler into his arms.

The lady Procula reclined on one of the couches, then smiled and examined Atticus's face with considerable concentration. "I have heard good things about you, Atticus Aurelius. Cyrilla tells me you care a great deal for this child, not minding that he is deaf, limited in usefulness . . . and a Jew."

Atticus shot a quick look at the girl, who held Quinn's uplifted hands as he practiced walking on the other side of the room. What, exactly, had she told her mistress?

Procula clasped her hands and looked at him with something fragile in her eyes. "Do not fear, soldier. As far as I'm concerned, the child is yours. But some people in my household would be happy to be rid of the Jews altogether, so we must keep certain facts to ourselves."

He bowed before the governor's wife. "I would never want to burden the army or your household, my lady, but it seemed . . . unkind to snuff out a life the gods have granted."

"I agree. And I wonder . . . would you be willing to take a break from your legionary responsibilities to do something for me?" The lady gave Atticus a careful look, with only a slight lift of her brow to indicate that she knew she might be treading on precarious ground. "This favor . . . would be an act of kindness."

He barely managed to restrain a gasp of surprise. As far as he knew, no governor's wife had ever singled out a soldier in this way. "I would be happy to serve you in any way possible—" he fumbled for words—"if the procurator and my centurion know and approve."

"Therein lies the problem." Procula lowered her voice. "The procurator and your centurion must *not* know of my request. Neither would approve, I'm afraid, and both would condemn us."

"If this request is not proper, then—"

"I sent for you, Atticus Aurelius, because I have it on good authority that you value honor more than blind obedience." Her brows lifted. "Have I misunderstood the sort of man you are?"

Some dim recess of his mind, a segment not occupied with seeking a way out of the situation, speculated that Flavius would claim Atticus's sword and possessions after his execution. Because if Procula's request required Atticus to act against the army, Gaius or another of the centurions would surely find out. The men of Mithras would not hesitate to kill him for disloyalty.

"Soldier?" The lady's voice cut into his thoughts. "Have I misunderstood?"

He shook his head. "My lady, I don't know what to say. I have vowed to serve Rome—"

"Say nothing for now, but listen. I know men, Atticus, and I know Romans. My husband and your centurion see yonder child as nothing more than a worthless slave, while I, who am well acquainted with the grief of a barren woman, would not willingly allow *any* child to suffer unnecessarily. So I will ask this favor . . . for the child's sake."

Atticus glanced at Cyrilla, who watched with wide eyes; then he knelt before the procurator's wife. "I will honor your wish," he said simply. "But I pray you—don't ask me to dishonor my cohort or my emperor."

"I would not ask that of you." Procula's calm voice warmed his troubled heart. "My request is simple—I want you to travel to

Galilee. Gaius is accompanying my husband's guard to Jerusalem, so he will not be aware of your absence. Though you are certainly a leader among your men—" her lips curved in a smile—"I do not think the recruits will forget how to march if you are gone for a few days."

Atticus propped his elbow on his bent knee. "What would you have me do in that region?"

The lady drew a deep breath, then stood and walked to the window. "The last time we visited Jerusalem, Pilate and I dined with Herod. The king introduced us to his steward, a man called Chuza, and later I had occasion to meet Joanna, the steward's wife."

Atticus nodded. Pilate and his household stayed at Herod's Jerusalem palace whenever they traveled to the Holy City. Because the palace lay only a short distance from the Temple and the Fortress Antonia, a single cohort could easily guard both rulers and control all three locations.

"Joanna," Procula continued, staring out the window, "told me of a healer from Nazareth, a man many of the Jews consider a prophet. They say he has turned water into wine."

Atticus struggled to stifle a snicker. Any drunk could be fooled into believing water was wine if he'd swallowed enough of the latter.

"They say," Procula went on, "he has opened blind eyes and deaf ears."

Atticus froze as comprehension seeped through his incredulity. A man who could heal the deaf?

Procula turned to face him. "I want you to take the child to this healer. But you cannot go as a soldier of Rome; you would attract too much attention. Put on plain clothing and take Cyrilla with you. Pose as husband and wife; take the boy and offer him to this prophet. See what can be done for the child."

Atticus blinked. "And . . . if nothing can be done?"

The lady's eyes shimmered with wetness. "At least we will have tried."

Atticus turned to Cyrilla, who gazed at her mistress with worry in her eyes. "Do you know how to locate this healer?"

Cyrilla's head bobbed. "From other servants I've heard that he travels through the lands around Galilee, teaching in various towns. Hundreds follow him, so I don't think he'll be hard to find."

Atticus returned his attention to his mistress. "When should we go?"

"Tomorrow at first light, I think. Gaius and Pilate are leaving tonight." She frowned slightly. "Have I forgotten anything, Atticus?"

"No. Thank you for trusting me with this task." He rose, then paused in the doorway before leaving. "May I ask one thing?"

"Ask."

"Why me? Any one of your servants could do this for you."

Her lips parted in a still, small smile. "Because you love the boy."

- ⋅→⋅⊨⊙⊨⋅←⋅ -

The next morning, Atticus rose before daybreak and pulled off his red tunic. Cyrilla had sent fresh clothing from the palace—a tunic of beige linen, a belt to tie at the waist, and a deep brown cloak. The clothing was finer than anything Atticus had worn before his army enlistment, but without his armor he felt curiously underdressed.

Flavius opened one eye, saw him dressed as a merchant, and sat up. "By Apollo's foul breath, what are you doing?"

Atticus pressed his finger over his lips. "Running an errand."

"Have you gone mad?"

"I'll be back in two or three days. While I'm away, say nothing. If anyone asks, I'm around the corner or in the barracks."

He moved to the doorway and peered into the courtyard. Cyrilla, dressed in a common cloak and unadorned tunic, waited in a wagon near the gate. The baby sat in her lap, drowsing against her shoulder.

Flavius crept up behind him and clicked his tongue against his teeth. "I see what you're up to. If it's the woman you're wanting—"

"It's not the woman." Atticus clapped his friend's shoulder in a farewell salute. "I'll tell you about it when I return."

He plucked a staff from a barrel near the doorway, stepped out into the courtyard, and strode off to join his temporary family.

⟨⟩⎯⎯◉⎯⎯⟨⟩

Nazareth and the Sea of Tiberias lay more than a day's journey from Caesarea, but as Atticus swatted the slow-moving donkey, he was grateful not to be marching in the stultifying heat.

Lady Procula had been wise to send them in a wagon instead of a chariot or a litter. The latter conveyances would have drawn hostile attention, and while no one would take them for Jews, at least they weren't readily identifiable as a soldier and a former harlot.

As the donkey clomped over the stone pavement, Atticus stared at the landscape and considered the task before him. How could he find one Jewish man among so many? He knew little about the Jews, but his centurion insisted they were a lazy, ignorant, and superstitious race. "They will not work on the seventh day," he'd once proclaimed to his century. "If you strike a Jew on a Saturday, he will not lift a hand even in his own defense. They exclude themselves from other people and will not let their daughters talk to strangers. They say these are the laws of their God, but there are no gods in their Temple, nor any in their synagogues. How foolish is that?"

Atticus wasn't certain he would be able to accomplish his mission among people who would scarcely speak to strangers, but as the gods would have it, they had set out on a Saturday and he *did* appreciate the nearly empty road.

He glanced behind him, where Cyrilla sat in the wagon with her legs tucked beneath her tunic and the baby by her side. "Everything all right back there?"

"We're fine." She ran her hand over Quinn's downy hair. "He really is a lovely boy, Atticus. The lady Procula is quite taken with him."

He looked away, lest she see how much her comment pleased him. "That's good."

"I'm fond of him, too."

"That's how it should be. A boy needs a mother."

"A boy also needs a father."

Atticus swallowed hard and flicked the donkey's reins. Conversing with Cyrilla was like treading over a beach dotted with quicksand . . . one thoughtless reply could land Atticus in unyielding muck.

"Do you think," she continued, "this healer will be able to help our Quintus?"

Our Quintus? With an effort, he dredged words from his throat. "I don't know."

"My lady Procula is most impressed with the stories she's heard. She'd go see this man herself, but her husband would not allow it."

"Well . . . it'd be hard to guarantee her safety. The Jews can be a troublesome lot."

"Yet you saved one of their babies."

Her voice had softened, and when he turned, he saw tenderness in her eyes.

"I don't think Gaius meant us to harm a child."

"You give him too much credit, Atticus. I know your centurion; I've heard other women speak of him. He can be a brutal man."

Atticus said nothing as the clomp of the donkey's hooves and the boy's drawn-out gurgle echoed over the empty road.

For a time they rode without speaking. Atticus kept the donkey at a steady pace and realized how pleasant it was to spend time with Cyrilla and Quintus away from the palace. The few minutes he'd been able to snatch with them in the garden paled in comparison to the pleasure of simple companionship.

When they stopped to eat in the shade of an oak, Quinn toddled over the grass, picking up leaves, trying to eat bark, and pointing at all sorts of curiosities he found on the ground.

"He walks well," Atticus remarked.

Cyrilla propped her head on her hand and smiled. "He does. He runs all over the house—at least until the governor comes in. Then Lady Procula makes me take Quinn to the servants' quarters, lest the governor be offended."

She waited while Atticus removed a piece of bark from Quinn's mouth and tossed it out of reach. The boy watched the bark fly away, a woebegone look on his face. Atticus pulled a piece of dried beef from his scrip and gave that to Quinn instead.

"I think she really wanted children," Cyrilla said, her voice soft. "And her husband is too proud to admit that their marriage isn't perfect. So Pilate pretends his wife is happy, and Procula watches Quinn with tears in her eyes. But she won't pick him up. She won't get too close."

Atticus shifted his gaze to the road, where a publican and his eagle-emblazoned collection box had just come into view. Another man, probably a Syrian, hurried by and shouted insults at the tax collector, but Quinn did not even glance toward the noisy pair.

"I could almost envy the boy," Atticus said, reclining in the shade. "Not hearing, I mean. We hear so much ugliness—the clash of swords, the cries of battle, the screams of men in pain."

Cyrilla laughed. "You have lived an odd life, soldier. The world is also filled with the sounds of women singing, children laughing, birds warbling in the trees." She looked up and pointed at a sparrow that hopped from branch to branch. Quinn saw her gesture and followed her gaze, then dropped his jaw.

Atticus grinned, convinced the child wasn't missing as much as Cyrilla thought. The bird began to sing . . . and the sweetly piercing sound snatched Atticus's breath away. How long had it been since he'd had an hour to sit and listen to birdsong? Far too long. And unless the Jewish healer could help, Quinn would never experience this exquisitely simple pleasure.

He stood and scooped up the curious baby, then handed Quinn to Cyrilla so he could gather the remnants of their meal. "We'd best be off. The day is fading fast."

Chapter Twenty-six

After sunset, as Atticus tended to the donkey in the courtyard of a house that served as the Nazareth inn, a group of newcomers came through the courtyard gate and gathered around the fire. The three men wore the beards and fringed shawls common to the Jews, and though they conversed in Aramaic, Atticus understood enough to realize that they were talking about a rabbi who'd been teaching on a hillside outside Capernaum.

Atticus pretended to fuss with the donkey's harness while he listened. He did not speak, afraid his accent would arouse their suspicions, but the travelers were so involved in their conversation they seemed not to notice him.

"This rabbi is different," a gray-bearded man said, holding his hands toward the fire. "Unlike the other teachers who'll give you a dozen different answers when you ask a question, he speaks as one who has authority."

"I hear he is from Natzeret," a thin man said, his eyes filled with doubt. "Can anything good come from this starving village?"

"Ask his mother." Gray Beard jerked a thumb over his shoulder. "His family lives not far from here."

The tallest man snorted. "His family thinks he is crazy. And if a rabbi's family does not support him, why should anyone else?"

"I heard—" the thin man stepped closer to the fire as he lowered his voice—"he went to the Jordan River to be immersed by the prophet Yochanan. When he came out of the water, some say they heard a voice from heaven! Some say a dove came to rest on his head."

Gray Beard shook his head. "Bah! I was there and I heard no voice. Yes, he was immersed and the heavens thundered. That's all. Not so uncommon a thing."

The thin man frowned. "And Yochanan? What has become of that prophet?" The three drew closer together. Atticus hated to be so bold in his eavesdropping, but since no one had questioned him, he soothed the donkey and moved toward the strangers.

"Yochanan has been arrested." The tall man lifted his brows. "On account of what he said about Herod taking his brother's wife."

Thin Man snickered. "I knew he'd get into trouble. The Immerser does not mince words."

"Surely Herod knows better than to harm him." Gray Beard looked around the circle. "He is safe in Herod's house, no?"

"Is anyone safe with Herod?"

The group fell silent as the fire cackled before them.

Taking advantage of the quiet, Atticus approached the group, his head bent in a submissive posture. "Peace to you, friends," he said, addressing them in Greek. "I have come to this territory in search of the prophet who heals. Do you know where I might find him?"

Thin Man lifted a brow. "You have need of healing?"

"Not me—my child."

The tight line of the man's mouth relaxed. "They are coming from

everywhere, some from as far as Syria. The man you seek is called
Yeshua; he teaches in the open fields around the lake. Set out tomorrow and head north on the main roads. Where you see the crowds,
you'll find Yeshua."

Atticus thanked him with a smile. "A good night's rest to you all."

"And to you," they murmured.

As he crept into the communal room and lay down next to a
stranger who smelled of sweat and horses, Atticus overheard
another fragment of the men's firelight conversation.

"A big one, that."

"Not from Galil, obviously."

"Syrian?"

"Too tall."

"Roman?"

"Too polite."

"Will Yeshua see him, do you think?"

"Hard to say. The prophet says he has come to the lost sheep of
Isra'el."

"He calls us lost sheep? How can he forget we've been chosen
from all the nations?"

"Chosen for *this*? What does HaShem have against us?"

They laughed.

⊹⟩══◎══⟨⊹

The next morning, Atticus turned his wagon toward the Sea of
Tiberias. By midday he expected to reach Herod's city, and from
there he could head toward any of several Jewish settlements that
circled the sea, among them Magdala, Gennesaret, Capernaum,
Chorazin, and Bethsaida. He planned to visit each one, if necessary,
until he found the healing prophet.

Cyrilla and Quinn sat quietly in the wagon, both of them drowsy from a restless night's sleep. Atticus sat behind the donkey's fuzzy rump and listened to the jolt and creak of the wooden wheels. Pedestrians and other conveyances crowded the road on this first day of the week, and they would not move aside for an anonymous merchant's donkey-drawn wagon.

Oblivious to his master's impatience, the donkey plodded forward, his head bouncing to the rhythm of his feet. When Cyrilla began to sing, Atticus glanced behind him—little Quinn watched her intently, focusing on her mouth. Though he joined her with a tuneless *"auuuuuuuu,"* Quinn gave no indication of hearing the lilting melody.

Atticus pressed his lips together and turned away. What would they do if this healer refused to help? Atticus supposed he could threaten the man with physical harm, but a true prophet would not be likely to use his power on behalf of a stranger who had bullied him.

They had passed Magdala and were nearing Gennesaret when Atticus noticed a marked increase in traffic. A throng clogged the road ahead, and they weren't all Jews. Among the crowd Atticus glimpsed several shaven faces and a pair of Roman uniforms.

"I think we've found him."

As Cyrilla cleaned the baby's face, Atticus urged the donkey off the pavement. After hobbling the animal and leaving him to graze in a grassy spot, Atticus lifted Quinn into his arms and led Cyrilla into the jostling crowd. They followed a footpath to a rocky knoll at the edge of the sea. Like the others, Atticus and Cyrilla sat in the grass and waited for the prophet's arrival.

While they waited, Atticus played with Quinn and strained to listen to the conversations around him. More than a few skeptics had come from Magdala, Gennesaret, and the Ten Towns, but several spoke of the prophet with reverent conviction.

During his service in Judea, Atticus had learned that though the
Jews sprang from a common ancestor, they were far from unified. In
this place, oddly enough, he saw Pharisees in their broad phylacteries and fringed shawls, Essenes in white tunics and trailing beards,
and even a few priests in embroidered tunics and showy turbans.
Beggars, children, women, cripples, and outcasts mingled freely
among the religious experts on the hillside, temporarily joined by
curiosity about the prophet.

At length a middle-aged man walked to the knoll and stood facing
the crowd. Like every other Jewish man in sight, he wore a beard
and a fringed prayer shawl. He also wore the plain tunic, robe, and
girdle of a typical Galilean.

After murmuring to some men behind him, the prophet—if
that's what he was—held up his hands. When the crowd grew quiet,
the one they called Yeshua spoke in an authoritative voice that echoed over the rocks.

"*Shema Yisra'el, Adonai Eloheinu, Adonai Echad!* Hear, O Isra'el, the
Lord our God, the Lord is one!"

Atticus flinched as the crowd around him responded by repeating
the same words. Was it a prayer?

He had no time to wonder, for the prophet immediately launched
into his lesson:

"Are you poor today? hungry? Are you grieving?" A glow rose in
his face, as though he contained a lamp that had just been lit. "Adonai
blesses you who are poor, for the Kingdom of God is given to you.
Adonai blesses you who are hungry, for you will be satisfied. Adonai
blesses you who weep, for the time will come when you will laugh
with joy. Adonai blesses you who are hated and excluded and mocked
and cursed because you are identified with me, the Son of Man.

"When that happens, rejoice! Yes, leap for joy! For a great reward awaits you in heaven. And remember, the ancient prophets were also treated that way by your ancestors."

The prophet's dark eyes swept over the gathering, then trained in on the children playing in the grass at his feet. "Do you see these little ones? The Kingdom of God belongs to such as these. Yes, I tell you, whoever does not receive the Kingdom of God like a child will not enter it."

Atticus turned to Cyrilla, who was watching the scene with wide eyes. "Does any of this make sense to you?"

A smile played at the corners of her mouth. "Not really. I understand one thing, though—look over there."

She pointed to the grass beneath the knoll where the prophet stood. When Atticus followed her finger, he first saw a group of Jews who had separated themselves with men on one side, women on the other. But Cyrilla had gestured to the children who toddled and ran and rolled in the grass at the prophet's feet. The listening men seemed oblivious to the little ones, though several of the women had stood to keep an eye on their offspring.

Yeshua stepped forward, his voice dropping to a lower tone as it increased in intensity. "If you are willing to listen, I say, love your enemies. Do good to those who hate you. Pray for the happiness of those who curse you. Pray for those who hurt you. If someone slaps you on one cheek, offer the other cheek as well. If a soldier forces you to carry his pack for one mile, carry it for two!"

Atticus nearly laughed aloud. Roman law allowed a legionnaire to enlist any civilian he encountered to help carry a burden from one mile marker to the next. And since a soldier on the march had to carry a lance, a shield, a saw and basket, a bucket and axe, a leather strap, a sickle, a chain, and rations for three days, rarely did a civilian obey without making a fuss.

Though many in his unit took advantage of the law, Atticus had stopped asking long ago. His shoulders were strong enough to bear what the army required; he would not ask another man to carry his burden. Especially not one of these resentful Jews.

Yet this rabbi wanted his people to volunteer for service to Rome? Unthinkable. Incredible. Impossible. Atticus felt his mouth twist in a grim smile when he saw signs of disbelief on other listeners' faces.

But not everyone responded with derision. Wonder lit more than a few expressions; confusion clouded others. Here and there Atticus spotted eyes that gleamed with yearning. What were they hoping for?

Surely . . . no. Gaius had told him that the most zealous Jews believed their God would soon send them a deliverer, a *messiah*, who would lead them to overthrow Rome.

But this rabbi was no military commander. Though the slender prophet looked fit enough, touches of humor lined his mouth and eyes, and the set of his jaw suggested a stubborn streak. He smiled too often at the gamboling children and spoke in too gentle a voice to command men.

If Yeshua dared challenge the emperor's authority, Rome would break him in an afternoon.

⟡

When the rabbi had finished speaking, the crowd stood and stretched. Frustrated mothers released their captive children, women gathered in conversational clusters, and men grouped themselves according to their station.

Atticus observed the social shifting with a tight smile, then felt a tug at his sleeve. Cyrilla, who'd stuck to him like a shadow until this moment, now stood an arm's length away, as if she'd suddenly become self-conscious in this segregated society.

"Quintus," she said, reminding him of why they'd come. "You must take the boy to the teacher."

Atticus looked toward the prophet. Yeshua had stepped behind a rock, forcing those who wished to see him to approach in a single line. The rabbi's disciples—a handful of ruddy, bearded Jews—struggled to bring order to the surging chaos.

"I'll take him." Atticus swung Quinn into his arms and strode forward, easily outpacing several others. When he reached the end of a snaking line, he hesitated. As a Roman legionnaire, he had every right to move to the front, but he was not wearing his uniform . . . and he was deep in Jewish territory.

Better to wait patiently.

So he stood, listening to the babble of Greek and Aramaic around him, while Quinn tapped at his chin and drooled on his tunic. Sound came from the child's throat, a toneless, continuous *uhhhhhhhh* that might forever mark him as a simpleton and cause him to be treated as an outcast, unworthy of love or attention. . . .

The first Quintus had talked, too, at about this age. But he had said "ba" and "da" and "ma"—until a fever intervened and he stopped speaking altogether.

Atticus stepped forward as the line moved. Ahead of him, close to the rabbi, an old woman danced with her hands lifted to the sky. A younger woman stood beside her, tears streaming down her cheeks while her bearded husband smiled in approval.

What were the limits of this healer's power?

Atticus watched, fascinated, as people left the prophet in groups of two and three. He saw a cripple stand erect and walk away without his crutch. A blind woman who'd been led forward by her daughter now walked independently, her eyes wide with wonder. A man who'd been weakened by fever and brought to the prophet on a stretcher left with the glow of health; a child who'd been covered with pox ran toward his father with unblemished skin.

"You." One of the disciples, a slender man with deeply tanned skin, nodded at Atticus. "Why do you wish to see the rabbi?"

Atticus shifted the child in his arms. "The boy . . . he is deaf."

The man frowned and tugged at his beard. "You are not Jewish."

"No."

"Well . . ." The disciple glanced behind him, as if seeking permission.

Atticus's breath burned in his throat. "Does this healer care only for Jews?"

The disciple blinked. "He came to us, the children of Avraham."

Atticus wavered, wondering if he should confess that Quintus was Jewish. If he announced the truth in this place, would he be allowed to walk away with the child he'd come to consider his own?

He frowned and met the disciple's gaze. "Does the healer not care for other children, too?"

Another fellow with short, curly hair stepped forward, tugged on the first disciple's sleeve, and jerked his head toward the prophet. "He wants to see all the children."

The second man smiled when his gaze crossed Atticus's. "A handsome boy." As the stranger peered at him, Quinn wormed his head into the crook between Atticus's neck and shoulder. "And a shy little thing."

Atticus smoothed the boy's long tunic. "He is."

"All right, then." The first disciple motioned to Atticus. "Come forward."

Atticus stepped up, then looked to his left, where dozens of people milled about, some congratulating the recently healed, others questioning the results with concerned looks and emphatic hand waving. Cyrilla stood alone, not mingling with the Jews or the

Syrians, but keeping a careful eye on Atticus. He nodded in acknowledgment of their bond, then moved closer to the rabbi.

Another disciple, a meaty man with a sparse beard, stopped him with an uplifted hand. "You'll have to wait. The master needs a moment to himself."

Atticus sighed heavily. The rabbi, only a few feet away, was saying farewell to a man and his aged mother. At a word from the disciple who'd stopped Atticus, Yeshua turned toward a thick stand of brush behind the rocks, seeking privacy.

Atticus looked away as understanding dawned. The rabbi had been standing before these people for hours without a break—no wonder he needed a moment.

"*Auuuuuuuuu.*" Quinn pulled on the neckline of Atticus's tunic. "*Auuuuuuuuu.*"

Atticus jiggled the baby. Soon the boy would be hungry and he had no food on hand. This prophet had better hurry.

The shrubs rustled and the rabbi reappeared. His mouth curved in a slow smile when he caught Atticus's eye. "I'm sorry you had to wait."

Not certain how much respect had to be paid to a healing Jewish rabbi-prophet, Atticus bowed his head. "I would wait all day if you can help this boy."

Yeshua approached with his hands outstretched. "How long has the boy been deaf?"

Atticus frowned as he handed the baby over. How did he know? No one looking at Quinn would guess he had a problem unless . . . He exhaled in a rush. Of course. The first disciple must have prepared Yeshua for this encounter.

Atticus folded his arms. "I think he's been deaf since birth."

Yeshua tossed the child into the air, then held the laughing boy against his chest. "Do you know why this child cannot hear?"

Atticus stared. Was this some sort of test? Did the prophet suspect Atticus was only pretending to be Quinn's father? He forced a laugh. "Who can say why these things happen? I must have done something to displease the gods, so they struck my son."

Yeshua glanced at Atticus, his eyes bright with confidence, his smile sly with knowing. "This child is not deaf because of your sin or his parents' sins. He was born deaf so the power of ADONAI could be revealed to you."

Before Atticus could wonder at the mysteries contained in that brief speech, the prophet returned the child to Atticus's arms, then placed his hands on Quinn's ears. The boy's pointed chin quivered as he stared into Yeshua's dark eyes; then the prophet lifted his hands and commanded, "Open!"

Quinn's eyes blinked, then widened. His bewildered gaze focused first on the prophet, then on Atticus. Then he twisted in Atticus's arms to look at a complaining crow that fluttered up from a bush and flew across the sky.

Yeshua rested his hand on the crown of the boy's head. "Like a seed dropped by a bird, he will grow to maturity apart from his people. But the purposes of God will be revealed in him, and he will know the truth."

Atticus had no idea what Yeshua meant, but the prophet could have promised that Quinn would become the next emperor and Atticus would have believed.

In the firm grip of a bottomless peace and satisfaction, he gave the prophet profuse thanks, then carried Quintus to Cyrilla.

Chapter Twenty-seven

QUINN, ORDINARILY A QUIET BABY, did not seem inclined to sleep on the journey back to Caesarea. He twisted in Atticus's arms, fidgeted on Cyrilla's lap, and fixed his eyes on everything that moved and made sound.

Cyrilla found the experience fascinating. "Can you imagine what must be going through his head? To live in a silent world and suddenly hear everything! Our little man must be shocked beyond all imagining."

Atticus smiled, but his thoughts went far beyond wonder. He had been thrilled to see the results of the healer's touch, but by whose power had the miracle occurred? The priests of Mithras—or at least the few he had been allowed to observe—made a great to-do of their rituals, performing their mysterious rites with powders, incantations, and extravagant bloodletting. Before they would even attempt something as important as a healing, they would first study the entrails of a goat or an ox to see if the day would be auspicious and the gods could safely be entreated. The petitioner would have to fast and endure testing to ascertain his worthiness of the god's attention. If at any point something went wrong or looked doubtful, the request would be denied.

This Yeshua, however, had looked at Quinn with the fond gaze of an old friend and said, *"This child is not deaf because of your sin or his parents' sins."*

Had Atticus heard the comment correctly? The healer could not have known that Quinn wasn't Atticus's son—the boy had been wearing a tunic that hid the evidence of his circumcision. In truth, Atticus felt like Quinn's father, and Cyrilla had developed real affection for the child. Yeshua could not have glimpsed any diffidence that might mark a pretend parent. So how had he known the truth . . . and how had he opened the boy's deaf ears?

The question hung in the air, shimmering like the reflection from the sea at Atticus's left hand. *"He was born deaf so the power of Adonai could be revealed to you."* Adonai had to be a name for the God of the Jews, the God who could not be found in their synagogues or their Temple. If he didn't live in their places of worship, how in the world did they reach him?

Atticus glanced behind him, wanting to ask Cyrilla if any of her people's gods had such power, but her head hung low, as if she were dozing. He turned back to the road and clucked at the donkey.

Cyrilla had changed since those days when she'd traveled behind the army. The garrulous, blunt girl had softened. Perhaps Lady Procula's refinement had rubbed off on her. Cyrilla took more care with her clothing and hair these days, and her nails were no longer bitten to the quick.

All in all, Atticus decided, any man would find the changes in Cyrilla attractive.

The crowds on the road thinned as they moved southward. Atticus gave the donkey a ripple of the reins and urged the beast to pick up his pace. If possible, he would like to spend the night in Tiberias, where the atmosphere was decidedly less Hebrew.

They had just passed the stout gates of Magdala when Atticus glimpsed a disheveled figure among the tombs outside the city walls. A woman, wild-eyed and straggle-haired, stood among the graves, her arms planted on a gravestone, her face haggard and lined. Unlike the modest Jewish women Atticus had observed earlier, she wore no veil.

Cyrilla nudged him, then moved closer, tightening her arms around Quintus. "Hurry, Atticus."

"Why should we fear a woman?"

"Don't argue; just whip the donkey. Only madwomen and devils live among the dead."

"Devils?" Atticus turned to give the woman another look, but Cyrilla snatched the flail and smacked the donkey's rump, startling the animal into a trot.

Atticus tightened his grip on the reins and let the beast maintain that pace until they passed the graveyard.

As the air turned gray and congealed with the softness of twilight, Atticus found himself envying the family groups who had left the road and headed home through various city gates. How pleasant it would be to have a wife and child of his own! If he had never joined the army, if Cyrilla were his wife and Quinn his son, he would take them to a sturdy house, bar the door, and make certain they settled down to sleep in safety. No man, soldier, or thief would come against their dwelling, for Atticus would guard it with his life . . . just as a certain Jewish father had tried to guard his home in Magdala.

A wave of guilt rose and threatened to engulf him, but he pushed it back. Why was he wasting time with foolish fantasies? He was a

Roman soldier; he had sworn to obey the emperor and defend the empire at all costs. Rome was the light of the world, the civilizing influence that had tamed barbarians and educated the poor.

The house in Magdala had belonged to an enemy. The uncooperative man was one of those rebels who had sworn to instigate revolt against the empire. If Gaius hadn't ordered them to strike that night, that man and his headstrong son might have attacked and killed four or five of Atticus's comrades.

Sometimes a leader had to make a preemptive move. And when a centurion commanded, a soldier had to obey.

Atticus took a deep breath and felt a dozen different emotions collide as he looked back and studied the child sleeping in Cyrilla's lap. He hadn't obeyed *every* order. Gaius had told him to deliver everyone in the house, and Atticus hadn't delivered the baby. But Quinn was no enemy. If given a chance, an education, and training, he might serve the Roman army as well and as ably as Atticus, Gaius, or even Pontius Pilate. . . .

"Atticus?" Cyrilla's voice cut into his thoughts. "Would you mind taking him? I'd like to stretch out."

Atticus accepted the sleeping child without speaking, then propped the toddler against his shoulder. They should find a place to spend the night, but maybe they shouldn't stay at an inn. Too many people, too many questions, and they no longer needed answers. They needed rest, and they could sleep in a grove as well as an inn.

He spied a spreading plane tree at the crown of the next hill and gestured with his free hand. "There. We'll stop there for the night and sleep in the wagon. Tomorrow we'll rise early and finish the journey to Caesarea."

He smiled when he heard Cyrilla's sigh of relief. The girl he'd once considered foolish and giddy had proven to be faithful and resourceful. She'd make a good mother. One day, if she'd wait, she might make a good wife.

With that thought uppermost in his mind, Atticus considered the road stretching toward the horizon and wished he were free to claim a wife of his own.

Chapter Twenty-eight

I WISH I COULD TELL YOU more about the days when I lived among the graves outside Magdala, but my memory of that time is cloudy. I remember darkness and pain, hunger and wretchedness, the breath of rough men in my face and the clawing of sharp-nailed hands on my heart. I remember being able to *smell* foul words as they escaped my lips. My eyes registered offensive sounds and obscene phrases. My nose inhaled a cacophony of noise and babble. I lived in complete confusion, frequently stumbling among the tombs and gravestones as if a host of pursuers nipped at my heels.

I felt as lived-in as a roadside inn that had been taken over by thieves and infidels. On some days my ears rang with silence; at other times the babble of inhuman voices made me scream and scratch at my skin in a desperate desire to be free. I became a shadow that slipped into villages at dawn and looked for scraps of food or tattered fabric with which to cover myself in the cold night.

I do remember one particular day. . . . I was between villages, walking alone on the road, when I saw a company of Roman soldiers coming toward me. Instantly, my thoughts cleared and my vision focused. I knew the centurion who walked out in front. I had seen him on a road before. I had seen his eyes glare from beneath his helmet and focus on my firstborn son.

I recognized the hard lines of his face and the confident strut of his walk. He had not changed.

I darted off the road and hid behind a bush. Between each convulsive breath I heard myself repeating a name: "Gaius. Gaius. Gaius." Murderer of my family.

I heard the centurion call a halt. I lifted my head and saw him step into the brush, a careless distance away from the men under his command. In the boldness of the eternally arrogant he had stepped aside to relieve himself, never dreaming anyone would notice him.

But I noticed. And so did my voices.

Look, there he is!

Who comes for you? The one you hate!

Rise, Miryam, rise and look!

He has come to kill you! Will you do nothing?

The one you hate is within your grasp!

The rattle of voices prodded me from my astonished state and focused my attention. Gaius, one of my enemies, stood only a few feet away.

I bent from the waist and crept toward him, using the roadside bushes as a screen. I halted two steps away and waited.

When Gaius had completed his business, he leaned against a tree and took a bit of bread from a scrip at his side. Below the leather pouch hung a dagger—pointed blade, steel hilt. Small enough for my hand.

Why do you wait? Have you no courage?

He presents his back to you, the fool! Rise and act! Take your revenge!

She's too weak; she won't do it.

She's strong! She will!

She won't!

"I will!" These words came from my own lips, and at the sound of them Gaius turned, his brows lifting as I rushed toward him like a whirlwind. Urgency fired my blood and I would not be stopped. The Roman tossed his bread away, but my hand was already fumbling at his waist, my fingers searching for the hilt of his dagger—

"As your sword has made women childless, so shall your mother be childless among women!"

I pulled out the dagger, drew it back, and felt his hand clamp around my arm. He shoved me down, his eyes burning into mine, his hand as rigid as the steel in my grip. I would have fallen to my knees, but by calling on the power of the gods within me I managed to resist his strength and push back until the blade kissed his neck. Color drained from his face and a strangled noise gurgled in his throat. Then something hit me at the back of the head, sending a shower of lights sparking through my skull like a swarm of fireflies.

I crumpled as if my bones had been made of parchment.

As the energy of my gods ebbed away, I closed my eyes and feigned death, not groaning even when a heavy foot kicked me and something at my center snapped like a twig.

"Shall I kill her?" a man asked in Greek.

My enemy coughed and cleared his throat before answering. "She's half dead already. Leave her. With any luck, the next unfortunate who attracts her attention will be a Jew."

Someone laughed and rolled me onto my back. I felt hands on my face and my tunic; I knew what would happen next. I prepared to withdraw into the dark well where I routinely escaped, but an unexpected voice intruded: "Leave her alone, soldier. Why would you add to this wretch's misery?"

Amazed that a Roman—*any* Roman—could show mercy, I opened my eyes. The blinding sun prevented me from seeing distinct faces, but I glimpsed two men—one dark-haired, one a hulking brute. My voices went silent as the brute's shadow fell over me; then they began to howl in maniacal glee.

Unable to endure their frenzy, I retreated into darkness.

I don't know why I didn't die during those months. I ate cast-off fish and grass and grubs. I drank from the lake. I took no care for myself because I cared nothing for myself, and the foreign gods within me delighted in my downfall.

Most of the time they gibbered in my head. Sometimes I could hear one voice above the others; sometimes I lost control of my tongue and the voices spilled from my own throat. When this happened, women drew their children close and hurried away; men stood in front of their courtyard gates and regarded me with folded arms and hard eyes. Even when my lips were silent, people who passed by would pull their cloaks around them lest we touch the same dust. Some spat on me as if I were an abandoned dog.

I must have reeked of idolatry and sin.

Most of those days are lost to me now, but I do remember waking one morning and finding my old neighbor in the Magdala graveyard. She was kneeling at my family tomb, cleaning dirt away from the inscription on the stone. For a long moment all I could do was stare; then I managed to speak her name: "Yudit?"

She recoiled as if she'd seen a ghost. "Miryam! You're—you're not well."

I staggered toward her, tearing at my tattered tunic as a guttural voice roared from my throat: "What have you to do with this place, daughter of Avraham?"

Fear radiated from my old friend like a halo around the moon. "Miryam . . . why are you talking like that? Are you—do you want something?"

"Want?" I tilted my head and stared at her. "I want everything. I want nothing. I want the sun and moon and stars to help me. I want to kill the Romans. I want to kill those who didn't stop them from murdering my family—"

I whirled as the graveyard gate creaked on its hinges. My lovely Hadassah stood at the entrance, a basket on her arm and a weight of sadness on her face.

My heart bounded upward. "Hadassah?"

"Miryam?" For an instant her face seemed to open so I could look inside and see the trail of her emotions. I saw joy, bewilderment, a quick flicker of fear . . . then grief. "Dear Miryam, what has happened to you?"

Yudit trembled as tears spilled over her cheeks. "Hadassah, don't."

"But, Mother, it's Miryam—"

"No. Run back to the gate."

"But, Mother—"

"Get out of here, now!" My best friend and neighbor grabbed up her tunic and squirmed through the tombstones like an eel, then grabbed Hadassah and dragged her through the gate. I followed them onto the road, cursing Yudit's cowardice with every step.

The elders at the Magdala gate, shamefaced and silent, retreated at my approach. I think they would have shut me out, but I was too close behind my fleeing neighbors. So the elders stood to the side as I stumbled into the city and skulked toward the ruins of my home.

There I knelt in the rubble and wailed the names of my lost loved ones.

The Law allows three days for weeping, seven for lamenting, thirty for abstaining from laundered garments and from cutting the hair. The rabbis say anyone who mourns longer than the allotted time is really grieving for someone else. Perhaps I grieved for my lost life. I no longer knew who I was or what I was supposed to be. But I did grieve.

I spent that night in the ashes of my past, and when the city gates opened the next morning, a stranger entered Magdala. Not a Roman, this man, not a Greek or a Syrian.

A Nazarene.

⟡══◉══⟡

I awoke at daybreak with a sense, unanchored but strong, that a storm was about to break. I looked up at the sky, expecting to see thunderclouds, but the heavens were a wide and faultless violet curve. Morning air floated around my bare arms, a blessedly cool welcome to the day.

So why did prickles of unease nip at the back of my neck?

The gods in my head whispered among themselves, but none of them spoke directly to me. When I trudged down the street and saw the watchmen opening the Magdala gates, I felt a surge of energy, a momentary alertness. I sensed that I stood on the threshold of some important occasion . . . and then the feeling slipped away. Gone. Like everything in my life.

I yawned, scratched at the insect bites on my arms, and idly wondered if I should be expecting a shipment of silk or a delivery of wool. No, no—my dyeing business belonged to my old existence, the life that had meaning.

My growling stomach turned my thoughts to food. Inside the city, I would have to rely on the charity of strangers or steal from stalls in the market; neither activity promised to be rewarding at this early hour.

I shuffled back to the courtyard of my home and sat in the spot where Yaakov's blood had stained the ground.

Qin-ah wakened within me and began her pitiful wail: *How can you sit there, Miryam? How can you let another day pass without avenging your husband? Rise from this place, coat your face with the dust that drank his blood, and take your vengeance on the first Roman you meet! Set out on the street, for there are Romans about; there are Romans to be had for the taking!*

I was wearily considering this proposition when I heard unfamiliar voices—*human* voices. I rose to my knees, peered through a gap in the wall, and saw that a group of travelers had entered Magdala, more than thirty men with several women trailing behind them.

The sight of the strangers threw my voices into an uncharacteristic silence. I shrank back, pressing my spine against the broken courtyard wall as the group passed. Their shadows glanced over me, strumming a shiver from my soul.

Natar began to growl. *Get out of this city at once,* she murmured in my ear, her voice low and filled with loathing. *Have nothing to do with these strangers, these sons of devils! They will spit on you, Miryam; they will hate you even more than your neighbors do!*

One by one, the others joined her rant: Ba-ath, Qin-ah, Avah, Azaph, Katakritos, and Ge-ah urged me to make haste and flee. I needed to get to the graveyard; I needed to leave the city; I needed to run as if my feet had caught fire. . . .

But I was tired of running . . . and I was starving.

Drawing on my small store of remaining strength, I pushed myself up and trudged to Yudit's house. Perhaps she would give me a small loaf out of pity—or out of a desire to see me gone. Either way, my belly would be full and I could leave the city.

I crossed Yudit's threshold, entered her courtyard, and beat upon her door. I stepped back and saw Hadassah's woebegone face behind the lattice at the window, but she did not let me in. I pounded again and again, calling for Yudit and Hadassah, but my neighbors, my onetime friends, did not want to know me.

Disappointment struck me like a blow in the stomach. I brought the back of my hand to my mouth and swallowed hard to choke down the bile that rose in my throat.

The Law commands us to love our neighbors. By loving others, the rabbis say, we honor those who are created in HaShem's image. When Yudit ignored my pleas, I knew that she saw nothing of the Holy One in me. I was no daughter of Isra'el, no rose of Sharon. I was a broken vessel, fit only for housing the pagan gods I'd invited to fill the emptiness of my life.

With one hand pressed to my chest, I stumbled out of my neighbor's unwelcoming courtyard. My voices wailed when I did not run immediately for the city gates, but thirst propelled me toward the well.

That's where I saw him.

Chapter Twenty-nine

As I ROUNDED THE CORNER and walked toward the well, the buzzing voices in my head piled on top of one another so furiously I couldn't think.

You'll never be anything again; you'll never be loved.

What do your neighbors want? Why are they ignoring you? Leave this place, leave now!

They want to hurt you. Don't you see the fear in their eyes?

That woman, that Yudit, has spread rumors about you.

You are better than her people, better than all of them!

By the light of the moon, by the light of the sun, all of them know everything you have done.

Kill them, kill them, destroy them all!

Through bleary eyes I peered at the band of strangers around the cistern. They were laughing, sharing a lively conversation as a woman poured water for them. At the sound of their amusement, my voices began to rage.

Run! Get away!

There is one here who means you harm!

Who do they think they are? That one . . . he is evil.

How can you think of approaching such men? Flee, Miryam, run!

They will spit on you, kick at you like a cur!

Curse them, Daughter of Darkness! Spit on them!

Turn away, do not let them look at you!

I hesitated, torn between my desperate thirst and the urge to flee. "It is wrong! It's not your time! Who do you think you are?" I shouted in a voice not my own. "The sun is hot; the day is long—you should be about your business and leave us alone."

A heavy silence fell over the group at the well. The woman lowered her eyes as if my shout had embarrassed her, and one of the men stiffened as if my presence were an offense. The others, however, turned to an unremarkable man of medium height and average appearance. He sat on the edge of the stone well and looked out at me from a sharply angled face with a prominent nose, high cheekbones, and smooth olive skin.

He focused on me, his eyes shining with an uncanny awareness.

My voices went wild when his gaze crossed mine. My limbs seemed to possess wills of their own; my hands tugged at my tunic while my legs trembled.

"Who are you to come here, Yeshua of Natzeret?" Natar's voice roared from my throat. "We know who you are, even if this woman does not. Leave us alone, Holy One."

My head tipped back of its own accord; the blue bowl of sky swept over me. My jaw clamped hard, and air rushed through my nose with a faint whistling sound. My hands clawed at my neck; my bones rattled as my body stiffened and fell to the ground. My head filled with a confusing bedlam unlike anything I had yet experienced. The world receded in a dizzy blur as I writhed in the dust like a cut snake.

Then the man spoke, and though he did not raise his voice, his words rang with authority: "Be silent! Come out of her, all of you."

My back arched; my mouth opened. My chest heaved as if I were surrendering my spirit . . . then a Shabbat stillness reigned over my soul.

And he touched me. The one Natar had called Yeshua and Holy One. The stranger risked talking to an outcast; he dared to take a broken woman's hand and help her to her feet.

Too amazed to speak, I shivered in the silence. I felt as though I had been scrubbed, and I stood before him as a shining, clean, and willing vessel.

I didn't know who he was, but I knew he was no ordinary man.

He looked at me with unguarded tenderness in his eyes. "Woman, your sins are forgiven."

Who *was* this man? I didn't know him, so I couldn't have done him harm. And while a man could forgive me for the wrongs I'd committed against him, only HaShem could forgive the sins I'd committed against his holy Law.

Nothing about that morning made sense, but my heart was grateful for release. My knees trembled as I knelt in the dust and stretched my grimy fingers to touch his sandals. "Rabbi," I whispered in my own raspy voice, "how can I thank you?"

When I lifted my head, his eyes had gone soft with kindness. "Miryam—" he spoke my name as naturally as if he'd known me all my life—"you are meant to follow me. But you must understand this—foxes have dens and birds have nests, but I have no home of my own, not even a place to lay my head."

"Then we are alike," I answered, relishing the freedom to speak openly with a man outside my family, "for I have neither home nor husband. What I do have are skilled hands, a strong back, and a grateful heart."

"Indeed," Yeshua answered, regarding me with a trace of amusement in his eyes. "Indeed you do."

Chapter Thirty

Yudit saw the difference in me at once. Drawn by the commotion, she came to the well and found me sitting calm and in my right mind. She took me to her house, allowed me to bathe and comb my hair, and gave me a clean tunic and a proper veil.

When Hadassah embraced me, once again I felt like a daughter of Isra'el.

While Yeshua spoke to several of Magdala's men, I sat by the well and studied the city with fresh eyes. The stone fence around Yudit's courtyard seemed to welcome me; the vine crawling over the broken wall of my house rioted with buds and vibrant green tendrils.

New eyes. What a gift.

I shifted my attention to the town center and the marketplace. My stall, still strong and well roofed, sat at the end of the row nearest the well. A woman was using it to sell her woolens—and why shouldn't she, since I'd had no will to work? But the sight of my stall reminded me of a fact I'd buried under my grief—I was a woman of means.

With no surviving children, I had inherited my husband's property: a ruined house, a marketplace stall, a boat and nets. I also owned the things I'd planned to share with Rachel—my knowledge of dyes, my techniques, my craft. I could still share that knowledge with someone . . . and leave them to oversee my business if I wanted to explore a new life.

I looked at the stranger, the man called Yeshua. He'd said I was meant to follow him, but who was he? His talmidim—*disciples* in your tongue—called him rabbi; but I knew he was more than a Torah teacher. He had to be a prophet sent from the Holy One, blessed be he. How else could he have freed me from the dominion of demons?

As a crowd filled the town center, one of the rabbi's men suggested that they go down to the lake where Yeshua could speak from a boat.

"What boats?" another man protested. "The fishermen are still out on the lake."

"I have a boat." I felt myself blush as every head turned in my direction. "My husband had a boat. I haven't seen it in some time, but if it's there, you may use it."

A short time later, I sat with a group of women while a pair of men pushed Yaakov's boat into the water with Yeshua aboard. Two other men sat behind him; they would steady the vessel while the prophet spoke.

A man on shore, a traveler I'd never seen before, waved for the prophet's attention. "We come from Yochanan the Immerser," he called. "He sent us to ask you a question."

Yeshua nodded. "Ask."

"Are you really the Messiah we've been waiting for, or should we keep looking for someone else?"

Yeshua lifted one eyebrow, then smiled. "Go back to Yochanan and tell him about what you have heard and seen—the blind see, the lame walk, the lepers are cured, the deaf hear, the dead are raised to life, and the Good News is being preached to the poor. And tell him: 'God blesses those who are not offended by me.'"

Yeshua's words provoked a memory that echoed through the years—my father, reading the prophet Isaiah to my brothers: "When he comes, he will open the eyes of the blind and unstop the ears of the deaf. The lame will leap like a deer, and those who cannot speak will shout and sing! Be strong, and do not fear, for your God is coming to destroy your enemies. He is coming to save you."

I felt a warm glow flow through me. The Immerser's representative had asked a blunt question and Yeshua, doubtless mindful of how close he was to Herod's prison in Tiberias, had answered tactfully. But any child of Avraham would understand. God was sending the Messiah to destroy Rome!

When the traveler and his companions turned to leave, Yeshua lifted his arms and addressed those of us who remained. "Those of you who have gone to see Yochanan—who is this man in the wilderness you went out to see? A reed swaying in the breeze? No? Then what did you go out to see? A prophet! Yes, and I tell you he is more than a prophet. He is the one about whom the Scripture says, 'See, I am sending out my messenger ahead of you; he will prepare your way before you.'"

Yeshua kept talking, but a phrase he used snagged my thoughts—*a reed swaying in the breeze*. No one in Galilee could think of reeds without thinking of Herod Antipas, for the man Rome appointed to rule over us had placed his symbol on his city, his ensigns, and our coins.

Yeshua was saying that neither Herod nor Yochanan was our promised king . . . but *he* was.

A thrill shivered through my senses as Yeshua began to pray:

"O Father, Lord of heaven and earth, thank you for hiding the truth from those who think themselves so wise and clever, and for revealing it to the childlike. Yes, Father, it pleased you to do it this way!"

I sat perfectly still, shocked by a realization I could not quite fathom. Yeshua prayed to the Holy One, blessed be he . . . as *Father*? We were people who did not speak HaShem's holy name; neither did we dare approach the throne of heaven with the ease of children seeking a parent. HaShem was too holy, and we—especially *me*— were too corrupt.

As the crowd murmured, the prophet lifted his head and looked toward a distant hill. I followed his gaze and saw a farmer walking behind a pair of oxen hitched to a plow.

"Come to me," Yeshua said, his gaze sweeping the gathering, "all of you who are weary and carry heavy burdens, and I will give you rest. Take my yoke upon you. Let me teach you, because I am humble and gentle, and you will find rest for your souls. For my yoke fits perfectly, and the burden I give you is light."

When he had finished, Yudit's elbow nicked my ribs. "Did any of that make sense to you?"

I frowned. Though it was a relief to think with only one voice— mine—in my head, I wasn't sure I could trust my interpretation of Yeshua's teaching. "I *think*," I said, whispering, "that he has been sent by the Holy One, blessed be he, to help us through this time of oppression. He is a prophet; he has power. But how he plans to use it . . . I don't know."

"Ah." Yudit's mouth twisted in a wry smile. "My thoughtful friend has returned from the land of grief." She tilted her head. "Are you sure you are well?"

I patted her hand. "Completely well. I have been set free."

One of the prophet's disciples came toward us, nodding in silent greeting. Yudit lowered her gaze as tradition demanded, but I smiled, encouraging him to speak.

"The day is warm." His dark eyes sank into nets of wrinkles as he squinted at the sun. "Would you be able to bring us some food and water?"

I nodded. "I could. My friend will help."

I ignored Yudit's gasp of surprise and pulled her up from the grass. We went into the city to fetch bread and water jugs. By the time we returned, the crowd had dwindled. Yeshua sat on the shore, resting with his disciples in the shade of an olive tree.

While Yudit distributed bread at the edge of the gathering, I passed around the water jug and pretended not to listen while I hung on every word.

I thought I recognized one of the disciples. Though I had never known his name, he and his brother were fishermen from Capernaum. Yaakov had often fished with the pair of brothers in the north part of the sea.

Yeshua nodded at the fisherman called Kefa, or Peter in Greek. "You had a question?"

Peter nodded, displaying two prominent front teeth. "Will you ever tell us what your stories mean?"

Yeshua smiled. "You are permitted to understand secrets about the Kingdom of God. But I am using stories to conceal everything about it from outsiders, so the Scriptures might be fulfilled."

The rabbi shifted the focus of his gaze to some interior vision I could not imagine, but I recognized his next words as a prophecy from Isaiah: "They see what I do, but they don't perceive its meaning. They hear my words, but they don't understand. So they will not turn from their sins and be forgiven."

With my water jug empty, I moved away, but my heart pondered what Yeshua had said. Why would a rabbi cloak his words in mystery? I could think of only one reason: Roman ears might consider his message seditious. His talk of the coming king wasn't hard to understand. The prophets had told us that HaShem intended Isra'el to be ruled by ADONAI himself through the administration of his anointed one, our Messiah. We had failed in the past and our kings had led us astray, but when ADONAI had finished chastising our nation, we would be liberated, restored, and allowed to fully possess the land promised to Avraham, Yitzhak, and Yaakov.

I leaned against a rocky outcropping and studied the knot of men on the hillside. If this Yeshua had come to lead us in revolt against Rome, he had come to the right place. Galileans were known for being quick-tempered, adventurous, and loyal to the death. They would follow any leader who proved himself capable of rousing the people's attention.

⟶⟦⟧⟵

Yudit linked her arm through mine as we walked back to the city. "What did you think of him?"

I drew a deep breath. "He knows the Scriptures. He knows our men; did you notice how their eyes lit when he spoke? He is a Galilean, so he also knows how we have suffered under the Herodians and the Romans."

Yudit nodded respectfully at the elders as we passed the gates. Three of the men gaped at me, obviously astonished at the change in my appearance and disposition.

I gave them a small smile—anything more would have appeared immodest—and didn't speak again until we had entered the city.

"I think Yeshua is a true prophet," I said as we approached the well. "Who else would have the authority to deliver me from foreign gods?"

"*Shedim*," Yudit said, whispering the awful word for demons. We set our jars down, and Yudit reached for the rope. She hesitated before pulling up the bucket. "I have missed you, Miryam."

My eyes brimmed with tears. She had turned me away in a time of need, but she must have been terribly frightened by my ravings. I might have done the same thing if the situation were reversed.

I squeezed her hand. "I missed you. And Hadassah."

"What will you do now?"

"I think—" I pushed my jar toward her for refilling—"I may travel with Yeshua for a while. I want to hear his plans for Isra'el. If he really is the Messiah, I want to help him destroy our enemies."

We fell silent as Yudit poured water into my jar; then I lowered my vessel. "I will probably sell the house and the boat. I have no use for them."

Her eyes went wide. "Where will you live?"

I laughed. "Birds of the air, Yudit. I'll live as one of the birds of the air."

Shabbat arrived with the sunset, and I spent it in Uriah's warm house. As Yudit lit the Shabbat lamps before our meal, I squeezed Hadassah's hand and peeked at her father. What would Uriah have thought if he'd been able to hear the prophet?

We gathered around heaping platters of fried locusts, fish, fruit, and pastries—a Shabbat feast. After giving thanks, we began to eat. Uriah, who peered at me every few minutes as if he expected me to burst into flames, remarked that he hadn't brought in a good catch. Yudit responded by saying that her day had been interesting.

Uriah's irritable mood did not improve when he heard that Yeshua had enticed several of the young men away from their work.

Yudit pointed to me as proof of Yeshua's calling as a prophet, but Uriah would not be persuaded.

"How many would-be messiahs and deliverers have we heard about in the last twenty years? A dozen? How many Israelites have been delivered from Rome? None. No, Yudit, I will not be glad about this Yeshua, and you are not to serve him or his tagalongs again. Let him leave Magdala in peace, but do not encourage him."

"He is doing great good among the people," Yudit countered, her voice low. "He has healed sick people from towns all around Galil. I spoke to one of the women who travels with him; she says blind men see and lame men walk at the prophet's touch—"

Uriah shook his head. "It's easy to fool a crowd. He has only to hire men to pretend they are lame."

Hadassah looked up, a glittery challenge in her eyes. "What about Miryam?"

Uriah studied me, sucking at the inside of his cheek as his thick brows worked like a pair of caterpillars. "Miryam was crazed by grief," he finally said, his voice gruff. "What woman wouldn't lose her mind in such a situation? But time has healed her and now she is home where she belongs."

Yudit exhaled, then caught my gaze and quietly rolled her eyes. In that moment, I knew she wouldn't be joining me when I left Magdala.

But I had made my plans. Abruptly, I told Uriah I wanted to sell my house, the boat, and Yaakov's fishing nets. "I will pay you to handle the sale."

He closed his eyes and opened his mouth, signaling that I had transgressed the bounds of womanly behavior. "You will need those things. You need a place to live."

"I'm not staying in Magdala."

"Then where?"

"I'm not sure."

He digested this. "What about your market stall? your business?"

"Yudit may have my stall—she's always admired it; now it's hers. I would also like to share my secret dye formulas with her and Hadassah; I can do some of that tomorrow. We will be partners in the business and you will deliver my portion of the proceeds every month or so."

When a livid hue overspread Uriah's face, I knew my forthrightness had confounded him. While Yaakov still lived, my husband had spoken for me; I doubt I had said ten words in Uriah's hearing. But with neither husband nor son, I had to speak for myself. If that upset Uriah, well, so be it.

Yeshua hadn't minded when I spoke directly to him.

Hadassah didn't seem to mind my decision. "You'll teach me how to dye fabrics?" she asked, her eyes widening. "Oh, Miryam, how wonderful!"

"I have always wanted to teach you." I patted her hand. "Now I can."

I lowered my gaze as a wave of sorrow rose in my chest. If not for the Romans, I would have shared my formulas with Rachel and Binyamin's wife; my dyeing techniques would have remained in the family. We would have spent the rest of our days either crushing crimson worms and stirring dyes or selling in the marketplace . . . now Yudit's courtyard would be scattered with dye pots and piles of crushed shells, not mine.

A cold, congested expression settled on Uriah's face. "As your late husband's friend, I must warn you that traveling with this so-called rabbi is not in your best interests. I have heard stories from Natzeret. Did you know his family does not accept him? Only his mother supports him. His brothers think he is insane, and I have heard that—"

"You are my late husband's friend," I interrupted, "and I thank you for your concern. But please arrange the sale of those things and keep the marketplace stall. Yudit deserves to enjoy a bit of shade as she works."

Uriah pinched his lower lip with his teeth, then drew his mouth into a tight smile. "And where shall I bring the money?"

"To me," I answered, my voice light. "I will be traveling with Yeshua."

◇━◉━◇

The night before I left Magdala, I lay awake and thought about Yeshua. He'd remained in Magdala for the Shabbat, and he'd spoken in our synagogue about the coming Kingdom of God.

As a woman, I had always preferred to leave theological discussions to Yaakov and Avram. But with a personal stake in the struggle between Isra'el and Rome, I wanted to learn more about the Messiah.

A memory flitted past my face like moth wings. One night at dinner, Yaakov and Avram had begun to discuss whether Herod Antipas might be the Messiah.

"Impossible!" Avram insisted. "The Messiah will fight for Isra'el, and Herod fights for no one but himself."

"But his father rebuilt the temple," Yaakov pointed out, a light in his eye as he stroked his beard. "And he won victories over the Parthians and Nabateans. So perhaps the Kingdom of God is already upon us."

"The father is not the son," Avram countered. "And as long as Isra'el is not properly observing the Torah, the Kingdom has not come. Unless the defeated pagans come to Zion for instruction as the prophets foretold, the Kingdom has not come."

But the Kingdom of God *was* coming . . . Yeshua the prophet had said so.

I felt like a child on the brink of a new life. I was too old to marry again. I had given birth and lost my children. I had built a home and a business and watched them go up in flames. I had been possessed by foul demons and I'd been freed. I'd be eternally grateful for my deliverance, but I wanted one thing more from Yeshua, the Holy One's true prophet.

I wanted to stand in his service when he ushered in the Kingdom of God. By helping him, I'd be doing something to overthrow the Romans and achieve justice for my husband, sons, and daughter-in-law. What I could not accomplish through Herod or my own strength, I could achieve by helping Yeshua. When he had driven the stench of Rome from our holy land, I could return to Magdala and die a satisfied woman.

With this thought uppermost in my mind, the next morning I joined Yeshua's group when they left Magdala. Hadassah threw her arms around me as I prepared to leave. "I will do my best to honor you with all you've taught me," she said, nodding toward the dye pots in her courtyard. "When you come home again, I hope to have a lovely piece of purple to show you."

"You'll do well," I said. "You have an eye for color."

"And I am so sorry," she whispered in my ear, "about how my mother treated you before . . . before . . ."

"Hush, child." I smoothed her hair away from her face, then kissed her forehead. "Everything's fine between us."

"Then why must you go? You've just come back and now you're leaving again—"

I clasped her hand and held it tight against my cheek. "Do you remember how much we loved Avram?"

"Of course!"

"I'm going away to help Yeshua set things right for us . . . for all of us. So be a good girl and I'll see you soon."

"You promise?"

"I do."

Though something of my heart remained behind as I walked out of Magdala, I knew I was doing the right thing. Yeshua had said so.

Since women usually keep to themselves, most men will scarcely notice if a woman travels behind them. But while the prophet's disciples might not have noticed my presence, the women who assisted the prophet could not avoid me. Four of them followed Yeshua when we left Magdala on the first day of the week—Yeshua's mother, also named Miryam; Joanna, wife to Herod's steward; Susanna, Peter's wife; and Salome, sister to Yeshua's mother.

The women of Yeshua's company proved friendly enough. They were prone to speaking in whispered voices, as if they didn't want to miss a word that passed Yeshua's lips. The men didn't treat him with that kind of respect, not when I first joined the group. Occasionally he'd say something that closed their mouths in thoughtful regard, but within a few hours they'd go back to bragging that they had been chosen to usher in the Kingdom of God.

Though I enjoyed watching the men, I walked with the women. We didn't talk much that first day—I think they were waiting for me to divulge my motives—and I was struggling to listen to any conversation that might reveal Yeshua's plan for the future. I couldn't hear much, though, walking behind the men, so after a while I slowed my pace and fell into step with Yeshua's mother.

The prophet's mother was a singer. She sang nearly all the time, usually in a voice pitched so low only those closest to her could hear it. I grew to love the sound of her musical murmur and listened for it at all hours of the day and night.

We camped that night in the wilds outside Capernaum. The sun had just vanished below the western horizon when Uriah trotted up on a donkey. He'd come to tell me he'd sold the boat and the house, and he handed me a purse filled with denarii. Of course, Peter invited him to enjoy a meal and the fire, so he stayed the night, though I suspected he wasn't happy about sharing a campfire with Yeshua.

I had just opened the purse when Judas, a broad-faced man from Kerioth, stepped forward and held out his hand. "I'll take that for you."

I clutched the purse to my chest and looked to Salome for confirmation. "It's all right," she said. "Judas handles the money for our group."

"It's not safe for women to carry great sums of silver," Judas said, looking at the stars, the rocks, the trees—everything but my eyes. "So if you will give me your purse, Miryam—"

I pulled out a denarius and placed it in his palm. "I'll give you that," I told him, "until I feel the need to give more."

"It's not safe—," he began again, as if I were hard of hearing.

"Young man," I interrupted, "I fear few things in this life. I am certainly not afraid of a thief."

I almost felt sorry for Judas when he finally met my gaze. How could he know what I'd endured in the wilds around Galilee?

I let him go without offering another word.

Joanna lifted a brow in silent inquiry.

"I'm not being greedy." I tucked my purse into the belt at my waist. "I don't trust that young man."

"If Yeshua trusts him—"

"Yeshua can trust him or not," I answered. "But I know business, and I want to wait."

"For what?" Susanna asked.

"For time to reveal what sort of man he is."

CHAPTER THIRTY-ONE

ATTICUS LEANS HIS ELBOWS ON his knees as the mention of a coin purse fills him with remembering. He had been ten the year his father knelt before him, placed a coin purse in his hand, and told him to take care of his mother and younger brother.

"I have to deliver a load of supplies to the army in Gaul," his father said, pride and tenderness mingling in his expression. "You will be the man of the house while I am gone, so you must look after your mother and little Quinn. Use these coins to buy whatever you need, all right?"

Atticus braced his shoulders, eagerly accepting the burden his father placed on them. His mother was easy to care for—soft-spoken and gentle, she drifted through life with the grace of a petal floating in a fountain. Caring for Quinn would be more challenging, but the little boy with the wide eyes spent most of his day squatting in the shadows, watching as Atticus practiced maneuvers with his shield and wooden stave.

His father kissed Atticus's forehead, then gave his shoulders a squeeze. "If you're a good boy, I'll bring you a present. So remember to say your prayers and obey your mother while I'm gone."

He had hugged his father and held his mother's hand as Varinus Aurelius rode off in the service of the empire.

Atticus never saw his father again. According to the letter they received a year later, Varinus had been supposed to meet up with a caravan at Lugdunum, but the caravan had not arrived a full week after the appointed time. Not wanting to delay further, Varinus pressed on alone, only to be robbed and killed by brigands on the highway.

Atticus's mother, who'd never been strong, could not bear the weight of her grief and the strain of providing for two sons, including one whose hearing and speech had been stolen by a raging fever. Atticus tried to help her, but he couldn't dispel the aura of melancholy that radiated from his mother's pale and delicate features. The coin purse had long been empty, and the money he brought in by selling sweetmeats from a street cart did not go far.

One winter day an older man, a merchant of patrician rank and considerable wealth, came to the house and proposed marriage, but Atticus's mother insisted on visiting a priest at the temple of Jupiter before accepting the merchant's offer.

That night she came home, placed her hand on Atticus's forehead, and said they'd soon be moving to the home of Titus Rutilius.

Atticus couldn't sleep after hearing the news. He stretched out on his bed and tried to persuade his eyes to remain closed, but excitement had fired his imagination. How wonderful to live in a big house, to have a pony, and go to school!

Unable to sleep and not wanting to disturb his mother, he crept to the chamber where Quinn slept, only to find his brother's pallet empty.

He found his mother, dressed in her cloak, tunic, and sandals, weeping on the moonlit portico. When he asked about Quinn, she shook her head and wept harder.

In a panic, Atticus flew through the house, searching all of Quinn's hiding places. Once he thought he heard his little brother's laughter, but when he turned the corner he heard only the splash of the fountain.

Where was he? Atticus was responsible for him; his father had told him to take care of the boy. How could he fail his father now?

With panic like a scent on him, Atticus slipped on his sandals and went out into the night. A cold fog had seethed into the city; it roiled over the cobblestones and cloaked his path. Atticus hurried from house to house, calling Quinn's name, his voice growing hoarse.

Somehow he found himself at the temple of Jupiter. The white-marble facade gleamed beneath a star-washed sky, imposing and unapproachable, but Atticus gathered his courage and climbed the steps of the portico.

A lone priest, a shriveled old man who huddled beneath a cloak, stood on the porch. His eyes narrowed as Atticus drew near, but he didn't speak until Atticus asked if he knew the priest who had advised his mother.

"And who is your mother?"

"Lithia Aurelius."

The priest frowned in a way that made Atticus wonder if he was trying to remember or trying to forget. "Why do you care about this?"

"Because my brother is missing and my mother weeps."

"Ah." The priest lifted one shoulder in a shrug. "She has done it, then."

Atticus felt cold fingers tiptoe down his backbone. "She has done
. . . what?"

"Do not concern yourself, boy. Go home. The sun will rise before
you've had any sleep."

"What has she done?" Atticus met the priest's indifferent eyes
without flinching, then put his hands around the man's skinny
throat. "Tell me what she's done!"

He didn't want to hurt the priest; he acted out of desperation to
save his brother. But he was a head taller than his peers even then and
unaware of his burgeoning strength. The priest tossed him a look of
pure terror, then waved in the direction of the street.

"What are you saying?" Atticus's hands tightened around the
man's throat. "Tell me!"

The old priest's face went the color of blood as he clawed at
Atticus's wrists. When he crumpled at the knees, Atticus released
him and stepped back, alarmed at what he and his anger had done.

But the old priest didn't look up to see the remorse on his face.
He leaned forward, supporting himself on his hands and knees, and
spoke in a wavering voice: "She can't . . . marry . . . with a mute son.
So she has . . . given him . . . back to the gods."

Atticus blinked. "What are you talking about? She didn't sacrifice—" He halted as a cold panic sprouted between his shoulder
blades and prickled down his spine. How many oxen and lambs had
he seen disemboweled on the altar of Jupiter? Surely his mother
wouldn't do *that*. . . .

"She surrendered him," the priest said, wheezing. "In the field
outside the Via Cornelia."

Atticus ran down the steps, his sandals slapping the marble. The
Via Cornelia ran through the northwest corner of Rome, a hard run
from the temple of Jupiter.

The first pale hint of sunrise had lit the eastern sky when he reached the city gate opposite the Via Cornelia. A broad field lay beyond the watchtower, a meadow that sloped away from the city.

Panting, Atticus reached out to steady himself on the stone wall. He lingered in the shadows until the changing of the guards and the opening of the gates; then he slipped through the gap and sprinted down the road.

He'd heard of little ones who mysteriously went away . . . but until that moment, he'd had no idea where the children went. Now he understood, and understanding brought him no peace. No youngster could survive in the cold for long; no child could survive in an area where wild animals and lawless men foraged.

He forced himself to walk at a slower pace, looking right and left while he waved his arms and called Quinn's name. Skirts of long grass and tufts of wildflowers grew along the edge of the road, but none were taller than Quinn. If only the boy would stand up . . .

The road sloped downward, following the curve of the hill, and Atticus spotted a ribbon of water at its lowest point. And there, among the rocks along the edge of the creek, he spied a small form.

Swallowing a cry, Atticus tore through the grass and sprinted down the incline. The meadow around him vibrated softly with insect life, but no sound came from the motionless boy.

Atticus splashed into the water, then turned the naked body toward the sun.

He'd found Quintus—alone, exposed, dead. The bruise on his forehead supplied the story—left to himself, the bewildered boy must have wandered to the stream, fallen in, and hit his head on a rock.

Atticus crumpled as everything inside him went soft. What must Quinn have felt after being abandoned here? Had he cried for Atticus? Had he suffered?

Imagined scenarios twisted and turned in Atticus's imagination, and he knew his dead brother's face would live in his memory forever. He pulled the boy close, anguish sweeping over him as he tried to rub warmth back into those pale, cold limbs. He had failed his brother, his father, and his mother. He was the eldest son, the first-born, and he had been charged with protecting the family.

The shock of defeat paralyzed him for the better part of an hour. Then, wincing from an unexpected and unusual pain in his breast, Atticus lifted the boy in his arms and returned to the city, walking silently past the guards at the gates and the merchants in their stalls. His teeth chattered and his limbs trembled as he carried his baby brother past the Pantheon and the Baths of Agrippa. Finally, he lowered his burden on the steps at the temple of Jupiter.

The old priest was waiting for him, and something in his stony gaze softened as he regarded Quintus's pale corpse. "Only the strong deserve to survive," the priest said, not looking at Atticus. "The weak should be returned to the gods. You were blessed with strength; your brother was not. Learn to live with your blessing."

Atticus had been struggling to live with it ever since.

CHAPTER THIRTY-TWO

NOT EVERY CITY WELCOMED Yeshua and those who traveled with him. In Natzeret, the prophet's home, we went to the synagogue on the Shabbat, where Yeshua read from the Scriptures: "The Spirit of ADONAI Elohim is upon me, because ADONAI has anointed me to announce Good News to the poor. He has sent me to comfort the brokenhearted and to announce that captives will be released and prisoners will be freed. He has sent me to tell those who mourn that the time of ADONAI's favor has come, and with it, the day of God's anger against their enemies."

Yeshua then lowered the scroll and told the people that the prophet Isaiah had been referring to *him*.

His statement caused a riot. The city elders grabbed him and dragged him to the edge of a nearby cliff. They planned to throw him over the edge as punishment for blasphemy, but somehow Yeshua managed to slip away.

When I heard that they had not been able to hold him, I rejoiced in his ability to outwit his enemies. When we marched against Rome, he might need to escape capture.

I had been thoroughly impressed by the prophet's powers. I watched in awe as he cast demons out of men and children who suffered from the same demonic darkness I had known. I saw him restore people who had been born lame; I saw him open blind eyes, just as the prophet Isaiah had foretold. We celebrated these healings, for not only had Yeshua eased the suffering of individuals, but he had given the gift of *shalom*, or wholeness, to those who had been excluded from the synagogue because they were ritually unclean.

While we celebrated, another thought occurred to me: with Yeshua in command of our army, we would have a leader who could heal the wounded with only a touch. How good of HaShem to plan for this contingency!

Yet not everyone believed; not everyone wanted to listen. Skeptics tried to explain Yeshua's works away, but even the Pharisees had to admit he possessed supernatural authority. Those who doubted were quick to say his power came from the devil, but I, who'd had firsthand experience with the forces of evil, saw no sign of that darkness in Yeshua. I saw nothing but light.

While not everyone was ready to hear the Good News, I was eager to spread the word. All Isra'el, from the southern tribes to those scattered in the north, longed for the Holy One, blessed be he, to redeem his oppressed people. I wanted to stand on a mountaintop and shout that HaShem, who was committed to the children of Avraham, Yitzhak, and Yaakov by unbreakable covenant, would soon enact the plan he had ordained from the foundations of the earth. He would establish his Kingdom, and he would keep his promises to Isra'el by punishing our enemies and reordering the world.

Oh, how I rejoiced in the prospect of Caesar's being dethroned.

When Yeshua reigned, Herod would be tossed out of Tiberias and his heathen palace destroyed. The *cohanim*—the high priests—who consorted with the enemy would be supplanted by righteous ministers. And the Romans who had murdered my family would be cast out of Eretz-Yisrael.

We knew the Romans despised us. Our customs—such as observing the Sabbath, circumcision, and abstaining from pork and meat sacrificed to evil spirits—elicited amazement, contempt, and ridicule from the pagans. Their attitude was nothing new—every man in Isra'el knew the Romans thought us beneath contempt. We had a saying: whatever is sacred to the heathen is profane to the Hebrews.

But the Holy One of Isra'el, blessed be he, specialized in defeating pagan tyrants. Hadn't he conquered Pharaoh, Balak, Og, and Sihon? Hadn't he flattened Jericho and made Ai a mound of ruins? The Holy One of Isra'el could conquer Rome.

I believed that soon, through his prophet Yeshua, he would do it.

And then I would have my vengeance upon the evil empire and her sons, Gaius Cabilenus and the Goliath known as Atticus Aurelius.

⋄⟩══◉══⟨⋄

In the marketplace of Capernaum, I saw an old woman wailing before a publican. She held her calloused hands open, indicating that she had nothing else to give, yet the tax collector, a bearded Israelite who worked for the Romans, frowned at her and showed no mercy.

Like a bolt of lightning through my chest, a surge of rage took me by surprise. I clamped my mouth shut, hoarding my anger like coals in a hearth, and tugged on the woman's sleeve. "Come with me."

She followed, probably hoping I would give her money, but I took her to Yeshua. He and his disciples had gathered around the well, where several of the village elders had come to question him. I hated to interrupt, and as a woman I had no right to approach, but I felt too tired and shopworn to worry about what strangers thought of me.

"Yeshua," I called, feeling my stomach tighten as I sought his attention, "this woman is being badgered by the tax collector. She has no money and he will not grant her relief. Can you help?"

I had expected him to gesture to Judas, who'd have to hand over a coin or two. The thought of tormenting our tightfisted treasurer brought me more than a little pleasure.

But Yeshua didn't even look at Judas. Instead he smiled at the woman and stood. "Will you lead me to him?"

With long strides the old woman and I led our rabbi to the market square. The tax collector sat at a small table under a shady stand, where he could harass people in comfort.

Yeshua took the old woman's hand, then walked up to the publican. I held my breath, expecting to hear a stream of condemnation, but Yeshua fixed his penetrating gaze on the man and said only two words: "Follow me."

The tax collector looked from the old woman to me, then back to Yeshua. He squinched his face into a bewildered expression; then he stood and followed Yeshua, who led us back to the well.

Yeshua left the old woman in my keeping. The poor creature turned, her tear-streaked face marked with trails of dust. "What do I do now?"

I smiled. "Is anyone asking you to pay a tax?"

"No."

"Do you have food in your house?"

"No."

I pulled a handful of coins from my purse and pressed them into her hand. "Buy yourself some grain and oil and go in peace."

The other women drew around her, offering words of encouragement and comfort, but I walked to the circle of men. The tax collector sat on the ground at Yeshua's feet, his brow wrinkled in thought.

Why hadn't Yeshua berated the publican? Everyone knew the tax collectors asked far more than Rome demanded, especially if they had something against the citizen standing before them. My Yaakov had frequently complained that the publican responsible for fleecing the people of Magdala had decided Yaakov and I were wealthy enough to subsidize his household as well as Caesar's.

I leaned against a wall and crossed my arms. Perhaps Yeshua had a plan for this particular publican. Perhaps he would wait for the right moment, then castigate the scoundrel before the entire assembly.

I waited, but Yeshua continued to talk about a farmer scattering seed. I was about to rejoin the women when he finally stopped and asked the publican to stand. I halted in midstep; the others watched with hooded eyes and suspicious smirks. The back of the man's neck flushed, but he obeyed.

"Friends—" Yeshua dropped his broad hand to the publican's shoulder—"this is Levi. Welcome him, for today he has become one of us."

As Levi stammered out an invitation to dine at his house, I stared in silence, stunned that Yeshua would display so much mercy toward one who had openly collaborated with our enemies. And dinner! To eat with someone meant you were at peace with him, and a covenant of peace made at a meal was binding.

When Yeshua accepted the publican's dinner invitation, I realized his generosity proved he had come to seek and to save the lost sheep of Isra'el. He had brought Levi into our group; he had forgiven the man's shameful sins.

For another child of Isra'el, I supposed I could do no less.

CHAPTER THIRTY-THREE

ONE AFTERNOON WE MADE camp outside Bethsaida. The spot where we stopped was as lovely as any in Eretz-Yisrael, with the sapphire sea to the east, the city to the west, a silken sky overhead, and a benign warmth that rose from the ground to comfort our tired bodies.

At sunset we gathered in a clearing and waited for the onset of darkness. One of the men began to sing—I think it was Andrew, for he possessed the strongest voice. As he sang, I sat with the other women and watched Yeshua. After a few weeks of traveling with the prophet, my feelings for him had ripened beyond respect. I had begun to love him—not the way a wife loves her husband nor the way a woman loves her rabbi.

I loved him in the gentle, tender way a mother loves a son.

I think I loved Yeshua because he reminded me of Avram. Like my firstborn's, his eyes could flash with intellect and feeling, and his heart burned with a passion for Isra'el. He had a way of standing

with his hands at his hips and his head thrown back in laughter—
that, too, reminded me of Avram.

In that gathering darkness, where no one could see the hunger in
my gaze, I looked at my rabboni and realized that if not for two
Roman dogs, my son could be helping Yeshua usher in the Kingdom of God. Avram had possessed enough heart for the task,
enough passion and goodness and courage. But evil men had
snuffed him out.

Earlier that day, when we had gritted our teeth and vacated the
pavement so a Roman chariot could drive by, I looked at Yeshua's
mother and wondered if she appreciated having such a son. I knew
she had suffered grief—she'd lost her husband the year before
Yeshua began to teach—but she seemed to move through her days in
a state of pensive wonder. When Yeshua laughed and celebrated with
his disciples, she merely smiled; when he grew angry with the criti-
cal Pharisees, she lifted a brow without comment.

What would she do when Yeshua conquered Rome? Would she
accept a position of honor in his new Kingdom, or would she go back
to Natzeret and live with her other children?

When I lifted my gaze to look at the prophet and his men again, I
felt a swell of pain that went beyond tears.

I had buried and mourned my loved ones, but I had not forgotten
them. My firstborn, my beautiful boy, had looked much like his
father, but in temperament, he had been too much like me. Unlike
my Yaakov, who'd been among the gentlest men in Magdala, Avram
had been quick of temper and swift to act. Every morning he'd gone
out to fish with his father, but in the afternoon, when the older men
sat in the shade to mend their nets, Avram had drawn the young men
around and ranted about Rome.

It was wrong, he'd said, for the children of Isra'el to remain silent under the bondage of foreign oppression. Would not the Judge of all the earth do right? If the Holy One, blessed be he, would have spared Sodom for the sake of ten, would he not free Isra'el for the sake of thousands?

Avram's zealous arguments often made my heart tremble because I suspected that his fervor sprang from the stories of Hezekiah, Josiah, and Judas Maccabaeus I'd told him as a child. All three of those heroes had cleansed the Temple and restored a proper worship of the Holy One, blessed be he, but when my son became a man, I regretted telling him of our heroes. In our time, nationalistic dreams could be dangerous; they invited suspicion and threatened our livelihoods.

When my son married, I warned him not to speak against Rome. When Rachel told us she was expecting a child, I asked Avram to swear he would keep his mind on fishing and leave the Romans alone.

He would not swear . . . and his actions killed him.

As much as Yeshua reminded me of Avram, I couldn't help but notice a major difference in the two men. My Avram, of blessed memory, had been hotheaded, but Yeshua was thoughtful and clever. He would not be taken in a Roman trap. Day after day I'd watched our rabbi tell cryptic stories that meant little to Romans, but resonated within Hebrew hearts.

Yes, Yeshua was wise. I was sure he would succeed where Avram had failed.

Swallowing the lump in my throat, I forced my lips to part in a smile as I joined in Andrew's song.

⟶══◆══⟵

One afternoon Judas and I got into an argument. A messenger had come from Magdala, and Judas, fox that he was, had caught the scent of money. After a brief interval—during which I barely had time to greet the messenger, offer him food and drink, and accept a payment from Uriah—Judas stepped into our women's circle and asked me for a contribution.

I stared as if I didn't know what he meant. "A contribution?"

"Miryam—" contempt laced his voice—"I know you receive payments from your village, so don't make me ask again. It's only right that I handle the money; I'm the treasurer."

"And I'm no fool."

Susanna gasped at my words, but Salome giggled.

Judas flushed. "I am the treasurer."

I rose to face him. He was not a tall man and I am not a small woman, so we stood eye to eye, equal in stature if not in station.

"You are not good with money," I told him. "How much did you pay for the chicken and bread in Nain? Ten denarii? That's outrageous. I could have talked the merchant down to five."

"I made a good bargain."

"Any woman in this circle could have done better. You should stick to negotiating the price of cattle and sheep; leave the food to us women."

Crimson patches appeared above his beard, as if I'd slapped him on both cheeks.

Joanna stepped to my side. "That's a wonderful idea; don't you agree, Judas? Leave the menial chores to us; you can help the rabbi with more important matters. You don't need to be bothered with food—we'll take care of that."

Any child could have seen through her blatant appeal to his pride, but Judas swallowed and backed away. "So be it. Keep the money for food, but if you have need, know I'll have other uses for the common purse."

"Understood," I called after him.

I forced a laugh as he walked away. "That one's a snake. I wouldn't be surprised if he hasn't been dipping into the community purse for his own pleasure."

"Why, Miryam!" Gentle Susanna's mouth dipped in a frown. "I'm sure Judas would never even consider such a thing. He's devoted to our rabboni."

Yeshua's mother came to stand by my side. "Sometimes I worry about you, Miryam." Her eyes searched mine, as if she could reach into my thoughts. "You have given all your income for this work. Shouldn't you hold something back? What will you do when our group disperses?"

I smiled at her in amused wonder. Hadn't she been listening to her son? That afternoon Peter had reminded Yeshua that we had left our homes to follow him. Our rabboni replied that everyone who had given up a house or wife or brothers or parents or children for the sake of the Kingdom of God would be repaid many times over.

I had given up my home, my city, and a few earthly goods, but I expected to be fully repaid when Yeshua reordered the Kingdom.

"I would give every last coin in my purse to support Yeshua's cause," I told her. "But I'm not here because I want money."

I want justice for my family.

I fell silent as a pair of Roman soldiers approached our resting place by the road. One of them jerked his chin at a traveler who'd stopped to meet Yeshua. The legionnaire pointed to the burden on his back, then shrugged out of the straps that held it in place.

That poor man would have to carry the soldier's burden to the next mile marker.

I forced a smile. "Every last quadrans," I repeated. "Nothing is too much to give for the cause."

One mild night, after the group had broken apart to seek places to sleep, I wrapped my cloak about my head and shoulders and left the women's circle for a walk along the shore. As grateful as I was to Yeshua for giving me a new chance at life, the sea would always fill me with a longing to turn back time.

I walked to the water's edge, closed my eyes, and could almost hear Yaakov's joyous greeting in the wind off the lake.

My smile faded as I stood with the breeze on my face. I had another life, another calling, and I loved the rabbi I served. I had never felt so close to HaShem nor to his people Isra'el.

Still . . . I missed my family.

I walked along the reeds and watched the stars come out as I thought about my loved ones. Though the Law would say I should not continue to mourn them, during quiet moments I enjoyed opening the windows of my heart to memories of Yaakov, Rachel, Avram, and Binyamin. Sometimes I heard their laughter in the chittering of insects; sometimes I saw their smiles in the lights winking from villages across the lake.

I was thinking of Avram when I stumbled upon Judas and Shimon the Canaanite talking with three men from a nearby village. No properly behaved man would acknowledge a woman walking alone in the night; most would turn and leave me to find my own way. Shimon and Judas did turn away, but not before giving me a piercing look that unnerved me while it aroused my suspicions.

I gave them a meaningless nod and moved through the shadows, then halted behind a rock and strained to listen. I didn't recognize the three strangers, but Shimon had made no secret of his sympathy for those Hebrews whose zeal for HaShem tended toward armed rebellion. And Judas—well, Judas never hesitated to stick his nose into matters that might cause trouble. So what could they be discussing?

A whisper of terror ran through me when I heard talk of daggers and swords; then I realized that I was witnessing a conspiracy. The three strangers might have been promising cooperation, money, or weapons. . . .

Did Yeshua know of their plans?

I pulled away, blending with the night shadows as I walked back to the area where the women had bedded down. Someone would have to tell those fools to be careful. My son had been zealous for God, too, and Avram's zeal had cost us dearly. One thoughtless action had resulted in the destruction of my entire family, so I could not let Shimon and Judas ruin the prophet's plans.

I had invested too much in Yeshua's cause; I would not want him to stumble over incompetent men.

Chapter Thirty-four

The heady scent of perfume clung to the young woman as she crept from the room where the men were eating. Hannah, Simon the Pharisee's wife, lowered her gaze in embarrassment as the woman stepped outside to join us; even Susanna looked away.

But how could I begrudge this creature any kindness? I had heard Yeshua's words; I knew he had approved her rash action. Our host, a Pharisee of the Pharisees, had criticized this girl as if she were as unfeeling as the alabaster jar in her hand, but Yeshua knew better.

I stepped closer and lifted the girl's chin with my fingertip. She flinched at this unexpected contact, probably anticipating a rebuke, but I met her red-rimmed eyes with a smile. "Are you hungry?"

She blinked. "H-hungry?"

"Surely you are." I slipped my arm around her slim waist and urged her toward the table where we women were working. "The hour is late and you've been waiting half the day."

The girl remained as if planted to the spot. "You . . . you saw me?"

"Of course, dear. I saw you hiding behind the courtyard wall. I would have urged you to come forward and join us but—" I gestured to the work on the tables—"my hands were required by others."

Her eyes darted toward a basket of bread. Her lips parted; then she averted her gaze and shook her head. "I cannot eat with you. These women would . . . would not welcome me."

"You think not?" I propped my hands on her shoulders—bony shoulders, I realized; the girl was much too thin. "Do you think—" I lowered my gaze to hers as I softened my voice—"that you are the only one with reason to be ashamed? All of us have secrets we keep from the world."

The girl's lip quivered. "The rich man at the table—he said the rabbi was a fraud. He said if Yeshua was a true prophet, he'd know what sort of woman knelt at his feet. He said it loudly, so everyone could hear. . . ."

I stroked her cheek, felt her tears burn my fingers like hot wax. "The rich man at the table," I said, well aware that Simon's wife was listening, "does not understand what Yeshua teaches. The Pharisee keeps the Law on the outside, while inside he is as black as the sins he sees in you."

Behind me, the other women fell silent. From the corner of my eye, I saw Susanna draw near, a reproachful look on her face.

But I didn't care. As the young girl peered at me through tear-clogged lashes, my thoughts drifted back to a sweltering day in Magdala before I met Yeshua. Starving and exhausted by the voices raging in my head, I had sought a bit of shade in an alley behind the market, but one of the merchants found my resting place. After glancing around to be sure no one watched, the brute pinned me in the dust and took his pleasure from me, then rose, sweating and grinning, and strolled back to his stall.

When I staggered onto the street, trembling and battered, I lifted my arm to accuse him. I had barely drawn a breath when he pulled his wife and daughter into the shadows. "Away with you," he scolded, stepping between me and his women. He lifted his chin, addressing anyone within earshot. "This creature *stinks* of harlotry!"

My arm fell to my side as the pressure of dozens of pairs of eyes assaulted my frame. In the hot glare of their unyielding disapproval, I felt more violated than I had in the alley.

An evil man attacks a woman privately. A devil strikes her in public.

"Come." I turned to the girl. "Sit with us and eat. Listen to our stories and you will learn that Yeshua is a true prophet indeed."

◄◦─══◉══─◦►

Though I wanted to speak to Yeshua about Shimon and Judas, the longer I thought about it, the more preposterous the idea of a conspiracy seemed. Yeshua was ADONAI's prophet—he had real power. What could Judas and Shimon possibly do to upset his plans?

So I said nothing.

We went to Jerusalem for the Passover. Yeshua performed several miracles, and many people believed in him. On the way back to Galilee, we stopped at Sychar in Samaria, where Yeshua wandered off alone and talked to a woman at the village well. She and her neighbors were so impressed with him that we remained in the area two days.

When we returned to Galilee, Yeshua called the disciples together and gave them authority to cast out demons and heal diseases. He sent them into the neighboring towns to heal the sick and tell everyone about the coming Kingdom of HaShem.

I could scarcely contain my excitement. This had to be Yeshua's call to arms! He could not be more open about his intentions lest he alert the Romans, but by sending the disciples as emissaries, he could spread the word, display his power as HaShem's prophet, and raise an army.

Surely the time was near.

While we waited for the disciples at Susanna's house, we learned that Herod had heard reports about Yeshua's work. According to the rumors, Antipas, who had executed Yochanan the Immerser, thought the dead prophet might have come back to life. He sent spies throughout the land to look for Yeshua.

I laughed like a drunken woman when I heard the news. Susanna stared at me as if I'd gone mad.

"Don't you see?" I wiped tears of mirth from my eyes. "This is good news! First, Yeshua will never let himself be caught by that horrid toad. Second, Herod is worried. He has caught a whiff of revolution and wants to know its source. By the time he discovers it, he will be overthrown!"

A faint line appeared between Joanna's brows. "What of my husband? Chuza works for Herod. If Herod finds out I am assisting Yeshua—"

Yeshua's mother placed her hand on Joanna's arm. "Do not worry about these things," she said, her voice calm. "Everything will be revealed when the time is right."

I closed my eyes and breathed in the comfort of her words. In time, all would be made plain to us.

I was counting on it.

⟡

The disciples returned to Capernaum with glowing reports of their progress. They had aroused people's interest and healed many with diseases. Crowds would soon be arriving from all the towns and villages throughout the region, and they were all eager to hear Yeshua speak about the coming Kingdom.

Messiah fever had finally gripped the people's hearts.

Yeshua welcomed his disciples and said he wanted to speak to them alone, so Susanna suggested that they go to the lake and take a boat to a remote spot. We agreed to join the master and his men at Bethsaida.

We women loaded several donkeys with supplies and set out. "Look," Salome said, nodding toward a group coming toward us on the road. "What a beautiful shade of blue that woman is wearing— it's the color of tzitziyot. Have you ever seen that dye used in a tunic, Miryam?"

I clicked my tongue against my teeth, about to suggest that someone had stolen the formula for my *tekhelet* dye, when I recognized the oval face beneath the blue veil. "Why, it's Hadassah!"

I flew down the road to meet her. After embracing her and greeting those who'd been kind enough to escort her, I took her hands in mine. "What are you doing here? Where are your parents?"

"I wanted to hear more about Yeshua," she told me. "When the sons of Zebedee came to tell us what he'd been saying, I knew I had to come, but Father wouldn't hear of it. Mother must have known I would sneak away, because she placed coins in my hand and told me to find you. She said you'd take care of me."

"Of course, my darling girl!" I hugged her again, then slipped my arm through hers and introduced her to the other women.

The others welcomed Hadassah, offering her water and a chance to rest. "I'm fine," she said, waving away their concerns. "Please, let's continue on the journey."

"We're on our way to Bethsaida," I explained, "But so many people are coming to hear Yeshua, I doubt the city walls can contain the multitude."

We met swarms of people on the road. Wandering like sheep without a shepherd, each group asked if Yeshua the prophet had gone to Capernaum or Bethsaida or if he had taken to the fields. We pointed them in the right direction, and by the time the sun had climbed halfway up the eastern sky, a crowd had formed outside Bethsaida.

"He's there!" Salome pointed to the lake, where a boat approached through the blinding dazzle of the sun's path on the sea. Twin anchors fell from the boat's nostrils; then Yeshua and his disciples splashed their way ashore. The crowd surged forward, forcing the disciples to link hands and herd them into a semblance of order. While the disciples restrained the crowd, Yeshua scrambled to a stony outcropping where he could be seen and heard.

When the crowd settled, he began to teach. He spoke of familiar topics and told stories I'd heard before, so I watched Hadassah. My young friend sat like an open flower that follows the sun; Yeshua's words filled her with light.

Yet I couldn't help feeling a twinge of guilt. Hadassah had come here without her father's permission, a serious offense in our culture. At seventeen, she was old enough to be married and living with her husband's family, but she had resisted her father's attempts to find her a husband. How much of her resistance, I wondered, came from her headstrong nature, and how much from my influence?

I knew she admired me . . . as Avram's mother and an older friend. And while I wanted her to be strong and competent, I didn't want her to suffer things I had suffered because of my stubborn independence.

At some point, I would have to return her to her father's care . . . and hope she didn't resent me for it.

The sun had just passed its zenith when Judas came to us. "You women wanted to be in charge of the food." His cold eyes sniped at me. "So how are you planning to feed this mob?"

I looked at Salome and Hadassah, then laughed. "We're not planning to feed them. All our coins combined couldn't begin to feed this many."

Judas stalked away, but Hadassah turned to me with wide eyes. "There's no food? So many of these people have little children with them—"

I patted her hand. "I'm not worried, dear one. Wait and see what Yeshua does."

I took Hadassah's hand and led her closer to the place where Yeshua stood. He had stopped speaking, probably to rest his voice, and a drowsy silence hung over the meadow where the people rested.

From where we stood we could see Philip and Judas clambering over the rocks, the communal purse in Judas's hand. When they reached the prophet, Philip's nasal voice cut through the silence, reaching even our ears: "You must send the people away to buy food. It's late and they have nothing to eat."

Yeshua looked at him. "You feed them."

Judas smacked the depleted purse. "With *what*? It would cost over two hundred denarii to feed this crowd!"

Yeshua looked around and smiled when he caught my eye. Then he squatted to address Peter and several others who stood on the grass below. "How much food do you have? Go and find out."

I hoped the disciples would discover that the people had brought food with them, but they returned with a dismal report: "We have five loaves of bread and two fish."

Yeshua gestured to the grassy field. "Have the people sit down in companies of fifty."

I slipped my arm around Hadassah as Yeshua took the five loaves and two fish, looked up to heaven, and recited the blessing of the bread: *"Baruch Atah Adonai Elohenu Meloch Ha'olam, hamotzi Lechem Min Ha'aretz."*

My young friend and I watched in silent wonder as our rabboni tore the fish and bread and gave pieces away, again and again and again. Everyone ate as much as they wanted, and the disciples gathered twelve baskets of leftovers. One basket, I realized, for each of the twelve tribes in the coming kingdom.

I squeezed Hadassah's shoulder. "Do you remember when a man brought Elisha a sack of grain and twenty loaves of barley bread? The prophet fed over one hundred men with that meager amount and had plenty left over."

Hadassah and the disciples marveled over Yeshua's power, but I daresay Judas, Shimon, and I saw the miracle from another perspective. A leader who could feed over five thousand men, plus uncounted women and children, with only the barest amount of bread and fish . . . could easily feed an army.

An army that would march victorious against our enemies.

Chapter Thirty-five

We were pressing toward Jerusalem when we heard that Pontius Pilate had murdered some Galileans as they sacrificed at the Temple. A ripple of horror moved through our group, and Shimon caught my eye as we gathered around our rabboni. Would Yeshua insist on leading us toward this dangerous Roman governor before we'd finalized our plan for a military campaign?

Our rabboni barely mentioned the tragedy in his teaching. I listened intently as Yeshua spoke, attempting to read between the lines and gauge his motivation. He taught in parables, as always—of fig trees, mustard seeds, narrow doors, and unprepared brides. He talked of ordinary things to ordinary people, and as I weighed his words, I became convinced that I had somehow missed his meaning.

Later that night, when the men had settled down to sleep and most of the women had retired to our circle, I found Yeshua standing by the shore, his cloak wrapped around his shoulders as protection from the chilly wind. His attention focused on something beyond the shoreline, and I would have given my last coin to read his thoughts.

"Something amiss, Miryam?" he asked without looking in my direction.

"You must know the sound of my footsteps."

He turned, the corner of his mouth dipping in a wry grin. "You have a question for me?"

I smiled, amazed at his insight. "Actually, yes. Today you said the Kingdom of God was like the leaven used by a woman making bread."

His chin dipped in a nod. "You listened."

"But I don't understand. We are commanded to rid our homes of leaven before the Passover feast; the rabbis say leaven represents sin, for sin permeates anything it touches. How, then, could the Kingdom of God be like leaven?"

"Miryam."

My heart warmed to the sound of patience and affection in his voice.

"Can you *see* the leaven at work in your bowl?"

I shook my head.

"Can you hear it?"

"No."

"Can you explain how the leaven expands a small lump of flour into a large loaf of bread?"

I laughed. "No."

"Neither will you be able to explain the advance of the Kingdom of God."

I had missed something, but he turned back to the lake, leaving me to carry his words into the night. I was sorting through them, trying to make his meaning fit with the coming revolution, when Susanna stepped into my path.

She lifted a brow when she saw me. "Have you seen Yeshua? Peter needs him."

I jerked my head toward the lake. "He's there."

"I suppose he was with John or one of the others?"

I stared at her for a full minute before the meaning of her arched brow hit home. By all that was holy, did she think I'd sought Yeshua . . . as a woman seeks a *man*?

I inhaled a deep breath and wrapped my tattered dignity around me. "He is a *prophet*," I said, my voice icy.

"You are a woman."

"Don't women deserve to understand?"

Susanna stared at me, her eyes alight with speculation; then she drew her veil tight around her throat. "Good night, Miryam."

My veil, of course, had slipped from my head while I stood in the wind talking to Yeshua. But Susanna's query hadn't sprung from my immodest appearance. She had stopped me because my reputation clung to me like an odor, poisoning everyone who had ever seen me wandering around Galilee when demons controlled my life. . . .

I had watched Yeshua restore a dead boy to his mother, but I had yet to see him kill a rumor.

⧓

We camped outside Natzeret before the Feast of Tabernacles. I thought Yeshua had brought us to that village to visit his mother, for she didn't always travel with us. Though our rabboni was her first-born, her other children—James, Joseph, Abigail, Simon, Judas, and Anna—demanded her attention and were not shy about offering their opinions on their elder brother's activities. The more Yeshua's fame spread throughout the region of Galil, the more outspoken his siblings became.

We had scarcely finished unloading the donkeys when Yeshua's brothers arrived and urged him to join the pilgrims on their way to the Holy City. "Leave," his brother James told him. "Go to Jerusalem where your followers can see your miracles. You can't become famous if you hide out here in the wilderness. If you can do such wonderful things, prove it to the world!"

Yeshua gave his brother a rueful smile. "Now is not the right time for me to go. You can go anytime and it will make no difference. The world doesn't hate you, but it does hate me because I accuse it of sin and evil. I am not ready to go to this festival because my time has not yet come."

The next day, however, Yeshua told us we would go to Jerusalem, but we would go quietly. "My time has not yet come," he repeated, and immediately I knew what he meant. We were not ready to launch a revolt.

My heart lightened as we joined hundreds of other pilgrims on the road to Mount Zion. Though we were not ready to strike against Rome, Yeshua needed to enlist the religious leaders in our cause, and most of them lived in the Holy City. How could we expect to defeat Rome unless our people united?

We traveled in groups of four and five, and Yeshua walked with his head covered so he would not be recognized. Hundreds of pilgrims filled the roads, traveling by donkey, camel, chariot, wagon, and on foot. As we walked, we sang the psalms of ascent: "How deeply loved are your dwelling places, Adonai-Tzva'ot! . . . Happy are those who are strong in Adonai, who set their minds on a pilgrimage to Jerusalem. . . ."

I had never felt such anticipation. We'd heard, of course, that certain misguided religious authorities were plotting Yeshua's death, but I was convinced they would join our cause once they'd had a chance to hear our rabboni's message.

I walked past a Roman legionnaire on the road and met his smirking expression with a steely gaze. Why should I cower before him? Victory was almost within our grasp.

⟡

Yeshua was the talk of the city when we reached Jerusalem. Some called him a prophet and a wise teacher; others insisted he was a deceiver and a fraud.

I was hoping Yeshua would court the religious leaders privately, meeting with them under cover of darkness as he had previously met with Nicodemus, an important leader of the Pharisees. I was on my way to speak to Judas about housing when Yeshua began to walk toward the Temple Mount.

A wave of apprehension swept through me as I hurried after him. Why had he slipped quietly into Jerusalem if he intended to address the festival crowds?

By the time I caught up, Yeshua had crossed the bridge that led to the Royal Porch. Moving as quickly as the mob would allow, I walked over the Royal Porch and followed Yeshua into the Court of the Gentiles.

That court, which any reverent person may enter, teemed with life. Money changers sat at tables; herdsmen offered goats, lambs, oxen, and pigeons for sale. I strode through the stench and clamor of that bustling space and paused only an instant before the marble tablets that warned Gentiles, on pain of death, not to proceed farther.

Yeshua had proceeded into the Court of the Women, so called because it was the farthest point a woman could venture. Ducking my head, I climbed the steps to that court and stood on the raised gallery that ran along three sides of the rectangular chamber.

I looked down on the hubbub and searched for Yeshua. Finally,

I spotted him standing beside one of the thirteen trumpet-shaped chests designated for charitable contributions and the required Temple tribute. He opened his arms and taught those who were willing to listen. Several priests stood at the edge of the crowd, their eyes scanning the assembly as they pretended not to listen to our rabboni.

"I haven't been teaching my own ideas," Yeshua was saying, "but those of him who sent me. If any man will do his will, he will know whether my teaching is from the Holy One or is merely my own. Those who present their own ideas are looking for praise for themselves, but those who seek to honor the one who sent them are good and genuine."

"What about your disciples?" one of the priests shouted. "They don't observe the Shabbat or obey the law of Moses!"

Yeshua's eyes blazed with sudden anger. "None of you obeys the law of Moses! In fact, you are trying to kill me."

The group released a collective gasp; then voices wrapped about Yeshua like water around a rock. When one of the priests accused him of being demon possessed, I wondered why these people couldn't accept what had been obvious to me from the day I met Yeshua: the Holy One had sent him to deliver us from the Romans. He *had* to be our Messiah.

A woman tugged at my sleeve. "Is that the man they are trying to kill?" She pointed at my rabboni. "Why do they hate him?"

"Do you think," another woman asked, "he *could* be the Messiah?"

"What do you think?" I answered, looking from one woman to the other. "Would you expect the Messiah to do more miraculous signs and wonders than he has done?"

The tinny sound of distant trumpets interrupted us. It was the seventh day of the Feast of Tabernacles, and we had entered the Temple in the midst of a beloved ritual. To commemorate Moses' drawing

water from the rock at Horeb, on the first morning of the Festival of
Tabernacles and every morning thereafter, a *cohen,* or priest, carried a
large golden jug from the Temple Mount to the spring of Siloam.
Surrounded by worshipers, he drew water from the pool, then
returned to the Temple and walked into the inner court.

I lifted my gaze in time to see the priest approach the altar with
the golden ewer in his grasp. Behind him, a procession of priests carried willow branches and chanted the closing verses of the Hallel:

Adonai, please save us! Adonai, please prosper us!

Blessed is he who comes in the name of Adonai!
We have blessed you out of the house of Adonai.
God is Adonai, and he has given us light.

Around the altar, sages juggled lighted torches while acrobats
performed somersaults. The joyous ritual, known as *Simchat Beit
HaSho'evah*, culminated as the priest poured the water over the altar,
washing away the blood of the morning sacrifices.

As the last of the water trickled into the font, I looked from the
spectacle to Yeshua's face . . . and saw that the observance had made
him smile, but with a distracted, inward look, as though he were listening to something only he could hear.

What was he thinking?

I understood his need to speak in riddles—with so many Roman
soldiers sprinkled throughout the Court of the Gentiles, he could
not speak openly of messiahs and revolt and sedition.

Yeshua strode through the Court of the Women, then stood at the
top of the steps and opened his arms to the mob in the Court of the
Gentiles. "If you are thirsty, come to me! If you believe in me, come

and drink! For the Scriptures declare that rivers of living water will flow out from within."

His words resonated within me, and doubtless with every worshiper who heard him.

As other priests blew the ceremonial trumpets at the conclusion of the water ritual, a choir of priests chanted the words of Isaiah: "Then you will joyfully draw water from the springs of *yeshua*."

Yes . . . *yeshua* means "salvation." And in that moment, some of us understood. The cohanim had been prophesying of our rabboni for years, and here he was, proclaiming himself the source of cleansing, living water.

But not everyone accepted his teaching. As my eyes scanned the congregation, I saw Yeshua's brother James. He stood among the pilgrims, his eyes fastened to Yeshua's face, his brows pulled into an affronted frown.

As the crowd began to disperse, I heard reactions to Yeshua's comment. Some declared, "This surely is the prophet Moses spoke of." Others wondered how he could be the Messiah from the royal line of David if his lineage didn't fit the ancient prophecy. The Scriptures said our Messiah would be born in Bethlehem, yet most people knew Yeshua came from Natzeret.

My rabboni stopped smiling when the temple guards, usually posted at the gates, surged toward him. My heart nearly stopped beating.

The guards halted before reaching Yeshua, though they kept wary eyes on him as he continued to speak. Scarcely able to breathe in the tense atmosphere, I slipped from the gallery and wandered back into the Court of the Gentiles. After a while, the guards drifted back to their posts, but the tension in the air remained.

I was about to search for Salome and Joanna when I heard one of the Pharisees accost a temple guard: "Why didn't you arrest him? You're the captain; you should have taken action!"

"I have never heard anyone talk like that," the guard answered. "He said nothing wrong."

"Have you been led astray, too?" Fire gleamed in the Pharisee's eyes. "Does a single one of us rulers or Pharisees believe in him? The crowds do, but what do they know about anything? A curse on their ignorant souls!"

I caught my breath as Nicodemus, the tall man who had sought a private meeting with Yeshua on one of our previous visits to Jerusalem, stepped forward and lifted a hand. "Caution, my friend. Is it legal to convict a man before he is given a hearing?"

The other Pharisee snapped back at him, "Are you from Galil, too? Search the Scriptures and see for yourself—no prophet ever comes from Galil!"

Chapter Thirty-six

Atticus did not need to be reminded of Jewish stubbornness. He'd seen evidence of it on an afternoon when his cohort had been stationed in Jerusalem for yet another religious festival. Flavius had entered the barracks with his hand on his sword and his cheeks flaming.

At the sight of his friend's heightened color, Atticus straightened on his stool. "What's wrong?"

Flavius released a stream of particularly colorful curses, then punctuated his exclamation by kicking an empty trunk. "Caesar should round up the lot of them! Use half of them for sport in the arena and sell the other half as slaves. That way they'd be doing the empire at least a little good!"

Atticus blinked. "Who?"

"The Jews." Flavius exhaled heavily, his nostrils flaring. "One of them had the gall to spit on me as I rode beneath a bridge. To *spit*!"

"Why didn't you arrest the man?"

Flavius's nostrils flared again. "I couldn't. The bridge was crowded with them, all jabbering and pointing and jeering. I'd have taken them all in, but by the time I could send men up to the bridge, they'd be long gone. They're like rats; they can vanish into the woodwork when it suits them."

Atticus pointed to an empty stool. "Sit down. Relax. This isn't the first time you've been spat on, and it probably won't be the last."

Flavius sat, his hands curling around the throat of an invisible opponent. "I'd like to find that weasly little Jew and strangle the breath out of him. Why don't these Hebrews act like ordinary people? like Romans?"

Atticus felt a half smile cross his face. "Well . . . perhaps it's because they're not."

Flavius ignored the comment. "Will we have to whip every one of them? They're conquered. It's about time they realized it."

"I'm not sure you or I would realize it if we were conquered by a superior army," Atticus remarked, pulling a polishing cloth from beneath his mattress. He withdrew his sword from its sheath, then ran the cloth along the sharp edge. "We would fight until the end, wouldn't we?"

Flavius scowled. "Fight, yes, with my dying breath. But these Jews don't fight. They *argue*. They withdraw into their silly rules and religious traditions. They play politics, and—"he glanced right and left, then lowered his voice—"you know there's nothing dirtier than a man who plays politics."

Atticus tilted his head, conceding the point. "I've heard," he said, taking pains to keep a pleasant note in his voice, "that most of the Jews don't fight because they are waiting for their God. Apparently he has promised to fight for them."

Flavius's expression changed as his anger shifted to surprise.

"How can anyone possibly believe that? Look at them—conquered, scattered, entire villages hungry and poor?"

"Even so, they believe. And if the Roman army hasn't been able to shake their faith, I doubt our cohort can do it."

Flavius snorted. "Fools, that's what they are. Any race that would follow an invisible God who leads his people into defeat—well, they deserve whatever happens to them."

Atticus held his sword up to the light, studying the long, sharpened edge. "Despite everything, they believe. So they might be foolishly stubborn . . . or they might be courageously faithful." He cocked a brow. "Though Caesar reigns here, these people are far from defeated. Until they bow in submission, how can we decide which they are?"

Annoyance struggled with frustration on Flavius's broad-boned face as he glared across the distance between them. "You've been too long in this province, my friend. These people have addled your brain."

Atticus slipped his sword back into its sheath. "I'll admit they can be trying. But they can also be . . . interesting."

Flavius rose, shaking his head. "I'm headed to the baths. I'd like to wash every last trace of this crazy place from my skin."

Atticus said nothing as he watched his friend go. Then he leaned forward and propped his hands on his knees. Flavius was right; the people of this place had affected him deeply. But a bath wouldn't help, for there was no way he could wash the imprint of Israel from his heart.

Chapter Thirty-seven

I GAINED A DAUGHTER SHORTLY after we left Jerusalem. We entered the region of Galil and I returned Hadassah to Uriah, but her father would not forgive her for leaving without his permission. Though she humbled herself and begged his pardon, Uriah glared at me and declared that Hadassah had exceeded the bounds of forgiveness. If she wanted to follow a prophet who associated with fallen women and ate with publicans, she would no longer be his daughter.

And so she became mine. As we left Uriah's courtyard, I put my arm around the weeping girl and looked back at the house. Uriah stood in the doorway, his red face set in anger, but Yudit stood in the window, tears glistening on her lined face.

Our eyes met and caught, and a promise was given and received. "Don't weep, dear one," I said, speaking as much to Yudit as to the girl in my arms. "You once said that you would be my family; do you remember? Now I will be yours."

Hadassah sniffed and nodded, but I knew she would mourn the loss of her loved ones. I would try to comfort her, but I knew some griefs could not be assuaged.

As I entered my third year of working for our rabboni, I sensed that our movement had begun to stagnate. We made little progress, Yeshua often looked weary, and tensions among the Twelve increased. Everyone sensed that Yeshua needed to act soon, but I did not believe we were ready.

For one thing, Yeshua had not recruited an army. He had followers in nearly every town around Galilee, including several Gentile settlements, but he had done nothing to establish military authority or train skilled soldiers. I had always assumed that the Twelve would become the commanders of his army, but even Peter, James, and John, Yeshua's closest friends, did not exhibit the sort of discipline necessary to lead an advance against Rome.

Tension thrived even among us women. Miryam, wife to Zebedee and mother to James and John, waited until after dinner one evening, then knelt respectfully before Yeshua. Like the others cleaning up, I would have been oblivious, but Hadassah saw her and gave me a hard elbow in the ribs.

I turned, my arms filled with empty bread bowls, and stared as Zebedee's wife asked if her sons could sit in places of honor once Yeshua had established his kingdom. "It would bring me great pleasure," she said, pressing one hand to her breast in exaggerated humility, "to know my sons sat at your right and left hand."

I sputtered wordlessly as Yeshua turned to James and John, our so-called sons of thunder. He studied them intently; then he asked if they were able to drink from the bitter cup of sorrow he was about to drink.

"Oh, yes," they answered, nodding. "We are able!"

A tinge of sadness filled Yeshua's eyes. "You will indeed drink from it, but I have no right to say who will sit on the thrones next to mine. My Father has prepared those places for the ones he has chosen."

Zebedee's Miryam rose with an abashed look on her face, and I glared as she scooped up a basket of leftover fruit and scurried toward the door. I wasn't offended because she wanted to promote her sons—well, perhaps I was—but rather because her sons had done nothing to prepare for the coming revolution. Peter had at least purchased a sword, but James and John seemed content to wander throughout the countryside as if the victory could be won with singing and persuasive teaching.

Even more disturbing was another recent development. Yeshua did not always speak openly; sometimes he took the Twelve apart and spoke to them about his plans. After one of these private meetings, I caught Peter looking through our supplies, probably trying to find something to eat.

I pulled a small fruit loaf from a basket, but hesitated before giving it to him. Shadows filled the usually optimistic fisherman's eyes.

"Peter?" I lowered my voice. "What's wrong?"

He glanced about to be sure no one could overhear. "Yeshua told us he would soon suffer many things. He said he would be rejected by the cohanim and Torah teachers. He said they would kill him."

I almost laughed aloud. How could they kill a prophet with Yeshua's power? But, respecting the worry in Peter's eyes, I nodded in sympathy. "Surely you misunderstood him."

"I thought I did. I pulled Yeshua aside and told him he shouldn't say things like that. But he looked at me and said—" Peter hesitated, his eyes filling with distress.

"He said what?"

"He said, 'Get away from me, Satan!' I stepped back, not under-standing how he could say such a thing to me, of all people. . . ."

I pressed my fingers to my lips and searched Peter's eyes. This man was close to Yeshua, closer than anyone but John, yet in many ways Peter resembled an overactive child. He must have done some-thing to annoy our rabboni, something he left out of the story. . . . I patted his shoulder as a mother comforts a son. "I'm sure Yeshua meant nothing by that comment, Peter. Don't worry about it."

"Do you think he will die?"

"I think he was testing your commitment. Are you willing to fol-low him even if the odds are stacked against us? If you are, then you are also ready to follow him to victory."

Peter looked at me with something like relief in his eyes. "I hope you're right."

"Of course I am. Do you really think Yeshua would be foolish enough to fall into a trap?" I laughed. "Not even my Yaakov, he of blessed memory and a simple nature, was so gullible."

<hr />

On our return to Capernaum, where we were to stay again at Peter's home, we met a group of Pharisees and Torah teachers who had been sent from Jerusalem to investigate Yeshua's activities. I took their presence as a good sign—apparently Nicodemus and others who supported Yeshua had made headway with the religious leaders. If these representatives carried a good report back to Jerusalem, our cause could advance quickly.

The fragile peace that had held since our meeting on the road shattered when we served the midday meal. As was our custom when we traveled, the men sat in a circle in the grass while we women offered bowls of fruit, bread, and cheese. After reciting the blessing of the bread, Yeshua and the disciples took from our bowls and ate, but the men from Jerusalem would not even touch the food.

Tension filled the air like smoke when their leader turned hot eyes upon Yeshua. "Why do your disciples disobey our age-old traditions? They do not wash their hands before eating."

I knew the answer to that question even if the Pharisee did not. Any water used for the washing of hands would have to be hauled from the lake on *my* back, as well as on Salome's, Joanna's, and Susanna's. Yeshua's decision to forgo the ritual hand washing was a kindness to us women, but these Pharisees apparently thought only of their tender consciences.

Yeshua turned to the Pharisee with smoldering eyes. "Why do you, by your traditions, violate the direct commandments of God? For instance, God says, 'Honor your father and mother' and 'Anyone who speaks evil of father or mother must be put to death.' But you say, 'You don't need to honor your parents by caring for their needs if you give the money to God instead.' And so, by your own tradition, you nullify the direct commandment of God."

Yeshua's voice went soft, but no one could miss the venom in his words. "You hypocrites! Isaiah was prophesying about you when he said, 'These people honor me with their lips, but their hearts are far away. Their worship is a farce, for they replace God's commands with their own man-made teachings.'"

The Pharisee to whom Yeshua had been speaking regarded our rabboni with a new expression. His face had been transformed, the pious and compassionate veneer peeled back to reveal the bitter ugliness underneath.

Yeshua lifted his voice so everyone in the vicinity could hear: "Listen to what I say and try to understand. You are not defiled by what you eat; you are defiled by what you say and do."

Like the others, I stared at Yeshua through an astonished silence.

Peter leaned toward him. "Do you realize you have offended the Pharisees by what you just said?"

Yeshua gave the Pharisee a quick, gleaming look before turning to Peter. "Every plant not planted by my heavenly Father will be rooted up, so ignore them. They are blind guides leading the blind, and if one blind person guides another, they will both fall into a ditch."

In that instant, my hope for rabbinical endorsement vanished like a mirage.

In the spring of that year, when we were near the Jordan River, we received word that Lazarus of Bethany, brother to Miryam and Marta, was sick. Yeshua nodded gravely when he heard the news but assured us that Lazarus's illness would not end in death.

After two days, Yeshua told us we would go to Bethany, which was only a short walk from Jerusalem. The disciples objected, for by that time the hostility between Yeshua and the religious authorities had flared into outright war, but Yeshua insisted we should go. Lazarus had fallen asleep, he said, and he needed to go wake him up.

Thomas, ever the pessimist, drew a deep breath and said we should go to Jerusalem . . . and die with our rabbi.

When we arrived in Bethany, a weeping Marta met us outside the city gate. "If you had been here," she said, "my brother would not have died."

Compassion struggled with grief on Yeshua's face as he regarded her. "Your brother will rise again."

"I know he will," Marta said, sniffing, "when everyone else rises on resurrection day."

"Marta." Tenderness vibrated in Yeshua's voice as he took her hand. "I am the resurrection and the life. Those who believe in me, even though they die like everyone else, will live again. Do you believe this?"

I did not hear her reply, for at that moment Miryam, Lazarus's youngest sister, ran through the city gates, trailed by a band of mourners. She fell at Yeshua's feet and repeated Marta's statement: "If you had been here, our dear brother would not have died."

Yeshua looked at the weeping women and the crowd beyond, all of whom were wailing. A troubled look crept over his face. He turned to Marta. "Where have you put him?"

She gestured to the nearby graveyard. "Come and see."

Yeshua went . . . and wept with every step. The disciples and I followed, and we couldn't help overhearing the words of the mourners:

"Look how he loved him!"

"If he loved him, why didn't he come in time to save him?"

"He healed a blind man, so why couldn't he prevent Lazarus from dying?"

When we reached the graveyard, Marta led Yeshua through the gate and pointed to the tomb. A stone had been rolled across the entrance.

Yeshua folded his arms. "Roll the stone aside."

"But, Lord," Marta cried, "he's been dead four days! By now the smell will be terrible!"

My stomach tightened into a knot as sorrow brushed the edge of my mind. I turned and pushed through the crowd, unwilling and unable to bear another moment at the tomb.

Too much pain. Too many memories. Not only did the images of Yaakov, Avram, Rachel, and Binyamin rise up to torment me, but I could never stand in a graveyard without reliving all those days I had lived among the dead because the living could not abide my presence.

I reached the edge of the mourners and shouldered my way to empty space, where I gulped breaths of fresh, clean air. The air at the tomb's entrance would be fetid and foul, and what did Yeshua hope to accomplish by viewing the decaying remains of his friend? I had seen him raise a boy from a funeral bier; I had seen him heal people whose souls hovered between this world and Sh'ol. But this was different. Lazarus had been four days dead.

The master's strident shout cut into my grief: "Lazarus, come out!"

My heart thumped against my rib cage as the crowd went silent. I closed my eyes and stifled a scream of frustration.

How would Miryam and Marta react when Yeshua failed to restore their brother? The Pharisees who stood at the edge of the crowd pretending disinterest would rejoice at Yeshua's failure, but Lazarus's sisters would suffer the grief of false hope as well as the grief of separation. I would try my best to comfort them; perhaps I could take them aside once we had gone inside the house—

"He's not coming," a man near the gate remarked, a smirk crossing his face. A flood of reproachful shushing drowned this cynical opinion, but I could find no fault with it. A man's soul might linger for a day, perhaps two, but every rabbi I knew said that no soul could resist the call of Sh'ol more than three.

I lifted my head as something moved near the tomb. Had Yeshua stepped inside? For I could see movement—

The still air of the graveyard quivered as feminine cries scattered the dust motes and shivered my skin. Miryam and Marta were sobbing; an instant later their voices were swallowed up by shouts of joy and disbelief.

"Unwrap him," I heard Yeshua call above the bedlam. "Unbind him and let him go!"

I looked at the cynical man by the gate. His eyes were still narrow, but his mouth hung open in a silent gape. Two of the Pharisees had risen on tiptoe; one Torah teacher supported himself on his companion's shoulder as he tried to peer over the crowd.

I rose, too, clinging to the graveyard fence as I struggled to glimpse the miracle by the tomb. I had just spotted Marta's head when the crowd stilled.

"Master."

The voice, deep and resonant, belonged to Lazarus of Bethany; I'd have recognized it anywhere.

"My friend Lazarus." A smile warmed Yeshua's greeting. "Shall we take you home?"

A cheer erupted from dozens of throats, and the crowd surged toward the gate. I stepped back, speechless, as Miryam, Marta, Lazarus, and Yeshua led the astounded group away from the tomb and toward the city.

I watched them pass and shivered as a new realization bloomed in my chest: I would never doubt the success of Yeshua's plan again. With a pulse-pounding certainty I *knew* the Holy One of Isra'el had sent Yeshua to lead us against Rome . . . because he had the power to bring even dead soldiers back to life.

Did the others comprehend what we'd witnessed? Did they *realize* what this meant?

Under Yeshua's leadership, victory would be ours. For not even Rome could boast of an immortal army.

CHAPTER THIRTY-EIGHT

SIX DAYS BEFORE THE PASSOVER ceremonies began, we returned to the house of Miryam, Marta, and Lazarus. The crowds heard of our impending arrival, and dozens of men, women, and children flocked to Lazarus's house to personally view the man who'd come back from the grave.

Word of what had happened to Lazarus had spread throughout Bethany and Jerusalem. During my visits to markets and city wells, I heard that eyewitnesses had reported the news of Lazarus's resurrection to the Sanhedrin, our religious council. Fearing the power of his influence, the council wanted Yeshua dead.

Furthermore, our rabboni had become quiet and withdrew from us even more than usual. He spent long hours in prayer, and I fretted for him. Was he worried about raising the support necessary to see his cause through? Did he fear the Romans? I wanted to assure him that I had absolute confidence in him, but as a woman, it was not my place to speak about such things.

I spotted a pair of Pharisees among the crowd at Lazarus's house and noted the look of scorn on their faces. How could they argue with a man who had been four days in the tomb? He had returned from Sh'ol because the word of Yeshua had brought him forth.

The sisters prepared a wonderful dinner in Yeshua's honor, and as the men ate together in the house, we women sat outside and nibbled at the feast. As hostess, Marta centered her attention on serving dinner, but I lingered with the younger sister, sensing that something lay heavy on her mind.

Finally Miryam met my gaze. "I don't know," she said, "how to thank him."

I knew what she meant—many times I'd been struck speechless when I thought of the immense debt I owed my rabboni.

I squeezed her arm. "I know how you feel. How can any of us thank him for what he's done?"

She smiled and shook her head. "No, not for what he's done. For what he's going to do."

I faltered in the silence that engulfed us. Yeshua was going to usher in the Kingdom and deliver us from our enemies . . . yet I'd never considered thanking him for that.

Miryam crossed her arms, thought working in her eyes. "I—I have to help serve dinner," she said, "but perhaps there is something . . ."

Marta called for her and Miryam stepped away. I paused outside the lattice-covered window and peeked inside the house. Lazarus, the picture of health, lay on the couch nearest Yeshua. He laughed and spoke like a man unafraid of anything, least of all the Pharisees who felt more threatened than ever by the prophet from Natzeret.

Lazarus's laughter stopped as a sudden silence settled over the group. The men turned to look at something or someone, and I saw Miryam moving toward Yeshua. Carrying a large jar in her hands, she knelt at the end of the couch where he reclined. Without speaking, she opened the jar and sprinkled perfume on his feet, then wiped his feet with her long hair.

The sweet fragrance reached even to the window where I stood.

I looked at the others—Peter watched with a wistful expression, John smiled at her with tenderness, and Andrew gazed at her in wonder.

But Judas wore a frown. "That perfume," he hissed, apparently not caring that Miryam could hear every word, "was worth a small fortune! It should have been sold and the money given to the poor."

Yeshua turned to Judas, hurt and rebuke shining in his eyes. "Leave her alone. She did this in preparation for my burial. You will always have the poor among you, but I will not be here with you much longer."

I felt my heart break for Miryam, who had flinched under Judas's harsh words. Tears flowed freely down her face, but whether she wept from Judas's condemnation or Yeshua's praise, I couldn't tell.

I wanted to rush in and wipe her tears away, but Marta was acting as hostess, so I could not walk into a room filled with men. I marveled that Miryam had found the courage.

But she didn't need to weep. Yeshua's hour of victory was almost at hand. He would be leaving us, but only to take his rightful throne as Messiah and deliverer of Isra'el.

⟿══◉══⟾

We observed the Shabbat in Bethany and left for Jerusalem on the first day of the week. The news of our approach preceded us, so a crowd of Passover visitors took palm branches and met us on the road with shouts of "Hosanna, son of David," which in our tongue means, "Deliver us, son of David!"

Not only did Jerusalem welcome Yeshua as Messiah that morning, but within the crowd Hadassah and I even spotted Gentiles who'd been caught up in the enthusiasm and were waving palm branches.

I had to restrain myself lest my excitement induce me to laugh aloud. The hour of victory was near; we could feel anticipation in the air. With Yeshua's ability to perform mighty works and this kind of popular support, no Roman legion could stand against us!

Someone offered Yeshua a young donkey. Because he was weary—I saw shadows beneath his eyes—he straddled the animal's bony spine and rode it through the city gate. He looked more like a tired and dusty traveler than a triumphant king, but still the crowd recognized their Messiah.

And as I followed, words from the prophet Zechariah rose on a wave of memory: "Rejoice greatly, O people of Zion! Shout in triumph, O people of Jerusalem! Look, your king is coming to you. He is righteous and victorious, yet he is humble, riding on a donkey— even on a donkey's colt."

⋅⟩⟩═◉═⟨⋅

Among those waving branches when we entered Jerusalem was a group of Greeks. Some of them knew Philip, and they asked for an audience with the prophet. I overhead Philip telling Andrew about their request; then they went together to ask Yeshua if he would speak to the Gentiles.

Yeshua agreed and went out to meet them. "The time has come," he told the Greeks, "for the Son of Man to enter into his glory."

I caught my breath. Yeshua had referred to himself as the Son of Man before, but I'd always assumed he was referring to his humanity. In that moment, for the first time, the phrase struck a chord—

Yaakov had often read to Avram from the writings of Daniel the prophet, who had written about the coming Son of Man.

I closed my eyes and was filled with remembering. Yaakov's voice merged with Yeshua's, and I heard the beloved words as clearly as if my husband were whispering them in my ear:

> "As my vision continued that night, I saw someone like a Son of Man coming with the clouds of heaven. He approached the Ancient One and was led into his presence. He was given authority, honor, and royal power over all the nations of the world, so that people of every race and nation and language would obey him. His rule is eternal—it will never end. His kingdom will never be destroyed."

A blush of pleasure rose to my cheeks as I watched my dear rabbi talk with the Gentiles. Yeshua had been cagey with the religious leaders, but with the Greeks he spoke plainly. The hour was near. Victory was nearly upon us.

I edged closer, hoping he'd extend a plea for their cooperation in his revolt against Rome, but instead his plain speech dissolved in to riddles. "The truth is," Yeshua continued, "a kernel of wheat must be planted in the soil. Unless it dies it will be alone—a single seed. But its death will produce many new kernels—a plentiful harvest of new lives. Those who love their life in this world will lose it. Those who despise their life in this world will keep it for eternity."

My burgeoning hope deflated like a dead puffer fish. What did he mean? Was he saying that we'd have new positions in the coming kingdom? I wasn't sure, but I didn't like this talk of death. I knew some men would die in the revolt—few revolutions have been bloodless—but I'd seen Yeshua raise a man four days dead. Surely he'd restore any losses we suffered.

"All those who want to be my disciples," he told the Greeks, "must come and follow me, because my servants must be where I am. If they follow me, the Father will honor them."

Watching him, I saw something that looked almost like regret enter his face. "Now my soul is deeply troubled," Yeshua went on. "Should I pray, 'Father, save me from what lies ahead'? But that is the very reason I came! Father, bring glory to your name."

What happened next is still a matter of debate among those of us who had gathered around Yeshua. Some claimed they heard a clap of thunder; some said they heard an angel. But I heard a voice. A rumble from heaven answered Yeshua's cry: *"I have already brought it glory, and I will do it again."*

Yeshua looked out at us as if his soul had grown tired. "The voice was for your benefit, not mine. The time of judgment for the world has come, when the prince of this world will be cast out. And when I am lifted up from the earth, I will draw everyone to myself."

Murmurs fluttered through the crowd:

"Is he saying he will die?"

"Scripture says the Messiah will live forever. And who is this Son of Man he's talking about?"

Yeshua looked down at his hands. "My light will shine out for you just a little longer. Walk in it while you can, so you will not stumble when the darkness falls. If you walk in the darkness, you cannot see where you are going. Believe in the light while there is still time; then you will become children of the light."

A Greek woman turned to me with a question in her eyes. "You follow this man?" She pointed at Yeshua. "Can you explain what he means?"

I could only shake my head.

Chapter Thirty-nine

Atticus was in Jerusalem during those days—he'd been sent there to guard Pilate, who, with Lady Procula, stayed at Herod's palace during major Jewish festivals.

On the first day of the week, Atticus reported on the run to tribune Claudius Lysias's quarters at the Fortress Antonia. Gaius sat before the patronizing tribune, a patrician's son with no patience for what he viewed as plebian incompetence.

"We've heard rumors," Claudius said, looking past Gaius to Atticus, "of potential trouble in Jerusalem this week. There's a new messiah in town, and this one is causing more trouble than most. The governor does not want trouble."

Atticus glanced at Gaius, who sat with his back straight and his expression unruffled. Gaius had undoubtedly heard this already . . . so why had the tribune summoned him?

He dipped his chin in a nod. "Understood, sir."

"They say," the tribune drawled, the hint of a smile curving his mouth as he looked at Gaius, "this one raises the dead. One of the Jews in Bethany had been dead and buried four days, but this Messiah called him out of the tomb with a word."

Atticus stiffened while Gaius laughed. "I wonder how much they paid the dead man to lie in his tomb and wait for his summons?"

"Not nearly enough, I'd wager." Claudius looked up at Atticus. "I hear you're a good man. Gaius Cabilenus thinks you'd make a good centurion."

Atticus stared wordlessly at the tribune as his mouth went dry. Him, a centurion? He had hoped for such an honor, but the potential for earning a promotion seemed remote this far from Rome and imperial favor. . . .

"Handle this assignment well, Atticus Aurelius," Claudius went on, shuffling through a package of parchments on his desk, "and you will be wearing a centurion's helmet within months. Gaius Cabilenus will give you further orders. Dismissed."

Atticus saluted the tribune, then stepped into the intense sunlight and leaned against the stone wall.

A moment later, Gaius came out of the room and grinned up at him. "Caught you by surprise, did he?"

"Yes."

"You're a natural leader, Atticus. And if you handle this week to Rome's satisfaction, you will deserve a promotion."

Atticus fell into step beside his centurion. "What do you want me to do?"

"The governor is worried about these Jews, of course. They are an unruly lot, as you know, and passions run unnaturally high during their Passover festival. This Messiah of theirs complicates things. Some of the religious leaders have already been to the governor with their concerns—they're afraid the mob will try to crown him king."

As they walked past a fountain in the courtyard, Atticus raised his voice to be heard above the sound of splashing water. "Shouldn't this be a problem more for Herod than Pilate? Herod's their king."

"The Jews *hate* Herod—and they like this Messiah. Rumor has it that he can raise the dead and feed thousands with one loaf of bread. The religious leaders think he could overturn Herod in a heartbeat, and most of them wouldn't care if he did. It's Rome they're worried about. According to some of their prophecies, this Messiah they've been waiting for isn't going to be content with Judea—the man intends to rule the world."

"Ah." Atticus nodded. "I'm beginning to understand."

"Good." Gaius's mouth twisted into a cynical smile. "The Jews have a temple guard, but I wouldn't place any confidence in them. I want you to take five contubernia and place them around the Temple Mount. Keep them out of the way, but advise them to be ready. If at any point this week you see signs of a riot, take this Messiah and his followers into custody."

Atticus bowed and saluted. "It shall be done."

⋆⟩━◈━⟨⋆

Later that night, Atticus stretched out on his mattress and looked across at Flavius, who had already closed his eyes. "You asleep?"

The other soldier grunted. "Not yet."

"What have you heard about this new Messiah for the Jews?"

Flavius opened one eye. "Why do you think I've heard anything?"

"Because I know you visit the Greek farmer's daughter in the market . . . and that farmer hears everything."

Flavius laughed, conceding the point. "He doesn't hear everything, but he has heard about this Jew. They call him Yeshua."

Atticus took a sharp breath. Yeshua . . . the healer. The gentle

Galilean who had lifted Quinn into the air and restored the boy's hearing with a word. He looked across the aisle. "Is this Yeshua supposed to be dangerous?"

"Not to my way of thinking. He's a storyteller, mostly. Goes about the country talking about the Jewish God and doing good."

"Then why do they hate him?"

Flavius pushed himself up on his elbows as a warning cloud settled on his features. "Maybe he keeps them up at night. Maybe he pesters them with questions when they're trying to sleep."

Atticus snorted, then folded his arms and stared at the ceiling. He didn't know much about the Jews' God, but he had been impressed by Yeshua. The things he'd said on the hillside that day . . . his words had rung with truth and honor. And his actions had illustrated compassion, a quality desperately lacking in those who worshiped Mithras.

He sat up and blew out the lamp. He hoped Yeshua and his followers behaved themselves during the festival. He owed Yeshua a great debt, and he didn't want to repay it by arresting the man.

⟡

The next morning, Atticus quietly pointed his men to positions around the outer courts of the Jews' Temple. Though the Jewish temple guards were a motley crew according to Roman standards, they did take one rule seriously: no Gentile, not even a Roman soldier, could venture past the Court of the Gentiles.

When he was confident that his men controlled every major entrance and exit, Atticus positioned himself near the widest court and rested his hand on the hilt of his sword.

He didn't have to wait long. Shouts and jubilant cries filled the air, and he heard people calling to one another, "It's Yeshua, the prophet from Nazareth in Galilee."

Atticus walked along the top of the steps and finally spied the man and his disciples. The disciples were all smiles, greeting and waving at those who welcomed their teacher, but in the years since Quinn's healing, lines of heartsickness and weariness had etched Yeshua's face. He climbed the steps leading into the Court of the Gentiles, then cast a glance of well-mannered dislike at the tables of money changers.

Atticus had once asked about those tables. A resident of Jerusalem had explained that since the Jews despised coinage with engraved images, any pilgrim to Jerusalem had to exchange the hated Roman coins for Tyrian. The money changers charged an exorbitant fee for exchanging coins, and the sellers of sacrificial animals often cheated the people as well.

Atticus moved to conceal himself behind a pillar as Yeshua stood in silence. The crowd around the prophet continued to stir, probably hoping for some sort of miracle, but Yeshua said nothing.

One of the money changers, a greasy-haired man with an unkempt beard, stood and tapped the prophet on the shoulder . . . and Yeshua whirled with a wordless shriek of fury.

Without warning, the gentle prophet from Galilee picked up the money changer's table and flipped it, then moved to the next. "The Scriptures declare," he shouted, his voice ragged with anger, " 'My Temple will be called a place of prayer,' but you have turned it into a den of thieves!"

Moving down the row, he upended tables and upset the benches of pigeon dealers. He stopped a man with a basket of pigeons and broke the basket open; then he spilled a leather purse of Roman coins, sending quadrantes, sesterces, and denarii rolling over the floor.

Atticus stared in stupefied amazement as the prophet overturned the last table, then glared at the astounded money changers. Behind him, a row of priests stood with their mouths agape, and Atticus realized that they were helpless to protest. Whatever the man had done, he had justified his action with words they could not refute.

Across the court, Atticus caught Flavius's eye. He had moved forward, his hand at his sword, but Atticus stopped him with a gesture. Whatever this was, it wasn't a riot. Yeshua had been the only man to act, and now an almost unnatural paralysis lay over the court.

Into this silence the prophet walked to a lame man who sat on a mat beneath one of the arched openings. Without saying a word, Yeshua bent and took the man's hand, then smiled as the lame man stood and straightened, at once perfectly whole. As the healed man shouted and leapt with glee, others surged toward Yeshua, who opened his arms and welcomed all who came to him—the blind, the deaf, the lame.

Atticus leaned against the pillar and watched in wonder as even little children joined those who were shouting Yeshua's praises.

He started when Flavius dropped a hand on his shoulder. "Thought you were going to see a bit of action there."

Atticus snorted. "So did I. But I'm glad . . . I'm glad we didn't."

A muscle flicked in Flavius's jaw. "Might do all of us good to lock a few hundred Jews away for the week."

"I don't know about that," Atticus answered. "And I'm beginning to wonder if you *could* lock up that prophet. He has power, Flavius. I've seen it."

"You've seen tricks. Clever magic stunts."

Atticus shook his head. "Nothing I've seen in a temple of Mithras comes close to what I've witnessed here today."

CHAPTER FORTY

A THRILL OF ANTICIPATION touched my spine when the Festival of Unleavened Bread arrived, the time when the priests sacrificed the Pesach lambs.

We had been staying at Lazarus's house in Bethany. Yeshua called Peter and John, and while they ambled toward us, he gestured to me and Hadassah. "Today," he told the men when they approached him, "I want you to go and prepare the Passover meal so we can eat it together."

Peter frowned. "Where do you want us to go?"

"As soon as you enter Jerusalem," Yeshua explained, "you will see a man carrying a pitcher of water. Follow him. At the house he enters, say to the owner, 'The teacher asks, where is the guest room where I can eat the Passover meal with my disciples?' He will take you upstairs to a large room already set up. Go prepare our supper there."

Peter and John promptly set off. Knowing that those two would have no idea how to properly prepare a meal, Hadassah and I followed a discreet distance behind.

Everything happened just as Yeshua predicted. I had been surprised when he mentioned a man carrying a pitcher of water—
water carrying was women's work—but we hadn't gone twenty
paces before we saw a young man with a jug on his shoulder. Peter
and John stopped him. I don't know if they recognized the young
man, but I did. His name was John Mark and he was the son of
another Miryam, a wealthy widow who owned a large inn on
Crooked Street. John Mark had often mingled among Yeshua's followers when we visited Jerusalem.

Without hesitation, John Mark led Peter and John to the inn.
Peter asked Miryam for a simple room, but she told her son to take
Peter upstairs to the best chamber in the house.

Peter came down a moment later, a satisfied expression on his
face. Seeing me, he lifted his voice so I would hear as well. "The
room is ready, already furnished with couches and a table. All we
need to prepare is the Pesach lamb."

I chuckled and shook my head. How like a man, to assume the
room would come furnished with everything necessary to prepare a
festival supper! Did Peter not see the things his wife did every year
to make ready for Pesach?

Hadassah and I ran over a list of items the master and his disciples
would need: wine for the four cups, cakes of unleavened bread, the
bitter herbs. They would also need a cup and the sacrificial lamb,
which, because it was small, would in no way feed the master and his
disciples. And we had to think of the *chagigah*, which we'd consume
with celebration on the afternoon following the seder. . . .

We pulled our veils over our faces as a camel lumbered by, emit-
ting a cloud of dander and dust. Judas should have given Peter and
John money to purchase the lamb at the Temple; had he given them
enough to buy a chagigah, too?

Hadassah and I followed Peter and John as they ascended the temple mount in a dense crowd of singing pilgrims. Worshipers from all over Eretz-Yisrael crowded the porches of the holy site. We had made it as far as the Court of the Gentiles when we heard the blasts from the priests' trumpets indicating that the Passover sacrifices were being slain.

While men of Isra'el brought their spotless lambs to the altar, the Levites chanted the Hallel and the children of Isra'el responded, "ADONAI, please save us! ADONAI, please prosper us! Blessed is he who comes in the name of ADONAI!"

As we listened, I couldn't help remembering Yeshua's entry into Jerusalem only a few days before. The crowds had shouted his name and sung those same words. Since then I had seen Yeshua cleanse the temple like Josiah, Hezekiah, and Judas Maccabaeus, other kings of Isra'el. He had acted like a king, freely wielding authority and power.

Why, then, did he seem so somber and preoccupied?

⸻

Perhaps it had been Miryam of Bethany's act of anointing Yeshua, or perhaps I wanted to lift my rabboni's solemn mood. No matter what my motivation, I caught him as he, James, and Andrew arrived at the inn. "Rabboni," I said, feeling my face heat as I pulled a package from behind my back, "I have a gift for you. It's a small thing, but I wanted to give you something for the festival . . . something to thank you for all you've done for me. For Isra'el."

His eyes softened as he accepted the package in my arms. "They apportion my garments to themselves . . . and for my clothing they cause a lot to fall."

I crinkled my brow, not understanding why my gift should cause him to quote a psalm, but he spoke so cryptically in those days. . . .

He unpeeled the linen wrapping, then shook out the tunic I'd taken great pains to select and purchase. The garment, composed of the softest linen I could find, had been woven in one piece, so it should wear well and last for years. The man who provided the garment had perfected his art, weaving tunics to the demanding standards of the Temple's high priests. This wasn't exactly a king's garment—I doubted Yeshua would wear anything made of silk or purple—but it was something he could wear with pride when he met with religious leaders and other dignitaries.

He held the tunic up, and his eyes moved into mine. "You too, Miryam?"

I frowned. "What?"

"Thank you," he said, smiling. "You have planned well."

⟶⟨⊙⟩⟵

As the master and his disciples prepared to eat the Passover together, I sent the other women away. Miryam, Yeshua's mother, went to eat the feast with her sister, Salome. The other Miryams—Zebedee's wife and the wife of Cleopas—went to enjoy Pesach with friends.

Hadassah and I went to John Mark's inn, where the young man's mother, another Miryam, welcomed Hadassah to their festival feast. Hadassah, I noticed, seemed thrilled by the invitation, for her eyes had been following John Mark all afternoon.

While the young man's mother entertained my young friend downstairs, I remained with our rabboni. I knew he would need a woman to light the lamps, and I wanted to remain close in case he needed anything else.

One by one, the disciples joined Yeshua in the upstairs room. Judas was the last to arrive; he came through the doorway breathless and with a flushed face.

Judas's intent expression sent a ripple of alarm through me. I knew that he and Shimon had been in touch with zealots in Galilee. Had he contacted revolutionaries in Jerusalem, too? Were they planning some sort of action on Yeshua's behalf? Or had we walked into a trap by coming to Jerusalem for the festival?

I lingered in the doorway at the top of the stairs and tried to decide how I could best help my rabboni. I had decided to go downstairs and ask John Mark to post a lookout at the gate, but when I turned to gesture my intent to Shimon, I saw Yeshua on his knees, his new tunic exchanged for a linen towel around his waist. He wore the clothing of a servant—no, a slave—and he held a washbasin filled with water. Obviously, he intended to begin the seder by washing his disciples' feet, but Peter would have none of it.

"What are you doing?" Peter lifted his legs from the floor. "This is not your job. We will ask John Mark to send a servant—"

Yeshua gripped one of Peter's ankles and gently pried off the leather sandal. "You don't understand now why I am doing it, but someday you will."

"No," Peter protested, "you will never wash my feet!"

Yeshua looked at the outspoken disciple with a smile hidden in his eyes. "If I don't wash you, you won't belong to me."

I hid a smirk behind my hand as the meaning of the master's words took hold and Peter blustered, "Then wash my hands and head as well, Lord, not just my feet!"

Yeshua splashed water over Peter's dusty ankles. "A person who has bathed all over does not need to wash to be entirely clean. And you *are* clean . . . but that isn't true of everyone here."

Yeshua proceeded to wash all the disciples' feet, but a chill ran down my spine as I looked around the circle. The men had taken their places on the low couches, leaving one couch empty for our teacher. What exactly did he mean? Who among them wasn't clean?

My rabboni stood and moved to the place where he'd left his new tunic; without speaking, he pulled it on, then let the wet towel fall to the floor. Looking up, he caught sight of me in the doorway and nodded.

My cue—time for a woman to light the lamps, to symbolically bring the light of God into the world.

As I filled my vessel with oil, I heard Yeshua speak to the men who had traveled and worked with him for over three years: "When I sent you out to preach the Good News and you did not have money, a traveler's bag, or extra clothing, did you lack anything?"

A dozen voices murmured no.

"But now," he said, "take your money and a traveler's bag. And if you don't have a sword, sell your clothes and buy one. For the time has come for this prophecy about me to be fulfilled: 'He was counted among those who were rebels.' Yes, everything written about me by the prophets will come true."

"Lord," Peter called, "we have two swords among us."

Yeshua hesitated. "That's enough."

My hand trembled as I moved to light the lamps. I didn't understand everything he meant, but perhaps I wasn't meant to.

One thing, however, was clear: Yeshua knew this night would be important, and he was ready to face it.

Chapter Forty-one

I left the men in the inn's upstairs room and took myself to bed. John Mark had kindly provided a small chamber off the first floor, so I lay down on a straw-filled mattress. The inn had larger chambers, of course, but they had been filled with pilgrims to the Holy City.

Before retiring to my room, I asked John Mark to wake me when the men left the upper chamber. Hadassah and I planned to walk with Yeshua and the disciples to Bethany, where Miryam and Marta waited to shelter us for the night.

I meant to rest only for an hour or two, but the stars had begun to fade behind a brightening sky when my eyes flew open. Hadassah slept on a mattress across from me, her hand pillowing her cheek.

My first reaction was indignation—had Yeshua and the disciples gone off and left us behind?—then I heard voices from the street outside. A pair of strangers spoke in quiet but intense tones, not the sort of conversation I'd expect during a joyous festival.

Then again, I didn't expect to hear anything before dawn.

I sat up and brushed straw from my hair, then tiptoed to the window. I stood in the shadows and held my breath, straining to hear the men outside.

"Where are they holding him?"

"The high priest's house."

"And his men?"

"Scattered like sheep."

I felt my stomach drop and the empty place fill with a frightening hollowness. *Whose* men had scattered like sheep? Surely not Yeshua's. His disciples were ready and armed . . . with two pitiful swords.

My heart began to thump almost painfully in my chest. I'd *known* they weren't prepared! Hadn't they noticed the extra guards at the Temple this week? Hadn't they felt the tension in the air?

The Romans must have taken Yeshua; the disciples must have turned and run. That's why John Mark hadn't wakened me—like the others, he was probably trembling in some dark corner, hiding from the authorities who had arrested the prophet of Isra'el.

I left Hadassah asleep as I grabbed my veil and hurried into the street. I didn't know this section of the Old City, but the Temple wasn't far away. Surely the high priest lived near the Temple Mount.

⸻◈⸻

At some point in my flight, rational thought returned. The other women were more familiar with Jerusalem than I; they would know how to find Caiaphas's house. They would know how to find Yeshua.

I went to the house where our rabboni's mother waited with relatives and found her awake, her veil on her head, her eyes red and circled with grief. She rose without a word when the door opened to me; a moment later her arm circled my waist.

Together we walked toward the Temple Mount; then she gestured toward the avenue where the high priest, Caiaphas, lived.

We halted when a pair of gates swung open. An official-looking procession of temple guards moved out in a knot, a bound prisoner at their center. Yeshua's mother and I stepped into the shadows, and I felt her body go limp when our eyes confirmed our fears—Yeshua walked at the center of this armed procession. Blood streamed from his mouth and nose; he staggered with the steps of a man too exhausted to lift his head.

He did, even so—and his eyes caught mine. And in that moment all my dreams and convictions of victory collided with a despairing reality. The world might as well have been turned on its head, for none of this was supposed to happen; none of it was even *possible*. How could the *prophet* who tossed money changers out of the temple walk like a lamb amid the same guards who had witnessed his fierce authority? How could the rabbi who commanded souls to break free of Sh'ol submit to being bullied by the religious rulers?

In that instant my heart sank with an emotion I never expected to feel toward my rabboni—shame. Why had Yeshua given up? Had he grown weary of the struggle? Had he surrendered when his men fled in the night? I would not have run; neither would his mother. I would have picked up a sword and fought the Romans until they stole my dying breath.

We had given up so much to enlist in his cause; we had left our homes and families and friends. We had believed in him; we had come to see him as the promised Messiah of Isra'el.

I looked away as the awful feeling mingled with disappointment and hurt and pain. Yeshua had power, so why hadn't he used it? I didn't understand anything, but a memory surfaced as he passed—

once again I saw myself lighting the lamps for the seder and felt the stirring of hope in my breast.

I might never feel such hope again.

CHAPTER FORTY-TWO

FOR THE BRIEFEST MOMENT, a criminal's battered face hangs in Atticus's mind's eye—faint at first, then as vivid as a portrait emerging under the hand of a skilled artist.

His contubernium had been called out to provide security for a trial, and for the better part of that morning, Atticus did not recognize the silent man who stood before Pilate. From his position, Atticus could see no more than the prisoner's plain robe and the back of his head. When the accused finally turned, his face had been so battered that Atticus still didn't realize who they were guarding.

He and his comrades escorted the prisoner from the praetorium to Herod's hall and back to Pilate's porch. Atticus had not been privy to the scene in Herod's throne room, but Herod wanted nothing to do with the criminal, and Pilate was clearly frustrated with the angry religious leaders who'd brought the beaten man to him.

When they brought the prisoner before Pilate again, he had moved his judgment seat to the open courtyard. With an exasperated grimace, the procurator of Judea leaned forward and asked in a rasping voice, "Tell me truly: *are* you the king of the Jews?"

In a voice cracking with weariness, the prisoner answered, "I am not an earthly king. If I were, my followers would have fought when the religious leaders arrested me. My Kingdom is not of this world."

At the sound of that Galilean accent, awareness ruffled through Atticus's mind like wind on water. He'd heard that voice before. In the Temple earlier that week, and by the Sea of Tiberias, where the wind had provided a haunting backdrop.

He was guarding the prophet Yeshua.

A flicker of horror coursed through him as he shifted his gaze from the procurator to the prisoner. Impossible to tell what the prophet had done to arouse the ire of the Jews clamoring behind the line of legionnaires, but he'd certainly done something.

Or had he?

Atticus looked at Pilate, who sat on the edge of his chair and drummed his nails on the armrest. His long face and glaring eyes, which could intimidate most men even from a distance, had filled with frustration and his voice had gone rough. He glanced left and right as if he could find an answer to his dilemma in the faces of his counselors, yet no one approached him except . . . Cyrilla.

Atticus tensed as Procula's maid bowed before the governor. Pilate saw her and, with a smile that proved he was grateful for any interruption, motioned her forward.

Atticus felt Flavius's eyes upon him as the girl walked toward the judgment seat, then bent to whisper something in her master's ear. A tiny flicker of shock widened Pilate's eyes, and for an instant panic tightened the corners of his mouth.

Cyrilla bowed and drifted away, leaving the governor to deal with the effects of her message. His hands tightened on the chair's armrests; then he lifted his chin and announced that in honor of the Jewish festival he would release a prisoner. Would the people prefer that he release the so-called king of the Jews, or Barabbas, a convicted rebel and murderer?

Atticus smiled at the wisdom in the procurator's words. Barabbas, leader of a bloody insurrection, deserved to die under Jewish and Roman laws, while this Galilean had done nothing but offend the sensibilities of a few religious leaders.

"We want Barabbas!"

Atticus stared, disbelieving, as the cry started among the Jewish leaders and spread through the crowd. "Give us Barabbas!"

Pilate stood and held up his hand. "Then what shall I do with this man you call the king of the Jews?"

"Crucify him!"

"Why?" Pilate answered. "What crime has he committed?"

The tenor of the shouting changed from disjointed responses to a unified and powerful thunder: "Crucify him! Crucify him!"

Pilate glanced toward the tribune Claudius Lysias, who stepped forward and saluted.

"Release Barabbas," Pilate commanded, "and flog this prisoner." In a lower voice that reached no farther than the Roman legionnaires, he added, "Perhaps that will satisfy their bloodlust."

Two of the soldiers who guarded Pilate's judgment seat descended the stairs and took the condemned man by the arms, turning him toward the Fortress Antonia. In that moment, Atticus glimpsed the prophet's eyes . . . and knew Pilate had made a grave mistake.

Fortunately, Claudius put another contubernium in charge of the flogging. They scourged the prophet, blow after blow, with a flagellum that tore the flesh from the thin man's back. Atticus winced with every strike, recalling how the flail felt when it had torn into his own skin. He still bore scars from his initiation into the Mithras cult, and he had borne only seven blows.

Yeshua took more than forty. When it looked as though the prophet could stand no more, Atticus swallowed hard and stepped into the barracks.

Flavius followed him. "What are you doing? You shouldn't desert your post—"

"He needs something," Atticus answered, searching through his chest. "We stripped him; he needs something to wear as he faces the procurator."

Flavius laughed. "Why are you so worried about this Jew? He's common enough, though I'll admit we don't get many would-be kings."

"Here's something." Atticus pulled a plain tunic from his belongings and shook out the folds.

"Don't waste a good tunic on him. We have a trunk over here, old things of the governor's, I think. Lady Procula sent it over last week." He walked to a chest against the wall and lifted the lid, then rummaged through the contents. After a moment, he pulled out a sliver of fabric. "I'd say *this* is fitting for a king."

Atticus watched as Flavius unfolded a length of shimmering crimson fabric. "Fine enough for a caesar, wouldn't you say?"

Atticus felt his mouth go dry. "You'd put that on a prisoner?"

Flavius tossed the material over his shoulder, then jerked his chin at the tunic in Atticus's hands. "Let him wear his own garments; don't spoil yours. Beneath this fine silk, no one will notice what he's wearing, anyway."

CHAPTER FORTY-THREE

THE PROPHET'S MOTHER AND I stood in the crowd, our hands touching as we gazed at the spectacle beyond the line of legionnaires separating us from Yeshua.

So many soldiers stood between us and our rabboni—probably an entire cohort. Most of them stood in a line, their armored backs a formidable wall between us and our beloved Yeshua. More Romans stood at ease in front of the fortress, sweat gleaming on their faces as they drank from gourds and hurled insults at the man they were beating.

I swallowed hard and squeezed Miryam's shoulder, wishing I could cover her eyes and shield her from this awful sight. Yeshua, I noticed, did not acknowledge the crowd or the taunting guards, though I knew he heard everything. How many times had I whispered a question to Peter only to discover later that Yeshua had heard every word?

Our anointed prophet had been so invincible, so powerful—how had things come to this? I'd watched him feed five thousand men and believed he could feed an army. I'd watched him heal diverse diseases and believed he would heal those who fought against Rome. I'd watched him raise the dead and believed he would resurrect anyone who died in the fight to free Isra'el from oppression.

I had never believed our Messiah could die before the battle began.

How could this be? God had ordained that we would conquer our oppressors; his prophets had foretold of the eternal reign of the Son of Man. Everything had been falling into place perfectly . . . so what had happened?

Yeshua's mother pressed her face to my shoulder, unable to look at her bloody son, but also unable to leave. The toothy flail rose again and again, striking my rabboni without pause or hesitation, but he did not lift his voice in anger or protest.

When at last the grinning legionnaire stopped to rest his arm, they cut the straps that held Yeshua upright between two posts. He folded gently at the knees and crumpled onto the pavement, his eyes closed, his lips moving as if in silent prayer.

A centurion, recognizable by his distinctive plumed helmet, stepped forward with something in his arms. Two of his men jerked Yeshua to his feet.

While a legionnaire tugged Yeshua's new tunic over that wounded head, the centurion unfurled a clump of scarlet fabric. Another Roman pressed a crown of thorns onto my beloved rabboni's brow, pricking his scalp so new trickles of blood flowed over his bruised face. As yet another soldier pressed a slender reed, the symbol of Herodian royalty, into Yeshua's hand, the centurion draped the shimmering scarlet over my master's shoulder . . . a lovely silk that warmed in the morning sun and deepened to a royal purple.

The color of bloody sacrifice, the color of royalty.

When have those two colors ever been meant for a single man?

A suffocating sensation tightened my throat as I gazed at my master. That silk could only have come from Magdala. From my dye pot.

And my hands.

Sadness pooled in my heart, accompanied by an anguish I hadn't felt even in my darkest hour with the demons. The shame I'd felt toward Yeshua turned to blacken my own soul. Our rabboni had told us he would die. He'd predicted this death, but I hadn't wanted to believe it. Nor could I believe what that morning revealed: the work of my prideful heart lay upon my master's back.

I clung to Yeshua's mother as grief welled within me, black and cold.

CHAPTER FORTY-FOUR

BECAUSE HIS CONTUBERNIUM had been charged with the execution of the criminals scheduled to die on that Friday, Atticus wrote out the signs for the three crosses in Hebrew, Latin, and Greek.

For the prophet's cross, he wrote:

Ἰησοῦ Ναζωραῖὸ βασιλεῦ τῶν Ἰουδαίων, or *Yeshua of Natzeret,* the King of the Jews.

With Flavius, Gaius, and the other men in their contubernium, Atticus walked beside the three prisoners as they staggered toward the usual place of execution—a dreary spot outside the city gates and near a garden graveyard. The forlorn location featured a domelike rocky plateau, hence the area's name: Golgotha, or "Place of the Skull."

Atticus had served on many execution squads, but never had he struggled with his conscience as he walked through the city streets. Roman justice was swift and sure, but in this case, he wasn't certain the governor had enacted justice. Neither was Pilate, for he had washed his hands of the affair before telling the guards to take the prophet away.

Due to the holiday, the shops and markets of Jerusalem were closed, but crowds still lined the street to observe the procession of condemned men. The first two malefactors were greeted with jeers, but when the onlookers spied Yeshua, men wept and women began to keen with sorrow.

Atticus turned to Flavius and lifted a brow. Where had these people been when Yeshua was standing before Pilate? Why had there been no lamentation for him then?

When they reached the gate of the city, Yeshua stumbled and fell beneath the weight of the *patibulum*, or crossbar. Flavius tapped a fellow coming in from the country and compelled him to carry the condemned man's burden.

Atticus knelt to lift the fallen prophet. When Yeshua met his gaze, the look of resignation in his eyes pierced Atticus's soul.

Once he was certain the prophet could walk, Atticus moved away and braced himself against the sturdy blocks of the city wall.

Flavius's voice rang over the keening crowd: "You all right?"

Atticus lifted his hand without turning. "I need a moment."

By the time Atticus's emotions had settled, Yeshua and his guards had moved to the Place of the Skull. Atticus swallowed the knot in his throat and joined them, then knelt at the cross of one of the condemned thieves. Flavius and Gaius could handle the prophet. Atticus couldn't look into the eyes of the man who had healed Quinn and still do his job properly.

Nodding to the other legionnaires who tended the first malefactor, Atticus bent the criminal's legs at the knees and twisted them back so the calves were parallel to the crossbar, with the ankles under the buttocks. He held the condemned prisoner in position while another soldier drove a spike through both heels into the *simplex*, or upright beam. The wrists had already been nailed to the crossbeam.

By the time Atticus joined Gaius at Yeshua's cross, blood from the wounds in the prophet's forehead had painted his face and clotted in his beard. The other legionnaires had shifted their attention from the condemned men to dividing the prisoners' possessions.

Four legionnaires had crucified the prophet and piled his clothing near the foot of the cross. Five pieces lay on the ground. Each soldier took one item: the outer robe, girdle, sandals, and turban. A single linen tunic remained, and the men hesitated when they saw it. The worn tunics of the two thieves were fit only for rags, but despite the bloodstains, the prophet's garment looked new—and it had been woven of a single piece.

"Let's not tear this one." Flavius shook out the bloodstained garment. "Let's throw the knucklebones to see who wins it."

Flavius won. And as Atticus watched Flavius celebrate his victory, he wondered how his friend could ever wear such a tunic.

He looked up as movement caught his eye. A group of the Jewish religious leaders came forward, their faces drawn into tight smiles. They called to the prophet and taunted him with mocking cries. "You saved others," one man jeered. "Save yourself, if you can!"

Atticus's hand went to the dagger at his belt. Yeshua had saved Quinn a lifetime of heartache; what good had these men ever done?

Flavius must have seen the ire in his eye, for he tugged at Atticus's arm. "Forget them," he said, tossing the prophet's tunic over his shoulder. "The Jews can't get along with each other *or* Rome. Leave them to their folly."

The morning sun dragged quietly into the afternoon, and the Jewish leaders moved away. When Atticus wondered aloud why they'd gone before witnessing the Nazarene's end, Gaius answered that the presence of death would make them unclean and unable to observe their holy festival.

As the prophet struggled to breathe, a group of women who had been keeping their distance moved closer. Two men walked with them. Most of the group were dressed in the plain garments of rural Galileans, but the older man wore a richly embroidered tunic like those favored by the religious leaders.

Yeshua spoke in a halting voice to the knot of weeping mourners. Then the younger man put his arm around one of the women and led her away.

Without warning, the wind rose, skirling across the stony knoll, an unseasonable chill in its breath. Blue sky retreated in the face of the blast, leaving the heavens gray and bruised looking. Far to the east, arteries of lightning pulsed, followed by a low throb of thunder. A slash of heaven's fire stabbed at the Jews' Temple; then the sky went black as the rocky promontory trembled in an earthquake.

The hair at the back of Atticus's neck rose as stones loosened and tumbled down the hill. Gaius stood from where he'd been kneeling, and Flavius shifted uncomfortably. "Atticus—" the centurion's dark eyes pierced the distance between them—"Flavius tells me you know something of this man. Who was he?"

"He was—"Atticus's voice, like his emotions, was in tatters— "a Jewish prophet. Some said he was their Messiah; some said he was the Son of their God."

Darkness pressed heavily on the hilltop as the man on the cross shouted, "Father, I entrust my spirit into your hands!" His chest rose and fell in a desperate exhalation. "It . . . is . . . accomplished."

With that last utterance, the prophet's head lolled forward in a heavy movement Atticus knew far too well.

He looked up at the dark sky, observed the stricken women, and heard the mourning howl of the wind. The heavens themselves seemed to be weeping for Yeshua of Nazareth, who had done nothing but good in his life.

Atticus had staked his future on the justice and light of Rome. On this day, however, darkness reigned and justice was not to be found.

"Surely," Gaius murmured, "this man was a son of God."

Atticus had to agree. Mithras and the emperors of Rome were supposed to be sons of gods, but the Jews' God had given this prophet power unlike anything Atticus had ever seen wielded by an emperor or a Roman priest.

How could a man with such power *die?*

CHAPTER FORTY-FIVE

STANDING AT THE FOOT OF THE cross in a day that had gone black as night, I felt the old feelings of grief tug at my heart. Like a powerful undertow that pulled at me against my will, the current of sorrow took hold and dragged me into the deep well of loss.

Why had Yeshua delivered me to face this? Why had he built up our hopes and dreams if he knew this fate awaited him? Because he *had* known—I could no longer deny it. He had known, and he had warned us.

But I hadn't wanted to listen.

My cheeks burned as I remembered his words: *"A kernel of wheat must be planted in the soil. Unless it dies it will be alone—a single seed. But its death will produce many new kernels—a plentiful harvest of new lives."*

So . . . what happened next? How would this shameful death produce a harvest of new lives? This was an awful death, gory and violent, and our law declared that anyone who hung on a tree was an anathema.

Yeshua had become a curse . . . and as I looked up at his bloody face, I couldn't understand why he had allowed it to happen. I had dreamed of the Lion of Judah overcoming the eagle of Rome, for, like David and Hezekiah, the Messiah was supposed to conquer our enemies. When word of Yeshua's death spread through Galil, everyone would know we'd been mistaken.

A messiah who suffered defeat . . . could not be the Messiah.

I pressed my hand over my mouth as the Roman legionnaires stood and approached the three crosses. The two thieves still lived, so the merciless Romans used the steel shafts of their spears to break the malefactors' lower leg bones. But the soldier who looked on Yeshua did not swing his spear. Instead he prodded my rabboni's lifeless head with the tip of his weapon; then he plunged the spearhead into Yeshua's side.

I smothered a cry as water and blood flowed from the wound. "He's dead," the Roman said, his voice flat.

I might have crumpled on the spot, but Yosef of Arimathea, a secret disciple and a member of the Sanhedrin, caught my shoulders. "I am here with Nicodemus," he whispered in my ear. "We have made arrangements."

For the first time I looked around. The other women had gone; even Hadassah had been overwhelmed by grief. No one stood with me but two members of the council who had condemned my rabboni to death.

I lifted my gaze to Yosef's face. "Who will care for him now?"

"We will." His brown eyes bored into mine. "You need to be strong, Miryam, for we must act quickly. Can you help us?"

After a long pause, during which I fought for self-control, I lifted my chin and squared my shoulders. "What do you need me to do?"

Yosef glanced at the cross, then turned to Nicodemus. "I'm going to Pilate for formal permission to take his body. If we don't get it, they'll toss him into a common grave."

I pressed my lips together to stifle a sob.

Nicodemus moved closer. "You and I, Miryam, must act now, even before Yosef returns. The Shabbat is approaching, so we must take his body down and care for him before sunset."

I sniffed, then nodded to Yosef. "Go, then. Hurry." I looked at Nicodemus as the older man hurried away. "Where are we taking him?"

Nicodemus gestured down the hill. "A tomb in yonder garden. It's not a long walk, and I've already arranged for the things we'll need. A merchant is about to deliver spices and linens . . . not enough for a proper burial, but enough to prepare him decently before Shabbat arrives."

Shock ran through me as our eyes met. "The markets were closed. How did you know?"

Nicodemus closed his eyes as a muscle quivered in his jaw. "Yosef and I . . . we have been studying the Scriptures. We read the prophets, and we realized he would die at Pesach. We were not at the council meeting last night because we were taking care of these matters."

I looked down the hill, where a twisted path curved among several flowering bushes and disappeared beneath a sprawling tree canopy. A restful place, and fitting for a prophet of Isra'el. "You go and wait for your merchant," I tell him. "I'll stay."

He shook his head. "You go. The tomb is a little hard to find, but you'll see the stone rolled away—"

I winced. "I'm not waiting in a tomb. You go; you know where it is."

"But how are you going to get his body—?"

"HaShem will provide a way. After all, he provided you."

Struggling to mask my dread, I managed a trembling smile. "I'll meet you in the garden."

⋄⊶⊷⊷⊶⋄

When Nicodemus had gone, I turned toward the cross. Blood still dripped from Yeshua's body, a slow arrhythmic patting that struck the stony ground.

Tears filled my eyes, blurring my vision. I knew a group of legionnaires crouched to my right. I could hear smothered laughs and the clink of weapons as they packed up and prepared to leave Golgotha.

Was this just another day to them? another prophet to execute? another nation to crush? Yeshua had embodied hope for Isra'el—even hope for the world. With everything in my heart I had firmly believed that only my rabboni could overthrow Rome and its caesars. Instead, the people who had conquered our nation and murdered my family had crucified my hope.

And Yeshua had allowed them to do it.

I stepped forward and placed my hands on my rabboni's wounded feet. His skin felt like cold marble beneath my palms.

From down the hill came the squeak of a saddle and the shudder of a horse; from somewhere quite close I heard the crunch of stones beneath sandals. I would never have asked an enemy for help, but no one remained in the area . . . except Romans.

"Please, sir," I said, speaking to the unknown soldier who hovered like a hulking shadow behind me, "will you help me take him down?"

The man did not answer, but the stones scrunched again and a pair of big hands covered mine. Almost tenderly, the soldier lifted my arms; then he stepped between me and Yeshua. I closed my eyes as the wood groaned and surrendered the spike. I covered my face as another man stood to help the first; together they brought Yeshua down and laid him at my feet.

When I could control myself, I blinked my tears away and looked at my teacher's lifeless body.

"What are you going to do with him?"

I had expected the Roman's voice to brim with contempt; instead, an almost kindly concern lined his words. I dashed wetness from my cheeks and pointed down the hill. "There's a path . . . and a garden. One of the council members has made preparations."

"Lead the way. I'll carry him for you."

Shock caused words to wedge in my throat. I looked up at the Roman, wanting to be sure he wasn't toying with me, but my eyes were too bleary to see anything but the seriousness of his expression.

I reached out, touched his hand. "You are . . . a gift from HaShem."

Heedless of the other soldiers who called out questions and jeers, the big man knelt and pulled Yeshua into his arms as if he were carrying a beloved son. I saw the metal of his helmet flash in the brightening sky as he nodded; then I turned and led the way down the hill.

And as I walked in a slow and stately pace, I couldn't help but remember the thousands who had lined the road and cheered him only a few days before: "Please, deliver us, Son of David."

Where had they gone? They were hiding. Weeping. Grieving.

They had abandoned their Messiah, leaving Yeshua to be buried by a former outcast, two council members, and a nameless Roman dog.

I did not sleep in the hours following Yeshua's death. Every time I closed my eyes I saw his face gazing at me from the cross; every time

I covered my ears I heard his rattling breaths. Throughout the long night I paced in the courtyard of the inn on Crooked Street and chewed my fingernails to nubs.

One thought filled my mind: I had failed my rabboni. I had walked and talked and lived with a prophet, but I had not listened to all he said. He had spoken of being pure of heart, but my heart had been filled with anger and resentment toward the Romans. When Yeshua realized that we were not strong enough to be the followers he needed, he had predicted his death. I had been too thickheaded to hear his warning . . . because I didn't *want* to hear. I had even felt ashamed of his weakness . . . because I was too focused on my goals to see his strength.

I could scarcely imagine how hard it must have been for him to submit to the indignity and pain of the cross. Yet he had done it. Because we failed him.

We didn't deserve rescue from the Romans.

The festival of Pesach, usually a time of rejoicing, filled our lives with despair. The sorrow of Golgotha clung to me like the smoke that had permeated my clothing as I watched my home go up in flames. The grief that had engulfed me at the cross remained with me when I washed my rabboni's body and wrapped him in linen. I would have remained through the night to tuck spices in among the grave wrappings, but Nicodemus, mindful of the setting sun, had urged me to hurry.

Jerusalem marked that day of rest with gloom. The people who had loved and supported Yeshua barely stirred from their houses, burdened not by the rules of the Shabbat but by an overwhelming sense of loss.

"O Jerusalem," Yeshua had said, weeping, "the city that kills the prophets and stones God's messengers! How often I have wanted to gather your children together as a hen protects her chicks beneath her wings, but you wouldn't let me."

My rabboni's words came back to me, proving that he had known what his fate would be. Still he had ventured into the city; still he had eaten with his spineless disciples and listened to them brag about being prepared to drink of his bitter cup.

On that dark Shabbat we learned other news—Judas had been the instrument of Yeshua's betrayal. Apparently he had come late to that final supper because he had been arranging to betray our rabboni for thirty pieces of silver. Peter told me, with tears, that Judas had led an armed mob to the garden of Gethsemane and signaled our master's identity . . . with a kiss.

After Yeshua's trial, Judas had been so overcome with remorse that he had killed himself.

On the first day of the week, before the sun pushed its way over the horizon, the other women and I gathered the additional spices we'd prepared and began the long walk to the tomb. On the way, Joanna worried aloud that we wouldn't be able to find a man to remove the stone blocking the entrance.

As we neared the garden in the half-light of dawn, an earthquake shuddered the ground beneath us. We clung to each other until the earth stopped shaking; then we drew deep breaths and steeled ourselves to our miserable task.

When we reached the sepulcher, we discovered that the stone had been rolled away. We bent and stepped into the crypt; then I cried out—the stone slab was bare, the graveclothes tossed on the ground, the other niches empty.

Had I come to the wrong garden? No—I distinctly remembered the vibrant yellow of the flowering shrubs beside the gate. Was this the wrong tomb? No . . . the linen graveclothes were the fabrics I had folded over my rabboni.

"Miryam—" Joanna's voice quavered—"where is he?"

"I don't know."

Frantic, I left the other women and hurried back to the inn. John Mark pointed me toward the chamber where Peter and John were sleeping. When they opened the door, my words spilled out in a tumble: "They have taken the Lord's body and I don't know where they have put him!"

To their credit, neither man hesitated. They ran toward the tomb as well, leaving me to follow on legs that felt as insubstantial as air.

By the time I arrived back at the garden, the two disciples had come and gone. I saw their footprints in the soft sand beside the entrance to the tomb. I could almost feel remnants of their alarm and confusion in the air.

I stood outside the sepulcher with my hands over my face and tears stinging my eyes. Once again, operating purely in vain hope, I peered inside the tomb. I had expected to see an empty stone slab, but my heart went into sudden shock when I saw two men in white—men who *glowed*.

The closest man's eyes warmed slightly, and with the hint of a smile he acknowledged the startling effect of his unexpected appearance. "Why are you crying?"

Somehow, I caught a breath. "Because they have taken my Lord away, and I don't know where they have put him."

Another smile tugged at the stranger's mouth, but he did not speak again. Instead, he tilted his head and looked behind me, so I turned to see who might be approaching. A man stood next to one of the shrubs; I supposed him to be the gardener. Perhaps he thought we had made a mistake by placing Yeshua in a rich man's tomb. . . .

"Sir—" my voice broke—"if you have taken him away, tell me where you have put him and I'll go get him."

The man stepped out of the shadows. "Miryam."

"Rabboni!" Yeshua's voice leapt into my heart like a living thing. Grateful beyond words, I fell at his feet and clutched his ankles— warm, *living* flesh—as if I might never let him go.

"Don't cling to me," Yeshua said, his voice as gentle as a breeze, "for I haven't yet ascended to the Father. But go find my brothers and tell them I am ascending to my Father and your Father, my God and your God."

Has any woman ever been charged with a more delightful task? I rose, weeping afresh, and backstepped to the garden gate, not wanting to tear my gaze from my teacher. Yeshua smiled at me, waiting, and though everything in me wanted to stay, I was determined not to fail him.

I ran back into the city and found the disciples at John Mark's inn. Peter and John had not yet returned, but the other disciples were red-eyed and weary from grief.

I laughed aloud, delighted to share my news: "Yeshua is alive! He called my name!"

I thought they would rejoice, but they didn't believe me. Neither did they believe Joanna, Salome, or Cleopas's Miryam, who had returned earlier with the same news.

What man, after all, trusts the word of mere women?

CHAPTER FORTY-SIX

As THREE-YEAR-OLD QUINN chased a ball across the empty chamber, Atticus looked at Cyrilla. The marks of grief were clear, etched into the lines beside her mouth and eyes. She had not smiled in three days, not since he'd seen her approach Pilate when the governor sat in judgment on the Galilean.

"What was it—" he squeezed her hand—"that sent you to him?"

She gave him a bleak, tight-lipped smile. "My mistress sent me to the governor with an urgent message. She had awakened late that morning because she'd been troubled by dreams about Yeshua of Nazareth. She bade me tell her husband he should have nothing to do with that innocent man." She squeezed Atticus's hand in return. "I can't believe it. I can't believe he's really dead. How could such a thing happen?"

Atticus couldn't answer. He watched as Quintus stooped to catch the wooden ball, then turned, crowing with delight. The little boy had caught up with other children his age; he spoke and sang and laughed like any other three-year-old. But if he'd never met the Nazarene prophet, he would be a far different child.

"I'm not sure," he finally answered, meeting Cyrilla's troubled gaze. "But if you'd been there . . . when he died, it was as though he meant to do it."

Grinning, Quinn ran over to Atticus, then dropped the ball into his hand. Atticus ruffled the little boy's dark hair and found it impossible not to return the child's smile.

"I have to go." He pressed his lips to Quinn's head, then kissed Cyrilla's cheek. "I'll see you two later."

When Atticus returned to the barracks, Flavius and several other legionnaires had gathered around a table playing knucklebones. Someone must have just told a joke, for they exploded into laughter as he approached.

Atticus paused by the gathering. "What's so funny?"

Flavius snickered. "Those Jews. They put their temple guards at the tomb of that Galilean prophet—you know, 'the king.' The undisciplined louts fell asleep on the job, and the prophet's followers stole his body during the night."

Atticus frowned. A Roman soldier who fell asleep at his post would pay a severe penalty, especially if the results were unfortunate. "What are they doing to the guards?"

Another soldier snorted. "That's the unbelievable thing—nothing! The dullards are getting away with little more than a slap on the fingertips. No wonder they're not afraid to take a nap on duty."

Atticus rolled his eyes and moved toward the latrine. The Jewish temple guards were controlled by the priests, who should be raging against their guards' ineptitude—so why had they let the men off so easily?

He pivoted on the ball of his foot and returned to the common area. "Flavius, have you heard anything else about the Galilean prophet?"

Flavius looked up from the game. "What do you mean?"

"Doesn't it seem odd that those priests aren't more upset over the theft of the prophet's body? They were terrified of his effect on the people."

Flavius tossed the knucklebones. "That's right—I nearly forgot about the women."

"What women?"

"There's a story going around about a group of women who went to the sepulcher and saw the Nazarene standing there, as healthy as you please. They say he came back to life and *walked* out of his tomb." He paused to scoop up a handful of coins. "Thank you, gentlemen. A pleasure to take your money."

"I heard a story." One of Flavius's companions turned a mischievous eye in Atticus's direction. "I'll tell it for a sesterius."

Atticus hesitated, then pulled out his purse and tossed a coin in the man's direction. Instantly, the man grinned. "The streets are full of the story of two men traveling to Emmaus from Jerusalem. As they traveled, their conversation ran wild with talk, of course, about the death, the darkness, the strange goings-on. They met a stranger who seemed not to know anything about what had happened, until they sat to eat a meal together. Then they looked at his wrists, saw the nail wounds, and recognized the prophet." The soldier leaned over the table and flashed Atticus a gap-toothed smile. "Rumor has it you can see the holes in his ankles, too."

Atticus felt a series of ghost spiders crawl across the back of his neck. Could the story be true?

Atticus was working in the armory later that afternoon, stacking shields and swords and tagging those that needed sharpening, when he saw a crumpled bit of cloth on the floor. He picked it up, felt the crust of dried blood in his hands, and realized what he'd found—the scarlet drape, the bit of royal silk they'd used to mock Yeshua, the king of the Jews.

Atticus sank to a low stool and winced as a stab of regret reminded him of his part in the prophet's execution.

Flavius rapped on the door and thrust his head into the room. "Almost done in here? We're supposed to leave at sundown."

Atticus looked up, distracted. "Why?"

"The meeting." Flavius lowered his voice. "Gaius wants to discuss new initiates."

Atticus brought his hand to his chin. The cult of Mithras, which had once seemed mysterious and powerful, no longer appealed to him. "Go without me," he said, gathering the silk to his chest.

Chapter Forty-seven

WE SAW OUR MASTER MANY times in the next forty days—in Galilee, on a mountain, by the shore of our beloved lake. Our rabboni's teaching had transformed our thinking, but one thing still troubled me—nothing had changed in our world. I had followed Yeshua because I wanted him to free us from our oppressors, but the Roman yoke remained heavy on our shoulders.

One afternoon as we sat by the shore of Galilee after Yeshua's resurrection, Peter asked, "Lord, are you going to free Isra'el now and restore our kingdom?"

"The Father sets those dates," Yeshua replied, "and they are not for you to know. But when *Ruach HaKodesh* has come upon you, you will receive power and will tell people about me everywhere—in Jerusalem, throughout Judea, in Samaria, and to the ends of the earth."

We didn't understand exactly what he meant, just as we hadn't understood when he told us about his impending death and resurrection. But we learned.

I wasn't with the disciples when Yeshua left them, but I believe their account. Our rabboni literally rose into the heavens and vanished into a cloud. Two angels appeared and asked the disciples why they were staring at the sky. Yeshua would come again, they said, and to the Mount of Olives, where he had left them.

On the day of the Feast of Pentecost, one hundred twenty believers gathered for prayer at John Mark's inn, including Yeshua's mother and his brothers, whose disbelief had turned to joyful acceptance. We were obeying the Lord and tarrying in Jerusalem, waiting for the Comforter he had promised.

Like the sound of a mighty windstorm, a rushing swept through the room as the Spirit indwelled our bodies and flames appeared on our heads—all of us, men and women alike. Great joy filled our hearts as we began to speak in languages we had never learned. We spilled onto the street and moved to the Temple, eager to share this wonderful news. Foreign pilgrims who'd crowded into Jerusalem for the festival heard us speaking in their languages—Parthians, Medes, Elamites, Mesopotamians, Judeans, Egyptians—everyone! They thought we were drunk, but Peter told them the hour was too early for drinking.

I can't remember that day without smiling. The Holy City gleamed in the bright glory of early summer. The markets brimmed with plenty, for most of the barley and wheat harvest had been gathered in, and the temple gates had been open since midnight, when the priests blasted their trumpets and announced the commencement of the festival.

Amid the joy of celebration, my brash friend Peter shared a message for everyone who gathered on the steps around us. He explained that this miracle had been predicted by the prophets. Yeshua of Natzeret had come to the children of Isra'el, performed signs and wonders, and died a cruel death. Yet all this happened as part of God's ordained plan.

"With the help of lawless Gentiles," Peter explained, "you nailed him to the cross and murdered him. However, God released him from the horrors of death and raised him back to life, for the grave could not keep him in its grip. Now he sits on the throne of highest honor in heaven, at God's right hand. And the Father, as he promised, gave him the Holy Spirit to pour out upon us, just as you see and hear today. So let it be clearly known by everyone in Isra'el that God has made this Yeshua whom you crucified to be both Lord and Messiah!"

Over three thousand people believed that day, and their excitement was contagious. Hadassah and I walked back to John Mark's inn and scarcely felt our feet touch the pavement.

In subsequent weeks, we worshiped at the Temple each day, telling anyone who would listen that the Messiah had come to Isra'el. Because he had come, we no longer had to fear to speak the name of God, for now we could call him *Abba* or Father. Anyone who would turn from sin and be immersed in the name of Yeshua the Messiah would receive the gift of the Holy Spirit.

For several months we lived in a continual state of excitement, overcome with joy and wonder. Hadassah and I shared our faith with others in the Court of the Women; we continued to serve the disciples as we met for meals at John Mark's inn.

But even though I loved my Lord Yeshua, I couldn't walk down the streets of Jerusalem without seeing Romans . . . and being reminded of the harm they'd done to me. At that point I held them responsible not only for the destruction of my family but for the cruel murder of my innocent rabboni.

Peter kept saying the Romans were a tool in God's plan, and

I believe he was right. But what woman loves the switch with which she disciplines her children?

My burning hatred of the Romans, which had cooled to embers while I traveled with Yeshua, flickered into flame.

⋄⟩═◈═⟨⋄

Shortly after Pentecost, Uriah and Yudit appeared at John Mark's inn. After a moment of shock, I welcomed them with open arms, but Uriah would not meet my gaze, and Yudit felt as stiff as a plank in my embrace.

"We have come," Uriah said, looking over my shoulder as if he addressed someone else, "to inquire about Hadassah. Now that this Yeshua is dead, it is time she came home. Jeremiah of Bethsaida has expressed interest in marrying her."

I glanced toward the chamber beyond, where Hadassah and John Mark's mother were preparing the midday meal. "I will get Hadassah for you," I said, folding my arms, "but you should know that Yeshua is not dead. He is alive and sitting at ADONAI's right hand."

Uriah's eyes darkened like thunderclouds. "Blasphemy! Yaakov, he of blessed memory, would rise up to curse you for saying such a thing."

I tilted my head and struggled to hold my temper. Hot words surged to my tongue, but this was not my fight. "Let me get Hadassah for you."

I went to the kitchen and told her she had guests; she stepped out a moment later, trailed by John Mark. I couldn't help but notice the way the young man's eyes followed her as she walked toward her parents with a light step.

"Mother! Father! It is good to see you!"

Uriah cast a glance of well-defined dislike in my direction, then turned to his daughter. "Hadassah, you will come home with us. This Yeshua is dead and I have found you a husband."

Hadassah, who'd been about to embrace her mother, lowered her arms. I expected her to look at me for assurance, but she didn't need my help.

"Father—" she spoke in a calm voice—"Yeshua said we must love him even above our family members. I want to honor you, truly I do, but I cannot dishonor my Lord. If obeying you means I must deny Yeshua, then I cannot obey."

Yudit, who'd managed to keep silent, burst into tears. "Hadassah!" she wailed. "If you do not come home, you will not marry. And how can you honor HaShem without creating a home and raising children?"

John Mark stepped to Hadassah's side. "I will marry your daughter and provide a home for her here in Jerusalem. You have my word that we will raise our children in a household that honors ADONAI and his Son, Yeshua the Messiah. If you want to draw up a marriage contract, I will promise to honor, support, and live with her."

As Uriah's eyes bulged and his face went pale, I felt a small surge of satisfaction. My former neighbor sputtered while Yudit clung to his arm.

John Mark looked around. "If we had cups, I would drink with you in celebration of our betrothal—"

"I will not have it!" Uriah peeled off his shoe and threw it to the floor. "I will not listen!"

Mindful of Yudit's anguished gaze, I turned to John Mark. "I will accept on Hadassah's behalf . . . if she is willing."

I shifted my gaze to my young friend's face—her eyes brimmed with tenderness and love as she regarded John Mark. I had sensed a connection between these two, so perhaps this encounter was part of HaShem's plan.

I took Hadassah's hand and placed it in John Mark's, then covered both of their hands with my own as I prayed: "Blessed are you, Lord our God, king of the universe, who has sanctified us with your commandments. Blessed are you, O Lord, who sanctifies your people Isra'el by consecrated wedlock."

Tears glistened in the wells of Hadassah's lovely eyes as she regarded her betrothed.

I gave Yudit a quick smile, then turned back to the happy couple. "May ADONAI bless you and keep you, may ADONAI make his face to shine upon you, and be gracious unto you. May ADONAI lift up his countenance upon you and give you peace."

Unmoved by his wife's sobs or his daughter's happiness, Uriah turned with a quick snap of his shoulders and left the inn.

I never saw him again, but in the spring of the year following our Lord's resurrection, Hadassah and John Mark stood beneath the *huppah* and were joined in marriage.

My heart warmed as I watched them beneath the wedding canopy. The Romans had stolen my family, but God had blessed me with Hadassah and John Mark, both of whom I loved with a mother's full affection.

———◦———

One night, after we had finished dinner, Peter and Susanna were in the courtyard talking to a mixed group of men and women. I waited until the conversation died, then I tugged on the sleeve of Peter's robe. "Peter," I said, taking care to include his wife in my gaze, "I have a question."

A wry smile flashed through the thicket of his beard. "Miryam, you know you may ask me anything."

"I wonder about the Romans. My heart remains hard toward them; I cannot see a Roman soldier without feeling my joy shrivel within me—"

Peter nodded as if he understood. "We who have been filled with the Spirit of God must still live in our corrupt flesh, Miryam. Yeshua knew how difficult it would be. That's why he sent the Comforter to teach and guide us."

"Still, I don't feel—"

"You cannot trust your feelings. You must surrender your hurts and let the Spirit of God love the Romans through you. Besides, think of all the good Rome has done for us."

I choked on the word. *"Good?"*

"Look around." He gestured toward the streets. "These fine roads are the work of Romans. Could we have traveled as easily in the master's work if these roads had not been built? And they are safe—in the day of my father's father, a man risked his life if he left the safety of his city walls. The Romans may not understand us, but they have made our land safer."

I snorted softly. "Safer for whom? We have always had a law. We could police our own people."

"Fair enough, but the Romans have given us a common currency. They have spread Latin and Greek as languages with which we can address the foreigner passing through Eretz-Yisrael."

"If not for the *Romans*—" I spat the word—"there wouldn't be foreigners in the land of Isra'el."

Peter laughed and draped an arm around his wife's shoulders. "We will always have foreigners among us. But Rome has given us a means to reach them with the news of salvation. I am going out to

spread the news in the next few weeks, and I'll be traveling on beautifully paved Roman roads."

I didn't answer, but grudgingly conceded that he might be right.
Perhaps Rome did possess glories that indirectly aided our cause.

My hatred of the nation cooled with that realization, but nothing
Peter said could erase my enmity toward a particular pair of
Romans. I didn't know where Gaius Cabilenus and Atticus Aurelius
were, but it wouldn't be easy to hide in an empire easily traversed on
beautifully paved roads.

Abruptly, I asked Peter and Susanna if they could use my help as
they traveled as Yeshua's emissaries.

CHAPTER FORTY-EIGHT

THE CONDEMNED WOMAN'S WORDS stir shadowy memories of a dark time in Atticus's military career. He shifts on the bench, recalling that Pontius Pilate had been a careful man the year of the Nazarene's execution, but he was not a careful man by nature. Three years after the prophet's crucifixion, once again the procurator overestimated his wisdom and underestimated his subjects.

Pilate had known that the Jews bore little love for the Samaritans, a group who worshiped at Mount Gerizim instead of the Temple in Jerusalem. Though the Samaritans venerated only one God, they had little to do with the Jews, preferring to believe that Moses had hidden sacred vessels on the mountain.

During a hot summer season, a Samaritan leader gathered a crowd on Mount Gerizim and promised to display the secret vessels of Moses. Alarmed that the assembling of such a crowd might result in a riot, Pilate ordered soldiers to block the road to the mountain. When the people charged the roadblock, the Romans pulled their swords and killed the insistent pilgrims.

The story of the Samaritan massacre flew to Rome on wings, and Tiberius wasted no time in recalling the governor of Judea.

A wind had come up, riding the edge of an approaching storm, when Atticus stood in the fortress courtyard to hear Gaius's announcement of Pilate's recall. Atticus had been made a centurion by that time, as had Flavius.

"Two centuria of the Cohors Secunda Italica Civum Romanorum," Gaius intoned, standing with his hands locked behind his back, "will accompany the procurator of Judea back to Rome. Atticus Aurelius and Flavius Gemellus—you and your men will leave Caesarea within the month."

Leave Judea? Atticus had begun to think he would remain in that outpost forever. He looked at Flavius, who wore a grin the size of a Jerusalem melon. For an instant excitement pulsed through his blood; then he remembered—a soldier could not have a family. If he went to Rome, Cyrilla and Quintus would not go with him. Pilate would undoubtedly take several members of his household staff, but not a pair of lowly slaves.

He nodded when Gaius dismissed them, then turned and stared at the ground. What was he to do? As a soldier, he had to obey orders, but he had established a family in Judea. Though those ties were tenuous, he couldn't sever them without breaking someone's heart. . . .

He stiffened as Flavius propped his arm on his shoulder. "What news, eh? We're leaving this dustbin for the marble streets of Rome!"

Atticus released a choked laugh. "Imagine that."

"Indeed! Imagine worshiping at a proper temple, attending games in the Colosseum, living in a decent barracks. I was beginning to think we were stuck—" He stopped and narrowed his gaze. "What's the matter, big man? One would think you weren't thrilled to be leaving this godforsaken place."

Atticus snorted. "I want to go to Rome. But . . . there's Cyrilla. And Quinn. I can't imagine leaving them."

Flavius stared at the ground for a moment, then slapped Atticus on the back. "Better make the break now, then. Let them get used to your absence."

"But—"

"Don't go soft. Softness will only hurt more in the end. Make a clean break, Atticus, like you should have done years ago. What did you think, you could pretend with them forever? Impossible. You're Roman; they're ... well, they're not. You'd better get used to the idea of severing unofficial ties."

With a final slap on the back, Flavius stalked away, whistling a tune.

※━◎━※

For three weeks, Atticus volunteered his men for patrols, escort duty, and posts at the port—anything that would take him away from the barracks at Caesarea. He found it easier to put Cyrilla and Quinn out of his mind if he didn't have to look across the courtyard and see Pilate's palace and the garden where they often met.

One rainy afternoon, he rode his horse into the stable after a march to Cana and back. The rain had been unusually insistent, and beneath his armor he was soaked to the skin.

His mare whickered and shook her head as he dismounted, jingling the bit in her mouth. Atticus gave her an appreciative pat on the flank, then gestured to one of the stable hands. "Take care of her, will you?"

"Do you take more care for a horse than for me?"

He looked up. Cyrilla stood next to the doorway, her head and shoulders covered with a soaked linen veil. Seeing her in this unexpected time and place, Atticus realized that the last traces of girlishness, uncertainty, and baby fat had evaporated from her features. She had become a woman . . . and from all appearances, an unhappy one.

The eyes she turned on him were hot with resentment. "Did you think you could just walk away?"

Atticus glanced around, then took her arm and led her away from the activity in the barn. Unfortunately, this meant walking back out into the rain.

"What do you mean?" he asked when they had left the barn behind.

"I heard," she said, her voice breaking. "My lady Procula is returning to Rome and so are you. Did you think I wouldn't find out?"

He pressed his lips together and looked away. "Cyrilla, you know I can't have a wife. I am a soldier."

"But you have a son. You have acknowledged him publicly."

"Many of the men in my cohort have sons. But they're not legal. There are no adoption papers—"

"You think I care about papers? I care about you, Atticus. I thought you cared about us."

"I do care."

"Then why aren't you doing something?"

It was a reasonable question, but Atticus flinched as though she had stabbed him with it. "What am I supposed to do?"

"I don't know!" The wet material gathered on her shoulder dropped over her arm as she flung out her hands. "But you could try something! Maybe we could stow away on a boat, or you could buy us passage—"

"Don't you think I've considered that?" He ran his hand through his wet hair. "What am I supposed to do with you once you get to Rome? I can't afford a house, so where will you live?"

Her chin rose. "I supported myself before we met you. I could support myself—"

"No. Not like that."

"Then *what?*"

She held her head up in the gray light of the rainy day, and for the first time he realized the full strength of her determination. By all that was holy, this woman deserved his effort.

A smile nudged itself into a corner of his mouth as he pulled her into his arms. "I don't know what to do, Cyrilla, but give me time, and I promise, I'll think of something."

With her face buried in his chest, her next words were muffled: "You promise you won't leave us?"

"I promise."

<hr />

Two days later, with his nerves strung as tight as a bowstring, Atticus approached the palace garden. Cyrilla and Quinn were tossing a ball by the fountain, maintaining a careful distance from Lady Procula, who appeared to be crying.

Atticus turned his back to the governor's wife, lest Procula think he wanted to see her. "Cyrilla?"

She rolled the ball to Quinn, then gave him a tentative smile. "I hoped you'd come."

"I came as soon as I could."

She gave him a quick, hopeful look. "Did you think of something?"

"I think so, but I need to know—are you *sure* you want to come to Rome?"

Cyrilla lowered her gaze. "I can't believe you'd ask that."

"Rome is not Judea. You'd be giving up everything familiar to you."

"But I'd be keeping you and Quinn, wouldn't I?"

Atticus took a deep breath. All right, then. He would ask Lady Procula if she would bring Cyrilla to Rome. His question, if interpreted incorrectly, could lead to trouble. If Pilate learned one of his legionnaires had taken the time to inquire after a servant and a child—

He strode toward the pale woman sitting by the trimmed hedges and knocked his fist against his breastplate. "My lady, may I have a word?"

When Procula lifted her head, he saw the faint tracks of tears on her cheeks. "Please do not—" She looked at him more closely. "Oh! It's Atticus, right?"

"I hate to disturb you, but I need to speak to you."

Her face crumpled with unhappiness. "Have you heard something about my husband?"

"No, my lady. I have not come on your husband's account."

"Then whose?" Her gaze softened when she looked toward Cyrilla. "Of course."

"I was wondering, my lady—will you bring your maid and the child with you to Rome?"

Procula tilted her head, regarding him with a look of faint amusement. "What do you think, centurion? Should I take Judeans to Rome? I have no need of them; my household will be well equipped with slaves."

"You will not have *these* servants." Atticus paused. She had to have guessed what he was thinking, so why was she being difficult?

She looked up at him through a fringe of curled bangs. "Tell me, Atticus—as a Roman soldier, have you never wanted to marry?"

He stiffened. "It is not permitted."

"And how does that make you feel? Do you ever want to rebel? run off and tell the entire Roman world to drown itself in the sea?"

"I serve Rome and its commanders with my whole heart. I have taken a vow and I intend to keep it."

"So there is no room in your heart for rebellion . . . or a wife and child?"

Atticus swallowed hard and tried not to reveal his irritation. "The army does not permit me to enjoy those things."

"But you have made room in your heart, Atticus. You do enjoy them. And I wonder how you have been able to pull it off."

He held his tongue. An answer would verify that he had established a family; a denial might result in a permanent break from Cyrilla and Quinn.

Procula ran her fingertip over the stiff bloom of a lily. "I shall try to help you. I'll ask my husband to bring the woman and the boy. Pilate has so many things on his mind, he'll scarcely notice my request . . . or me. He is too worried about his future."

Atticus bowed. "Thank you, Lady Procula."

"You're welcome."

He bowed again, but not before flashing Cyrilla a hopeful smile.

Lady Procula, Atticus later learned, proved herself both faithful and insightful. She kept her promise to ask Pilate if Cyrilla and Quinn could accompany her to Rome, and as she had predicted, the governor gave his absentminded consent.

The news had thrilled Cyrilla, and not until the matter was settled did Atticus realize how desperately he'd been hoping for the procurator's permission. He had sworn to leave all for the military, but abandoning the woman and the boy would have been a painful sacrifice.

He and Cyrilla had been aboard the transport ship for little more than a week when she pulled him aside and motioned to Quinn. "You need to speak to the boy."

"About what?"

The tip of her nose went pink. "He has just realized that he . , , is not like you. Because you've been with him . . . you know . . . more often since we've been at sea."

Atticus blinked, then drew in a deep breath. He had known this moment would come sooner or later. He hadn't expected it to arrive when Quintus was only seven years old.

And what should he say? He knew nothing of what fathers told their sons about such intimate matters. The men in his garrison were frank enough with their thoughts and comments, but how did a man talk to a child at such a tender age?

He walked forward, took Quinn's hand, and led him toward the bow. Smiling, he lifted his son onto a block, then braced the boy's hands on the rail as a sudden gust struck the boat, heeling the vessel over enough to bring their fingertips within a foot of the foaming sea.

To his credit, Quinn laughed. Atticus chuckled, glad the boy wasn't afraid, and nestled the child against his chest as the ship breasted the swell and straightened.

"Your mother," Atticus said, glancing down at his son's face, "tells me you had a question."

Quinn looked up, his eyes wide; then he scrunched his nose and nodded.

"You want to know why we look different . . . in a way that has nothing to do with why I'm tall and you're small."

The boy's chin dipped in another nod.

"Well." Atticus braced himself against the railing. "Have you seen the brand on my back?"

Quinn's eyes flicked to the armor over Atticus's shoulder, then moved away as if afraid to rest there. "The dog and snake?"

"It's a dog, a snake, and a scorpion. The brand of a Roman soldier."
Quinn digested this information, his eyes serious, then looked
back at Atticus. "Did it hurt?"

"Yes, it did. But it doesn't hurt now. And anyone who sees my
back knows I'm a soldier. Not all soldiers have this brand, only the
ones who worship Mithras."

The boy slid his hands beneath Atticus's as the sea spat at them in a
sudden white plume. "Will . . . will I have to get a brand?"

"No. In fact, I have left the people who worship Mithras, but my
body still bears his mark. Taking the brand was part of a ritual.
You've seen rituals, haven't you?"

Quintus nodded.

"Good. When you're old enough to go to the public baths, you'll
see that men look different in many ways. Some groups of people,
you see, perform rituals on babies and cut away part of their skin.
Some perform these rituals when boys become men. And some
groups never perform these rituals at all."

Quinn looked up at him again. "And me?"

"When you were a tiny baby, you lived with people who cut part
of your skin away in a ritual. I'm sure you don't remember it, but
that's all right. It doesn't hurt you anymore, does it?"

"No." Quinn remained silent for a long moment. He didn't look
up when he asked, "Didn't I come from your people?"

Atticus squeezed the child's arm. "You came from special people,
Quintus, but the gods brought you to me and your mother. Are you
glad they did?"

Again the small face tilted, the nose squinched, and the mouth
curled into an impish smile. "I am."

"Me, too." Atticus dropped a kiss onto the top of the boy's head
and inhaled the scent of sea salt in Quinn's hair. "Very glad."

Chapter Forty-nine

For the next several years I worked with Peter and Susanna, spreading the gospel wherever people would listen. My hair, which had been a rich and glossy ebony, became threaded with gray. I watched lines appear in Susanna's face and knew that even deeper tracks were finding a home in my own.

But no matter how wearying the work, we always found occasions for joy.

Seven years after the resurrection of my rabboni, in a coastal town called Joppa, Peter raised a woman named Tabitha from death. The miracle opened the villagers' hearts to our message, and Peter, Susanna, and I took jobs in the town so we could continue to share the good news about Yeshua.

We stayed with Shimon, a leatherworker, and often laughed at how far we'd come from our beginnings. No pious Hebrew would ever work with dead things, but the skins of dead beasts enabled us to earn a living and gain respect among the people of Joppa. The palms of our hands took on a golden glow from handling the various dyes and agents used to soften animal skins. I was delighted to be working with dyes and colors again.

One afternoon, while Susanna prepared the midday meal and I mixed a new dye, Peter went up to the roof of Shimon's house to pray. Before Susanna could call the men to eat, three strangers approached the courtyard gate.

I saw them first, and though I had been perspiring all day, I felt suddenly damp, slick with the cool, sour sweat of fear. A horrible sense of déjà vu swept over me, for although two of them wore the simple garb of household servants, one man wore the red tunic and armor of a Roman soldier.

I retreated into the shadows, forcing Shimon's wife to answer their summons. Dusty from their journey, they asked if this was the house where they could find Simon, also called Peter. Startled, the leatherworker's wife nodded.

I would have flown up the stairs to warn him, but I had no time. Peter had heard their inquiry from the rooftop; he came downstairs and, as thoughtless as ever, identified himself. The men explained that they had been sent by Cornelius, a Roman in Caesarea. An angel, they said, had told the centurion to send for Peter.

I did not believe their story. A Roman soldier sending for a follower of Yeshua? How could Peter possibly believe them?

We'd heard many stories in the days since Yeshua's resurrection. We'd heard about Sha'ul, a Pharisee from Jerusalem who ordered the stoning of many believers, including Stephen, a leader among Yeshua's followers in Jerusalem. Shortly after Stephen's death, we'd heard that Sha'ul had seen Yeshua on the road to Damascus . . . and the shock had been so great that Sha'ul had believed in Yeshua and received the Holy Spirit. I had doubted that story, too, until Sha'ul came to Jerusalem and met with the other disciples. After the meeting, Peter explained that the Lord had called Sha'ul just as he had called us, so we should accept him as a brother.

After listening to Peter, I could welcome my Hebrew brother Sha'ul, but *Romans*? I closed my eyes and tried to picture Peter preaching to the legionnaires who had driven the nails into our rabboni's wrists, but I could not even imagine it.

But Peter always blurts out the first thought that crosses his mind. Before I could give him a private word of warning, he had invited the men for dinner and asked them to be our guests for the night. Though I grumbled privately and rolled my eyes at every comment the Gentiles made, Peter made them feel welcome, and Shimon preened as though their presence brought honor to his humble house.

That night, as I lay between Susanna and the wall—the farthest position I could take from the Gentile dogs under our roof—a startling thought occurred to me. Peter and the strangers were leaving for Caesarea the next morning . . . and Caesarea was home to the Italian cohort, the same group that had come through Magdala and murdered my family ten years before.

A lot had happened in those years: I had given myself over to darkness and been brought back to wholeness, I had walked with Yeshua and witnessed his death and resurrection, and I had been baptized and filled with the Holy Spirit. But the resentment and hatred that had burned within me in the months following my family's deaths had not grown cold.

If I went with Peter to Caesarea, I could slip away and make inquiries at the fortress. I could see if anyone there knew Gaius Cabilenus or Atticus Aurelius. I might actually find those men. If I

did, and if this centurion who'd sent for Peter proved sympathetic
to our cause, he might be willing to see that I received long overdue justice.

I rose on one elbow and peered at the thin curtain dividing the
room. Perhaps the prophets were right. Perhaps, like our father
Avraham, at times we really did entertain angels unaware.

⋯⟩══◈══⟨⋯

The next morning we rose and prepared for the journey. Peter lifted
his brows when I told him I wanted to go along, but he had too many
things on his mind to protest.

Other believers from Joppa joined us, including Shimon the
leatherworker and his wife.

The uneasiness that had filled my soul faded to a sunny cheerful-
ness. Memories of my days traveling with Yeshua flooded my mind
as we set out on the road that led north to Caesarea, and I think even
Peter was caught up in nostalgia. He told stories of Yeshua as we
walked; he even told the Romans that I was the first to see our risen
Lord on the morning of his resurrection.

Two days after leaving Joppa, our party walked through the tall
gates at the Roman fortress at Caesarea. Susanna and the people
from Joppa kept whispering and pointing at the sights of the thoroughly Roman city, but I'd been to Tiberias, so heathen marvels held
no attraction for me.

The three Romans hurried away to fetch the centurion who had
sent for Peter, while we waited in an open courtyard. A profound
and peaceful weariness settled over me like a blanket. I had come
many miles and waited ten years for justice, so I could wait a few
hours more.

A group of servants hurried out of the barracks, eager to show us to rooms where we could wash and rest. Tomorrow, they assured us, we would meet Cornelius at his house.

⟡

"It's not that I don't want to meet this centurion," I told Peter the next morning. "But I'd like to make inquiries among the soldiers about some people I knew from Magdala."

Peter looked down, his lashes hiding his eyes, and hesitated. "Are you sure this is what you should do?"

Something in his voice—something decidedly *un*-Peter—gave me pause. "I've come a long way," I finally answered. "What harm will it do for me to ask a few questions?"

"Go, then," he said, nodding at someone behind me, so I knew he was already thinking about his meeting with the centurion.

So I left him and walked toward the barracks.

I hesitated outside the wide stone arch that led into the legionnaires' area to take a deep breath and wind the raveled fabric of my nerve. A uniformed equestrian walked by, leading a horse whose hooves clomped over the stone pavement in time to the thumping of my heart.

Was I nervous because I'd waited so long for this moment? Or was I afraid because I was a Hebrew woman—alone—among people who didn't respect women or Hebrews?

Gulping back my fear, I slipped along the passageway like a shadow. When I had traversed the stone entry, I found myself in a paved courtyard surrounded by colonnades on two sides and a single arched entry to my left. Because I could see men moving in the areas behind the roofed porches, I darted toward the entry.

I found myself in a rectangular hall with a wooden ceiling supported by wide beams. Benches ran down the center aisle, facing each other, and a painted image of a large man slitting the throat of an ox stood behind a set of three altars, each of which steamed with live coals—

I cried out as a rough hand gripped my arm. "What are you doing here?"

I grimaced at the soldier who held me, his eyes bright beneath the rim of his helmet. Brass cheek guards covered most of his face, leaving only his nose, eyes, and chin exposed.

"I am a guest of the centurion Cornelius," I told him in Greek. "I would like to speak to someone in charge."

His brows raised at the mention of the centurion's name, but he did not loosen his grip. "We do not allow women in the temple of Jupiter."

"I didn't know this was a temple. Excuse my ignorance, please."

"You Jews don't excuse a man's ignorance." He glared at me, his eyes hot with resentment. "If a man takes one step out of that Court of the Gentiles in your Temple, your guards would strike him dead."

I gaped at him. "True—but there are warnings posted on the walls. There are no warnings here, nothing at all."

His expression darkened with unreadable emotions; then he pulled me out of the chamber. "We're going to see the commander of the garrison. We'll let him decide what to do with you."

⊰═◉═⊱

My mind raced as the brute led me—half walking, half stumbling—toward the marble palace to the north of the barracks. I went along without speaking, my misgivings increasing by the minute.

The soldier thrust me through a door and I stumbled forward, then caught my balance. Two legionnaires sat behind a table, both wearing ornate uniforms. They frowned when they saw me. "Who's this?"

"Found her snooping around in the barracks temple. She says she's here to see Cornelius."

The younger of the two men, a man with thinning brown hair, jerked his head toward the small houses that stood behind the barracks. "Cornelius is in his quarters, and he does have guests."

"Yes." I glanced back at the brute who'd found me. "We're from Joppa."

He bared his teeth. "You speak like one of those stubborn Galileans."

"I'm from Magdala. But I've come here from Joppa."

As if that statement confirmed my untrustworthiness, the soldier shoved me forward. "I think she's a spy. Perhaps you should send her to Syria to stand before the legate."

A wave of grayness passed over me. "Ask what you will; I'll tell you what I was doing. But I am no spy."

"All right, then." The silver-haired officer, obviously the commander, crossed his arms. "Why were you in the temple?"

"I was looking for someone . . . who could help me find a pair of Roman soldiers."

The silver-haired man turned to his companion and lifted a tufted brow. "She's a little old for that, don't you think?"

For a moment I didn't understand; then a blush burned my cheek. "This is not what you imagine! I don't know these men. I only know *of* them."

"Then why do you need them?"

"I want to report them for misconduct."

The second centurion laughed. "By which law are you defining this misconduct? Jewish or Roman?"

I crossed my arms too, determined to match their stubbornness. "I'll not say more until I know whether Gaius Cabilenus and Atticus Aurelius are garrisoned here."

The names meant something; I could tell. The men at the table looked at each other again, but this time with faces as blank and smooth as sleeping babies'.

"Atticus Aurelius *was* here," the commander said. "He has been transferred to Rome."

"And Gaius Cabilenus?"

"Dead." His mouth dipped into an even deeper frown. "Broke his neck last year when he was thrown from his horse."

I studied the officer carefully. Roman soldiers looked out for each other, so this man might well be lying for his brothers in treachery. "Have you any proof?"

The commander sighed, then nodded to the younger man, who stood and left the room, returning a moment later with two unfurled scrolls. He laid them on the table and pointed to a hand-written line on the first parchment.

"Here." He tapped the writing. "The honorable Gaius Cabilenus, buried on the fourth day of the sixth month, killed in a training accident." He picked up the second scroll, searched the scrawled lines, then turned the parchment toward me. "There—two centuries of the Cohors Secunda Italica Civum Romanorum escorted Pontius Pilate, procurator of Judea, to Rome. One century commanded by Atticus Aurelius; the other commanded by Flavius Gemellus." He named the date and the ship they had sailed on, but I scarcely heard him.

I stared at the names on the parchments and realized that HaShem had removed Gaius Cabilenus from my reach . . . and my only remaining hope of justice had sailed away four years earlier.

⟨⟩

I'd had no success in my quest, but Peter's meeting with Cornelius had gone better than anyone expected. The centurion and several of his men not only accepted Peter's testimony, but the Holy One poured out his gift of the Holy Spirit as Peter was telling the Gentiles about what Yeshua had done.

Peter, Shimon, and the other men from Joppa celebrated that night, praising God and singing as they sat at dinner with the Romans. Shimon's wife, Susanna, and I kept to ourselves and watched from an alcove. I shared their gladness in the goodness of God, but my heart remained shadowed with the disappointing news I'd received earlier.

Though I would never admit it to my believing brothers and sisters, I couldn't help but question the Holy One. How could Roman legionnaires be blessed with fullness of Spirit while my arms remained empty?

CHAPTER FIFTY

PESACH HAD TAKEN ON NEW meaning since our Lord's death, yet during one particular festival, eleven years after Yeshua's resurrection, we found it difficult to celebrate. I looked around the circle and noticed several missing faces. Were the others mourning . . . or hiding?

Herod Agrippa, our new king, realized he could win favor with the religious authorities if he silenced the leaders of the Hebrew believers. As the first step in his plan, he sent soldiers to arrest James, John's brother. Before we could decide how to react, Herod had the son of Zebedee run through with a sword.

The news of James's execution left us numb with grief and shock. With heavy hearts, we met at John Mark's inn to observe Pesach. In a gathering that included many of the elders, we stood in the dullness of despair and prayed for comfort. Peter had raised the dead, but God had not willed the resurrection of James. Yeshua had not hurried to Tiberias to restore the Immerser after Yochanan's beheading, but he had raised Lazarus after four days in the tomb.

Why did one man deserve a miracle while another man didn't? I couldn't see an answer, and I didn't dare voice my question.

But every time I closed my eyes, the backs of my eyelids filled with images of James and John, the loud, laughing brothers who rarely parted from each other. I remembered how they had wanted to call down fire from heaven when a Samaritan village refused to give us shelter for the night, and how, with Peter and John, James had been part of Yeshua's inner circle. The three of them had been privy to things withheld from the rest of us . . . and for what? All the things James had witnessed died with him.

Pain squeezed my heart when I recalled how furious the other disciples had been when Zebedee's Miryam asked Yeshua if her sons could sit at his right and left hand in his kingdom. I hadn't seen Miryam in months, but I knew this news would break her heart. And John? Of the two men, he was the more sensitive. I couldn't imagine how he would handle the death of his beloved brother.

We were in the midst of prayer when someone knocked on the door. Rhoda, one of the servants at the inn, answered the summons, then came to tug on my sleeve. "A Roman," she whispered, her eyes as round and white as a panicked colt's. "He wishes to speak to a woman called Miryam."

John Mark's mother and I looked at each other. Miryam was such a common Hebrew name, the Roman probably had no idea how to differentiate between us.

Both of us went to the door. John Mark's mother opened it. I wouldn't have been surprised to see an entire company of armed men at the door, all set upon our extermination. But the fellow before us had barely entered manhood; he was probably no more than fourteen or fifteen. He looked barely old enough to grow a beard. He wore a plain white tunic, bordered at the edge with a scrolled pattern, while a scarlet cloak hung over one shoulder.

Miryam didn't invite the Roman to enter. Instead we stepped outside and waited for the young man to state his business.

He nodded at us, then lifted a brow. "Miryam?"

"We are both known by that name," John Mark's mother said. "And we are like sisters, so anything you have to say to one can safely be said to the other."

The youth hesitated, then lowered his voice and moved closer— so close, in fact, that I would have retreated had the door not blocked my way.

"I have been sent to warn you," he said, glancing over his shoulder. "Herod has arrested Peter and is holding him at the Fortress Antonia. The king intends to bring Peter out for public trial after the festival and then to execute him."

My hostess gasped and clung to my shoulder, but I fastened steely eyes on the unlikely messenger. "Why should we believe you?"

He blinked as if surprised by my question. "Why would I lie?"

I would have smiled at his innocence if the situation weren't so serious. "Who sent you to us?"

He lifted his hand and took a step back. "That's all I can say. I have to go."

"But who sent you?"

He backstepped again, looking at me with brown eyes that glowed beneath his curled bangs. "Someone who would ask one other thing—that you pray."

Without another word, the Roman youth turned and moved into the bustle of the street. I stepped out and watched him thread his way through the boisterous crowd, then turned back to John Mark's mother, who clung to the doorpost.

A tremor touched her lips. "Do you believe him?"

I tilted my head, then nodded. "I think I do."

"Then we should tell the others."

"And we should pray."

CHAPTER FIFTY-ONE

ATTICUS LOOKED UP AS QUINN entered the barracks and made a beeline for the bench where he and Flavius were playing senet.

As always, his gaze ran over the boy's form, making sure he had not come to any harm; then he smiled. "Did you find the Miryam who owns the inn?"

Quinn nodded. "I found two Miryams, both at the inn on Crooked Street. I gave them the news."

Atticus squeezed his son's arm. "You did well. Here, take a denarius for your trouble."

Quinn waved the gift away. "I don't need anything, Father."

Atticus tucked the coin back into his belt, grateful that the boy had grown into a sense of honor. "Sit and talk to us. Sometimes I think you spend entirely too much time in the company of women."

Quinn grinned. "If you'll excuse me, Father, I think I'd rather go to the stable. The cavalry commander has just accepted delivery of a fine stallion."

Atticus waved him off. "Go, then."

Because Empress Messalina wanted to visit Jerusalem during the spring festivals, Atticus's and Flavius's centuries had spent the last three months serving as military escorts. Though he hated to leave Cyrilla in Rome, Atticus had been grateful for an opportunity to revisit the land of Quinn's birth.

Flavius had loathed the thought of returning to Jerusalem, but he had had no choice. Across the bench, he scowled at Atticus. "You take too many chances. What if one of Herod's men discovers that you have warned those people?"

Atticus shrugged. "I am sworn to serve Rome, not Herod."

"You seem to have forgotten the terms of the sacramentum. Your actions are to be governed by the rule of your commander, and Governor Vitellius has warned us not to offend Herod."

"I haven't offended him."

"*Those people* offend him." Flavius leaned forward and lowered his voice. "I hear there are thousands in Jerusalem alone. They say the Nazarene has followers even in Rome."

"I'm sure of it. I can't be the only one who realizes that his power came from God."

Flavius shook his head back and forth, like an ox stunned by the slaughterer's blow. "You are a fool, Atticus Aurelius. First you lose your heart to a child, then to a woman, then to a Jewish prophet—"

Atticus pulled a coin from the purse strapped inside his belt. He held it between his fingers, displaying the superscription as well as the image of Caesar. "Do you see this?"

Flavius blinked. "What of it?"

"They once asked Yeshua whether it was lawful for a Jew to pay taxes to Rome. He asked for a coin like this one; then he said a man should render unto Caesar what was Caesar's, and unto God what was God's." Atticus grinned and slipped the coin back into his purse. "I will give Rome everything I have promised, and the invisible God whatever he demands. As I learn *what* he demands, that is. I know so little about him."

Flavius's jaw shifted, bristling the whiskers on his cheek. "What if they ask for opposite things?"

Atticus hesitated. "Then I must obey God, I suppose. After all, he has outlived several caesars."

Flavius scooped up the game's throwing sticks. "Before I win your last denarius, I need to know—are you going to do anything else for this Peter? anything that's going to earn the entire cohort a scourging?"

"Have no fear." Atticus shifted on the bench, making room for Flavius to toss the sticks. "I'm going to pray. I don't think they'll scourge me for that."

CHAPTER FIFTY-TWO

I HAD NOT BEEN SO FRIGHTENED since the morning I learned of Yeshua's arrest. Would Herod come after all of us who believed? How much blood would have to flow before he called off his crusade?

Hadassah and I moved through our usual routine, helping John Mark's mother care for her guests at the inn, but my stomach churned with anxiety and the urge to flee. Hundreds of people knew where the believers regularly gathered, so how safe were we at the inn?

At one point I suggested that we leave. Miryam might have agreed, but Hadassah stopped and put her hands on our shoulders. "We are not going anywhere." Her voice was like velvet edged with iron, and as she spoke, she looked up at John Mark, who had entered the hall. "In faith we will pray for Peter and trust God to protect us . . . if that is his will."

We were praying in the upstairs room when Rhoda interrupted. "Excuse me," she said, her whisper breaking into our anguished entreaties, "but I think Peter is standing outside the door."

One of the elders looked at her with eyes narrowed in derision. "You're out of your mind, girl."

John Mark's mother pressed her hand to her throat. "You didn't open the door, did you?"

"I didn't open it," Rhoda insisted. "I listened. The man outside sounds just like Peter."

John Mark's mother turned to me as terror drained the blood from her face. "Herod has killed him. It must be his angel at the gate."

Several of the women broke into tears, but I pulled out of the circle and hurried down the stairs. I stopped in the hallway and stared at the door, my heart beating hard enough to be heard an arm's length away. Rhoda wasn't crazy; I could hear someone knocking.

Had the Roman boy led Herod's soldiers straight to us?

John Mark's mother appeared beside me; then she squeezed my hand. "Soldiers don't knock," she said, reading my thoughts. "They batter their way in."

She opened the door.

I stood in shocked silence. Peter—the flesh-and-blood Peter— stood on the threshold, a look of grateful wonder on his face. We led him upstairs to the others, who immediately broke out in a clamor of confused questions. He told us to calm down, and then he said an angel had entered the prison and set him free, going before him to unlock gates and doors.

Peter didn't linger, but he had a parting word for us: "Tell James, the Lord's brother, what happened."

As I watched the darkness swallow him, I wondered if I'd been praying in faith or despair. If I truly believed God would rescue Peter, why had I been so surprised to receive an answer to my prayers?

CHAPTER FIFTY-THREE

ATTICUS, TOO, HAD SPENT THAT night in prayer. He stood at his window and watched as dawn rose in a violent splash of color, spreading streaks and slashes over the sleeping city. In the judgment hall of the palace, Herod would soon be taking his seat and calling for the man known as Simon Peter. A group of Herod's guards would arrive at the Fortress Antonia and demand the prisoner.

Within an hour after sunrise, Claudius Lysias, chief captain of the cohort stationed permanently in Jerusalem, received Herod's guard and dispatched his aides to see what was keeping the jailers. They ran down the stairs and found the dungeon empty except for a handful of frantic guards. Simon Peter, who had been securely locked into his cell at sunset, had vanished, leaving a trail of open gates and unlocked doors.

When the news reached the visiting centuries, Flavius pulled Atticus into a quiet niche. "Tell me," he said, his voice like iron. "Tell me you didn't walk him out."

"Surely you don't believe that!"

"I don't know what to believe anymore."

Atticus shook his head. "I swear to you, I didn't leave my bed last night."

"Quinn, then. You sent Quinn."

Atticus gritted his teeth. "You think I'd risk my son's life?"

"I don't know. You'd risk yours easily enough."

"I promise you, Flavius—neither Quinn nor I had anything to do with this."

The trembling captain of the guard went in to face Claudius. "This Peter is no ordinary man," he told Claudius, a quaver in his voice. "By all the gods, I swear we took every precaution. He should be here. He should not have escaped."

Claudius jerked his head in an abrupt nod. "You'll have to explain yourself to Herod."

If possible, the jailer's face went a shade paler. He summoned his men, adjusted his uniform, then soberly presented himself to Claudius's escort.

Out of pity for the unfortunate jailers, Claudius's men marched across the pavement to Herod's palace with measured and unhurried steps. Atticus watched from a distance as the ill-fated men entered the king's hall; he wasn't surprised to hear Herod condemn every man to death.

Yet Atticus couldn't help feeling relieved for Yeshua's followers when Herod issued another command later that afternoon: he and his retinue would return to Caesarea as soon as possible. The empress Messalina would accompany him.

Agrippa had had his fill of Jerusalem.

Apparently, God had also had his fill of Agrippa. Not long after Atticus's return to Caesarea, Herod entertained Messalina and a group of sycophants from Tyre and Sidon. Dressed in embroidered purple robes and a heavy crown, he sat on his throne and made a ponderous speech that threatened to put his audience to sleep. But the fawning merchants, eager for royal approval, responded with enthusiastic shouts, proclaiming they had heard the voice of God, not a man.

Atticus and his men stood at attention as Herod rose and accepted the applause with languid waves. Midway through his acknowledgment, however, a grimace twisted his face. The king bent over, clutching at his gut, while he shrieked in pain and Messalina went pale with fear. Atticus and his men charged forward, fearing that an assassin in the crowd had hurled a weapon at the king, but Herod's physician could not find any evidence of a knife or a dart.

The king's bowels, the royal physician later reported, had been devoured by worms. A rumor circulating among the people blamed Agrippa for his own demise—he'd been stricken, the priests of several religions claimed, because he accepted worship rightfully belonging to God.

Frightened by the instability of the region, the empress Messalina returned to Rome, taking with her two centuries from the Cohors Secunda Italica Civum Romanorum.

Atticus stood at the stern of the transport ship and gratefully watched Judea slide away.

Chapter Fifty-four

With Flavius and Cyrilla, Atticus sat on a bench and watched as the commanding legate administered the oath of the sacramentum to a group of new recruits. Dressed for the first time in the bloodred tunic of the legionnaire, eighteen-year-old Quintus stood at attention and stared straight ahead as he echoed the first recruit's vow: *"Idem in me."* The same in my case. Not until he had fulfilled his promise of twenty-five years' service would he again wear the white toga of a civilian.

Atticus had helped Quinn don his tunic and armor, explaining that the color symbolized blood that should not stain his conscience as long as it was shed in defense of the empire.

"Some of the men who will be training you will say the Roman soldier is only a tool of war," Atticus told his son. "Though you possess dignity and honor, some centurions would have you abandon all thought in order to obey your commander. They will tell you to flinch from nothing and feel neither cruelty nor mercy. Some would have you become a cold, calculating, killing machine."

Quinn's dark eyes met and held his. "What would you tell me, Father?"

Atticus had smiled. "I would have you remember that you have vowed obedience to the emperor, but a higher authority reigns above whoever occupies the Roman throne. There is a God in heaven who scoffs at gods made by human hands. He sent his prophet to earth, and that man died upon a Roman cross. Yet he walked out of his tomb, and because he lives, those who believe in him shall also conquer death. This truth will enable you to live courageously and to temper your strength with mercy. Remember this always, Quinn . . . my son."

After the induction ceremony, Atticus and Cyrilla followed Quintus to the camp where he would train before being dispatched to his first posting. Cyrilla dabbed at her eyes, then rested her hands on the young man's shoulders. "It's been my greatest pleasure to watch you grow," she said, sniffling. "I know you will make us proud."

Quintus kissed her cheek, then turned to Atticus. "Any last words, Father?"

Atticus studied the boy he'd adored for the last eighteen years. Quintus looked every bit a man. His eyes were bright, his shoulders broad. Even at this moment of parting, the quaver in his voice was barely noticeable; only the tightening of the muscles in his throat betrayed the depth of his emotion.

Atticus gripped Quinn's hand. "We've talked enough. Go, Son, and remember all your mother and I have taught you."

Quintus threw his arm around Atticus, squeezed him tight, then pulled away for a final smile. "I'll write you."

The young man picked up his bag and strode toward the garrison, his shoulders broadening and settling as he drew responsibility around him like an invisible mantle.

Flavius slammed his cup down on the table and glared at Atticus. "By the putrid wax in Apollo's ears, I won't have it! This time you ask too much."

Atticus blanched before the fire in his friend's eye. "What do you mean? Quinn can't serve in my century; the other men would think me unfair no matter what I did."

"So you'd have him serve in mine?"

"Why not? You could keep an eye on him—"

"I won't allow it. I won't have a Jew among my men."

Atticus stared, caught off guard by the force of Flavius's reply. "What do you mean? Quintus has been raised Roman; he's as fine a recruit as any man in this barracks—"

"He's a Jew, Atticus. He doesn't deserve to be a legionnaire. By all rights he should be in the auxiliary troops in one of the outer provinces. If not for your soft heart, the boy wouldn't even be in Rome."

Atticus sat without moving—blank, amazed, and shaken. Flavius had never approved of his relationships with Cyrilla or Quinn, but he had never reacted with this sort of vehemence. Atticus leaned forward and placed his hands on the edge of the table. "What is *wrong* with you?"

"Nothing."

"What do you mean, nothing? You've never been like this before—"

"I can't believe you can be so blind!" Flavius's eyes went black and dazzling with fury. "You spent years over there with those people and yet you can't see anything wrong with them. You know what they do to their babies. You have seen their empty Temple; you have heard their superstitions. You save one of their maimed infants and cart him off to some soothsayer from a poor village;

then you believe the silly stories about the man walking out of his tomb—"

"It's not a silly story." Atticus felt his own temper spike. "And Quinn is not maimed."

"He's still a Jew." Flavius rose and leaned over the table. "And I won't have him in my century."

"He's my son." Atticus stood and met Flavius's glare. "And I want him to serve where I can keep an eye on him."

"You think that's what he wants?"

"I don't care what he wants. I'm his father; I want what's best for him."

"What's best for him is to go back to the land of his birth."

"Who are you to say? You've never cared for anyone but yourself!"

"I care for my men. And I won't require them to tolerate a Jew in their midst."

"What if I go to the tribune and ask that Quintus be assigned to your century?"

"You do and I'll tell the tribune the truth about what you did in Magdala. Who knows what will happen then?" Flavius's mouth curled in an expression that was not a smile. "You've lived a lie for years, and for that you'll be at least demoted and flogged. And Quinn? They could toss him out of the army or sell him as a slave. But the entire world will know there's no way he could be your son."

Atticus stared as Flavius's words fell with the weight of stones in water, spreading endless ripples of betrayal. More than twenty years of friendship had shattered in the last moment, but perhaps he had never really known the man who sat across from him.

He drew a deep breath, then looked down at his fisted hands. "Let Quintus finish his training in Rome. I'll request that he be stationed in Jerusalem, under Claudius Lysias."

"One of the auxiliary cohorts would be more appropriate."

"The auxiliaries are mainly Samaritan! That won't do."

The two men glared at each other for another long moment; then Flavius nodded. "I don't care, as long as he's not serving in Rome. Rome must be defended by Romans."

Atticus nodded slowly.

Cyrilla listened sympathetically as Atticus told the story; then she pulled his head into her lap. "I know," she said, her fingers brushing hair from his forehead, "how much it has cost you to allow Quinn to join the army. You will miss his company, his love . . . and now it would appear you have lost Flavius's friendship."

Atticus snorted softly. "I thought Flavius was a better man. I thought he stood for Roman ideals—"

Cyrilla dropped her arm on Atticus's chest. "Even Rome is not all it should be."

He caught her hand and looked into her eyes. "I will miss both of them," he said, enjoying the chance to speak freely of the matters on his heart. "But I'm grateful to have you. When I think of how I nearly left you in Caesarea—"

"You were young and foolish then." She eased into a smile. "You have improved remarkably in the last few years."

He lifted her arm, encased her small palm between his big hands, and thanked God for bringing her to him. The invisible God worked in astounding ways, but he worked with power and authority.

"I'm going to marry you," he said, studying her left hand. "When I am out of the army, I will place a ring on this finger and claim you as my wife."

Her eyes lit with mischief. "You'd better. I've been waiting a long time."

From another room, a servant's sandals made soft popping sounds as she walked across the porch and into the garden. "You are too good to me, Atticus," Cyrilla whispered.

He turned to better see her face. "Do you ever think it was a mistake? That I should have left Quinn at the house in Magdala?"

"I haven't thought that since we met Yeshua." Her eyes left no room for doubt. "What did the prophet tell you?"

Atticus pulled the prophecy from the well of memory: "'He will grow to maturity apart from his people . . . but the purposes of God will be revealed in him, and he will know the truth.'"

"Yeshua was right," Cyrilla said. "Wait, and you'll see."

⸎

When he returned to his quarters in the barracks, Atticus pulled a sheet of parchment from his lap desk and addressed a letter to Quintus: *Atticus Aurelius to his dear Quintus, greetings.*

These are dangerous times, he wrote, careful to choose inoffensive words in case a commander might read over Quinn's shoulder. *So live as an honorable man and remember what you have been taught.*

> *Quintus, my dear son, be strong with the special favor God gives you. You have heard me speak of many things that have been confirmed by reliable witnesses. Teach these truths to trustworthy people who are able to pass them on to others.*
>
> *You are about to be tested, so endure suffering as a good soldier. Do not let yourself become entangled in imperial politics, for then you cannot satisfy the one who has enlisted you in his army. Follow the Lord's rules for doing his work,*

just as an athlete either follows the rules or is disqualified and wins no prize.

Know that I pray for you daily and I remain,
Your loving father,
Atticus Aurelius

CHAPTER FIFTY-FIVE

I AM ABOUT TO CONTINUE WHEN the scribe pounds his desk. "She must stop," the man says, lowering his stylus.

The centurion at the table looks at him, a frown between his brows. "On whose authority do you order her to halt?"

"Mine," the scribe says, holding up a glass vial. "I have run out of ink."

The centurion exhales heavily as the scribe slides from his stool and waddles away.

I lick my dry lips and clasp my hands. I have been talking for a long time, but though my voice is raspy, I am not tired.

I lower my gaze, sensing rather than seeing the Roman on the bench to my left. He has not spoken one word during my recitation, and I wonder what he is thinking. Does he now hate me as thoroughly as I have hated him?

The centurion shifts in his chair, glances at the single silent observer, then looks at me. "Do you need water?"

I shake my head. "I'm fine. I am ready to finish my testimony."

The gap-toothed guard at my right cracks a smile. "In a hurry, old woman? The arena will wait."

I close my eyes and exhale a quiet chuff. That ignorant fool has no idea of the depth and breadth of my tale—how it spans years and miles and countries and emperors.

But it is nearly finished. And I am ready to die.

I clear my throat and lift my chin. "You have been patient, and I thank you for that. But I am eager to conclude."

The centurion lifts a finger as the scribe pants back into the room, a cup in his hand. "Thank the gods for fresh ink. This woman will talk forever."

I glance at the big man on the bench, who watches me with a wrinkled brow. Something moves in his eyes, some emotion I can't interpret.

I nod at my judge. "I'm ready."

CHAPTER FIFTY-SIX

IF IN THE FOLLOWING YEARS I had thought only about Yeshua and the Holy One's magnificent provision, I would not be standing before you today. But, in truth, a woman's world is filled with conflicting purposes and desires. I wanted to serve my Lord; I wanted to be a good friend and a compassionate believer. After learning that my particular enemies were beyond my reach, I should have been able to bury my grievances . . . but the emperor Claudius prevented me.

After Herod returned to Tiberias, John Mark's mother and I had a long talk. She was growing older, as was I, and she said she would welcome my help at the inn. So I agreed to join her in managing the business. I was privately delighted that I'd be able to see John Mark, Hadassah, and their children every day.

I had only one request, I told Miryam: if she wanted my help, the inn on Crooked Street could not accept Romans beneath its roof. Since she'd never had anything but Hebrew guests, she agreed.

I spent several wonderful years working at the inn. I was blessed to watch Hadassah develop into maturity and her children grow from my knee to my elbows.

Three years after our agreement, however, John Mark bade me and his mother sit down. He had agreed to join Sha'ul and Barnabas on a missionary journey, he said, and he would be taking Hadassah and the children with him. They planned to go to Antioch, and from there they would proceed to Cyprus and other cities, however the Spirit led.

His mother and I gave the couple our blessing, though our hearts broke as we said good-bye. Miryam and I stood with our arms around each other as the small family loaded a few belongings on a wagon and headed out.

They hadn't been gone a year when we heard troubling news. Apparently John Mark and Sha'ul—as headstrong a man as I've ever met—had some sort of falling out in Pamphylia. John Mark left the work. Afterward, Sha'ul and Barnabas separated, and John Mark went with Barnabas to Cyprus.

Before sailing for Cyprus, though, Hadassah and the children came to Jerusalem for a visit. Miryam and I welcomed them with joy.

One morning, as Miryam remained behind to play with her grandchildren, I took Hadassah shopping. We were walking among the colorful wares, exclaiming over the sheer size of the market-place, when Hadassah gave me a twisted smile.

"I had forgotten how vast Jerusalem is," she said, her gaze drifting over dozens of booths in a single line. "I do believe a woman could find almost anything here."

I squeezed her arm. "An Indian tunic, an Arabian veil, a Persian shawl—ask what you will, Hadassah, and I'll get it for you."

"I don't need anything." Her eyes crinkled at the corners as she pointed to a booth across the aisle. "Though John Mark could use one of those."

I followed her pointing finger, then laughed. "A false tooth?"

"There's too much sand in our bread; it has ruined his teeth." She shook her head. "Not every city is as civilized as Jerusalem."

We walked in silence for a while; then her expression stilled and grew serious. "He's been talking about working for Peter."

"Peter is a good man."

"Peter wants to work . . . in Rome."

I gripped my basket and struggled to control my swirling emotions. "Why would he want to go to such a heathen place?"

"Peter says there are believers in Rome. They need teaching and encouragement."

"Let someone else encourage them. Rome is not a good place, Hadassah; I wouldn't send my worst enemy to such a city."

My worst enemy lives there already.

Hadassah drew a deep breath, then slipped an arm about my shoulder. "I don't know where we'll go. We have to finish the work with Barnabas, and John Mark will continue to seek ADONAI's will. I just wanted you to know what we were thinking."

I embraced her, though I also resolved to pray that my darling Hadassah would never set foot in my enemy's pagan city.

Back in Magdala, when I sold dyed fabrics, a woman once came to my booth and wanted to buy a length of fine wool to make a new tunic for her son's wedding. I told her the price and she smiled. "I can't afford that," she said, "but you will give me the wool as a *mitzvah* commanded by HaShem."

I bit down hard on my lower lip and tried to disguise my annoyance. In truth, I might have given her the wool or sold it at a reduced price, but because she told me to give it as an act of obedience to Adonai, my spirit rebelled.

It is pleasant to do a good deed when the urge springs from the heart. It is far less agreeable to do good because you've been commanded to do so.

I looked at the woman and her open hands. "Giving my fabric away is not a mitzvah; it is bad business. Now go away and don't bother me again."

Did I feel guilty? I might have, but later I saw her offer a fistful of coins to the merchant at the salter's booth. If she had money for fish, I reasoned, she had money for wool.

In the same way, my heart might have softened toward Atticus Aurelius, but life intervened.

⋅⟡⋅

One afternoon a young couple came to the inn on Crooked Street. They had been among those evicted from Rome and were on their way to Corinth, where they hoped to establish themselves as tentmakers.

We had listened to stories of the eviction with disbelief and sorrow. According to the rumors, Claudius Caesar, who had initially treated our people with respect, began to listen to those who thought us a seditious race. If the emperor had stopped with merely thinking us peculiar, we would be no worse off than usual, but apparently someone had alarmed Claudius with a story about a riot instigated by Hebrew followers of one called "Chrestus." Worried by these inflammatory stories, the emperor ordered all Hebrews out of Rome. Every descendant of Avraham had to abandon his house and business, gather what he could, and move his family elsewhere.

In Jerusalem, Miryam and I anxiously waited for news of John Mark and Hadassah, who had been living in Rome. We sat to eat with Aquila and Priscilla, but I knew Miryam and I were both wishing we were sitting across from our loved ones instead.

We had been making pleasant conversation when Aquila suddenly lowered his cup and gripped the edge of the table. As a visible quiver ran through the man, I braced myself for bad news.

"I don't know how to say this," Aquila said. "But I did not come to Jerusalem only to worship at the Temple. I also bring word from John Mark."

Miryam recoiled from his troubled eyes and tried on a trembling smile. "Don't tell me he's gone on to Cyprus. I knew he wouldn't come here, so I'm not too disappointed—"

"He is with Peter in Alexandria. Uriah and Abel are with him as well."

"And Hadassah?" I spoke calmly but with that odd sense of detachment that descends with the awareness of impending disaster.

He looked at me and blinked hard. "Hadassah is dead."

For a moment color ran out of the world and the sounds of the servants faded. I looked at Aquila through a face as frozen as those engraved on Herod's palace walls. Miryam clutched my hand.

I didn't move as Aquila told the story. Apparently a cohort of legionnaires had been sent to drive the last Hebrews from the quarter of the city where they lived. John Mark and Hadassah had not left their house because Hadassah was in labor, struggling to give birth to their third child. When the soldiers approached, John Mark ran out and tried to explain, but in the noise and confusion he couldn't find the centurion in charge.

As he ran down the road, searching for the officer, one of the legionnaires spied young Uriah in a window. To force the boy out of the house, the soldier shot a flaming arrow onto the thatched roof. Though Uriah was able to rescue his brother from the burning building, he was not able to reach his mother. By the time John Mark returned, Hadassah and the baby had died.

Miryam covered her face and sobbed as Aquila's voice dissolved in a thready whisper, but my sense of loss went beyond tears. The old pain in my heart, which had been covered over by my new life, became an aching, fiery gnawing.

I stared at the floor where I had knelt so many times in prayer. "Did he ever find him?" I asked, my voice odd and hollow in my own ears.

Aquila's brow furrowed. "Who?"

"The centurion. Did John Mark ever find the man?"

Our guest exhaled a heavy breath. "Yes, but too late. The centurion carried Hadassah out of the house." He rubbed a hand over his beard, then shook his head. "He was a big man, too, and easy to spot—a Roman called Atticus Aurelius."

⊰⊱═◉═⊰⊱

After leaving the Temple, instead of turning down the familiar alley that would take me to Crooked Street, I lifted my chin and strode toward the gates of the Fortress Antonia.

I had come to a decision. No longer would I let my grievances fester; I would deal with them. Rome prided itself on discipline and justice, so I would lodge a complaint and be sure it was sent to someone with the authority to crush a centurion.

I only needed to know how to proceed.

I crossed the garrison's dusty courtyard and walked into a small chamber built into the gate. A pair of guards sat around a game of some sort, and one of them looked up and frowned when he saw me. "What do you need, woman? You shouldn't be here."

Despite his rudeness, I forced a smile. "I wanted to inquire about a Roman centurion known as Atticus Aurelius. I believe he serves in Rome."

A younger man at the back of the room turned. He shot me a sideward look that I didn't like and couldn't read; then he grinned. "I know Atticus Aurelius."

My breath caught in my lungs. "You . . . know this man?"

The young fellow waited until the gruff guard went back to his game, then walked toward me and offered a conspiratorial smile. "He's my father."

I stiffened. A Roman soldier . . . with a son? I shouldn't have been surprised. After all, Romans like their women, and children are a natural result of such liking. I took pains to keep my expression smooth and calm. "Is he here, by chance? in Jerusalem?"

The young man laughed. "He's in Rome." The soldier leaned against the wall and narrowed his eyes as he smiled. "How do you know him?"

"We've never met. But I have heard of his . . . exploits." I held up my hand when I realized I was babbling. "Will you give me a moment? I must think about what to do."

I turned and pulled my veil forward to shield my face from the young man's observant eyes. How should I handle this? How could I file a formal complaint with the man's son? If I wrote a letter, he'd destroy it. If I told him what his father had done, he'd deny the truth. If I asked to speak to his superior officer . . . no. The gruff men sitting on the bench had not granted me even a token measure of respect.

Nothing to do, then, but take my leave. For the present.

I turned and nodded at the young man. "Thank you for your help, but it's not likely I'll be going to Rome anytime soon."

"Is there anything I can do for you?" The young legionnaire tilted his head. "Are you in need of protection? some kind of assistance?"

Again I smiled. "Thank you, no. I wanted to speak with the centurion about a matter from the past. But what's done is done."

Before he could quiz me further, I pulled my veil tight beneath my chin and slipped into the street.

Chapter Fifty-seven

On the first day of the week, I stood with John Mark's mother on the women's side of the synagogue and lifted my voice in a *tehillim* of praise. Even though a shadow of grief hung over us, we were comforted in the presence of other believers.

I nudged Miryam with my elbow as a young soldier edged into the synagogue and stood at the back of the men's section. "Do you know that one?"

She peered over her shoulder, then shook her head. "Not his name, but he comes almost every week. A handsome youth, don't you think?"

I bit my lip, unable to believe my eyes. I hadn't been able to forget meeting the son of Atticus Aurelius; the knowledge of his existence had been gnawing at the edges of my contentment ever since I returned from the Fortress Antonia.

Why did Atticus Aurelius get to enjoy a child after stealing two sons from me? How could the Holy One allow the offspring of a brutal legionnaire to attain maturity while my Binyamin lies in his tomb?

These worrisome thoughts chased themselves through my mind as we sat to hear from James, Yeshua's brother.

He unfurled a scroll and began to tell us a story from the writings of Samuel. "Scripture tells us," James said, "that David was Isra'el's best king, the only one who truly followed God. Though he was a great leader, he took another man's wife, a woman called Bathsheba, and she conceived a child. In order to hide his sin, David sent her husband to the front lines of battle, where he met his death.

"Nathan the prophet called David to account for his sin, and the king paid a steep price—the baby born to Bathsheba died soon after birth."

I looked down at my hands and suppressed the urge to roll my eyes. David had lost a baby . . . yes, a tough loss, but I had lost an entire family, not due to my sin but someone else's! Though it felt blasphemous to think so, I was beginning to believe God owed me the freedom to commit a sin or two.

"Most people think the story ends there," James continued, "but years passed and Absalom, one of David's sons, rebelled against his father. He employed runners to go before his chariot and praise him to the skies; he sat in the city gate and prejudiced people against his father the king.

"When Absalom was certain of his influence, he went to Hebron and established a throne there. When the people began to support him, David and his loyal followers had to flee for their lives. One man remained in Jerusalem, however—David's friend Ahithophel. He had been one of the king's most trusted counselors.

"Grateful for the older man's experience, Absalom asked David's counselor for advice. Ahithophel told him to go to the royal palace and sleep with David's concubines on the roof of the house . . . so all Isra'el would see what Absalom was doing.

"Why would he advise this?" James let the question echo as his gaze roved over us. "Because Ahithophel had a son named Eliam, and Eliam had a daughter named Bathsheba. Ahithophel had burned with fury for years, knowing his granddaughter had been publicly shamed and her husband murdered. But what could he do against a powerful king? Only one thing: wait for the proper time to strike."

As a murmur rustled through the room, James lifted his hand for emphasis. "You have heard that revenge is a dish best served cold, but Yeshua told us to forgive our enemies."

The Lord's brother continued to speak, but the subject of his story flooded my mind. Like Ahithophel, I had been waiting for a proper time to strike at the Romans who destroyed my family. Gaius Cabilenus was beyond my reach and Atticus Aurelius was in Rome, but I could exorcise the emotions in my festering heart if I could punish the man who had destroyed my family.

Like Ahithophel, I might not be able to reach the mighty man, but I could reach his son.

⟡═◉═⟡

That afternoon I paced in the hall of the inn and considered my options. After our morning worship, I had made subtle inquiries and discovered the young legionnaire's name: Quintus. He had been a soldier for six years, a talkative woman told me, so he had to be about twenty-four years old.

He'd been born the year my son died.

God might forgive the unfortunate timing of his birth, but I couldn't.

Forgiveness is a lovely idea . . . until you have an offense to forgive. Though the Spirit of Christ urged me to move on, the spirit of woundedness paralyzed me. Justice had not been achieved. No one had acted to avenge my family. Herod wouldn't help, Yeshua had ignored politics, and no one in Jerusalem wanted to remember the awful things that had happened when Pilate governed Judea. I might have been able to release those past sorrows until a heavy Roman arm had snatched Hadassah from me too.

If I had been braver, if I had done something to avenge Yaakov, Rachel, Avram, and Binyamin, would HaShem have spared Hadassah? I didn't know, but her loss had awakened the slumbering voices of my loved ones. They haunted my dreams, reminding me that the family tomb outside Magdala had been filled far too soon.

What was I to do? The Law commanded me to avenge my loved ones; Yeshua had told me to submit to my enemies. I wanted to obey my rabboni, but how would obedience ease my anger and grief and frustration?

If I didn't act, how was I to find peace?

Peace, I realized, would come at a price.

I would have to strike the son to wound the father.

To take my revenge.

Why should it matter that Quintus was winsome and a believer? My Avram had been handsome and bright; my husband had been a devoted son of Avraham. Rachel had died in the full flower of woman-hood; her baby had been wanted and loved. And my precious Binyamin . . . I had cherished him even more passionately because he needed me more than the others.

I see the look in your eye; I know you think me hard-hearted. Is it surprising to find such an emotion in the breast of one who follows Yeshua? Perhaps.

My rabboni told us to love our enemies, but I could not love a man I could not forgive.

So Quintus Aurelius would have to die.

Chapter Fifty-eight

Once I decided to strike the Roman's son, relief settled over my shoulders like a warm woolen cloak. My life no longer mattered; I lived for vengeance and knew what it would cost.

Throughout the following week I went about my work and considered the best way to accomplish my goal. I was no warrior; at sixty-three I lacked the strength to accomplish murder. Yet Jerusalem was a sprawling city, and the Romans had not managed to eradicate every trace of lawlessness. In certain quarters I knew I could find zealots who hated the occupiers; in other areas I might find criminals who could be persuaded to attack a pair of Romans on their nightly patrol.

Arranging the murder would be easy. But how would Atticus feel upon receiving word that his son had been killed? He would mourn, of course, but he wouldn't receive the correspondence for weeks, perhaps months, depending upon the speed of whatever sailing vessel or caravan carried the news. The blow, though severe, would be muted by time and distance. Atticus Aurelius would not hold his son's broken body in his hands as I had held Avram, he would not feel his son's precious blood spilling over his fingers.

More to the point, he would not realize his own rash actions had birthed the fatal blow. The report would say that Quintus had been attacked by brigands or enemies of Rome, so the centurion would have no idea that he'd paid an installment on the debt he had assumed one hot night in Magdala.

My initial plan was good, but too indirect. I needed something more personal, more involving.

I needed Atticus Aurelius to come to Jerusalem.

⟡

The next week, as our assembly of believers dispersed, I tugged on the young Roman's sleeve. He turned, surprise on his face, and smiled when he saw me standing beside John Mark's mother. "A blessed morning to you! Christ is risen!"

I would not have been more startled to hear Greek words from the mouth of a toad. Miryam, however, summoned the grace for a proper reply: "Christ is risen indeed."

I tucked my hands into my sleeves and bowed my head. "We were hoping, sir, that you would come to dinner. Several of the others are joining us for a meal."

Miryam shot me a look of amazement, then smiled. "At my inn," she added. "The one on Crooked Street."

"I know the place." Something that might have been a smile flitted into his dark eyes, but I couldn't be sure. "I'd be delighted."

"Bring a friend, if you like," Miryam said. "We'll be eating at about the sixth hour."

I could not look at him again but managed to echo, "By all means, bring a friend." What was one more detestable Roman at the table?

Miryam nudged me as we walked away. "What happened to your rule?"

"What rule?"

"You said we should never have Romans at the inn, so I never dreamed you'd invite —"

"Times are changing, Miryam." I led her through the street without haste, but with an urgent purpose.

⋆⟶☰⟵⋆

Miryam was thrilled and honored when Quintus Aurelius not only came for dinner, but presented her with a freshly filled wineskin.

Atwitter with delight, she led him to a place of honor in the center of the room. I watched in silent horror as the son of my dearest enemy reclined on a couch and ate with the elders of the congregation at Jerusalem. We women wandered in and out, refilling goblets and replenishing plates. Only when our guests had finished did I find the courage to ask the question that had lingered on my lips all afternoon. "Tell us, Quintus, about your father. He is stationed in Rome, is he not?"

His youthful face brightened. "Indeed he is. And I must know, Miryam—how do you know his name?"

I smiled. "Your father makes an impression wherever he travels. His century once came through my village in Galilee—a place called Magdala."

I looked to see if he had caught the meaning hidden in my words, but Quintus's expression remained pleasant. "My father's century traveled all over Galilee. Sometimes I think there's not a foot of Judean soil my father's foot has not trampled."

I gritted my teeth as I lifted the pitcher. "More wine?"

"Please."

"Does your father ever come to Jerusalem?" I asked, insinuating a friendly note into my voice as I splashed liquid into his cup. "Surely a centurion is free to travel as he pleases."

Quintus lifted his hand. "That's enough, thank you. Actually, Father rarely travels without his men. I'm not likely to see him anytime soon."

"Do *you* hope to make the army a career?"

"If I can. Though I have to admit, lately I've been wondering how it's possible for a follower of Yeshua to belong to the emperor's army." He shot a look at James, who reclined on the couch next to him. "My father always said we owe one sort of allegiance to Caesar and another sort to God. But I've never been sure how to reconcile those two."

James smiled. "Your father is right, but you might consider something else as well. Our law, which was fulfilled by Yeshua, tells us not to *murder*. Killing is not always murder. When repentant soldiers came to Yochanan the Immerser, he told them to turn from their sin, but he did not tell them to leave the army. When centurions came to Yeshua, he healed their diseases without telling them to quit their occupation—which he would not have hesitated to do, for he frequently admonished people to stop sinning."

Quintus swallowed hard. "So it is right, then, for me to use my sword in the defense of Rome?"

James tugged at his beard. "Defense may be the best use of a sword. Yeshua told his disciples they might bring swords for their journey to aid in their defense. Then again——" his eyes darkened with emotion——"Yeshua did not strike at those who arrested him in the garden, and he freely laid down his life for all mankind. Stephen did not defend himself; nor did James, the brother of John; nor did

the Immerser. Yeshua said we should love our enemies and turn the
other cheek to those who would strike us."

The leader of the Jerusalem congregation took a deep breath and
adjusted his smile. "I think, young Quintus, that the Holy Spirit will
direct you when such a time comes. Listen to that still, small voice
and you will not fail to honor the Lord."

I felt James's gaze settle on me, but I did not meet his eyes. I had
heard such comments before; I knew what Yeshua would have me
do. But knowing and doing are different things, and I had set my
heart on achieving justice.

As a child, my father would not allow me to play with the Passover lamb lest I become attached. The holiness of our just God
demanded sacrifice, which we had to give without hesitation.

So I would not open my heart to Quintus Aurelius.

⊰⊱═◉═⊰⊱

Quintus began to appear regularly at our synagogue and the inn
where so many believers gathered. He took so naturally to our conversations that one day James joked that Quintus must have been
born an Israelite. Everyone around the table thought this terribly
funny—everyone but me and Quintus, whose jovial expression
faded and became somber.

The suggestion lodged in my brain, however, and I found myself
studying Quintus's face. He *did* bear a resemblance to some men of
Isra'el I had known—I saw it in the curve of his nose and the slight
stretch of his dark eyes—yet the deliberate curling of his short hair
and his clean-shaven jaw overruled those features. The young man
was as tall as James and wide-shouldered, but that effect could have
come from his soldier's red toga, which he wore in all public places.

Miryam teased the young man and welcomed him with open

arms. She confided to me that Quintus was a blessing from the Holy One, for he had entered her life when she missed her son most. We heard only occasionally from John Mark, who was working with Peter.

"He is writing," Miryam told us after one dinner, scarcely able to hide the pride in her shining eyes. "John Mark is writing an account of Yeshua's life."

James nodded. "These things should be written down. We who are eyewitnesses should not tarry because . . . well . . ."

He didn't have to finish his thought. No one had to remind us that we wouldn't live forever.

I cleared my throat. "John Mark wasn't with Yeshua at the beginning. So how can he——?"

"Simon Peter," Miryam answered. "Peter is telling him all the things Yeshua said and did, and Mark is translating them into Greek."

"How I wish I remembered," Quintus said. He looked up, his cheeks flaming as if he hadn't meant to enter the conversation. "My father met Yeshua once. I was born deaf, you see, and my father took me to see the healer. He told me that Yeshua touched my ears, then held me up and said the purposes of God would be revealed in me." A fleeting look of discomfort crossed his face. "I've often wondered what he meant."

No one spoke as we absorbed the news. We had never doubted Quintus's faith, but I doubt any of us had imagined that his father might have met Yeshua. Still, hundreds of people had encountered our rabboni and had gone away without believing. . . .

"The purposes of God are revealed in all of us." James's eyes caught and held those of the young Roman. "But how much better it is when we bring him glory instead of shame. You do your father credit, Quintus."

The men kept talking, but John Mark's mother turned and placed her hand on my arm. "You had a baby born deaf, didn't you?"

I picked up an empty platter. "We have more fruit. Would anyone like something else to eat?"

⋄⊹═◎═⊹⋄

One day slid seamlessly into the next; one festival merged with another. We moved from Yom Teruah to Yom Kippur and prepared to reconcile ourselves to relatives and friends we had wronged in the past year.

I confessed petty annoyances to Miryam and Rhoda, her servant, but the Holy One, blessed be he, did not send anyone to confess the wrongs done to me.

We were preparing to celebrate Sukkot, the Feast of Tabernacles, when I received the news for which I'd been praying: Atticus Aurelius would be among the hundreds of pilgrims crowding Jerusalem for the festival. Quintus came to the inn and eagerly shared his announcement, expecting us to rejoice with him.

I welcomed the news, but hearing it from Quintus brought me no joy. I stood on the threshold, saw the light in his eyes, and heard my heart break—a small, distinctive sound, like the snapping of a twig.

Quintus must have seen sorrow enter my gaze. "Miryam," he asked, his eyes alive with calculation, "have I done something to offend you? I've searched my conscience, but I can't see what I've done."

I held up my hand and stepped back. "I have to go."

"Miryam, please." He caught my wrist and held it. "You are so . . . so *motherly* with the others; your love spills out on them. Why are you so distant with me?"

"Release me, please." My heart was squeezed so tight I could scarcely draw breath to speak. "I have work to do."

"Miryam!"

I stepped into the cool shadows of the hallway and closed the door, then leaned against it, my palm pressed to the rough wood. On the other side, I heard shuffling steps, then a muffled oath as Quintus kicked the courtyard gate.

I had not planned to torture this boy; I bore him no ill will. If not for my shredded heart, I might have loved him almost as much as I loved John Mark and Hadassah.

But I had vowed to obtain justice for my family, and I would honor my vow. That boy in the courtyard, that winsome young man, would pay for his father's sin just as David's son had paid for his father's sin with Bathsheba.

After the blow had been struck, I would go to the Roman fortress and confess my part in his murder. Because I was not a Roman citizen, they would probably execute me without a trial. They might force me to stand before the man I'd wronged.

If so . . . all the better. Atticus Aurelius deserved to know what he'd done.

I might enter eternity with a stain on my conscience, but I had been stained worse than this when I met Yeshua. He'd forgiven me and delivered me from the darkness of my sin.

I would beg him to forgive me again.

CHAPTER FIFTY-NINE

WHEN A WOMAN HAS MURDER on her mind, nearly every man she meets appears capable of the deed.

During the Feast of Tabernacles, amid the rejoicing of Jerusalem, I walked into the poorer parts of the city and wended my way through the temporary booths erected along the narrow, winding streets. I brought my veil to my face and peered over the edge at families who devoutly celebrated the festival while others reclined on mats and drank themselves into a stupor.

I went out alone, not wanting to endanger or involve any of my brothers or sisters. In truth, I feared for my life with every step. Hard men loitered in this part of the city, Gentiles and Hebrews who cared nothing for the virtue of women or the holiness of HaShem.

If I had met with misfortune and been murdered in the street, my friends would have assumed I'd gone to that part of town in search of a lost soul.

They would have been right.

A notion had occurred to me a few weeks before: I *knew* a murdering thief; everyone in Jerusalem did. I had never personally met him, but his name had been branded into my brain when Pilate had asked what prisoner he should release in honor of the Passover. Instead of asking for Yeshua, the innocent Lamb of God, the crowd, bribed by the religious authorities, had demanded the prisoner Barabbas.

Barabbas—convicted murderer, thief, conspirator—had been released to walk free while Yeshua died in shame. I had not heard much about Barabbas since my rabboni's death, but if he still lived in Jerusalem, I knew I'd find him in this decrepit quarter.

Keeping my veil tight around my face, I made a few discreet inquiries and was finally directed to a spot where four mud-brick houses slumped into ruin. No booths lined the road at the end of that decaying street; no one celebrated in those grim shadows.

I knocked on a grime-coated door and was admitted by a woman with loose hair and a black eye—the sort of companion I'd expect to keep company with a murderer.

Barabbas reclined on a soiled mattress inside the drab room, his eyes closed, one hand across his bare chest. A huge belly bulged over the belt at his loincloth; a bowl of foul-smelling stew lay on the floor beside him.

A goat in the corner lifted its head as I approached, then went back to chewing its feed.

I stood by the man for a long moment, then cleared my throat. When he didn't respond, I nudged his leg with the toe of my sandal.

His eyes flickered open.

Barabbas had been a young man when Pilate released him. He should still have been in the prime of his life, but the man on the mattress had forfeited the strength of his youth. Something brutal lay about his mouth; something feral gleamed in the deep-set eyes that glared at me. "Who are you, woman, and why do you disturb my nap?"

I pulled a pouch of silver coins from my belt and dropped it by his side. "I have a favor to ask."

He studied the bag, then lifted it and felt its heft. "Most people make me work harder for their money."

"You will work—for that bag and another twice its size. But you cannot tell the authorities what I'm asking you to do."

His eyes narrowed and he pushed himself up. "What do you want?"

I tucked my hands into the safety of my sleeves. "There is a Roman legionnaire called Quintus Aurelius stationed at the Fortress Antonia. His father, Atticus Aurelius, has joined him for the festival of Sukkot. What I ask is this: wait until the two are together, then stop them in the guise of a robbery. Take their money if you wish, but stab them both. Kill the younger man; leave the older man to bleed."

Barabbas gaped at me like a fellow faced with a hard sum in figures. "Which of them do you really want dead? Let me lie in wait for that one and kill him when he is alone."

"I want both of them to feel the bite of your blade. If possible, I want the older man to watch his son die."

Barabbas's eyes widened; then he tilted his head as his mouth twisted in a grudging smile. "And they say women are the weaker sex. You surprise me."

"I don't expect you to understand."

"I don't care about understanding." He scratched the grizzled beard at his chin and regarded the purse in his hand. "Killing a Roman soldier won't be easy."

"No, it won't. The older man is big, but you'll have the advantage of surprise. You can bring a companion if you like—bring ten men. I don't care. Just do what I ask."

Outside, his woman moved past the window, her shadow rippling over Barabbas like water over a sunken rock. He showed no more expression than a rock, either, as he considered my request.

Finally he looked up. "You want I should tell you when it's done?"

"You won't have to—I'll hear about it. When I do, I'll deliver the rest of the money. Do we have an agreement?"

His dissipated face showed no more than mild interest, but his eyes gleamed in their shadowy caves. "I can keep anything I take from the Romans?"

I sighed. "You wouldn't tell me if you took a pound of gold. I don't care—take it all."

"I never cared for those Roman pigs." He brought the bag of coins to his lips, kissed it, then settled back on his mattress. "I'll find the ones you want and I'll do as you asked. Then I expect the rest of my payment, or I'll find you and kill you, too."

Though I had no fear of him—I expected to be in Roman custody long before the thug could hurt me—his threat sent a chill up the ladder of my spine.

But I lifted my chin and met his glittering gaze head-on. "Done."

⊰⊷⊜⊶⊱

The bruised and swollen sky burst into rain before I reached the inn. A rising wind whooshed past me, lifting the veil from my shoulders and whipping my tunic around my legs. I ran through the deluge and wondered how much longer I'd be able to consider the inn my home. A week? Two days?

The knowledge of what I had done turned and twisted within

me as I hurried through the streets. How easy to bribe certain men to kill. With no concern for others, they cared only for gold and silver and what it could buy. But I cared about more than pleasure. I cared about justice and vengeance and the satisfaction of debts.

I had just come through the courtyard gate and our Sukkot shelter when Rhoda strode toward me, her eyes alight. "You have a visitor," she said, pulling my wet veil from my head. "Someone who has ventured out into the storm to see you and the other Miryam."

I brushed water from my tunic and wondered if the stench of Barabbas's house remained on my clothing. "Someone from the assembly?"

Rhoda's entire face spread into an approving smile. "Young Quintus."

I turned away with a feeling of unease, my hand rising to my stomach. "Give him my regrets, will you? I'm not feeling well."

"But he has a gift for you, and he's braved the rain—"

I turned toward my small chamber but hadn't taken two steps before Miryam and Quintus appeared in the hall.

"Oh, good, here she is." Miriam caught my sleeve. "I was hoping we'd catch you."

"I'm not feeling well—"

"That's all right; I can't stay." The young man smiled, then thrust a fabric-covered bundle toward each of us. "I hope you like them. I thought with the change in the weather, you might be able to use something that repels water."

My fingers felt paralyzed, but Miryam had no trouble opening her package. Within a moment the wrapping fell away, and she shook out a beautiful square of lightweight gray wool. I had to admit it was a good piece of material.

"Yours is like it, but blue." Quintus focused on the unopened bundle in my hands. "I've noticed you favor that color."

I gave him a wintry smile. "You shouldn't have bothered."

"It's the least I can do for women who feed me almost every week. I've told my father about you. He can't wait to meet—"

Abruptly, I said I needed to lie down.

CHAPTER SIXTY

ATTICUS LEANED BACK ON HIS couch, lifted his goblet, and smiled at Quintus across the rim.

His host, Longinus Priscus, chuckled at this sign of his guest's pleasure. "Is the wine not delicious, my friend? I told you Jerusalem could rival Rome's sensory delights."

"The wine is good," Atticus admitted after taking a sip. "And I have always enjoyed the city."

"And your son? He finds Jerusalem to his liking?"

"I do." Quintus lifted his bronze cup. "I find the place delightful, though I am often confused by the Jews."

"Who isn't? The Jews are an odd lot indeed." The merchant set his cup on the table, then picked up a pastry and popped it into his mouth. "Have you seen the ragtag collections of tents on the streets and rooftops? They stay in those things for a week, commanded to live outdoors by their God. They actually pretend to enjoy such lunacy!"

Atticus caught his son's eye and smiled. "I don't understand the reasons behind the tents, but they do seem to take pleasure in them. And I can't say their traditions are any odder than some of ours."

The merchant clapped his fingertips to his pursed lips and widened his eyes. "Oh, dear centurion, don't let anyone hear you speak such heresy! If the idea is Roman, it has to be brilliant. We are, after all, the masters of the world."

Atticus smiled, not certain if his host meant to be honest or sarcastic. In either case, better to say nothing than to err at a rich man's table.

He reached for a sliver of roasted chicken and dropped it into his mouth. Longinus might be trying, but he did set a good table. Quintus would undoubtedly find this a better meal than the frumentum he would have had back at the garrison.

"Now—" Atticus pushed himself up on one elbow—"let's talk about the business that brings us together, shall we? You are concerned about one of your shipments."

"Indeed I am." The merchant's fat face melted into a buttery smile. "But I am sure you can alleviate those concerns. I have gathered a great collection of delicacies, and I must transport them from Jerusalem to Rome. They will sail from the port of Sebastos, of course, and I will be at the mercy of the gods while we are at sea. I need your help, my dear centurion, to be sure my shipment and I travel safely from Jerusalem to Caesarea."

Atticus exchanged a subtle look of amusement with Quinn, then smoothed his face into confident lines. "The highway to Caesarea is safe. It is regularly patrolled by our legionnaires."

"Regular patrols will not suffice." The merchant's face screwed into the look of a petulant child. "I must have extra protection, and I am willing to pay for it."

"What, may I ask, are you transporting?"

Longinus glanced left and right, then lowered his voice. "Jewels and pearls, purple cloth, silks and linens, scented woods, ivory, cinnamon, incense, wine, oil—"

"Those goods, while valuable, are not unusual."

"—and slaves." The merchant lifted a fat finger. "Nearly a dozen of the finest artisans I could procure. The slaves, you see, are why I need an extra guard. I must not only take care to be sure I am not robbed, but the slaves must not be allowed to run away."

Atticus drew in his breath, then picked up his goblet and slowly swirled the wine at the bottom of the cup. He had little interest in slaves, but Longinus was a Roman citizen who deserved to have his property protected.

"My friend," he said, offering the merchant a smile, "while I cannot promise an entire century, I can promise this: when my visit in Jerusalem has concluded, I will personally escort your caravan to Caesarea. If the ship is loaded in a timely manner, I may be able to travel with you all the way to Rome—"

"The gods be praised!" Longinus sat up so suddenly that the bulk of his toga slipped from his shoulder, but he scarcely noticed as he lifted a pitcher. "Let me pour you more wine to celebrate our agreement."

Atticus blew out his cheeks, then looked across the table at his grinning son. Before lifting his cup to be refilled as well, Quinn mouthed a message to his father: *Now you've done it.*

Indeed he had. If Longinus Priscus didn't talk Atticus to death tonight, he would surely do it before they reached Rome.

⌁⌁⌁◉⌁⌁⌁

Night had spread her velvet robe over the ancient city by the time Atticus and Quintus walked back to the Fortress Antonia. With a

shiver of vivid recollection, Atticus found himself walking on the ancient street leading from Herod's palace to the garrison. How many
years had it been since he last crossed these flagstones? He would
have stopped to count, but both he and Quinn were feeling sluggish
from the merchant's rich food and wine.

Quinn, Atticus noted, had handled himself admirably in what
could have been an awkward social situation. An officer in the
Roman army ought not to take bribes, but a centurion could do a
reasonable favor for a citizen without violating his conscience.

Atticus tossed a grin at his son. "What did you think of my friend
Longinus?"

Quinn laughed. "He's an odd one. He sits in his house and mocks
the Jewish people, but his words tell me he hasn't spent much time
in their company."

"You're right. He's content to ridicule and fleece them, but I
believe he's actually terrified of what he doesn't understand. That's
the real reason he wants a guard."

They stopped talking long enough to proceed single file through a
noisy row of booths. Quinn pointed to a dark and narrow alley. "This
way's clear."

Atticus followed. He turned to his son, about to ask another question, but a sudden stench tightened his nerves—the sharp smell of
terrified sweat. He turned, but before he could call out a warning,
brigands leapt from the shadows. Atticus's mind went blank with
shock; only fools would attack Roman soldiers within a few yards of
the fortress.

He counted at least a half-dozen men, though in the confusion he
could scarcely keep track of their shadowy forms. A silver dagger
flew at him from the right; he pulled his sword and lopped off a
man's hand without thinking. He thought he called Quinn's name,

but he could hear nothing specific through the haze of violence that enveloped them. The air went thick with curses and knots of men who pushed and shoved, punched and stumbled in their attempt to—what?

He thought of the purse tucked inside his belt. Did they want his money? If so, Jerusalem's bandits had fallen to a new level of thick-headedness. You didn't have to kill a man to take his purse; you only had to hold a knife to his throat.

The alley rang with the clash of iron on iron. Atticus whirled to see Quinn's sword knock a dagger from an opponent's hand. Another fiend launched himself at Quinn's back, pointing his blade toward the vulnerable spot beneath a soldier's arm yet above the leather bands of armor—

"Quintus!"

His son's name ended in a gurgle as a hand closed around Atticus's throat. He brought his wrists up between his attacker's arms and knocked the man away; then he spun and elbowed his assailant in the face. The man flew back and landed so heavily that Atticus heard bones crackle like dry twigs.

He turned. Quinn faced a single opponent, his sword drawn and ready. Both men seemed to swell, sizing each other up. Then the bearded assailant lunged forward. Quinn thrust with his sword in what would have been a fatal hit if he hadn't hesitated at the last instant.

Atticus stared in horror as the smaller man's dagger slipped between the bands of Quinn's armor and penetrated flesh. For an instant the two of them stood motionless, the attacker grinning like a maniacal fiend.

Atticus drew back his sword and struck with all the passion in his anguished heart. His ears registered the hollow thump of the man's head falling to the flagstones, but his thoughts centered on Quinn.

His son's eyelids had closed, but as Atticus reached for the dagger, Quinn squinted at him through one eye. "I didn't want to kill him—"

"Don't talk, Son."

Atticus caught him as Quinn's knees buckled. All caution and reason fled as the centurion grappled with his inert son and hoarsely called for help.

CHAPTER SIXTY-ONE

SCRIPTURE TELLS US THAT AFTER Ahithophel gave Absalom advice on how to defeat David, the old man saddled his donkey, went home, set his affairs in order, and hanged himself.

I had no donkey to saddle, and Jerusalem had become my home. To set my affairs in order, I wrote a long letter thanking Miryam for her many kindnesses and asking her to distribute my few possessions. I placed the letter beneath my mattress and waited to hear that my plan had succeeded.

I would not hang myself. At the right time I would turn myself over to the Romans, because Atticus Aurelius had to know the reason he'd been attacked. He had to know that he had paid for his sin, as I would pay for mine.

I was scrubbing the floor in the upstairs room when news of the assault reached us. I heard Miryam shriek and Rhoda wail; by the time I reached the bottom of the stairs, the Galilean guest who had brought the news was smiling at the dire effects of his report.

I comforted my grief-stricken friends and asked the Nazarene to repeat himself. After composing his face into serious lines, he told me that three days earlier, the infamous Barabbas and a gang of brigands had set upon two Roman legionnaires, one a centurion. Barabbas lost his head in the struggle, and the younger man, Quintus Aurelius, suffered a fatal wound. "The centurion," he finished, "has gone back to Rome."

Miryam wept aloud, rubbing her arms as she rocked back and forth. I embraced her and Rhoda, then retired to my room, where I sat on the edge of my bed and shivered as a skein of remorse unwound in my chest.

What had I done?

Until that moment, revenge had been an idea that fluttered ahead of my fingertips, always out of reach. Even when I'd gone to see Barabbas, something in me couldn't believe that the fool on that grimy mattress would actually complete the task I'd given him.

But he had. My idea had become a deed, and my deed a sin I would carry for the rest of my life.

Atticus Aurelius would suffer. He would never see a curly haired youth without thinking of his lost son; he would never don his uniform without thinking of the soldier who had died in his arms.

He would suffer . . . and so would I.

I had thought the act of retribution would bring me satisfaction, that revenge would restore order to my world, but Barabbas's violence only made my heart knot in sorrow. I was not sorry Barabbas had died—he deserved his fate. And Atticus the Roman had murdered my family, so he deserved to suffer the worst grief life could offer.

But Quinn . . . the lamb I had kept at arm's length had done nothing to warrant the evil I'd instigated.

Instead of satisfaction, loneliness seeped through my chamber like a fog. The burning rock in the pit of my belly wasn't going anywhere, so I needed to be away from this blessed place.

I stood and pulled the square of blue wool, Quintus's gift, from the peg on the wall and settled it over my hair. Like the scapegoat who carried our sins into the wilderness at Yom Kippur, I would wear it to the fort as a symbol of my guilt.

I paused at the inn's threshold and looked behind me one last time. My hand trembled as I latched the gate, but I could not weep.

Later, the others would weep for me. They would ask why I had done this terrible thing; they would not understand.

Let them remember the prophet Jeremiah's words: "The human heart is most deceitful and desperately wicked. Who really knows how bad it is?"

God knows. And so do I.

In that moment, I finally grasped the truth: Yeshua had not come to save us from the Romans but from our sinful selves.

⟡

The grizzled guard at the Fortress Antonia blinked when I said I wanted to confess. "Confess what, woman?"

"Murder."

He glanced at his companion, who smirked at me. "And whose murder would you be confessing to?"

"Quintus Aurelius. I hired the assassin Barabbas to attack him and the centurion."

The older man's mouth curled and rolled like he wanted to spit. The younger man sank to a stool.

"It's all right." I folded my hands at my waist so they could see

I carried no weapon and meant no further harm. "I'll sit on this bench and wait until you decide what should be done with me."

The grizzled guard chewed a stalk of straw, but the younger soldier ran out of the room, his sandals slapping the pavement as he rushed away.

I lowered my gaze as a single drop of sweat traced the course of my spine. Would they execute me immediately? I wasn't sure how the Romans killed women. I'd never seen them crucify a woman, but one never knew what to expect with these people. . . .

I didn't want to die in front of my friends. Bad enough that they would hear what I'd done. I didn't want them to weep for me as they had wept for Yeshua and James and Stephen. Those men had been blameless; I was guilty.

Let them run me through with a sword and toss my body into a pauper's grave. I deserved nothing better.

The younger soldier returned, breathless and wide-eyed. "She's to be taken to Caesarea," he told the other. "Then to Rome."

I took a wincing breath. "Rome?"

"That's where he's gone." The older soldier fixed me in a steely-eyed stare. "You don't deserve a trial, but Atticus Aurelius has the right to confront you before you die. So as a favor to the centurion, we're sending you to him."

CHAPTER SIXTY-TWO

I SHIFT BENEATH THE WIDE-EYED gaze of Flavius Gemellus, the Roman centurion who has listened to my story. "Is there anything else you want to know?"

At his desk, the scribe stops scribbling and eyes me as if I were a bad smell. "How can you hold your head up in the same room as a fine man like Atticus Aurelius?"

Even now, my temper flares. "He is not guiltless in this! I had grievances; my family was murdered!"

The scribe rolls his eyes, signaling that I am beneath his contempt. He is such a Roman.

"I regret I am not a better woman." I lift my chin and realize that stores of pride still surge within me. "And I would have Atticus Aurelius know I regret striking his son. God will forgive my sin and Rome will take my life. When I breathe my last breath, I will consider my debts settled."

"Miryam." The soldier on the bench speaks, his voice gruff with emotion. "Do you not recognize me?"

I turn to face Atticus Aurelius and am startled to see the sheen of tears in his eyes. How could he expect me to recognize him? I ransack my memories of Roman soldiers but cannot find his face among so many tattered images.

"I stood with you on Golgotha the day they crucified the Nazarene."

I stare at him, my heart pounding. My hated enemy at the Crucifixion? Impossible. The Romans at the site had paid little attention to Yeshua as the day wore on; they had gambled and laughed and taunted our rabboni.

"You cannot—" I halt as a memory knifes my heart.

Not all the Romans had scorned us that awful day. One centurion looked at the untimely dark and recognized the work of the Almighty. And another soldier, a big man, brought Yeshua down from the cross.

"Lead the way," he'd said, nodding to me. "I'll carry him for you."

I'd heard the sound of grief in his voice, but I'd been so focused on my task that I'd scarcely noticed.

"I am Atticus Aurelius," the big man says now, "and I served in a century under Gaius Cabilenus. I remember the night we raided your house in Magdala. I remember . . . and I know you suffered a great loss."

He stands and nods at the scribe. "Antonius, this has nothing to do with you. You may go."

The scribe hesitates, then glances toward the centurion at the desk. "Most irregular, sir. All words from the prisoner should be recorded—"

"Her history has been taken down." The centurion clasps his hands. "If Atticus Aurelius wishes to speak privately with the woman who wronged him, it is his right. His words will make no difference in the outcome of this trial."

The scribe nods stiffly, then stands and shuffles out of the hall.

Left with the man whose son I conspired to murder, my heart congeals into a lump of terror. Will he strangle me with his bare hands while his comrade looks on with approval?

Atticus Aurelius waits until the scribe's footsteps fade from our hearing; then he lifts his gaze from the floor and looks at me. "The men in my contubernium obeyed Gaius the night we went to Magdala. But I have never been the sort to obey blindly. I came away from your house with a secret— a secret I have kept for years."

I feel a sudden coldness in my belly. What could he have done in my house? Did he torture my husband and son before killing them? Did he take his pleasure from Rachel?

He sinks back to the bench and props his elbows on his knees, then folds his hands. "As I cleared the house, I found your baby . . . and carried him safely away."

My heart stops dead at his words. For an instant I gape at him, unable to believe, but something in his eyes assures me he is telling the truth.

"You took Binyamin?"

"I did not know about you. I saw a dead woman and assumed she was the child's mother. I had to smuggle the baby out of the city to avoid Gaius's displeasure, and I couldn't hide him forever in the camp . . . so I gave him to a girl who raised him in Caesarea. Cyrilla noticed he was deaf . . . and she accompanied me when we went in search of Yeshua the healer."

An icy memory chills the chain of my spine: *"My father met Yeshua once. I was born deaf, you see."*

No.

"Yeshua healed him. The boy grew tall and strong, as bright a lad as any you could meet. My cohort was attached to Pilate's household, so he learned how to read and write. He became quite skilled."

My heart is beating heavily; I can feel each thump like a blow to my chest. "Please, say no more."

"The year Yeshua was crucified, my century was dispatched to Jerusalem to help control the Passover crowds. My centurion and I witnessed the events on Golgotha, and we knew Yeshua was no ordinary man. When I saw you, Miryam, I couldn't believe such strength could exist in a woman. Everyone around you crumpled with grief, but you stood unbowed and unbroken at the foot of the cross."

I can't speak. The Roman probably means to compliment me in some way, but in his words I hear an indictment of my fierce anger and pride. I hadn't bowed because I cherished suffering; I hadn't broken because I focused on revenge. Even as my beloved rabboni died, I had wept knowing that I would count this death as another offense the Romans had committed against me.

"When we heard that Yeshua had risen from the dead," the centurion continues, "we believed the story. We have believed in his power since those early days—Cyrilla, myself . . . and my son."

A scream rises in my throat and I choke it off. *Impossible.*

"I had mixed feelings when my son decided to join the army. I was proud he wanted to serve Rome, but I despaired of him traveling such a great distance. I found consolation, however, in knowing he'd be serving in Jerusalem, where I knew he would find a community of believers."

My tears, which are barely dammed, well up and overflow.

"As I'd hoped, my son found a community that loved him. His letters brimmed with praise and affection for the congregation in Jerusalem, for they took him into their fellowship and welcomed him as a brother. He spoke with special fondness of two women, both called Miryam, who had helped provide for Yeshua during his ministry."

Oh, God of mercy, kill me now.

"You, Miryam, know the joy of my life and the son of your womb as Quintus Aurelius."

The words, once he gets them out, strike through my heart, sharp and sudden as a thrown dagger. I cover my face with trembling hands and give vent to the agony of bitter realization.

I have murdered my son. . . . Not only have I killed him, but I have fervently *desired* his death. I have plotted, I have planned, I have taken joy in the destruction of the vulnerable boy I loved most—

The child God preserved for me.

Someone, somewhere, is keening, but I am focused on the memory of my son, Binyamin. Quintus Aurelius. The young man who had looked at me with such longing in his great dark eyes that it had taken all my strength to resist him.

Yet I *did* resist him and for that I can never forgive myself. I closed my heart to him, and now my heart will forever be locked with shame.

When I can speak over the constriction in my throat, I fall to my knees and thrust my manacled wrists toward Atticus Aurelius. "Take my life now. I know you want to."

The centurion stands and comes toward me. I expect his broad hands to wrap around my throat; instead they support my shoulders and lift me to my feet, then pull me into his arms.

Then I, a despised Jew and a traitor to Rome, sob within a Roman's embrace. The centurion pats my back, comforting me as he must have comforted my son in younger days. "Shhh, hush now." His breath fans my ear. "You did not know."

"I *should* have known." I can scarcely speak over the ache in my throat. "You did me good, not evil, but look how I repaid you! I should have forgiven you. Yeshua told us to forgive so we might be forgiven, but I have never been able to *forget*—"

"I forgive you."

He speaks the words into my hair, and I'm so surprised I push away and stare at him through watery eyes. "How can you? How can God forgive me? I had him *killed*, your son and my son—"

"Our son lives, Miryam. The wound was not fatal."

I blink at him. His mouth has moved; words have fallen upon my ear, but what I heard cannot be the truth. "But—at the fortress, they told me he was dead. The rumors . . . everyone said Quintus had been killed."

"I knew that whoever attacked us had more than robbery in mind. I wanted our enemy to think they had been successful, so I had Quinn transferred to Rome while he recovered from his injury."

Relief rushes over me in a wave so strong my knees buckle. I sink to the end of the marble bench and close my eyes as my heart thumps in a stuttering rhythm. My skin is clammy, my breathing quick.

I may die before I reach the arena.

Atticus Aurelius sits beside me. "I think I would forgive you even if Quinn had not survived," he says, his smile tinged with a touch of sadness. "It wouldn't be easy, but I'd try my best. Because, you see, God has forgiven me of much."

I meet his gaze as my mouth twists in a bleak smile. "Rome won't forgive me."

"But God already has." He pulls a scroll from a bag hanging on his belt. "I have been reading a copy of a letter from an evangelist called John Mark. He ascribes these words to Yeshua: 'But when you are praying, first forgive anyone you are holding a grudge against, so your Father in heaven will forgive your sins, too."

I can't stop a smile. "I remember Yeshua saying that."

The door at the back of the hall opens with a complaining screech. "Atticus Aurelius?" a voice calls. "Someone to see you, sir."

Atticus stands, leaving me alone.

⊱─═══◯═══─⊰

After Atticus Aurelius leaves, I look at Flavius Gemellus, the centurion who has heard my case. He is reading parchments, apparently more interested in documents than in what is happening in his judgment hall.

I slide to the damp floor and prop my elbows on the marble bench, then lift my eyes to heaven and address the Lord who has been crowded out of my heart for too long.

What can I tell him that he doesn't already know? He knows I am an unfit vessel. When he delivered me from demonic bondage, he knew I would rather nurse my wounds than accept healing and extend forgiveness.

After walking with the eternal Son of Man, I turned a deaf ear to his Spirit and cherished my pain more than his leading.

I loved Yeshua dearly, but I loved my grief far more.

My rabboni begged heaven to forgive the Romans who nailed him to the cross, but I had kept an account of offenses ranging from murder to scornful looks cast in my direction.

Yet my heavenly Father responded with mercy. He preserved the son I thought I'd lost; he protected Binyamin from my own manipulations. The Lord poured grace upon me from an unexpected source, and now he wants me to . . . forgive.

Forgive Gaius Cabilenus for murdering my family.

Forgive Atticus Aurelius for taking my son.

Forgive myself for being too blind to see what God restored . . . and for trying to destroy that precious gift.

I press my cheek to the cold marble; I am poured out like wax, shapeless and used up. If God has a purpose for my suffering, I can't see what it is.

Perhaps Yeshua can still make something good from my life. After all, he used me in his service when I had nothing to offer. I have less than nothing now, for I will not live to see tomorrow's sunrise—

Don't cling to your life, Miryam. Trust in me.

Though over twenty years have passed since I heard his voice, I recognize it at once. Yeshua. Still living, still powerful, still my Lord and rabboni.

And waiting for me.

⋯⋯◉⋯⋯

I have regained my composure by the time steps echo from the outer passageway. I hear the clatter of swords and the tread of many feet— a company.

It's time for me to go.

I stand and smooth my tunic, then swipe my palms over my damp cheeks. The door opens and a pair of guards enters, followed by the scribe and other legionnaires. Behind them walks Atticus Aurelius, and with Atticus is . . . Quintus.

Binyamin.

Beneath the surface of my son's face there is a suggestion of movement and flowing, as though a hidden spring would like to break through.

He knows. Atticus has told him everything.

The soldiers flank the door; the scribe returns to his desk.

Atticus escorts Quintus to my side, then steps back to give us room for an almost-private conversation.

"At least," Quintus says, a wry smile twisting his mouth, "now I understand why you avoided me."

My trembling hand floats up and touches his face with tenderness. "My son. If I had known——"

"I understand."

"I should have known." I look into his eyes, which are dark and wild with distress. "But more important, I should have *loved*. No matter whose son you were."

A tremor passes over his face, and a sudden spasm of grief knits his brows. "It's not fair," he says, his voice husky. "To find you and lose you in a single hour——"

"We will have eternity." I place my hands on his shoulders. "We will sit down and trace the plan of God through our lives. And we will see——if God so wills——how even our deaths brought him glory."

His arms slip around me, clutching me so tightly he nearly steals my breath. The guards start forward, eyes alert, so I lift my hands to show I mean Quintus no harm.

"It's time," another soldier calls from the hallway. "The prisoner must make ready."

I squeeze my son as hard as I dare, then push him away and blink back fresh tears. The corners of his mouth are tight with distress, his eyes shiny. The thin line of his lips clamp tight, and his throat bobs as he swallows.

"I heard," he said, his voice low in my ear, "that before Herod's executioner killed James, the disciple promised that the blood of Christ's martyrs would be seed. John says a time of affliction is coming, so we should not be afraid of what we are about to suffer. If we remain faithful even when facing death, Yeshua will give us the crown of life."

I wipe a trickle of tears from my cheek, then manage a smile for my son. "I have lived foolishly," I tell him, "more foolishly than most. But as some people's lives are examples of how we should live, let mine be an example of how we should not. You have a record—" I nod toward the scribe—"so share my story so others may learn from my mistake. But know this—better that my name fall into obscurity than Yeshua's glory be eclipsed. The hope of Isra'el has come, my son, and our rabboni will come again."

Atticus Aurelius steps to Quintus's side, then offers me a bundle of linen. I feel an odd twinge of recognition in the gesture—Quintus had held out a package in the same way when he presented me with the veil that now covers my head.

"I wanted to give you something that might . . . *comfort* you in the arena," Atticus says, his eyes shadowed. "I thought of this."

I unwrap the linen and find myself holding a rectangle of scarlet silk. Sections of it are dark and crusty, and I know without being told that this fabric will glow like a caesar's purple when I wear it in the sun.

Just as it did when Yeshua wore it.

I look up and study the Roman's face, feature by feature. My dearest enemy has become a font of God's blessing. There's no way he could know the original source of this material, but ADONAI knows. And he is with me.

I pull the long rectangle over one shoulder, tie the ends in a loop at my side, and smile at Atticus Aurelius through my tears. "Thank you."

The guards move into position on my right and left; they take my arms and lead me toward the door. When we reach the hall, I turn and see Quintus trailing behind us.

"No." I send him back with a smile. "You will follow me, perhaps soon, but not today. So wait with your father and know that ADONAI will keep watch between us while we are apart."

I look up and meet the tallest guard's eyes. "I am ready."

Epilogue

Flavius Gemellus, owner of Yeshua's linen tunic, hanged himself shortly after Miryam the Magdalene perished in Nero's arena. The tunic was found on the floor, under his body. His friend Atticus Aurelius mourned his loss.

Though Rome became aware of Christianity as early as Claudius Caesar's reign, wholesale slaughter of believers did not begin until the Neronian persecution of AD 64.

During the night that fell between July 18 and 19 of that year, Rome began to burn . . . and the fires raged for nine straight days. The cause of the conflagration was never proven, but because Nero had often spoken of his admiration for the spectacle of a burning city, he was publicly accused of incendiarism.

Over 17,450 buildings were destroyed in the fire, including the homes of 98,500 people. Men and beasts perished by the score, and entire sections of the city were laid waste by the inferno.

To divert suspicion from himself, Nero cast the blame upon the Roman Christians. The citizens of Rome, who had been terrorized, displaced, and bewildered, swallowed the lie and demanded justice. Even cultivated and educated Romans such as Tictus, Suetonius, and Pliny, stigmatized Christianity as the populace surrendered to paranoid hysteria.

Christians were rounded up and arrested. Most of them were not charged with arson, but with the crime of *"odium generic humani,"* or "hating the human race." Because believers abhorred heathen Roman customs, maintained an indifference to politics, and sprang from Jewish roots, they were viewed as intolerant misanthropes. Hundreds of Christians were crucified, including the apostle Peter, who died with his head down, deeming himself unworthy to be crucified in the same manner as his Lord. Peter's wife, Susanna, was martyred before her husband, who cheered and encouraged her as she walked to the place of execution.

Enflamed by bloodlust, the carnage continued. Those responsible for killing Christians sewed some believers into the skins of wild beasts and exposed them to mad dogs in the arena. In the imperial gardens, executioners coated Christian men and women with oil and nailed them to pine posts, which were lighted and burned as living torches while Nero drove around them, displaying his prowess as a charioteer.

Clement, a believer, mentions a "multitude of the elect," who "became a most noble example among ourselves" and the Roman historian Tacitus speaks of a "vast multitude" of Christians who perished.

Tacitus had little respect for Christians but was nonetheless convinced of their innocence. Despite his indifference to the Christian faith, he couldn't help pitying the believers because they had been sacrificed only to appease the ferocity of a cruel tyrant.

Atticus Aurelius, who had publicly confessed his belief in the Jewish Messiah, perished in the persecution with his wife, Cyrilla. Quintus Aurelius, who had by then been sent back to Judea, survived and continued to spread the gospel of Yeshua the Messiah, who had come to redeem Hebrews and Gentiles alike.

ABOUT THE AUTHOR

Christy-Award winner Angela Hunt writes books for readers who have learned to expect the unexpected. With over three million copies of her books sold worldwide, she is the best-selling author of *The Tale of Three Trees*, *The Note*, *Unspoken*, and more than 100 other titles.

She and her husband make their home in Florida with mastiffs. One of their dogs was featured on *Live with Regis and Kelly* as the second-largest canine in America.

Readers may visit her Web site at www.angelahuntbooks.com.

An Interview with Angela Hunt

Q: *Don't you find it a little intimidating to write a novel where you're putting words into Jesus' mouth?*
A: Absolutely! That's why I tried to use his actual words, or slight paraphrases, whenever possible.

Q: *Okay—I have to know. Mary Magdalene was a real person, and of course I recognized the names of the disciples, but what about all the other characters? Which are fictional and which are real?*
A: The challenge of a historical novelist is to flesh out the story world with fictional characters and events while not contradicting the historical record. So yes, Mary Magdalene is real, as were the other women around Jesus, the disciples, the emperors, and several other names you'll recognize from the New Testament, including Claudius Lysias. Incidentally, Peter did have a wife who traveled with him, so she must have been one of the women around Jesus. Which one? I chose Susanna, but I could be wrong.

The fictional characters? Of the major figures: Atticus, Flavius, Gaius, Quintus/Binyamin, and Hadassah.

Q: *Where'd you learn the names of Jesus' half brothers and sisters?*
A: The brothers are named in Matthews 13:55 and Mark 6:3. The sisters' names I used are fictional, but from those Scriptures we know Jesus had sisters, too.

Q: *You chose not to depict Mary Magdalene as a fallen woman, but that's how I've always heard her described.*
A: Poor Mary! She really has been falsely accused all these years. Tradition has furnished us with much information about Mary that is almost certainly inaccurate. First-century history does *not* portray her as a prostitute, an adulterous woman, or Jesus' wife. The *only* thing Scripture tells us specifically about Mary from Magdala is that Jesus delivered her from seven demons.

We can assume other things about her from the biblical record. First, she was probably an older and much-respected woman because she is listed the first seven of eight times when Scripture names the women present with Christ. Those who would portray Mary Magdalene as a prostitute, an adulteress, or Jesus' wife have taken their cues from misguided sources.

Q: *Didn't the pope say Mary was a fallen woman?*
A: Many people, including Pope Gregory I, have confused Mary of Magdala with the unnamed "sinful woman" who anointed Jesus' feet at Shimon's house (Luke 7:36-39) and Mary of Bethany, who anointed Jesus' feet at *her* house (John 12:1-7). But in 1969, the Catholic church quietly admitted that Gregory was mistaken— clearly, Luke and John were not talking about Mary Magdalene.

Others have tried to portray Mary Magdalene as the woman taken in adultery (John 8:1-11), but this could hardly be Mary, as this scene happens outside the Temple, and Mary lived in Magdala before meeting Jesus. Furthermore, the most ancient Greek manuscripts do not include John 7:53–8:11, so the story may be apocryphal.

Q: *Seems like there's a lot of mumbo jumbo about Mary today—she's a goddess; she's the female apostle; she's part of a new-age religion.*
A: And all of that "mumbo jumbo" is nothing but second-century man's attempt to reduce salvation, an act of God, to an act of man. The Gnostics elevated Mary in their doctrine, particularly in apocryphal works such as the Gospel of Philip and the Gospel of Mary. (Gnosticism is the attempt to attain salvation through *gnosis*, or "knowledge" rather than faith. Such knowledge regularly dealt with the intimate relationship of the self to the transcendent source of all being, and this knowledge, according to Gnostics, was often conveyed by a "revealer."[1]) They have tried to depict Mary as a prophet in her own right, or even as an "apostle to the apostles," but nothing in Scripture validates such a concept.

Q: *But since the publication of* The Da Vinci Code, *everyone's been saying that Mary Magdalene was Jesus' wife . . . or at least his lover.*
A: Was Mary Jesus' lover? Don't think so!

I love the way my friend Liz Curtis Higgs handles this topic in her book *Mad Mary*:

> Jesus loved Mary Magdalene, certainly. He knew her well.
> But he used the same words for all his disciples—*to love,*
> *to know.* Same Greek words, same emotions. In a sense he
> knows us all "very well." The psalmist confessed for all of us:
> "You know when I sit and when I rise; you perceive my
> thoughts from afar. You . . . are familiar with all my ways"
> [Psalm 139:2-3, NIV].[2]

Many contemporary feminists and goddess worshipers have attempted to elevate Mary Magdalene by linking her with Jesus sexually . . . a contradiction in approaches if ever there was one.

Bottom line: Jesus lived a sinless life that included abstaining from fornication and distraction. He was wholly dedicated to the Father's will and his purpose of redeeming mankind. In repeated dealings with men and with Satan, he refused to allow himself to become entangled with the affairs of this world.

Q: *You've portrayed Mary M. as quite the businesswoman. Isn't that a little out of keeping with the role of women in those times?*
A: Not necessarily. The virtuous woman of Proverbs 31 runs a home and a business. From what Scripture tells us, I think we can assume Mary had a source of income and could have even been wealthy. Luke wrote that the women who traveled with Jesus provided financial support for his ministry (Luke 8:1-3).

From the fact that Mary had the freedom to travel and money of her own we can surmise that she might have been a widow with no surviving children—otherwise, her children would have inherited her husband's property.

Q: *You used some Hebrew names and some Greek names—why the mix?*
A: I wanted to give the story an authentically Jewish flavor, but I ran into difficulty with names. First, so many of them are repeated—Miryam was an extremely common name, as were John (Yochanan) and Simon (Shimon). If I thought the Hebrew name might cause a contemporary reader to stumble, in some instances I opted for the more common name, hoping to clarify the differences between characters.

Actually, the characters themselves would have answered to several names. Galileans lived in a bilingual region that had been

rated with ▨ ▨oke Greek, the lingua
▨d Peter's name used in
▨ter, Petros, and the

▨ently referred to as
▨ch age, but I tried

Q: ▨ ▨and references for the story?
A: ▨s of reference books, few of the
exper▨ ▨h a consensus of opinion. Few references a▨ ▨es of Jesus' birth, death, and years o▨
ministry, ▨ ▨e remarkably close. For the record, th▨
book suppos▨ ▨began his ministry in AD 30 and was cr▨
fied in AD 33.

Q: *I was hoping you'd include the scene of Jesus in Gethsema▨*
A: As much as I would have liked to portray every even▨
ministry, the limited scope of a novel made that task imp▨
Plus, I was working from Miryam's and Atticus's limited ▨
spectives, so I could only record events they might have seen a▨
experienced.

Q: *You have Gaius the centurion stand at the cross and say, "Truly this man was a son of God." But my Bible says, "Truly this man was the Son of God."*
A: The Greek text literally says "truly this man was Son of God," so whether it's *the* son or *a* son is a matter of debate. In any case, it's hard to imagine that the centurion would have had a complete understanding of what he witnessed. First, the Romans were poly-

theistic; they didn't believe in only one God. Second, they were accustomed to the idea that great men were "sons of God"—their emperors regularly claimed to be divine. Third, at that time few of the disciples understood the concept of God-in-flesh—such an idea was almost inconceivable until *after* the Resurrection.

The disciples had accepted that Yeshua was the Son of Man prophesied by the prophet Daniel; they knew he was the Son of God. But Scripture called Isra'el God's firstborn, so Hebrew men had always considered themselves sons of God in the sense that Israelites were HaShem's earthly representatives. They accepted the idea that Yeshua was their Messiah, the one who represented God to them.

But after the Resurrection, when they saw Yeshua conquer death, the phrase "Son of God" took on new meaning. You must understand that the Shema—"Hear, O Isra'el, the Lord our God, the Lord is one!"—was recited by devout Hebrews practically every day of their lives. They lived in a world where the Gentiles worshiped entire pantheons of gods, and they knew that the universe had been called into being by *one* God, HaShem.

Suddenly, after the Resurrection, the disciples were faced with a puzzling reality—HaShem was *one*, but he was also more than one, for they had seen his Son, the only begotten of the Father, full of grace and truth. And Yeshua had promised to always be with them because he would soon be sending the *Ruach HaKodesh*, or the Holy Spirit.

As they puzzled over the *Tanakh*, the Scriptures, they began to understand why the word *Elohim* was plural and why HaShem had said, "Let *us* make humankind in our image, in the likeness of *ourselves*."

They realized that Yeshua had been with HaShem even at the beginning of time. He had appeared to Avraham and Yaakov as the angel of ADONAI. And the Scriptures even mentioned the *Ruach HaKodesh* in the form of the *Spirit of Adoniai Elohim*.

Q: *When Jesus meets Mary outside the tomb, my Bible says that he said, "Touch me not." But you have her clinging to his feet.*
A: I read several sources and translations, and the best meaning of Jesus' words is "Don't cling to me." So Miryam must have touched him. She probably wanted to cling to him, but Jesus had something important for her to do . . . just as he has an important task for each of us.

There are other things I interpreted that might come as a surprise to the modern reader: *baptize* literally means "immerse," *Hosanna* means "please deliver us," and the first Lord's Supper was a seder. Our word *hallelujah* comes from the *Hallel of Egypt*, Psalms 113–118, which was sung at many Jewish festivals. Read those prophetic psalms as you think about the Lord's death and resurrection, and you'll see how clearly they point to Jesus as the Messiah.

Q: *As I read about Atticus and the baby, I kept wondering—what did they use for diapers in the first century?*
A: You know, I wondered the same thing! Scripture talks about swaddling clothes for newborns, but there's no way you're going to keep a toddler swaddled.

So I did a little research and discovered a technique called—are you ready for this?—elimination timing. Apparently it's still in use all over the world. As I read the overview, it occurred to me that it's pretty much like training a puppy—you pay close attention to the child's signals and, after waking or eating, you give them an opportunity to, well, eliminate. It's helpful if the child wears a tunic and nothing underneath.

Oh, the things I learn in this job . . .

Q: *So what was the most interesting thing you learned?*
A: Tough question. All of it was interesting, but my eyes were opened to how radical Jesus' preaching was and how much my faith owes to Judaism. For years I've read Jesus' words in Matthew 9:16-17 and not really understood the metaphor:

> "Who would patch an old garment with unshrunk cloth? For the patch shrinks and pulls away from the old cloth, leaving an even bigger hole than before. And no one puts new wine into old wineskins. The old skins would burst from the pressure, spilling the wine and ruining the skins. New wine must be stored in new wineskins. That way both the wine and the wineskins are preserved."

After researching this book, the analogy became clear. Jesus was presenting a new way to relate to God, and the Jews who followed him had to accept some radically different ideas—that God was One and also a Trinity, that the God whose name is too holy to be spoken could be addressed as "Abba" or "Daddy," and that women, who were never taught the Law, could sit and learn at the Savior's feet.

Faith in Jesus (the patch) had to be adapted to Judaism (the coat) and Judaism (the former wineskins) had to be reconditioned in order to hold the new wine (faith in Christ). As Jeremiah wrote (31:31-37), the new covenant would be written on the hearts of the people of Isra'el.

Q: *Anything else you'd like to add?*
A: As always, I need to acknowledge some folks: first, a huge thanks to Terri Gillespie for making sure the manuscript had a proper Jewish perspective. Like me, Terri has a deep and abiding love for

Isra'el. She is director of donor relations for the Messianic Jewish Alliance of America, an amazing organization that can be found at www.mjaa.org. Thanks also to Susan Richardson for proofreading part of an early draft, and to Randy Ingermanson, who helped me make sense of several ancient manuscripts.

1. P. J. Achtemeier, *Harper's Bible Dictionary* (San Francisco: Harper & Row, 1985).

2. Liz Curtis Higgs, *Mad Mary* (Sisters, OR: WaterBrook Press), 2001, p.189.

Discussion Questions for Book Groups

1. What did you know about Mary Magdalene before you read this novel? Did the story shatter any of your previously held ideas?

   Think about this—when Peter protested after Jesus talked about dying, the Savior replied, "Get away from me, Satan! You are a dangerous trap to me. You are seeing things merely from a human point of view, and not from God's" (Matthew 16:23). With that example in mind, what do you think Jesus would have said to any woman who tried to tempt him to sexual sin?

2. Did you begin to read this story with the eyes of a twenty-first-century Christian? Did you stop to consider that the people of Jesus' day didn't know who he was in the beginning? First-century Hebrews were firmly sold on the concept of "one God and only one God." If Jesus had proclaimed himself as God from the outset of his ministry, how do you think he would have been received?

3. Before reading this, did you realize that Jesus's many references to himself as the "Son of Man" pointed to Daniel 7:13-14? Why would this have been significant to a Jewish audience?

4. Have you stopped to think about how salvation differed in the time of Christ? The book of Acts indicates that people gathered pieces of information about repentance, salvation, and the Holy Spirit gradually. How would this have affected someone like the Roman centurion at the cross?

5. Neither Miryam nor the apostles became perfect people after Jesus' ascension and the coming of the Holy Spirit. Scripture tells us that Paul and Barnabas had a falling-out over John Mark (Acts 15:37-39), and Paul freely admitted that he remained a slave to sin after his salvation experience (Romans 7:21-25). Do you, like Miryam, struggle with a sin that prevents you from following Christ in perfect obedience? How has the Lord worked in your life regarding that sin?

6. This story is written in only two viewpoints: Miryam's and Atticus's. How did this enhance or detract from your enjoyment of the story?

7. How did Yeshua revolutionize the role of women in society? Would a person like Miryam be grateful for this changing role?

8. Where do you think Angela Hunt got the idea for a silk fabric that shifts from crimson to purple, depending on the light? Hint: see Matthew 27:28 and Mark 15:17. How was this fabric used as a symbol in the story?

9. Misunderstanding is a frequent theme in this novel—Miryam misunderstands what happened in Magdala; she and many others misunderstand Yeshua's plan and purpose; and Gaius misunderstands how Atticus came to have a son. What other characters or groups of people misunderstand a truth of the story?

10. If this were a movie and you could play any role, which role would you like to play?

References

Achtemeier, Paul J. *Harper's Bible Dictionary*. San Francisco: Harper & Row & Society of Biblical Literature, 1985.

Barclay, W., ed. *The Gospel of Matthew: Volume 2*. Philadelphia: Westminster Press, 2000.

Barclay, W., ed. *The Letter to the Romans*. Philadelphia: Westminster Press, 2000.

Barclay, W., ed. *The Letters to Timothy, Titus, and Philemon*. Philadelphia: Westminster Press, 2000.

Barclay, W., ed. *The Revelation of John*. Philadelphia: Westminster Press, 2000.

Bellevie, Lesa. *The Complete Idiot's Guide to Mary Magdalene*. New York: Alpha Books, 2005.

Boucher, Francois. *20,000 Years of Fashion*. New York: Harry N. Abrams, 1962.

Bruce, A. B. *The Training of the Twelve; Or, Passages Out of the Gospels, Exhibiting the Twelve Disciples of Jesus under Discipline for the Apostleship*. Oak Harbor, WA: Logos Research Systems, Inc., 1995, c1877.

Caselli, Giovanni. *The Everyday Life of a Roman Soldier*. New York: Peter Bedrick Books, 1986.

Coleman, William. *Today's Handbook of Bible Times and Customs*. Minneapolis: Bethany House, 1984.

Coogan, Michael D. *The Oxford History of the Biblical World.* New York: Oxford University Press, 1998.

De Boer, Esther. *Mary Magdalene· Beyond the Myth.* Harrisburg, PA: Trinity Press International, 1997.

Douglas, J. D., Comfort, P. W., & Mitchell, D. *Who's Who in Christian History.* Wheaton, IL: Tyndale House, 1997.

du Toit, A. *The New Testament Milieu.* Orion: Halfway House, 1998.

Easton, M. *Easton's Bible Dictionary.* Oak Harbor, WA: Logos Research Systems, Inc., 1996.

Edersheim, A. *Sketches of Jewish Social Life in the Days of Christ.* Bellingham, WA: Logos Research Systems, Inc., 2003.

Edersheim, A. *The Temple, Its Ministry and Services as They Were at the Time of Jesus Christ.* Bellingham, WA: Logos Research Systems, Inc., 2003.

Edersheim, Alfred. *The Life and Times of Jesus the Messiah.* Bellingham, WA: Logos Research Systems, Inc., 2003.

Elwell, W. A., & Comfort, P. W. *Tyndale Bible Dictionary.* Wheaton, IL: Tyndale House, 2001.

Freedman, David Noel. *The Anchor Bible Dictionary.* New York: Doubleday, 1996.

Freeman, J. M., & Chadwick, H. J. *Manners & Customs of the Bible.* North Brunswick, NJ: Bridge-Logos Publishers, 1998.

Gansky, Alton. *Uncovering the Bible's Greatest Mysteries.* Nashville: Broadman and Holman, 2002.

Gonzalez, Justo L. *The Story of Christianity.* San Francisco: Harper San Francisco, 1984.

Gower, Ralph. *The New Manners and Customs of Bible Times.* Chicago: Moody Press, 1987.

Gundry, Robert H. *A Survey of the New Testament.* Grand Rapids: Zondervan, 2003.

Hagee, John. *His Glory Revealed, A Devotional.* Nashville: Thomas Nelson Publishers, 1999.

Haskins, Susan. *Mary Magdalene: Myth and Metaphor.* New York: Harcourt Brace & Company, 1993.

Henry, M. *Matthew Henry's Commentary on the Whole Bible: Complete and Unabridged in One Volume*. Peabody, MA: Hendrickson, 1996.

Higgs, Liz Curtis. *Mad Mary: A Bad Girl from Magdala Transformed at His Appearing*. Colorado Springs: WaterBrook Press, 2001.

Janson, H. W. *History of Art*. New York: Harry N. Abrams, Inc., 1968.

Jenkins, Simon. *Nelson's 3-D Bible Mapbook*. Nashville: Thomas Nelson, 1985.

Josephus, Flavius, & Whiston, W. *The Works of Josephus*. Peabody, MA: Hendrickson, 1996.

Kaiser, W. C. *Hard Sayings of The Bible*. Downers Grove, IL: InterVarsity, 1996.

Keppie, Lawrence. *The Making of the Roman Army: From Republic to Empire*. Norman, OK: University of Oklahoma Press, 1998.

Kiehl, Erich and Klinck, Arthur. *Everyday Life in Bible Times*. St. Louis: Concordia Publishing House, 1995.

Malina, B., & Joubert, S. *A Time Travel to the World of Jesus*. Halfway House: Orion, 1997.

Martin, Malachi. *Hostage to the Devil*. San Francisco: Harper San Francisco, 1992.

McGarvey, J. W. *The Four-Fold Gospel*. Oak Harbor, WA: Logos Research Systems, Inc., 1999.

Mills, M. *The Life of Christ: A Study Guide to the Gospel Record*. Three Volumes: 1. *The Advent of Jesus* 2. *The Beginning of the Gospel* 3. *Jesus Presents Himself to Israel*. Dallas: 3E Ministries, 1999.

Moltmann-Wendel, Elisabeth. *The Women Around Jesus*. New York: Crossroad, 1982.

Mounce, R. H. Vol. 27: *Romans. The New American Commentary*. Nashville: Broadman & Holman Publishers, 1995, 2001.

National Geographic Society. *Everyday Life in Bible Times*. National Geographic Society, 1967.

Negev, A. *The Archaeological Encyclopedia of the Holy Land* (Third ed.). New York: Prentice Hall Press, 1996.

Newman, Carey, ed. *Jesus and the Restoration of Israel*. Downers Grove, IL: InterVarsity Press, 1999.

Pfeiffer, C. F., & Harrison, E. F. *The Wycliffe Bible Commentary*. Chicago: Moody Press, 1962.

Philo, O. A., & Yonge, C. D. *The Works of Philo: Complete and Unabridged*. Peabody, MA: Hendrickson, 1996.

Ricci, Carla. *Mary Magdalene and Many Others*. Minneapolis: Fortress Press, 1994.

Richards, L. *The Bible Reader's Companion*. Wheaton, IL: Victor Books, 1991.

Richards, Larry and Susan. *Women of the Bible*. Nashville, TN: Thomas Nelson Publishers, 2003.

Roberts, A., Donaldson, J., & Coxe, A. C. *The Ante-Nicene Fathers* Vol. VIII: *Translations of the Writings of the Fathers Down To A.D. 325. Fathers of the Third and Fourth Centuries: The Twelve Patriarchs, Excerpts and Epistles, the Clementina, Apocrypha, Decretals, Memoirs of Edessa and Syriac Documents, Remains of the First Ages*. Oak Harbor: Logos Research Systems, 1997.

Robertson, A. *Word Pictures in the New Testament*. Vol.V ©1932, Vol. VI ©1933 by Sunday School Board of the Southern Baptist Convention. Oak Harbor: Logos Research Systems, 1997.

Santosuosso, Antonio. *Storming the Heavens*. Boulder, CO: Westview Press, 2004.

Schaff, P. *The Nicene and Post-Nicene Fathers*. Second Series Vol. XIV. *The Seven Ecumenical Councils*. Oak Harbor: Logos Research Systems, 1997.

Schaff, P., & Schaff, D. S. *History of the Christian Church*. Oak Harbor, WA: Logos Research Systems, Inc., 1997.

Sproul, R. *Following Christ*. Wheaton, IL: Tyndale House, 1996.

Stern, David H. *Jewish New Testament*. Clarksville, MD: Jewish New Testament Publications, Inc., 1989.

Stern, David H. *Jewish New Testament Commentary*. Clarksville, MD: Jewish New Testament Publications, Inc., 1992.

Stern, David H. *Complete Jewish Bible*. Clarksville, MD: Jewish New Testament Publications, Inc., 1998.

Strobel, Lee. *The Case for Christ*. Grand Rapids: Zondervan, 1998.

Tan, P. L. *Encyclopedia of 7700 Illustrations*. Garland, TX: Bible Communications, 1996.

Telushkin, Rabbi Joseph. *Jewish Wisdom: Ethical, Spiritual, and Historical Lessons from the Great Works and Thinkers*. New York: William Morrow and Company, 1994.

The Treasury of Scripture Knowledge: Five Hundred Thousand Scripture References and Parallel Passages. Oak Harbor: Logos Research Systems, Inc., 1995.

Unterman, Allan. *Dictionary of Jewish Lore & Legend*. London: Thames and Hudson, 1991.

Van Biema, David. "Mary Magdalene: Saint or Sinner?" *Time Magazine*, August 11, 2003.

Walvoord, J. F., Zuck, R. B., & Dallas Theological Seminary. *The Bible Knowledge Commentary: An Exposition of the Scriptures*. Wheaton, IL: Victor Books, 1983, 1985.

Watson, G.R. *The Roman Soldier*. Ithaca, New York: Cornell University Press, 1969.

Wiersbe, W. W. *The Bible Exposition Commentary*. Wheaton, IL: Victor Books, 1989, 1996.

Willmington, H. L. *Willmington's Bible Handbook*. Wheaton, IL: Tyndale House, 1997.

Wood, D. R. W., Wood, D. R. W., & Marshall, I. H. *New Bible Dictionary*. Downers Grove, IL: InterVarsity Press, 1996.

Wright, N.T. *Jesus and the Victory of God*. Minneapolis: Fortress Press, 1996.

Wright, N.T. *The New Testament and the People of God*. Minneapolis, MN: Fortress Press, 1992.

Young, R. *Young's Literal Translation*. Oak Harbor: Logos Research Systems, 1997.

Other Novels by Angela Hunt

HISTORICAL
The Shadow Women
The Silver Sword
The Golden Cross
The Velvet Shadow
The Emerald Isle
Dreamers
Brothers
Journey

CONTEMPORARY
The Novelist
A Time to Mend
Unspoken
The Truth Teller
The Awakening
The Debt
The Canopy
The Pearl
The Justice
The Note
The Immortal
For a complete listing, visit www.angelahuntbooks.com

DaVinci
DIDN'T CONVINCE ME

COMPELLING FACTS	CONVINCING FICTION

The Da Vinci Code: Fact or Fiction? *Hank Hanegraaff & Paul Maier*	**Divine** *Karen Kingsbury*
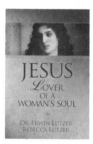	
Jesus, Lover of a Woman's Soul *Dr. Erwin & Rebecca Lutzer*	**Magdalene** *Angela Hunt*
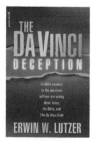	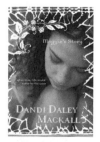
The Da Vinci Deception *Dr. Erwin Lutzer*	**Maggie's Story** *Dandi Daley Mackall*

Expect the **Un**expected—July 2006

ANGELA

HUNT

EXPECT THE UNEXPECTED

UNCHARTED

Prologue

PRESENT DAY
The Hamptons, New York

The secret of sex appeal, sixteen-year-old Sarah believes, is an even
tan, and the key to an even tan is remembering to turn over at eight-
minute intervals between one and two p.m. Most of her friends opt for
spray-on fake-n-bakes, but Sarah has always preferred the real thing.

As the second hand of her watch sweeps over the twelve, she flips
from her stomach to her back, then inhales the delicious fragrance
of sea salt.

"You're going to regret lying there," a voice calls from beneath a
nearby umbrella. "You'll be burned tonight and freckled next week.
When you're thirty you'll have wrinkles, and when you're forty you'll
have skin cancer."

Sarah rolls her eyes. "Transmission received! You sound like Miss
Pratt."

The woman beneath the umbrella lowers her book and peers over
the top of her reading glasses. "Who's Miss Pratt?"

"My Health teacher."

"Oh." The book rises again, eclipsing the pale face beneath a wide straw hat. "Well, Miss Pratt is correct."

Sarah sighs loudly, then flips back onto her stomach. Truth is, she's bored with the pursuit of the perfect tan. She has nothing to listen to because she left her iPod in the city, and umbrella woman won't let her bring the CD player down to the beach . . .

She pushes herself up and jogs toward the water, splashing away a pelican that climbs from the shallows and flaps his way toward a distant dock.

"Be careful!" the straw hat calls.

Sarah ignores the warning. The woman is hyper-paranoid; a certified over-worrier. Enough to drive a girl crazy.

Especially one who's had more than her fair share of things to worry about.

Sarah wades forward until the water touches her bare belly, then she turns to brace against the breakers. After gasping at the first cold splash on her sun-warmed back, she swims beyond the waves, then backstrokes in an area where the swells rise and fall in a gentle rhythm.

She loves the ocean. She'd never admit this to a living soul, but if mermaids could exist, she'd exchange every shoe in her closet for a tail and flippers.

Floating lazily, she positions ankle to ankle and knee to knee, then kicks, sputtering as the awkward movement plunges her beneath the water.

She surfaces, laughing and spitting. It's not easy to kick both legs simultaneously, but she could probably get the hang of it if she had time to practice.

She swims a little farther and treads water, then lifts her arms and lowers a tentative toe. She can touch the sandy bottom only until a swell pushes in, then she's picked up and set back down as gently as you please. The ocean is quiet today; due to the heat, more people are shopping than swimming.

To the east, the white fleck of a sailboat streams against a vibrant blue sky while to the west, a sleepy line of gulls squabble over a ripple on the sea—probably a fish, maybe an entire *school* of fish.

A glimmer on the water grabs Sarah's attention. Beyond the slanting line of the glassy waves, a shiny object rises and falls.

Sarah stretches out and swims. The object is a plastic container, a two-liter bottle that once held Coke or Sprite. No—Sprite comes in *green* bottles, and this one is transparent. The cap is missing, though, and in its place is a wad of some unidentifiable material.

Sarah closes the gap with one stroke, then grasps her prize. The container is nothing special; the wad is dried grass and something black—tar maybe, or gum? A few pages of densely printed paper curl inside the mostly waterproof ride. One edge is ripped, so these must be pages torn out of a book.

She turns the bottle. She's not much of a reader, having been forced to read too many classics over the summer while her friends were touring Europe, but a handwritten message in the margin catches her eye. The brown ink is blurred, but one word is legible: *Sarah.*

"Hey!" Sarah waves to catch the straw hat's attention. "Hey, look!"

The woman is too engrossed in her book. Either that or she can't hear above the steady crash of the surf.

Sarah's mouth twists. *Good thing I'm not drowning.*

But she is a good swimmer, and umbrella woman knows it. Sarah tucks the bottle under her arm and sidestrokes toward the shore, then catches a wave and rides it until she reaches shallow water. She tugs her wet bathing suit back into place as she approaches the umbrella, then drops to her knees in the powder soft sand.

"Look at this." She holds the bottle horizontally between her hands. "I found it in the water, and guess what? Someone wrote my name on these pages."

The book falls. "What—oh, gross! That's trash, Sarah, throw it away."

"But it's got—"

"You don't know *what* it has. Some nasty drunk probably pitched it off a sailboat."

Sarah points to the message. "But that's my name, see? Can you read the rest of what it says?"

A pair of perfectly arched brows furrow for a moment. "Ugh! That looks like dried blood."

"But—"

"Drop it, and don't touch it again. You don't know where that's been or who's handled it. They could have HIV or AIDS, or something even worse."

Sarah drops the bottle and wipes her hands on her bathing suit while the pale face warily regards the sun. "Look at how late it's getting. We'd better go. When we get back I think we ought to write a letter to let someone know this beach is becoming unfit for swimming. I know they can't stop riffraff from boating here, but there *has* to be a law against tossing trash into public waterways . . ."

Accompanied by an inexplicable sense of guilt, Sarah picks up her towel, shakes out the sand, and wraps it around her. Before following the bobbing straw hat to the house, she gives the odd bottle one last look.